Klaus Petrus (Eds.)
On Human Persons

METAPHYSICAL RESEARCH

Herausgegeben von / Edited by

Uwe Meixner • Johanna Seibt
Barry Smith • Daniel von Wachter

Band 1 / Volume 1

Klaus Petrus (Eds.)

On Human Persons

ontos
verlag

Frankfurt · London

Bibliographic information published by Die Deutsche Bibliothek
Die Deutsche Bibliothek lists this publication in the Deutsche Nationalbibliographie;
detailed bibliographic data is available in the Internet at http://dnb.ddb.de

©2003 ontos verlag
Postfach 61 05 16, D-60347 Frankfurt a.M.
Tel. ++(49) 69 40 894 151 Fax ++(49) 69 40 894 169
www.ontos-verlag.de

ISBN 3-937202-31-5 (Germany)
ISBN 1-904632-20-3 (U.K.; U.S.A.)

2003

Alle Texte, etwaige Grafiken, Layouts und alle sonstigen schöpferischen
Teile dieses Buches sind u.a. urheberrechtlich geschützt. Nachdruck, Speicherung,
Sendung und Vervielfältigung in jeder Form, insbesondere Kopieren, Digitalisieren, Smoothing,
Komprimierung, Konvertierung in andere Formate, Farbverfremdung sowie Bearbeitung
und Übertragung des Werkes oder von Teilen desselben in andere Medien und Speicher
sind ohne vorherige schriftliche Zustimmung des Verlages unzulässig
und werden verfolgt.

Gedruckt auf säurefreiem, alterungsbeständigem Papier,
hergestellt aus chlorfrei gebleichtem Zellstoff (TcF-Norm).

Printed in Germany.

To all animals,
nonhuman and human

Contents

Contributors ... 7
Preface ... 9

Eric T. Olson
Warum wir Tiere sind ... 11

Lynne Rudder Baker
The Difference That Self-Counsciousness Makes ... 23

Brian Garrett
Some Thoughts on Animalism ... 41

Paul Snowdon
Some Objections to Animalism ... 47

Kevin J. Corcoran
Biology or Psychology? Human Persons and Personal Identity ... 67

Käthe Trettin
Persons and Other Trope Complexes. Reflections on Ontology and Normativity ... 89

Michael B. Burke
Is My Head a Person? ... 107

Klaus Petrus
Human Persons. Some Conceptual Remarks ... 127

Daniel Cohnitz
Personal Identity and the Methodology of Imaginary Cases ... 145

Daniel von Wachter
Free Agents as Cause ... 183

Thomas Spitzley
Identität und Orientierung ... 195

Contributors

Lynne Rudder Baker, Department of Philosophy, 352 Bartlett Hall, University of Massachusetts/Amherst, Amherst, MA 01003-9269, U.S.A., lrbaker@philos.umass.edu

Michael B. Burke, Department of Philosophy, Indiana University, 425 University Blvd, Indianapolis, IN 46202-5140, U.S.A., mburke@iupui.edu

Daniel Cohnitz, Philosophisches Institut, Heinrich-Heine-Universität Düsseldorf, Universitätsstraße 1, D-40225 Düsseldorf, cohnitz@phil-fak.uni-duesseldorf.de

Kevin J. Corcoran, Department of Philosophy, Calvin College, 3201 Burton Street SE, Grand Rapids, MI 49546, U.S.A., kcorcoran@calvin.edu

Brian Garrett, Philosophy, School of Humanities, ANU, ACT 0200, Australia, brian.garrett@anu.edu.au

Eric T. Olson, Department of Philosophy, University of Sheffield, Sheffield S10 2TN, U.K., e.olson@shef.ac.uk

Klaus Petrus, Institut für Philosophie, Unitobler, Länggaß-Straße 49a, CH-3000 Bern 9, petrus@philo.unibe.ch

Paul Snowdon, Department of Philosophy, University College London, Gower Street, London, WC1E 6BT, U.K., p.snowdon@ucl.ac.uk

Thomas Spitzley, Universität Duisburg-Essen, Institut für Kulturwissenschaften, Lotharstraße 65, D-47048 Duisburg, thomas.spitzley@t-online.de

Käthe Trettin, Johann-Wolfgang-Goethe-Universität, Institut für Philosophie, Grüneburgplatz 1, D-60629 Frankfurt am Main, 320081108325-0001@T-Online.de

Daniel von Wachter, Philosophie-Department, PF 42, Ludwig-Maximilians-Universität, Geschwister-Scholl-Platz 1, D-80539 München, daniel@von-wachter.de

Preface

Whenever it's about persons, it's about *us*. For we are all persons. In a certain sense, we cannot be anything that is not a person. I, for instance, couldn't be a dog. If I were one, something would be seriously wrong, at least according to my understanding of myself. For it is part and parcel of our self-understanding that we are persons, with everything – everything! – that constitutes us (according to this picture, neither our right hand nor our brain alone is the person we are). But is what we are according to our self-understanding also what we are in terms of our nature or essence? Are we indeed, as it is often put, essentially or most fundamentally persons? The answer to this depends, among other things, on what exactly persons are. Philosophers, we know, have been agonizing over the issue through the ages. The most famous definitions are probably those of Boethius, Locke, Kant and Strawson, since they touch on nearly all of the important facets of the subject.

Thus Boethius mentions, apart from reason or rationality, *individuality* as a defining characteristic of persons – an aspect which, abeit modified, also becomes an issue in the guise of authenticity, understood as the ability to lead an unmistakably individual life (cf. the contribution by Thomas Spitzley).

Locke puts the emphasis, in modern terms, on self-consciousness, and touches on something that has since been discussed intensely, indeed excessively, up to the present day: the problem of *personal identity* across time (Kevin J. Corcoran). No small part of the debate centers around the effectiveness of the sometimes pretty complicated and awkward *thought experiments* that are supposed to clarify our intuitions as to the criteria for classifying and reidentifying entities as persons (Daniel Cohnitz).

Kant, for his part, drew attention to the close connection between the concept of a person and that of an *action*, and therewith raised a problem that is still seen as a challenge in contemporary philosophy: namely, the clarification of what it is for persons to act freely (Daniel von Wachter). In some respect, the mind-body problem makes its appearance here (in one of its multiple manifestations), and with it the entire issue of the relation between person and body.

Strawson's well-known view is that persons cannot be identified as such if they lack bodies. The relation between persons and their bodies concerns the *metaphysics* of persons, and thus ultimately the question of what it is that makes us what we are: is it a specific, precisely locatable part of our body – our head or brain – (Michael B. Burke)? Or is it, if anything at all, a complex of certain properties (Käthe Trettin)? Are we, in essence, and therefore fundamentally, mere animals (Eric T. Olson)? Or is there something like a specific capacity of ours which makes us persons, and distinguishes us from everything else (Lynne R. Baker)? Questions of this sort not only require a careful evaluation of pros and cons (Brian Garrett, Paul Snowdon). It is also expedient to clarify which *concept* is in play when we ponder ourselves (Klaus Petrus).

Of course, these selected problems only highlight a few facets of the topic. But they are nevertheless among the crucial ones. The essays of this volume complement their discussion with amendments and objections, and in doing so demonstrate perfectly how rewarding it can be to think about things that are of concern to us all.

*

Thanks to the *Stiftung zur Förderung der wissenschaftlichen Forschung an der Universität Bern* for financial support, to the authors for being on board, and to Rafael Hüntelmann for his commitment.

Berne, in the hot summer of 2003   Klaus Petrus

Eric T. Olson

Warum wir Tiere sind*

Was sind wir? Wie immer man sich zu dieser Frage stellt, eines scheint offenkundig: Wir sind Tiere, genauer gesagt: menschliche Tiere, Mitglieder der Art *Homo sapiens*. Dabei mag es überraschen, daß viele Philosophen diese vermeintlich banale Tatsache abstreiten. Plato, Augustinus, Descartes, Locke, Berkeley, Hume, Kant und Hegel, um nur einige herausragende zu nennen, waren alle der Meinung, wir seien keine Tiere. Es mag zwar sein, daß unsere Körper Tiere sind. Doch sind wir nicht mit unseren Körpern gleichzusetzen. Wir sind etwas anderes als Tiere. Kaum anderer Meinung sind Denker nicht-westlicher Traditionen. Und rund neun von zehn Philosophen, die heutzutage über Probleme der personalen Identität nachdenken, vertreten Ansichten, die ausschließen, daß wir Tiere sind.

Ich werde zunächst darlegen, wie die Auffassung, wir seien Tiere, zu verstehen ist und welches die Alternativen sind. Dann will ich zu zeigen versuchen, weshalb sie derart umstritten ist. In der Hauptsache aber möchte ich begründen, warum wir Tiere sind.

1. Animalismus

Daß wir Tiere sind, heißt, daß jeder von uns mit einem Tier numerisch identisch ist. Es gibt einen bestimmten menschlichen Organismus, und dieser Organismus ist es, der ich bin. Er und ich sind eins. Diese Auffassung wird *Animalismus* genannt. So einfach sie auch ist, läßt sie sich doch leicht mit anderen Positionen verwechseln.

Zum Beispiel ist Animalismus nicht gleich Materialismus. Letzterer besagt, daß wir materielle Dinge sind, also einzig aus Materie bestehen. Tiere sind materielle Dinge. Wenn wir Tiere sind, so sind wir materiell. Der Umkehrschluß jedoch gilt nicht. Es könnte nämlich sein, daß wir materielle Dinge sind, aber keine Tiere. Diese Idee mag merkwürdig erscheinen. Was für materielle Dinge, wenn nicht Tiere, sollten wir dann sein? Und doch ist gerade sie, besonders unter englischsprachigen Philosophen, stark verbreitet. Wir sind, so heißt es, durch Tiere "konstituiert" (Shoemaker 1999; Baker 2000). Dahinter verbirgt sich in etwa der Gedanke, daß ich mich zwar an demselben Ort befinde und aus derselben Materie bestehe wie ein Tier, im Prinzip aber von diesem Tier abgetrennt werden kann; da jedoch kein Ding von sich selbst getrennt werden kann, kann es nicht sein, daß ich mit diesem Tier identisch bin.

---

* Ich danke Astrid Degen und vor allem Klaus Petrus für ihre Hilfe bei der Übersetzung.

Der Animalismus besagt, daß *wir* Tiere sind. Das soll nicht heißen, daß alle Personen Tiere sind. Ich will nicht ausschließen, daß es Personen gibt – Götter z.b. oder Engel –, die völlig anorganisch sind. Wir *menschliche* Personen aber sind Tiere. Daß wir Tiere sind, bedeutet ebenso wenig, daß sämtliche Tiere – selbst alle menschlichen Tiere – Personen sind. Denn es könnte sein, daß Menschen, die sich in einem irreversiblen vegetativen Zustand befinden, zwar Tiere, aber keine Personen mehr sind. Gleiches gilt für menschliche Embryonen: sie sind menschliche Tiere, aber vielleicht noch nicht Personen. Der Animalismus besagt nicht, daß Personen definitionsgemäß Tiere einer bestimmten Art sind. Er sagt überhaupt nichts darüber aus, welche Kriterien erfüllt sein müssen, damit etwas eine Person ist. Das ist ein anderes Thema.

Daß wir Tiere sind, läßt auch offen, ob wir substanziell Tiere sind, also nicht existieren könnten, wären wir keine Tiere. Wenn das Tier, das ich bin, substanziell ein Tier ist, so bin ich dem Wesen nach ein Tier; ist es hingegen bloß akzidentiell ein Tier, so bin ich es nur akzidentiell. Auch darüber schweigt sich der Animalismus aus.

Folgt aus der These des Animalisten, daß wir *nur* Tiere, also nichts anderes als biologische Organismen sind? Das ist ein heikles Thema. Die Frage ist nämlich: Kann ein Tier überhaupt "mehr als nur ein Tier" sein? Falls wir mehr als nur Tiere sind, können wir dann noch Tiere sein?

Wenn jemand darauf hinweist, daß die Fakultät mehr ist als nur der gegenwärtige Dekan, so will er damit wohl sagen, daß der Dekan allein die Fakultät nicht ausmacht, sie vielmehr noch aus anderen Mitgliedern besteht. Sind wir, in diesem Sinne verstanden, mehr als nur Tiere, so sind wir keine Tiere. Vielleicht sind wir mit Teilen ausgestattet – mit einer immateriellen Seele z.B. –, die nicht Teile eines Tieres sind. Andererseits sagen wir: Descartes war mehr als bloß ein Philosoph; er war auch Mathematiker, Franzose, Katholik und anderes mehr. Und doch war er auch ein Philosoph. Wir könnten mehr als "nur" Tiere, aber immer noch Tiere sein, insoweit wir auch über nicht-biologische Eigenschaften verfügen. Daß wir Tiere sind, schließt demnach nicht aus, daß wir Mathematiker, Franzosen, Katholiken und anderes mehr sind. So gesehen ist der Animalist nicht auf die These festgelegt, daß wir ein ausschließlich "tierisches" Wesen besitzen oder daß es keinen nennenswerten Unterschied zwischen uns und anderen Tierarten gibt. Wir sind zwar besondere Tiere; doch auch besondere Tiere sind Tiere.

2. Alternativen

Was könnten wir sein außer Tiere? Welches sind die Alternativen zum Animalismus?
Nun, wir könnten immaterielle Substanzen sein. Oder wir könnten aus zwei Teilen bestehen: aus einer immateriellen Substanz und einem biologischen Organismus.

Auch könnten wir, wie schon erwähnt, durch Tiere konstituiert sein. Ich teile mit dem Tier, das hier sitzt, zwar all meine physischen Eigenschaften, doch bin ich kein Tier. Ferner könnten wir Teile von Tieren sein. Ich bin vielleicht ein Gehirn: streng gesehen wiege ich nur eineinhalb Kilogramm und sitze in meinem Schädel. Oder wir könnten zeitliche Teile oder "Phasen" von Tieren sein: Tiere und andere persistierende Objekte existieren zu verschiedenen Zeitpunkten, indem sie verschiedene zeitliche Teile haben, die zu diesen Zeitpunkten existieren; und eine Person besteht aus Phasen eines Tieres (oder in Gedankenexperimenten: aus Phasen mehrerer Tiere), die psychisch miteinander verknüpft sind. Da es nun nichts gibt, womit die embryonalen Phasen jenes Tieres, das ich bin, psychisch verknüpft sind, sind sie entsprechend auch nicht Teile meiner selbst. Mit anderen Worten bin ich später entstanden als dieses Tier. Man könnte diese beiden Auffassungen – wir sind räumlich sowie auch zeitlich kleiner als Tiere – auch miteinander kombinieren (Hudson 2001, Kap. 4).

Wir könnten, wie Hume gesagt hat, Bündel von Wahrnehmungen sein. Demnach bestehen wir nicht aus Fleisch und Knochen, sondern bloß aus psychischen Ereignissen. Es ist fraglich, ob Hume derlei wirklich geglaubt hat; doch es gibt andere, die das sehr wohl tun (z.B. Quinton 1962).

Oder wir könnten, wie neuerdings zu hören ist, so etwas wie Computerprogramme sein. Ich bin ein gigantischer, in meinem Gehirn realisierter Informationskomplex. Somit könnte man, wie Lewis Caroll einst scherzhaft bemerkt hat, als Meldung per Telegraph versandt werden. Dies würde bedeuten, daß wir nicht konkrete Einzeldinge, sondern Universalien sind (andernfalls wäre diese Ansicht bloß eine Variante der vorherigen). Genauso wie es mehrere Exemplare von *WriteNow 4.0* gibt, könnte es auch von mir mehrere Exemplare geben.

Schließlich könnten wir überhaupt nichts sein: Zwar gibt es Wahrnehmungen, Gedanken und Handlungen, aber nichts, das wahrnimmt, denkt oder handelt. Das klingt zwar paradox, doch gehören immerhin Parmenides, Wittgenstein (1995: 5.631), Russell (1985: 50) und Unger (1979) zu denen, die ihre eigene Existenz bestritten oder zumindest bezweifelt haben.

Es gibt noch andere Ansichten darüber, was wir sein könnten. Doch scheinen mir dies die wichtigsten Alternativen zum Animalismus zu sein. Sind wir nicht Tiere, dann muß eine dieser Auffassungen wohl richtig sein. Denn irgendetwas müssen wir sein. Wenn es etwas gibt, das hier sitzt und diesen Text schreibt, so muß es von irgendeiner ontologischen Art sein.

Für jene, die sich an metaphysischen Gedankengängen erfreuen, mögen diese Auffassungen ihren Reiz haben. Doch sind sie von dem, was wir normalerweise über uns denken, weit entfernt. Demgegenüber mutet die Idee, daß wir schlicht Tiere sind, ver gleichsweise vernünftig und vertraut an. Umso seltsamer ist es, daß sie unter Philosophen so wenig Zustimmung findet.

3. Warum der Animalismus umstritten ist

Daß der Animalismus in früheren Zeiten so unbeliebt war, liegt wohl in erster Linie an der Abneigung gegenüber dem Materialismus. So haben sich Philosophen über lange Zeit hinweg schwer damit getan zu glauben, materielle Gegenstände seien – egal, wie komplex sie gebaut sind – zum Denken fähig. Nun sind Tiere materielle Gegenstände; und da *wir* offensichtlich zum Denken fähig sind, gelangt man leicht zum Schluß, daß wir etwas anderes sein müßen als Tiere.

Warum ist diese Auffassung auch unter zeitgenössischen Materialisten dermaßen verbreitet? Der wichtigste Grund ist vermutlich dieser: Wer über das Problem der personalen Identität nachdenkt, fragt meist nicht danach, was für Dinge wir sind. Es geht nicht darum herauszufinden, ob wir Tiere sind, oder in welcher Beziehung wir zu jenen Tieren, die wir bisweilen unsere Körper nennen, stehen, oder was wir sonst sein könnten, wenn nicht Tiere. Zumindest geht es um all das nicht in erster Linie. Traditionell lautet die Frage also nicht, was wir sind, sondern, worin unsere Identität über die Zeit hinweg besteht. Was ist notwendig und hinreichend dafür, daß eine Person, die zu einem bestimmten Zeitpunkt existiert, mit etwas identisch ist, das zu einem anderen Zeitpunkt existiert?

Die wohl beliebteste Antwort lautet: Unsere Identität über die Zeit hinweg besteht in einer Art psychischer Kontinuität. Demzufolge bin ich in etwa jenes künftige Ding, welches meine psychischen Eigenschaften erbt (meine Erinnerungen, Meinungen, Wünsche usw.); und ich bin jenes Ding aus vergangenen Zeiten, dessen psychische Eigenschaften mir vererbt wurden. Auf welche Weise diese Vererbung genau zu erfolgen hat, ist strittig. Manche glauben, die einschlägigen psychischen Eigenschaften müßten kontinuierlich physisch realisiert sein (z.B. Unger 1990: 147-52); sollte mein Gehirn zerstört werden, bedeutet dies mein Ende – auch dann, wenn es (wie in *Star Trek*) später neu zusammengebaut wird. Andere halten eine kontinuierliche physische Realisation für unnötig (z.B. Shoemaker 1984: 108 ff.). Die Mehrzahl der Philosophen ist heutzutage aber der Meinung, personale Identität habe in irgendeiner Weise mit Psychologie zu tun. Die Identität eines menschlichen Tieres jedoch hat damit nichts zu tun (Olson 1997: 89-93, 114-19).

Jedes menschliche Tier war irgendwann einmal ein winziger Embryo. Dieser Embyro aber wies keine psychische Eigenschaften auf. Entsprechend gibt es keinerlei psychische Kontinuität zwischen einem erwachsenen menschlichen Tier und einem Embryo. Daraus folgt, daß psychische Kontinuität für die Persistenz eines menschlichen Tieres nicht notwendig ist.

Ein bekanntes Gedankenexperiment zeigt, daß sie hierfür auch nicht hinreichend ist. Man stelle sich vor, mein Großhirn würde in einen anderen Kopf verpflanzt. Somit stünde derjenige, der mit diesem Organ versehen wird – und nur er allein – in einem kontinuierlichen psychischen Zusammenhang mit mir. Diese Kontinuität wäre auch kontinuierlich physisch realisiert. Sollte nun irgend eine Art von psychischer Kontinuität hinreichend dafür sein, daß ein späteres Ding mit mir identisch ist, würde ich meinem Großhirn folgen, bzw. nicht mit einem leeren Kopf zurückbleiben.

Was aber würde aus jenem menschlichen Tier werden, mit dem ich so eng verbunden bin? Würde es dem Großhirn folgen? Würden die Ärzte zunächst an ihm herumschnipseln, bis ein kleines Stück faltigen Gewebes zurückbleibt, es sodann verpflanzen, indem sie es mit neuen Teilen – mit einem neuen Kopf, Rumpf usw. – versehen? Wäre dieses Tier zuerst ein ganzes Tier, dann bloß ein Teil von einem Tier und zuletzt wiederum ein ganzes Tier? Wohl kaum. Ein isoliertes Großhirn ist, wie auch eine abgetrennte Leber, kein Organismus. Das Ding ohne Großhirn allerdings ist ein Organismus (und zwar einer, der durchaus lebensfähig ist, falls sein Kleinhirn intakt ist). Gleiches gilt von jenem Objekt, in das mein Großhirn verpflanzt wurde. Demnach sieht es so aus, als hätten wir es mit zwei Tieren zu tun: Dem einen kommt erst sein Großhirn abhanden, dann wird ihm ein leerer Kopf beschert; das andere ist zunächst hohlköpfig und erlangt später ein Großhirn. Dabei wird nicht etwa ein Tier in ein anderes verpflanzt. Vielmehr wird bloß ein bestimmtes Organ von einem Tier ins andere transplantiert. Wenn dem so ist, stellt psychische Kontinuität keine hinreichende Bedingung für die Persistenz eines menschlichen Tieres dar. Denn wir haben hier einen Fall, in dem ein Tier in einem makellos kontinuierlichen psychischen Zusammenhang mit einem anderen Tier steht.

Nun, wird diese Geschichte richtig erzählt, so kommt man leicht zu der Auffassung, ich würde dem transplantierten Großhirn folgen. Derjenige, der nach der Operation mit diesem Organ ausgestattet ist, würde denken, fühlen und handeln wie ich. Er würde denken, er sei ich. Warum auch nicht? "Mein" Tier jedoch – das Tier, das ich wäre, wäre ich überhaupt ein Tier – würde dem Großhirn nicht folgen; es bliebe zurück. Dies wiederum bedeutete, daß mein Tier und ich getrennte Wege gehen können. Ein Ding aber kann sich nicht von sich trennen.

Wenn ich also meinem transplantierten Großhirn folgen würde, so wäre ich mit diesem Tier nicht identisch. Dies Tier ist ein Ding. Ich bin ein anderes. Mithin wäre ich nicht bloß dem Wesen nach kein Tier. Ich wäre nicht einmal akzidentiell ein Tier. Nichts, was auch nur akzidentiell ein Tier ist, bewegt sich von einem Kopf in einen andern. Das menschliche Tier bleibt, zumindest in der so erzählten Geschichte, wo es ist; ihm kommen allenfalls gewisse Organe abhanden oder es werden ihm neue beschert.

Das Argument, das zeitgenössische Philosophen zur Ansicht verleitet, wir seien keine Tiere, ist demnach in etwa dieses (man könnte es das "Transplantationsargument" nennen): Ich würde meinem transplantierten Großhirn folgen. Ein menschliches Tier würde das nicht tun. Anders gesagt: Unsere Identität über die Zeit hinweg, nicht aber die Identität menschlicher Tiere, besteht in einer Art psychischer Kontinuität. Also sind wir keine Tiere.

Wären wir Tiere, wären wir den Identitätsbedingungen von Tieren unterworfen. Diese Bedingungen aber haben mit Psychischem nichts zu tun. Somit hätte auch unsere Identität mit Psychischem nichts zu tun. Entsprechend wäre so ziemlich alles, was seit Locke über personale Identität gesagt wurde, falsch. Das zeigt, daß der Animalismus keine banale Binsenwahrheit ist, sondern eine gewichtige metaphysische Position mit Konsequenzen, die keineswegs harmlos sind.

4. Denkende Tiere

Daß wir Tiere sind, ist nicht bloß intuitiv einleuchtend; es gibt hierfür auch Gründe. Ich komme damit zu meinem Argument für den Animalismus.

Es scheint offenkundig, daß es ein menschliches Tier gibt, welches aufs Engste mit mir verbunden ist: Es ist jenes Tier, das ich im Spiegel sehe und das jetzt auf meinem Stuhl sitzt. Ferner scheint es evident, daß menschliche Tiere fähig sind, zu denken und zu handeln (zumindest jene, deren Nervensystem normal ausgebildet und intakt ist). Es gibt demzufolge ein denkendes, handelndes menschliches Tier auf meinem Stuhl. Ich aber kann denken und handeln. *Ich* bin das denkende Wesen auf meinem Stuhl.

Aus diesen vermeintlich platten Bemerkungen folgt, daß ich ein Tier bin. Grob gesagt, lautet das Argument so (man könnte es das "Argument des denkenden Tieres" nennen): (1) Es gibt ein menschliches Tier, das hier sitzt. (2) Dieses Tier denkt. (Falls es mehr als eines gibt, so denken sie alle.) (3) Ich bin das denkende Wesen, das hier sitzt. Das einzige denkende Ding auf meinem Stuhl ist nichts anderes als ich. Also bin ich dieses Tier. Das betrifft übrigens nicht bloß mich: wir alle sind Tiere.

Das Argument ist logisch gültig. Man vergleiche: Ein Hund kam in die Küche. Der Hund, der in die Küche kam, stahl dem Koch ein Ei. (Falls es mehr als einer war, so taten es alle.) Fritz, und nur er allein, kam in die Küche und stahl dem Koch ein Ei. Folgt daraus nicht, daß Fritz ein Hund ist? Wer hinter dem Argument eine List vermutet, betrachte seine logische Form:

1. $(\exists x)(x$ ist ein Tier & x sitzt auf meinem Stuhl)
2. $(x)(x$ ist ein Tier & x sitzt auf meinem Stuhl) $\to x$ denkt)
3. $(x)(x$ denkt & x sitzt auf meinem Stuhl) $\to x =$ ich)
4. $(\exists x)(x$ ist ein Tier & $x =$ ich)

Mithin ist jeder von uns mit einem Tier identisch.

Daraus wiederum folgt, daß wir die Identitätsbedingungen von Tieren aufweisen. Worin die Persistenz eines menschlichen Tieres auch bestehen mag, es ist zugleich das, was unsere Identität ausmacht. Im vorhergehenden Abschnitt habe ich zu zeigen versucht, daß die Persistenz menschlicher Tiere nichts mit Psychologie zu tun hat. Wenn dem so ist, gilt das auch für unsere Identität. Allerdings ist die Frage, ob wir Tiere sind, von der Frage zu unterscheiden, worin die Identität eines Tieres besteht. Ich könnte Recht haben, daß wir Tiere sind, mich aber über die Identitätsbedingungen menschlicher Tiere irren. Hier geht es bloß um Ersteres.

Mein Argument ist verblüffend einfach – *zu* einfach, möchte man vielleicht meinen. Andernfalls ist nicht recht einzusehen, weswegen es überhaupt Philosophen gibt, die keine Animalisten sind. Daß nur wenige Philosophen Animalisten sind, scheint mir daran zu liegen, daß sie dieses Argument nicht kennen (dazu später mehr). Wie dem auch sei: Das Argument hat drei Prämissen, und entsprechend lassen sich drei Einwände erheben, bzw. drei Strategien anwenden, um der entscheidenden Schlußfolgerung zu entgehen: Man behauptet, daß kein menschliches Tier hier sitzt; oder man sagt, das betreffende Tier denke nicht; oder man bestreitet, daß ich das einzige Wesen bin, welches hier sitzt und denkt. Wer der Meinung ist, wir seien keine Tiere, hat zwischen diesen Optionen zu wählen. Eine andere Möglichkeit hat er nicht. Sehen wir sie uns also der Reihe nach an.

5. Gibt es menschliche Tiere?

Was könnte dafür sprechen, daß hier kein menschliches Tier sitzt? Vermutlich, daß es überhaupt keine menschlichen Tiere oder sonstige Organismen gibt. Denn wenn es menschliche Tiere gibt, so gibt es hier, wo ich bin, ein solches Tier. Wer die erste Prämisse des Arguments bestreitet, scheint sich also darauf festzulegen, daß es streng gesehen keine Lebewesen gibt.

Derlei metaphysische Thesen gibt es zuhauf. Zum Beispiel sind die Idealisten der Auffassung, es gebe überhaupt keine materiellen Gegenstände (jedenfalls verstehe ich sie so). Andere meinen, daß kein Gegenstand einen Wechsel seiner Teile überleben kann; demzufolge gibt es nichts, das zu verschiedenen Zeitpunkten verschiedene Teile aufweist (Chisholm 1976: 86-113 und 145-58; siehe auch Unger 1979). Nun, wenn wir überhaupt etwas über Organismen wissen, so gehört dazu, daß sie einer Veränderung ihrer Teile unterliegen können. Ist das unmöglich, kann es keine Organismen geben.

Allerdings leugnen nur wenige Gegner des Animalismus die Existenz von Tieren. Das ist auch nicht weiter verwunderlich. Einmal davon abgesehen, daß eine solche Auffassung nur schwer zu glauben ist, würde damit die Existenz der meisten anderen Dinge, die wir stattdessen sein könnten, bestritten. Gibt es keine Tiere, so auch keine räumliche oder zeitliche Teile von Tieren oder Gegenstände, die durch Tiere konstituiert werden;

und ist die Annahme, daß es Tiere gibt, problematisch, so wohl auch jene eines Bündels von Wahrnehmungen. Sollte es keine Tiere geben, ist schwer einzusehen, was wir überhaupt sein könnten.

6. Können menschliche Tiere denken?

Die zweite Möglichkeit besteht darin einzuräumen, daß ein Tier auf meinem Stuhl sitzt, hingegen abzustreiten, daß es denkt (unter "Denken" sei hier Glauben, Wollen, Hoffen usw. verstanden). *Ich* denke, das Tier aber nicht. Der Grund für diese Auffassung kann nur darin bestehen, daß das Tier nicht in der Lage ist, zu denken. Denn wäre es dazu fähig, würde es jetzt denken. Wenn *dieses* Tier aber nicht denken kann – trotz seines gesunden und normal entwickelten Gehirns, seiner Bildung, seiner sprachlichen Fähigkeiten, seiner sozialen Umgebung, seiner passenden evolutionären Geschichte usw. –, kann kein Tier, welcher Art auch immer, jemals denken. Kann kein Tier denken, ist auch nicht einzusehen, wie ein Organismus überhaupt psychische Eigenschaften haben könnte.

Der Gedanke läuft also darauf hinaus, daß Tiere, selbst Mitglieder der Art *Homo sapiens*, genauso wenig denken und empfinden können wie Pflanzen. Das aber ist schwer zu glauben. Warum sollten Tiere nicht denken können? Was sollte ein Tier daran hindern, mit seinem Gehirn zu denken? Ist nicht gerade dies die Funktion eines solchen Organs?

Traditionell gesehen, sind Tiere deswegen nicht fähig zu denken, weil materielle Gegenstände dazu prinzipiell nicht in der Lage sind. Das hat etwas für sich: Wenn überhaupt ein materieller Gegenstand zum Denken fähig ist, dann ein Tier. Denkende Wesen müssen immateriell sein. Also sind wir immateriell. Freilich, wer bestreitet, daß kein materieller Gegenstand fähig ist zu denken, hat damit noch lange nicht erklärt, warum dem so ist. Allerdings glauben nur wenige Gegner des Animalismus, wir seien immateriell.

Man könnte auch so argumentieren: "Dieses Tier auf meinem Stuhl ist bloß mein Körper. Und es wäre abwegig zu behaupten, daß es mein Körper ist, der in diesem Augenblick über ein philosophisches Problem nachdenkt oder einen Text verfaßt. Was da nachdenkt oder schreibt, muß also etwas anderes sein als ein Tier. Das aber heißt nicht, daß ich immateriell bin; ich könnte einfach ein anderer materieller Gegenstand sein als mein Körper."

Es mag vielleicht falsch sein zu sagen, daß mein Körper denkt. Jedenfalls ist an solchen Aussagen irgendetwas nicht in Ordnung. Weniger klar ist aber, ob dies daher rührt, daß sich der Ausdruck "mein Körper" auf ein Ding bezieht, und zwar auf ein Tier, das ich in einem gewissen Sinne habe, das zu denken nicht in der Lage ist (vgl. Olson 1997: 142-150). Wie dem auch sei, das Argument liefert so oder so keine Erklärung dafür, weshalb menschliche Tiere nicht fähig sein sollten zu denken.

Wer behauptet, manche materiellen Gegenstände könnten denken, Tiere aber nicht, hat es schwer. Shoemaker (1999) begründet dies mit den Identitätsbedingungen von Tieren. Was ihre Identität ausmacht, ist seiner Auffassung nach nicht damit verträglich, daß sie über psychische Eigenschaften verfügen. Derlei Eigenschaften weisen nämlich spezifisch kausale Rollen auf, und diese Rollen setzen voraus, daß psychische Kontinuität für die Persistenz der Träger psychischer Eigenschaften hinreichend ist. Da aber keine Form von psychischer Kontinuität für die Persistenz eines Tieres hinreichend ist, können Tiere, menschliche Tiere eingeschlossen, keine psychischen Eigenschaften aufweisen. Entsprechend sind sie weder in der Lage zu denken noch zu empfinden. Hingegen sind jene materiellen Objekte, die über die passenden Identitätsbedingungen verfügen, zum Denken fähig und Organismen können solche Dinge "konstituieren". Ich habe mich an anderer Stelle mit Shoemakers Vorschlag auseinandergesetzt (Olson 2002a) und will hier nicht weiter darauf eingehen.

7. Wieviele Denker?

Angenommen, ein menschliches Tier sitzt auf meinem Stuhl und denkt. Könnte man dennoch darauf bestehen, daß ich etwas anderes bin als eben dieses Tier? Daß dieses Tier denkt, ich hingegen nicht, kann man kaum sagen. Ebenso wenig, daß ich nicht existiere, solange es ein Tier gibt, das meine Gedanken hat. Daß ich etwas anderes bin als das denkende Lebewesen auf meinem Stuhl, könnte nur dann sein, wenn ich nicht der einzige bin, der hier denkt. Ich denke. Das Tier denkt. Dabei verfügt es vermutlich über dieselben psychischen Eigenschaften, die auch ich habe. Dieses Tier aber ist nicht ich. Wo es so schien, als gebe es bloß ein denkendes Wesen, finden sich in Wirklichkeit deren zwei. Zwei Philosophen, ein Tier und ich, sitzen hier und verfassen diesen Text. Man ist nie allein: wo immer du bist, ist ein wachsames Tier mit dir.

Es fällt schwer zu glauben, daß es doppelt so viele denkende Wesen geben soll, wie die Volkszählung uns berichtet. Doch ist die drohende Überbevölkerung nicht die einzige Schwierigkeit dieser Auffassung. Wenn es wirklich zwei Wesen – eine Person und ein Tier – sind, die denken, was ich denke, oder tun, was ich tue, so muß ich mich ernsthaft fragen, welches von beiden ich bin. Ich könnte glauben, ich sei die Person (jenes Wesen also, das nicht ein Tier ist). Doch hält sich nicht auch das Tier für eine Person? Es hat dieselben Gründe, das zu glauben, die auch ich habe. Und doch hat es unrecht. Wenn ich das Tier wäre und nicht die Person, würde ich dennoch glauben, ich sei die Person. Nach allem, was ich weiß, bin ich derjenige, der im Unrecht ist. Selbst wenn ich eine Person wäre und kein Tier, ich könnte es niemals wissen. Aus meiner Sicht liegt die Wahrscheinlichkeit, daß ich eine Person und kein Tier bin, höchstens bei 50%.

Es geht noch weiter. Falls das Tier in der Lage ist, zu denken, sollte es doch auch als Person gelten. Es verfügt über dieselben psychischen Eigenschaften wie ich. (Andernfalls hätte man zu erklären, weswegen es hier einen Unterschied gibt.) Tiere sind intelligent, sie haben Vernunft, Selbstbewußtsein, sind Träger moralischer Verantwortung und dergleichen mehr. Entsprechend erfüllen sie die herkömmlichen Kriterien für Personenhaftigkeit. Und doch wäre es unklug, anzunehmen, daß jenes Tier, welches hier sitzt, eine numerisch von mir verschiedene *Person* ist. Denn dies würde der Auffassung widersprechen, daß Personen – sämtliche Personen – über psychische Identitätsbedingungen verfügen. Genau diese Auffassung war aber Anlaß zu glauben, wir seien keine Tiere.

Sollten menschliche Tiere trotz ihrer Intelligenz usw. nicht als Personen gelten, wären die gängigen Definitionen von 'Person' zu freizügig. Um eine Person zu sein, würde es nicht ausreichen, über psychische und moralische Eigenschaften zu verfügen, wie du und ich sie haben. Mithin könnte es intelligente, rationale, moralisch verantwortliche Lebewesen geben, die keine Personen wären, ja, es würde zu jeder echten Person mindestens eine solche Nicht-Person geben. Ob jemand eine Person ist, wäre damit psychologisch oder moralisch gesehen schlicht von keinem Interesse (mehr zu diesen Themen findet man bei Olson 2002b).

8. Einwände und Fragen

Da mir all diese Auffassungen unglaublich erscheinen, halte ich uns für Tiere. Anders gesagt: Auf unserem Planeten leben etwa 6 Milliarden menschliche Tiere. Diese Tiere sehen uns recht ähnlich. Sie sitzen auf unseren Stühlen und schlafen in unseren Betten. Sie reden, gehen zur Arbeit, fahren in Urlaub oder verbringen die Zeit mit Philosophie. Sie verfügen über dieselben physischen und psychischen Eigenschaften wie wir. Danach jedenfalls sieht es aus. All dies macht es schwierig zu behaupten, daß wir etwas anderes als diese Tiere sind. Die mutmaßliche Existenz von denkenden menschlichen Tieren kommt den Gegnern des Animalismus höchst ungelegen.

Ich möchte mich abschließend einem Einwand sowie einer heiklen Frage widmen. Der Einwand ist dieser: Ich habe behauptet, daß wir mit Tieren identisch sind und deshalb die Identitätsbedingungen von Tieren aufweisen. Nun könnte man mit gleichem Recht sagen: Wir sind mit anderen Dingen, *Philosophen* z.B., identisch, und teilen folglich ihre Identitätsbedingungen. Entsprechend würde das Argument lauten: Hier sitzt ein Philosoph. Dieser Philosoph denkt. *Ich* bin das denkende Wesen, das hier sitzt. Also bin ich ein Philosoph. Das heißt, ich bin mit einem Philosophen identisch. Also muß ich die Identitätsbedingungen eines Philosophen besitzen. Das scheint aber mit dem Animalismus unverträglich zu sein. Denn wie sollte es möglich sein, daß ein Ding den Identitätsbedingungen von Tieren als auch jenen von Philosophen unterworfen ist?

Ich will keineswegs bestreiten, daß wir Philosophen sind. Habe ich recht, so sind die Identitätsbedingungen von Philosophen – von menschlichen Philosophen zumindest – auch die Identitätsbedingungen von Tieren. Falls (menschliche) Personen Tiere sind, so ist Personenidentität nämlich Tieridentität. Und falls (menschliche) Philosophen Tiere sind, so ist Philosophenidentität Tieridentität. Wir sind Tiere, Personen, Philosophen, Europäer, und vieles andere mehr. Unsere Identitätsbedingungen aber verdanken sich dem Umstand, daß wir Tiere sind, und nicht dem Umstand, daß wir Personen oder Philosophen oder Europäer sind. In diese Richtung jedenfalls habe ich in Abschnitt 3 zu argumentieren versucht.

Viele glauben, daß wir die Identitätsbedingungen haben, die wir nun einmal haben, weil wir Personen sind. Ihrer Auffassung nach besteht unsere Persistenz in einer Art psychischer Kontinuität, weswegen für sie die Identitätsbedingungen von Personen mit denen von Tieren unverträglich sind. In ihren Augen sind wir keine Tiere. Gerade deshalb ist die Frage, ob wir Tiere sind, eine interessante und wichtige Frage. Wer sie mit "Nein" beantwortet, hat sich dem Argument des denkendes Tieres zu stellen.

Ich habe weiter oben behauptet, daß unsere Identitätsbedingungen mit Psychologie nichts zu tun haben. Das wiederum hat mich veranlaßt, mich mit dem Transplantationsargument auseinanderzusetzen, das Generationen von Philosophen zwingend erschien. Und damit zur heiklen Frage: Warum haben sie sich derart gründlich geirrt?

Einenteils wußten sie nicht, zu welchen Problemen ihre Ansicht führt. Das rührt daher, daß sie sich nicht mit den richtigen Fragen befaßt haben. Sie haben nicht gefragt, was wir sind. Vielmehr haben sie sich für Probleme der Identität über die Zeit hinweg interessiert; sie haben nach Identitätsbedingungen gesucht, die ihnen plausibel erschienen, sie haben sich damit zufrieden gegeben und sich anderen Themen zugewandt. Um die metaphysischen Folgen dieser Auffassung haben sie sich nicht gekümmert.

Ein weiterer Grund ist dieser: Wenn es zwischen einem Ding und mir einen kontinuierlichen psychischen Zusammenhang gibt, so ist dies ein starkes Indiz dafür, daß dieses Ding mit mir identisch ist. Das gilt umso mehr, als es ja niemals vorkommt, daß eine andere, von mir verschiedene Person in einem kontinuierlichen psychischen Zusammenhang mit mir steht: Gehirntransplantationen gibt es nur in der Fantasie. Hinzu kommt, daß wir uns meistens für psychische Kontinuität weit mehr interessieren als für die Frage, ob es einen kontinuierlichen physischen Zusammenhang zwischen einem Lebewesen und mir gibt. Hören wir einer Geschichte zu, ist es uns meist egal, welche Charaktere am Ende der Erzählung dieselben Lebewesen sind wie die, von denen zu Beginn die Rede war. Spannender ist für uns z.B. die Frage, wer sich noch an welche Begebenheiten oder Taten zu erinnern vermag.

Derlei mag uns leicht zu dem Gedanken verleiten, daß unsere Identität in psychischer Kontinuität besteht, vor allem, wenn man blind ist für die immensen Probleme, die eine solche Auffassung in sich birgt. Sieht man hingegen ein, daß wir Tiere sind, sollte auch klar werden, daß man damit einen Fehler begeht – wenn dieser Fehler auch verständlich ist.

Die Gegner des Animalismus können sich natürlich auf dasselbe Spiel einlassen. Sie können versuchen, uns verständlich zu machen, weshalb die Prämissen *meines* Arguments offenkundig erscheinen, obgleich sie falsch sind. Wie geht dieses Spiel weiter? Ich schlage vor, das Transplantationsargument mit jenem des denkenden Tieres zu vergleichen. Was ist plausibler: Daß es keine Tiere gibt? Daß kein Tier jemals in der Lage ist zu denken? Daß ich eines von wenigstens zwei vernunftbegabten Wesen bin, die hier sitzen und denken? Oder daß ich doch nicht meinem transplantierten Großhirn folgen würde?

Literatur

Baker, L. R. 2000. *Persons and Bodies: A Constitution View*. Cambridge: Cambridge University Press.
Chisholm, R. 1976. *Person and Object*. La Salle: Open Court.
Hudson, H. 2001. *A Materialist Metaphysics of the Human Person*. Ithaca: Cornell.
Olson, E. 1997. *The Human Animal: Personal Identity Without Psychology*. New York: Oxford University Press.
–. 2002a. What does functionalism tell us about personal identity? *Noûs* 36: 682-98.
–. 2002b. Thinking animals and the reference of 'I'. *Philosophical Topics* 30: 189-208.
Quinton, A. 1962. The soul. *Journal of Philosophy* 59: 393-403.
Russell, B. 1985. *The Philosophy of Logical Atomism*. La Salle: Open Court (Originalausgabe 1918).
Shoemaker, S. 1984. Personal identity: a materialist's account. In S. Shoemaker und R. Swinburne, *Personal Identity*. Oxford: Blackwell.
–. 1999. Self, body, and coincidence. *Proceedings of the Aristotelian Society,* Supplementary Volume 73: 287-306.
Unger, P. 1979. I do not exist. In G. F. MacDonald (Hrsg.), *Perception and Identity*. London: Macmillan (auch in M. Rea (Hrsg.), *Material Constitution*. Lanham, MD: Rowman and Littlefield, 1997).
–. 1990. *Identity, Consciousness and Value*. New York: Oxford University Press.
Wittgenstein, L. 1995. *Tractatus Logico-Philosophicus. Werkausgabe Band 1*. Frankfurt am Main: Suhrkamp Verlag (Orginalausgabe 1921).

Lynne Rudder Baker
The Difference that Self-Consciousness Makes

With all the attention given to the study of consciousness recently, the topic of *self*-consciousness has been relatively neglected. "It is of course [phenomenal] consciousness rather than ... self-conscious that has seemed such a scientific mystery," a prominent philosopher comments.[1] Phenomenal consciousness concerns the aspect of a state that *feels* a certain way: roses smell like *this*; garlic tastes like *that*; middle C sounds like *this*, and so on. Although phenomenal consciousness is surely a fruitful area of scientific investigation, I hope to demonstrate here that investigation of self-consciousness offers its own rewards, ontologically speaking.

My aim here is two-fold. First, I want to show that self-consciousness is what distinguishes persons from everything else. Second, and more controversially, I want to argue that, not only is self-consciousness definitive of us persons, but also that self-consciousness makes an ontological difference. By an 'ontological difference,' I mean a difference in the inventory of the world. The coming-into-being of a new person is the coming-into-being of a new entity; it is not just a change in an already-existing entity. I shall begin by discussing consciousness and self-consciousness; then I shall give a very brief account of my view of persons as necessarily self-conscious. Although we human persons are the only kind of thing that we know to be self-conscious, on my view, anything that is self-conscious – Martians, computers, or whatever – is a person. Next, I shall discuss a view of human persons that opposes my view. (The opposing view is called 'Animalism;' I call my preferred view 'the Constitution View.') Finally, I shall discuss and defend the claim that the difference that self-consciousness makes is an ontological difference.

Consciousness and Self-Consciousness

Many kinds of nonhuman animals, I think, are conscious: they feel pain, they spit out the medicine with apparent distaste. As subjects of experience, conscious beings not only feel things, but they perceive the world from certain points of view, from which things seem one way or another to them. Experience is perspectival. For example, the dog digs there (in the garden) rather than here (by the house), because she saw you bury the bone there in the garden and she wants it. A conscious being has a certain perspective on its surroundings with itself as "origin." If the dog could speak, she might say: "There's

---

[1] Ned Block, "On a Confusion About a Function of Consciousness," *Behavioral and Brain Sciences* 18 (1995): 227-247. Quotation is on p. 230.

a bone buried over there, and I want it." This fragment of a practical syllogism would explain the dog's problem-solving behavior in terms of its perspectival attitudes. The dog has her own point of view that we can identify by attributing the word 'I' to the dog. But this use of 'I' does not indicate that the dog is self-conscious.

Merely sentient beings, like dogs (that are conscious without being self-conscious) have subjective perspectives, but they are not aware of themselves as having subjective perspectives. Dogs may have beliefs and desires (simple ones, anyway); but they cannot think of themselves as having beliefs and desires. They may have points of view (e.g., "danger in that direction"), but they cannot conceive of themselves as subjects of such thoughts. Nonhuman animals, like persons, can have conscious experience of their environments (e.g., that there's danger over there). But persons, unlike nonhuman animals (as far as we can tell), also can have conscious experience of their thoughts and attitudes (e.g., that they are hoping that there's no danger over there).

To be self-conscious, a being must not only have a perspective, but also must realize that she has a perspective. To be self-conscious, a being must not only be able consciously to experience things, but must also realize that she experiences things. Merely to have a perspective, or to be a subject of experience, is not enough. One must be able to recognize that one is a subject of experience; one must be able to think of oneself as oneself. One must be able to think of one's thoughts as one's own, and to have immediate access to her thoughts in that she can know without evidence that she is entertaining a thought that so-and-so.

There are several kinds of self-consciousness, from the simple realization that if I don't get some food soon I shall starve to death to the sophisticated project of constructing a narrative self. Underlying all these forms of self-consciousness is what I call *the first-person perspective*. The first-person perspective – itself sufficient for the simplest kind of self-consciousness – is the defining characteristic of all persons, human or not.[2] To have a first-person perspective, one must not only be able to distinguish between oneself and other things (as perhaps chimpanzees can be taught to do),[3] but also to conceptualize the distinction between oneself and everything else. One must have a first-person concept of oneself.

In English, the ability to conceive of oneself as oneself is marked grammatically by a sentence with a first-person subject of a psychological or linguistic verb and an embed-

---

[2] For a more detailed account, see Chapter 3 of *Persons and Bodies: A Constitution View* (Cambridge: Cambridge University Press, 2000) and my "The First-Person Perspective: A Test for Naturalism," *American Philosophical Quarterly* 35 (1998): 327-348.
[3] See Gordan Gallup, Jr., "Self-Recognition in Primates: A Comparative Approach to Bidirectional Properties of Consciousness," *American Psychologist* 32 (1977): 329-38.

ded first-person reference.[4] English speakers not only use first-person pronouns to refer to ourselves (e.g., "I'm happy"), but also to attribute to ourselves first-person reference (e.g., "I wonder whether I'll be happy in 10 years"). The second occurrence of 'I' in "I wonder whether I'll be happy in 10 years" directs attention to the person per se, without recourse to any name, description or third-person referential device to identify who is being thought about. Use of first-person pronouns embedded in sentences with linguistic or psychological verbs – e.g., "I wonder how I'll die," or "I promise that I'll stay with you" – provides linguistic evidence of a first-person perspective.

It is only from a first-person perspective that one can evaluate one's goals, or take responsibility for what one has done, or entertain thoughts about oneself as oneself. If I wonder whether I'll be happy in ten years, I am wondering about myself as myself – not myself as a philosophy professor, or as a married woman, or as LB. From a first-person perspective, I do not need to pick myself out as one object among many. I could still have this thought even if I had total amnesia. The first-person perspective opens up a distinction between thinking of myself as myself, on the one hand, and thinking of myself as Lynne Baker, or as the person who is writing this paper, on the other. The first-person perspective is the ability to consider oneself as oneself in this way. This is the basis of all forms of self-consciousness.

Although many nonhuman animals are conscious and are subjects of many intentional states, they lack the first-person perspective that allows them to know that they are subjects of intentional states. There are many kinds of intentional states that only a being with a first-person perspective can have – namely, those that require one as the thinker to conceive of oneself as oneself. A squirrel, lacking a first-person perspective from which it can think about itself qua itself, cannot assess its goals. It cannot consider whether stockpiling nuts really is the task that it should undertake; nor can a squirrel hope that it has enough nuts to get through the winter. If a dog, *per impossibile*, came to have a first-person perspective, then the dog would come to constitute a canine person. If a gorilla (like Koko?) were taught a language sufficiently close to English that we could recognize embedded first-person references, then that gorilla would come to constitute an ape person. Anything that has a first-person perspective is a person.

So, what distinguishes human persons from animals is not consciousness; nor is it the ability to have intentional states like fearing or desiring. The ability to have intentional states is a necessary, but not a sufficient, condition for being a person. To be a person

---

4 Hector-Neri Castañeda developed this idea in several papers. See Hector-Neri Castañeda, "He: A Study in the Logic of Self-Consciousness," *Ratio* 8 (1966): 130-157 and "Indicators and Quasi-Indicators," *American Philosophical Quarterly* 4 (1967): 85-100. For a study of philosophy from a first-person point of view, see Gareth B. Matthews, *Thought's Ego in Augustine and Descartes* (Ithaca, NY: Cornell University Press, 1992).

– whether God, an angel, a human person, a Martian person, an artificial person – one must have a first-person perspective.

The Constitution View of Persons

The Constitution View of persons aims to recognize our animal natures without taking us to be identical to animals. Human persons are *persons* in virtue of their capacity for self-consciousness; they are *human* in virtue of being constituted by human bodies (i.e., human animals).

First, consider the notion of a capacity for self-consciousness. A being has a capacity for self-consciousness (of the relevant kind) if it has the structural properties required for a first-person perspective, and either is in an environment conducive to the development and maintenance of a first-person perspective, or has manifested a first-person perspective at some time in the past. These conditions allow for a person to begin existence at or near birth, and to continue to exist in a coma as long as the structural (e.g., neural) properties remain intact. The conditions for personhood are metaphysical, not epistemological. We may well not know whether a particular being is a person or not.[5]

Second, consider the idea of constitution. The guiding idea of this view of persons is that we are constituted by human animals – just as (certain) statues are constituted by pieces of marble. But since the pieces of marble could have existed without constituting statues, and the human animals could have existed without constituting us, the statues are not identical to the pieces of marble; nor are we identical to the animals that constitute us. The piece of marble did not constitute a statue before it reached the sculptor's workshop. Since the same piece of marble that constitutes the statue now did not constitute the statue before the sculptor saw it, the statue is not identical to the piece of marble. Similarly, when the organism that constitutes me now was an embryo, I did not exist. Since the same organism that constitutes me now did not constitute me at some other time (when it was an embryo), I am not identical to that organism. Identity is necessary; constitution is contingent.

Constitution is a relation intermediate between identity and separate existence.[6] I

---

[5] In that case, we should err on the side of personhood. However, there is no question that a human animal without a neocortex fails to have the structural properties required for a first-person perspective.

[6] Any believer in the Christian Trinity is committed to there being some such relation. I'm not suggesting that a believer in the Christian Trinity will endorse constitution as I construe it; rather, a Christian is in no position to reject my view on the grounds that the idea of a relation between identity and separate existence is incoherent. I define 'having separate existence at t' in "On Making Things Up: Constitution and its Critics," *Philosophical Topics*, forthcoming.

have gone to some lengths elsewhere to give a technical account of the notion that absolves it of charges of incoherence and obscurity.[7] Here I just want to give an informal description. On the one hand, we need constitution to be similar to identity in order to account for the fact that if x constitutes y at t, then x and y have many of the same properties at t. For example, if a particular 6-foot piece of pink marble constitutes a statue, then the statue and the piece of marble are located in exactly the same place; and the statue, as well as the piece of marble, is 6-foot and pink. If the statue is worth a million dollars at a certain time, then so is the piece of marble. (The statue is pink wholly in virtue of being constituted by a piece of marble that is pink; hence the statue has the property of being pink *derivatively*. The piece of marble is worth a million dollars wholly in virtue of constituting a statue; hence the piece of marble has the property of being worth a million dollars *derivatively*. In general, if x constitutes y at t, x borrows some of its properties at t from y, and y borrows some of its properties at t from x.) On the other hand, we need constitution *not* to be the same relation as identity in order to account for the fact that that piece of marble might have existed wihout ever constituting a statue. A certain piece of marble might have remained in the quarry and never have constituted a statue, even if in fact it does constitute a statue now. Similarly, a certain human organism might have miscarried and never have constituted a person, even if in fact it does constitute you (a person) now.

According to the Constitution View, the relation between a human person and her body (the relation that I am calling 'constitution') is exactly the same as the relation between a statue and the piece of marble that makes it up. Nothing that is a statue could exist in a world without art; nothing that is a person could exist in a world without self-consciousness. The difference between a piece of marble and a marble statue is the relation to an artworld (or, perhaps, to an artist's intentions); the difference between a human body and a person is self-consciousness. When a piece of marble is suitably related to an artworld, a new thing – a statue – comes into existence. When a human body develops self-consciousness, a new thing – a person – comes into existence. The human body does not thereby go out of existence – any more than the piece of marble goes out of existence when it comes to constitute a statue. Moreover, a human person is as material as Michelangelo's *David* is. When a human body comes to constitute a person, the body has the property of being a person derivatively (in virtue of constituting something

---

[7] See *Persons and Bodies* and "Unity Without Identity: A New Look at Material Constitution," *New Directions in Philosophy,* Midwest Studies in Philosophy 23, Peter A. French and Howard K. Wettstein, eds. (Malden, MA: Blackwell Publishers, Inc., 1999): 144-165. I have given a completely general definition of 'x constitutes y at t.' Here I'll drop the reference to time when no confusion will ensue. I have a revised definition in "Replies," *Philosophy and Philosophical Research* 64 (2002): 623-635.

that is a person nonderivatively); and the person has the property of being a body derivatively (in virtue of being constituted by something that is a body nonderivatively).

There is much more to be said about the idea of having properties derivatively, but to pursue that topic here would take us too far afield. From now on, I shall omit the qualifier 'nonderivative.' Unless otherwise noted, when I say 'person' or 'body' or 'human animal,' I mean things that have the properties of being a person or a body or a human animal nonderivatively – i.e., without regard to their constitution relations. And when I speak of the bearer of a property, I shall mean something that has the property nonderivatively.

The property of having a capacity for self-consciousness is a property that persons – like you and me – have essentially. The property of being organic is a property that human bodies have essentially. On the other hand, you and I, being constituted by human animals, have the property of being organic contingently. (If our organic parts were gradually replaced with bionic parts, then we persons would still exist, but we would no longer be constituted by organic bodies.) So, you are a person essentially, and organic contingently; and the human body that constitutes you is organic essentially, and a person contingently. You and I have our persistence conditions in virtue of being self-conscious; our bodies have their persistence conditions in virtue of their organic properties. (Persistence conditions are the conditions under which a thing can continue to exist.)

The persistence conditions of animals – all animals, human or not – are biological; and the persistence conditions of persons – all persons, human or not – are not biological.[8] Persistence conditions are determined by ontological kinds: If x and y have different persistence conditions, then x and y are of different ontological kinds. So, on the Constitution View, *person* is an ontological kind defined by self-consciousness. Human persons are constituted by human bodies; Martian persons (if any) are constituted by, say, green-slime bodies. But human persons and Martian persons are essentially self-conscious, and only contingently do they have the kinds of bodies that they have. I am ontologically more similar to a Martian person than I am to a human embryo. According to the Constitution View, self-conscious beings – persons, whether human, Martian or something else – make up an ontologically distinctive category.

Let me explain what I mean by saying that *person* is an ontologically distinctive category. Contrast the proposition that something is a person in virtue of being self-conscious with the proposition that someone is a wife in virtue of being a married female. Necessarily, if x is a wife, then x is a married female. But it does not follow that if x is a wife, then necessarily, x is a married female. I am a wife, but I might have been single; I am not a wife essentially. According to the Constitution View, being a person is not like

---

[8] For an extended defense of this claim, see *Persons and Bodies*.

being a wife. A new person (i.e., a new self-conscious being) is a new entity in the universe; a new wife is just a change in an already-existing entity.

The reason that persons are an ontologically distinctive kind of entity is that the first-person perspective (self-consciousness) brings into being a new kind of reality: the reality of what we might call 'inner lives.' The subjectivity of non-self-conscious consciousness is a step in this direction, but consciousness that is not self-conscious is not sufficient for the rich inner lives that persons have. The subjectivity of persons is not just a matter of experiencing "qualia," but of experiencing stretches of narrative coherence. We not only react to stimuli from the environment; we evaluate possible courses of action. Unlike entities that are conscious without being self-conscious, we can evaluate our own motives. The property of self-consciousness that enabled Augustine to write his *Confessions* is, as far as we know, unique in the universe. Inanimate objects do not have it; nonhuman animals do not have it.[9] Self-consciousness makes us human persons the kind of beings that we are.

Self-consciousness is ontologically but not biologically distinctive. Biologically speaking, human animals are closer to chimpanzees than chimpanzees are to other nonhuman primates. Even if not biologically significant, self-consciousness expands the field of reality. According to the Constitution View, the difference that self-consciousness makes is to define a new category of being. Persons are as different from human animals as statues are from pieces of marble.

So, according to the Constitution View, human persons are constituted by human bodies in the same way that marble statues are constituted by pieces of marble; and what makes something a person is self-consciousness.

The Animalist View vs. The Constitution View

The claim that self-consciousness makes an ontological difference in the world is not a popular one. With the emphasis on biology today, many philosophers find it overwhelmingly plausible to hold that, ontologically speaking, we are animals, period. "Sure," they may say, "We are self-conscious, but self-consciousness is just a property that some animals have during some parts of their existence. Being self-conscious is like being a wife; just as a wife is not ipso facto an ontologically different kind of thing from a non-wife, so to a self-conscious being is not ipso facto an ontologically different kind of thing from a non-self-conscious being. We are most fundamentally organisms," say these philosophers. "We have the persistence conditions of human organisms. We persist as long as

---

[9] Chimpanzees come close. I discuss this point in Ch. 3 of *Persons and Bodies*. See also Gordon Gallup, Jr., "Self-Recognition in Primates."

the organisms that we are persist; self-consciousness has nothing to do with it."

Let us call those who espouse such a view "Animalists." According to Animalism, the kinds of properties that make us the kind of beings that we are our biological properties – the properties that figure into the taxonomy of biological theories. Animalists would regard the properties that we have in virtue of being animals as determining the kind of beings that we are. It follows from Animalism that, in contrast to the Constitution View, persons are not essentially self-conscious. Animalists cannot hold that persons are essentially self-conscious, for this reason: if persons have the persistence conditions of human animals, as Animalists all hold, then persons are essentially human animals; and if persons are essentially human animals, then persons cannot also essentially be self-conscious. Since there are human animals that are not self-conscious (e.g., an early-term human fetus), human animals cannot be essentially self-conscious.

The difference between Animalism and the Constitution View is stark. According to the Constitution View, we are essentially self-conscious and contingently animals; according to Animalism, we are only animals and contingently self-conscious. On the Constitution View, if there are nonhuman persons, then they are ontologically like us; they have first-person perspectives that determine their persistence conditions. On the Animalist View, if there are nonhuman persons, they are ontologically different from us; they have the persistence conditions of whatever they are made of. Suppose that there were a Martian person (a self-conscious being), with very different internal mechanisms from humans. A Constitutionalist would hold that I am ontologically more similar to that Martian person than I am to a groundhog (an organism without self-consciousness). An Animalist would hold that I am ontologically more similar to a groundhog than I am to that Martian person.[10]

According to Animalism, what makes us the kind of beings that we are are our biological properties (metabolism, etc.), and a person's continued existence depends on the continued functioning of biological processes. According to the Constitution View, what makes us the kind of beings that we are is our capacity for self-consciousness and a person's continued existence depends on its continued capacity for self-consciousness.[11] Relatedly, an Animalist holds that the persistence conditions of human persons reside in the continuation of their biological functions.[12] A prominent Animalist, Eric Olson, puts

---

[10] An Animalist might well hold that I am *psychologically* more similar to a Martian person than to a groundhog, but from an Animalist point of view, psychological similarities are ontologically irrelevant.

[11] For a Constitutionalist account of our persistence conditions, see Ch. 5 of *Persons and Bodies*.

[12] There are several versions of Animalism. Some Animalists hold that a human animal ceases to exist when it ceases functioning (i.e., at death). Other Animalists hold that a dead animal is still an animal. For the first version, see Eric T. Olson, *The Human Animal: Personal Identity Without Psychology* (New York: Oxford University Press, 1997). For the second version, see Fred Feldman, *Confrontations*

the matter sharply: "What it takes for us to persist through time is what I have called *biological continuity*: one survives just in case one's purely animal functions – metabolism, the capacity to breathe and circulate one's blood, and the like – continue."[13]

Here is the contrast: According to Animalism, self-consciousness is ontologically irrelevant. According to the Constitution View, self-consciousness is ontologically significant: Two possible worlds as alike as possible, except that one contains self-conscious beings and the other contains no beings that are self-conscious, are *not* ontologically on a par. According to the Constitution View, the difference that self-consciousness makes is thus an ontological difference. A self-conscious being is a fundamentally different kind of thing from anything else in the world.

The Constitutionalist holds that development of self-consciousness in a human organism should be understood in terms of that organism's coming to constitute a new entity – a person. The Animalist disagrees: The development of self-consciousness in a human organism should be understood in terms of the acquisition of a contingent property by an organism that is basically nonpersonal.

Before giving reasons to prefer the Constitution View over Animalism, let me emphasize that the issue here is not over whether or not self-consciousness is a product of natural selection, nor is it over whether or not self-consciousness has some particular kind of neural basis. The issue concerns the *status* of self-consciousness: Does self-consciousness make an ontological difference, or is it just a contingent property of some already existing thing (like an animal)? The Constitution View need not deny that self-consciousness is a property that animals have evolved by natural selection. The Constitutionalist's claim is that when it did evolve by natural selection (if it did), it was sufficiently different from every other property in the natural world that it ushered in a new kind of being.[14] Where an Animalist would say that there is a single animal, unself-conscious at one time and self-conscious at another, the Constitutionalist would say that there is an animal that does not constitute a person at one time and does constitute a person at another. If self-consciousness is a product of natural selection, according to the Constitution View, it still makes an ontological difference. The moral to draw in that case would be that ontology does not recapitulate biology. So to say that self-consciousness is a product of natural selection does not settle the issue between the Animalist and the Constitutionalist.

---

with the Reaper (New York: Oxford University Press, 1992). But whatever persistence conditions animals have, we persons have the same ones, according to Animalism.

[13] Olson, *The Human Animal*, p. 16.

[14] The reason that I do not say that self-consciousness ushered in a new kind of animal is that biologists do not take self-consciousness to distinguish species, and I take the identification of new kinds

The Constitution View vs. The Animalist View

Regardless of the origin of self-consciousness, or of its physical basis, the question is this: Is self-consciousness just a contingent property of an already existing animal, or does the appearance of self-consciousness mark the coming-to-be of a new kind of entity? Does self-consciousness really make an ontological difference – as the Constitution View holds and the Animalist View denies?

I want to offer considerations in favor of saying that self-consciousness really does make an ontological difference. Then, I shall discuss the methodological principle that underlies my position. Self-consciousness is both unique and significant in a way that I claim is ontological. By saying that self-consciousness is unique, I mean that self-consciousness – one's having an inner life – is not an extension of, addition to, or modification of any other property. A first-person perspective is irreducible to third-person properties.[15] By saying that self-consciousness is ontologically significant, I mean that a world lacking self-conscious beings would be lacking in a kind of reality that our world enjoys. In order to argue for the ontological significance of self-consciousness, I shall consider ways in which self-consciousness makes possible what is distinctive about human persons. Manifold manifestations of self-consciousness attest to its uniqueness and significance:

First, consider natural language and culture. Natural language itself is connected to the first-person perspective in complicated ways. Let me speculate about our evolutionary ancestors: In order for there to be natural language at all, there had to be beings with at least rudimentary first-person perspectives. The first-person way of distinguishing between oneself and everything else is a prerequisite of having a natural language. Then, as natural language developed, the first-person perspectives of its users became more sophisticated. Acquisition of a language enabled its users to entertain increasingly complex thoughts (first-person and otherwise). One lacking self-consciousness could not learn to speak a fully developed natural language – a language that contained such ordinary locutions as 'I believe that I know the answer to number four' or 'I hope that I will get home safely.' To be able to entertain the thoughts that these sentences express requires self-consciousness.

Cultural achievements are further consequences of self-consciousness. The ability to wonder what sort of thing we are, to consider our place in the universe – these are specifically first-person abilities that motivate much of science, art and architecture, philosophy and religion.

Second, self-conscious beings are bearers of normativity in ways that nothing else is:

---

of animals to be within the purview of biology.
[15] See *Persons and Bodies*, Ch. 3.

Self-consciousness is required for rational and moral agency. A rational agent must be able to evaluate her goals. In order to evaluate her goals, she must be able to ask questions like "Is this a goal that I should really have?" Asking such questions is an exercise in self-consciousness, requiring that one can think of herself as herself, from the first person. A moral agent must be able to appreciate the fact that she (herself) does things and has done things in the past. Such appreciation requires that one have a concept of herself as herself.

Third, in contrast to nonself-conscious beings, we have control over nature, at least in a limited way. We are not only the products of evolution, but also we are the discoverers of evolution and interveners in evolutionary processes, for good or ill. We clone mammals, protect endangered species, devise medical treatments, stop epidemics, produce medications, use birth-control, engage in genetic engineering and so on. Reproduction is the great biological imperative, which we can and do flout. Animals that do not constitute persons can attempt to survive and reproduce, but – being unable to conceive of themselves in the uniquely first-personal way – they cannot try to change their natural behavior.

Fourth, any reflection on one's life requires self-consciousness. Any thought about one's desires or other attitudes – "What do I really want?" – requires a first-person perspective. Being anxious about the future, wondering how one is going to die, hoping that one is making the right decision about going into a certain profession, and on and on – are depend directly on self-consciousness. Things that matter deeply to us as individuals – our values, our futures, our ultimate destinies – could matter only to beings with first-person perspectives. Furthermore, we care in a more intimate way about groups that we are members of (social or biological) than of other groups. (One may care about any country's waging war that does not meet the criteria for a "just war;" but one cares in a quite different (and more wrenching) way about one's own country's waging such a war. One may care about wholesale destruction of the natural environment and the extinction of countless species by any cause whatever; but, again, one cares in a quite different (and more wrenching) way about wholesale destruction of the natural environment by one's own species.)

Fifth, there is a way in which self-consciousness itself brings into existence new reality – the "inner world" that Descartes explored so vividly in the first part of the *Meditations*. Although I do not accept Descartes' reified conception of the realm of his thoughts nor its independence of the "external" world, I do agree that there are facts of the matter – e.g., that Descartes was thinking that he existed – and that the existence of these facts would be logically impossible in the absence of self-conscious beings. Descartes' certainty was that he (himself) existed, not that Descartes existed. His quest in the *Meditations* was ineliminably first-personal. It is not just that Descartes spoke in the first-person for heuristic purposes; rather, *what* he discovered (e.g., that he himself was a thinking thing) was first-personal. The appearance of such first-personal facts implies that self-consciousness has ontological implications, in which case it is seems to be more than just another contingent property of animals.

Here, then, are five ways in which self-consciousness makes us the kind of beings that we are: Self-consciousness is required: (i) for natural language and culture, (ii) for normativity in rational and moral arenas, (iii) for control over our destinies as individuals and as a species (and over the destinies of other species), (iv) for understanding of ourselves as individuals and as members of social and biological groups, and (v) for the existence of our "inner lives."

Contrast the difference that self-consciousness makes with the difference that, say, wings on birds make. The appearance of wings makes possible new facts about flying. But there is a big difference between facts about flying and facts about self-consciousness. Many different species (e.g., of birds and insects) fly, and facts about flying are on a continuum with other kinds of facts – say, about swimming, running, and jumping. The appearance of self-consciousness also makes possible new facts. But the facts that self-consciousness makes possible (e.g., deciding to change one's life) are not on a continuum with other kinds of facts. Nor do we find self-consciousness among different species. Self-consciousness is novel in a way that wings are not.

Mere consciousness, too – it may be argued – is also novel. I agree, but self-consciousness is novel in a unique way. In the first place, consciousness seems to come in degrees: a housefly may feel pain (else why shouldn't schoolboys pluck off their wings?), but your beloved dog makes finer discriminations – discriminations that we presume to have a conscious aspect. Consciousness is spread over many different species, and seems to come in different degrees in different species. But only one species supports self-consciousness. In the second place, self-consciousness brings in its wake all the achievements and abilities that I have just enumerated. Consciousness brings in its wake nothing new in terms of achievements and abilities. (If consciousness brought in its wake new achievements and abilities, we could detect which of the lower organisms are conscious by their achievements and abilities.) We do not even know exactly which beings feel pain, say, at all. There is no clear mark of consciousness the way that there is of self-consciousness.

In short, the difference in abilities and achievements between self-conscious and nonself-conscious beings is overwhelming, and overwhelming in a more significant way than any other single difference that we know of. The abilities of self-conscious, brooding and introspective beings – from Augustine in the *Confessions* to analysands in psychoanalysis to former U.S. Presidents' writing their memoirs – are of a different order from those of tool-using, mate-seeking, dominance-establishing nonhuman primates – even though our use of tools, seeking of mates and establishing dominance have their origins in our nonhuman ancestors. With respect to *the range of what we can do* (from planning our futures to wondering how we got ourselves into such a mess, and with respect to *the moral significance of what we can do* (from assessing our goals to confessing our sins), self-conscious beings are obviously unique.

The uniqueness of self-consciousness, together with the kind of significance that it has, counts in favor of taking self-consciousness to have ontological significance: Self-consciousness makes us the kind of beings that we are.

I have been arguing for the ontological significance of self-consciousness. But it is equally important for my view that we are wholly constituted by animals and so have biological natures. The animals that constitute us are part of the seamless animal kingdom which sees no discontinuity between human animals and other higher primates. Darwinism offers a great unifying thesis that "there is one grand pattern of similarity linking all life."[16] Human and nonhuman organisms both find their place in this one grand pattern.

Considered in terms of genetic or morphological properties or of biological functioning, there is no gap or discontinuity between chimpanzees and human animals. In fact, human animals are biologically more closely related to certain species of chimpanzees than the chimpanzees are related to gorillas and orangutans.[17] So, *biologically considered*, there's no significant difference between us and higher nonhuman animals. But *all things considered*, there is a huge discontinuity between us and nonhuman animals. And this discontinuity arises from the fact that we, and no other part of the animal kingdom, are self-conscious. (If I thought that chimpanzees or computers really did have first-person perspectives, I would put them in the same category that we are in – namely, persons.)

These two considerations – the uniqueness of self-consciousness and the seamlessness of the animal kingdom – may now be seen as two data:

(A) Self-consciousness is unique in the universe – in that self-consciousness (one's having an inner life) is not an extension of, addition to, or modification of some other property. Self-consciousness is an extremely significant feature of human persons. As self-conscious beings, human persons have vastly different abilities from nonself-conscious beings.

(B) The animal kingdom is a seamless whole, revealing no important biological (morphological, genetic, etc.) discontinuities between human and nonhuman animals. Human persons are, in some sense, animals – biological beings.

[16] Niles Eldredge, *The Triumph of Evolution* (New York: W.H. Freeman, 2000): 31.
[17] Daniel C. Dennett, *Darwin's Dangerous Idea* (New York: Simon and Schuster, 1995): 336. Dennett is discussing Jared Diamond's *The Third Chimpanzee*.

I believe that these two data can be much more naturally accommodated by the Constitution View than by the Animalist View. According to the Animalist View, the sense in which human persons are animals is identity; human animals (= human persons) are just another primate species – along with chimpanzees, orangutans, monkeys and gorillas. The fact that human persons alone have inner lives (and all the abilities discussed) is not a particularly important fact about persons. Animalists have nothing to say about what distinguishes us from nonhuman primates. From an Animalist perspective, self-consciousness is just a contingent property of organisms that are fundamentally nonpersonal. The significance of self-consciousness is rendered invisible by Animalists. So, I do not think that Animalists do just to datum A.

On the other hand, the Constitution View explains both these data: The Constitution View explains datum A – that we are self-conscious beings in a world apparently lacking self-consciousness elsewhere. It explains this datum by taking self-consciousness to be what makes us ontologically distinct. The property of having an inner life – not just the property of sentience – is so extraordinary, so utterly unlike any other property in the world, that beings with this property are a different kind of thing from beings without it. Only self-conscious beings can dread old age or discover evolution or intervene in its otherwise blind operations. Since first-person perspectives are essential to us, it is no mystery that we human persons are self-conscious.

The Constitution View also explains datum B – that we are biological beings in an animal kingdom that is seamless – by holding that we are constituted by human animals that are on a continuum with nonhuman animals and then explaining what constitution is. The continuity of the animal kingdom is undisturbed. Well, almost: human animals that constitute persons do differ from other animals, but not in any essential way. Person-constituting human animals have first-person-perspective properties that non-person-constituting human animals lack; but the animals that have these properties only have them derivatively – wholly in virtue of their constitution relations. To put it more precisely, human animals have first-person-perspective properties wholly in virtue of constituting persons that have first-person-perspective properties independently of their constitution-relations. So, the Constitution View honors the continuity of the biological world and construes us as being part of that world in virtue of being constituted by human animals. Unsurprisingly, I conclude that the Constitution View gives a better account of human persons than does the Animalist View.

To sum up: Animalism cannot do justice to datum A. The Constitution View can do justice to both datum A and datum B. It can agree with Animalism that considered biologically, human animals are just another primate species – not very special from a biological point of view. So, there is no difference between the Constitution View and Animalism with respect to datum B. However, the Constitution View is far superior to Animalism with respect to datum A. Whereas the Animalist simply denies the relevance of self-consciousness (or of any psychological properties) to our being the kind of entities that we are, the Constitution View brings forward the ways in which self-consciousness is significant that we have discussed. According to the Constitution View, self-consciousness is sufficiently different from everything else known to us in the natural world that it is reasonable to say that the difference that self-consciousness makes is an ontological difference. This conclusion is more than adequate to explain datum A.

The issue between the Constitution View and Animalism is this: What kind of beings are we most fundamentally? The Animalist says that we are most fundamentally biological beings, and has nothing to say about our mental and moral properties. The Constitutionalist says that we are fundamentally moral beings, and still can explain our biological properties. To hold with the Animalist that human persons are fundamentally animals, and not essentially self-conscious, is to make properties like *wondering how one should live* irrelevant to what we most fundamentally are, and properties like *having digestion* central to what we fundamentally are. I think that what we most fundamentally are is a matter of what is distinctive about us and not what we share with nonhuman animals.

Methodological Morals

This discussion raises some important methodological issues, two of which I want to discuss briefly. First, my position implies that ontology need not track biology. Second, my position implies that the fundamental nature of something may be determined by what it can do rather than by what it is made of.

With respect to the first issue – that ontology need not track biology – my position is to take biologists as authoritative over the animal kingdom and agree that the animal kingdom is a seamless whole that includes human animals; there are no significant biological differences between human and higher nonhuman animals. But from the fact that there are no significant *biological* differences between human and higher nonhuman animals, it does not follow that there are no significant differences, *all things considered*, between us and all members – human and nonhuman – of the biological kingdom. This is so, because we are constituted by animals without being identical to the animals that constitute us. For example, the evolutionary psychologist Steven Pinker writes, "A Darwinian would say that ultimately organisms have only two [goals]: to survive and to reproduce."[18] But he also points out that he himself is "voluntarily childless," and comments, "I am happy to be that way, and if my genes don't like it, they can go jump in

---

[18] Steven Pinker, *How the Mind Works* (New York: W.W. Norton and Company, 1977): 541.

the lake."[19] These remarks indicate that Pinker has a first-person notion of himself as something more than his animal nature as revealed by Darwinians. The Constitution View leaves it open to say that although biology fully reveals our animal nature, our animal nature does not exhaust our complete nature all things considered.

Thus, we have a distinction between ourselves regarded from a biological point of view, and ourselves regarded from an all-things-considered point of view. We know more about ourselves all-things-considered than biology can tell us. For example, the quotidian considerations that I mustered to show the uniqueness and importance of self-consciousness are not learned from biology: that we are rational and moral agents; that we care about certain things such as our own futures; that we have manifold cultural achievements; that we can interfere with the blind workings of evolution; that we enjoy inner lives. These are everyday truths that are constantly being confirmed by anyone who cares to look, without need of any theory. These truths are as firmly established as any in biology. So, they are available for our philosophical reflection – understood, as Wilfrid Sellars put it, as "how things in the broadest possible sense of the term hang together in the broadest sense of the term."[20] With this synthetic ideal, it is clear that we cannot just read ontology off any of the sciences. Everything we know – whether from science or everyday life – should go into determining the joints at which we are pleased to think that nature is carved.

This kind of methodological consideration underlies my holding that there is an ontological division that is not mirrored by a biological division. As Stephen Pinker and others point out, small biological differences can have big effects.[21] I agree. Small biological differences can even have ontological consequences. Biologically similar beings may be ontologically different. Indeed, that is my view.

Now turn to the second methodological issue: My position is that what something most fundamentally is – its nature – is more nearly determined by what it can do than by what it is made of. This is obvious in the case of artifacts: What makes something a clock has to do with its telling time, no matter what it is made of and no matter how its parts are arranged. Similarly, according to the Constitution View, what makes something a person has to do with its being self-conscious and its ensuing abilities, no matter what it is made of.[22] Self-consciousness can make an ontological difference because what self-

---

[19] How the Mind Works, 52.
[20] "Philosophy and the Scientific Image of Man," in Science, Perception and Reality (London: Routledge and Kegan Paul, 1963): 1-40. (Quote, p. 1)
[21] Steven Pinker, How the Mind Works, 40-1.
[22] I reject Humean metaphysics, according to which the identity of a thing is determined entirely by its 'categorical' properties that are independent of what the thing can do, and according to which what a thing can do is determined by contingent laws of nature.

conscious beings can do is vastly different from what nonself-conscious beings can do. We persons are ourselves originators of many new kinds of reality – from cathedrals to catheters, from bullets to bell-bottoms, from cell-phones to supercomputers. One reason for this for this methodological stance is that it allows that the nature of something is tied to what is significant about the thing. What is significant about us – as even some Animalists agree[23] – are our characters, memories, mental lives and not the respiration, circulation and metabolism that we share with nonhuman animals. To understand our nature is to understand what is significant and distinctive about us, and what is significant and distinctive about us is clearly our self-consciousness.

Conclusion

So, according to the Constitution View that I endorse, the difference that self-consciousness makes is an ontological difference. The Constitution View offers a way to set a traditional preoccupation of the great philosophers in the context of the "neo-Darwinian synthesis" in biology.[24] The traditional preoccupation concerns our inwardness – our abilities not just to think, but to think about our thoughts; to see ourselves and each other as subjects; to have rich inner lives. The modern synthesis in biology has made it clear that we are biological beings, continuous with the rest of the animal kingdom. The Constitution View of human persons shows how we are part of the world of organisms even as it recognizes our uniqueness.[25] What sets us apart ontologically is our self-consciousness.

---

[23] A prominent Animalist, Eric T. Olson, insists that a mental life is irrelevant to what we most fundamentally are. Supposing that there could be a transfer of your cerebral cortex into another body, while your cerebrumless body still carries out biological functions like respiration, circulation, etc., Olson argues that the cerebrumless body is actually you and that the person with your memories, character, and mental life is actually not you. Nevertheless, he says that it is rational for you to care selfishly about the person who has your cerebrum (who is not actually you), rather than the cerebrumless body (who actually is you.) See *The Human Animal: Personal Identity Without Psychology* (New York: Oxford, 1997): 52.

[24] Variations on this term are widely used. For example, see Ernst Mayr, *Toward a New Philosophy of Biology: Observations of an Evolutionist* (Cambridge, MA: The Belknap Press of Harvard University Press, 1988); Philip Kitcher, *Abusing Science: The Case Against Creationism* (Cambridge MA: The MIT Press, 1982); Daniel C. Dennett, *Darwin's Dangerous Idea: Evolution and the Meanings of Life* (New York: Simon and Schuster, 1995).

[25] For further arguments in the same vein as this article, see my "The Ontological Status of Persons," *Philosophy and Phenomenological Research* 65 (2002): 370-388. Some of the sentences in the paragraph to which this note is appended came from that article.

Brian Garrett
Some Thoughts on Animalism*

Animalism

Animalism is the doctrine in the theory of persons according to which each of us is (numerically identical to) an animal, *viz.*, the animal we share our matter with. So if the animal I share my matter with is labeled 'A', then Animalism implies that I am A (and so, *mutatis mutandi*, for everyone else).

Animalism has the initial attraction of being, or seeming to be, a piece of commonsense. Is not man simply flesh and blood? Are we not obviously biological creatures, part of the animal kingdom? Nonetheless, Animalism flies in the face of much traditional philosophical doctrine. Clearly it is at odds with Cartesian Dualism and with religions which emphasise the survival of the soul after bodily death. But there is also a more recent philosophical tradition, inspired by Locke, which eschews Cartesian dualism, yet still refuses to identify persons with animals. Clearly, I and the human animal A stand to each other in a very intimate relation (sharing the same space as, sharing the same matter as, constitution, or whatever), but, according to the Lockean tradition, this relation falls short of strict numerical identity.

In this brief discussion piece, I shall outline the powerful theoretical motivation in support of Animalism, recently outlined convincingly by Eric Olson in his book *The Human Animal* (Oxford University Press, 1997). However, I shall then give reasons why Animalism cannot be true, drawing on considerations advanced by the Lockean tradition. I shall then describe a model from elsewhere in metaphysics (the theory of artefacts and art works) in terms of which we can understand how Animalism might be false and its motivation flawed.

Since I am in no position to refute Olson's main point (his theoretical case for Animalism), my conclusion is that, until more is said, we have a paradox on our hands: powerful theoretical considerations support the view that we are identical to animals, yet equally powerful intuitive considerations support the opposite view.

Why it's true

The central case for Animalism (outlined clearly by Olson in Chapter Five of his book) proceeds by *reductio*: if we suppose Animalism to be false, we end up with an absurdity; so Animalism is true.

* Thanks to Eric Olson for helpful discussion of these issues.

Thus suppose Animalism false: suppose, in particular, that I and A are numerically distinct. I am a person. But is A, the animal composed of my biological matter, body, organs, brain etc., also a person? Most philosophers in the Lockean tradition have assumed that the answer to this question is 'no'. Such philosophers assumed that, strictly speaking, the person is the bearer of mental states (sensations, emotions, beliefs, desires etc.), but that, strictly speaking, the animal is the bearer of no mental states, and hence is not a person.[1]

However, Olson makes vivid how uncomfortable and just plain wrong that answer is. The animal A has my brain, body, abilities etc. Why deny the full panoply of mental life to A? Certainly, such a denial will seem irrational to anyone who believes in the supervenience of the mental on the physical (since I and A would be physical identical, yet mentally utterly dissimilar). But, even without relying on supervenience, the denial of mentality to A flies in the face of the well-confirmed scientific belief that mentality results from, and depends on, brain structure.

In other words, it seems entirely *ad hoc* to deny mentality to A. So we should concede that A has just the mental life that I have, and so is a self-conscious subject of experience. But this discussion proceeded on the assumption that I and A are distinct. In which case, if both I and A are subjects, there are two subjects in my shoes, not one! More generally, the population of the world is twice what we thought it was. But this is absurd.[2] What led to this absurdity? The assumption that I and A are numerically distinct. So this assumption must be rejected. But this is just another way of saying that Animalism is true.

It might be thought that there is a way of living with the consequence that I and A both have mental states. Could it not be that I and A *share* the same mental states, just as a 1kg bronze statue and the bronze lump which constitutes it share the same matter? In the latter case (see below), the statue and the lump are numerically distinct; but we

---

[1] Why have Lockeans thought this? Maybe they thought that, since a human animal is not essentially a mental being (e.g., it can remain alive even when all mentality has been irretrievably extirpated), so it is not a bearer of mental states at all. But is this not a fallacy?
No. Or, rather, not if mental beings are essentially mental. For then it's true that if an animal is not essentially mental, it is not mental at all. A is not a mental being since A lacks a property (an essential property) had by any mental being. In which case, we are not forced to the conclusion that A is identical to a person. This Lockean position has the consequence that, *contra* the point made in the following two paragraphs in the text, A has all my physical properties, yet none of my mental properties. To say the least, this commits the Lockean to a view uncongenial to most contemporary philosophers of mind.
[2] In correspondence Olson has suggested that there is an additional epistemological absurdity: if I'm not A, how can I *know* that I'm not A? However, even if there is an epistemological worry here, the metaphysical consequence is absurd enough.

avoid the conclusion that the statue and lump together weigh 2kgs by appealing to the fact that they share the same matter.

Similarly can we not avoid the double-counting consequence by claiming that I and A share the same mental states? When I think "Canberra is in Australia" so does A: but there are not two thoughts here, just one shared thought. The problem, however, comes with indexical and demonstrative thoughts. Suppose I think "this thinker lives in Canberra". Does A think this (token) thought too? No. Thoughts are individuated by truth-conditions, and thoughts about different subjects have different truth-conditions. If I and A are distinct subjects/thinkers, we cannot share such a thought. In which case, two demonstrative thoughts are expressed, and this seems one too many. So the double-counting worry remains.

Why it can't be true

Nonetheless, Animalism cannot be true. There is a host of thought-experiments, the most plausible descriptions of which imply the falsity of Animalism. I will outline some of these thought-experiments now.

First, we have brain-transplant cases. Suppose that my brain, or cerebrum, is transplanted into the (brainless) skull of my now dead twin brother. My old (and cancerous) body is simply allowed to die. The resulting person is fully psychologically continuous with me, and has the kind of body that can allow for the exercise of all my abilities and dispositions. The most plausible description of this case is that I am the resulting person; I survive with my brain and my brother's body. But no human animal has survived, only part of an animal. The human animal (A) is allowed to die. But if I can survive a scenario which A cannot, then I cannot be identical to A. (Of course, Olson wants to resist this description of the case, but that is implausible. That is, it's implausible to think that I die with A, and that a new person comes to occupy my twin brother's body.)

Second, we can imagine a slightly different scenario. Suppose that my cerebrum is removed from my skull and the rest of my body destroyed. My cerebrum is kept alive by a machine, and I am conscious, and self-conscious, throughout. If a self-conscious being has survived, then a person has survived. I have survived, albeit in a vastly denuded condition. But no animal has survived; the animal was destroyed. Again we seem to have a scenario in which I survive, yet A does not. So I cannot be A.

Third, we can imagine that technology has reached such an advanced stage that all animal organs, including the brain, can be replaced with bionic organs which serve the very same functions as the animal originals, including psychological functioning.[3] (This at

---

[3] This is not to assume that mental processes are computational. John Searle, who famously denied

least seems metaphysically or logically possible, which is all that matters here.) So we could imagine that I go through a process of total bionic replacement. Every part of me is (gradually) replaced with a bionic part. At the end of the process no animal part, hence no animal, remains. Provided the replacement process in no way interferes with my psychology, abilities and appearance, it is very plausible to say that I survive. Yet, given the plausible essentialist thesis that if x is an animal, x is essentially and (hence) at all times an animal, no animal has survived; so, again, I cannot be identical to A.

Fourth, we can imagine an even more compelling thought-experiment along similar lines: *Mutation*. I am a space man on the first mission to Mars. The mission is successful; we spend 6 months on Mars then return. There are no (unaccountable) changes in my abilities, appearance or psychology. I go for a routine check up, and the doctors find something quite extraordinary. Apart from my appearance, there is nothing human, or animal, about me at all. My biological matter has mutated into that of a non-animal, silicon-based life-form. Given the essentialist thesis of the previous paragraph, it follows that the animal that left for Mars (A) no longer exists. But I still exist. Hence, Animalism is false. (And notice that, unlike the previous example, this transformation is entirely natural and law-governed: mutating from a carbon-based life-form to a silicon-based one in that way is what happens to people like us who go to Mars.)

What our reactions to these thought-experiments suggest is that, at least in these and similar cases, a continuing line of (non-branching) psychological continuity is sufficient for personal identity; and this sufficient condition, together with other plausible assumptions, implies the falsity of Animalism. (And note that one can endorse this sufficient condition while agreeing with Olson (Chapter 4) that psychological continuity is not everywhere necessary for personal identity, since, e.g., "I once existed as a fetus".)

A familiar analogy

There is a familiar example which, by analogy, tells against Animalism. This is the example of the statue and the lump. Consider a bronze statue. Call the statue 'Statue' and the bronze lump of which it is composed 'Bronze'. It seems uncontroversial that Statue and Bronze are distinct, even though made of the very same matter. They are distinct because they have different properties. For example, Bronze presumably existed prior to Statue; and nothing can exist prior to itself. So, in general, coinciding does not imply identity.[4]

this assumption, took pains to point out that he wasn't thereby denying the possibility of a thinking machine. (See his "Mind, Brains and Programs", *Brain and Behavioural Sciences*, 1980.)

[4] The case of the Ship of Theseus provides another motivation for the thesis that an artefact and its constituting matter are numerically distinct. See my *Personal Identity and Self-Consciousness* (Rout-

Of course, conceding that Statue and Bronze are distinct does not force us to conclude that I and A are distinct, for there may be relevant differences between the examples. But there is the following complication. It seems that, just as in the case for Animalism, we can pose the following question in the statue/lump case: why, when I'm admiring Statue, am I not admiring two beautiful objects? The statue is beautiful; the lump is arranged in the very same way as the statue, so surely the lump is beautiful too; the statue is not the lump; so there are two beautiful things before me.

I'm not sure how to respond to this line of reasoning. But note that we do not respond by saying: "That consequence is absurd – I'm obviously not looking at two beautiful things; so the statue and the lump must be identical after all." We don't respond like that because we know, for the reason described above, that the statue and the lump are distinct. That belief we will not give up. So, if the "over-crowding problem" is not a decisive reason for identifying Statue and Bronze, why do Animalists think it *is* a decisive reason for identifying myself with A?[5]

Conclusion

My conclusion is hardly satisfactory. There are powerful considerations in favour of Animalism, yet powerful considerations against. The analogy with the statue example may tip the scales against Animalism. But more needs to be said.

---

ledge, 1998), pp. 65-67.

[5] The expedient – suggested in correspondence by Olsen – of denying the existence of artefacts such as statues seems to me a desperate response to the just mooted argument from analogy. There is another strategy worth considering here. It's not obviously absurd to think that the statue is not a real entity in its own right: it is rather the form or shape of the lump. Could one resolve the paradox about persons by claiming that persons are similarly not substances? However, the non-substantiality claim about the statue is plausible only because the statue could not exist without the lump existing: it depends on the lump. But the analogous claim in the case of persons would, of course, be disputed by the Lockean (who thinks that I can exist even if A does not).

Paul Snowdon
Objections to Animalism

The main purpose of this paper is to provide (in §2) a classification of different objections to animalism, and then (in §3) to discuss some recent examples of what emerges as one particular sort of objection. Thus, it is only in §3 that objections to animalism are critically examined, and then it will only be examples of one sort. The arguments which provide the examples to be discussed come from, or have been read by me into, Professor Baker's recent book *Persons and Bodies*. My hope is, of course, that the grouping or classification of objections will ultimately aid in their general evaluation. Now, by 'animalism' I mean the thesis, uncontroversial and obviously correct in the opinion of some, and obviously incorrect in the opinion of others, that we are, essentially and fundamentally, animals. (This formulation, particularly in its employment of the term 'fundamentally' cuts some corners, but that does not matter at this point.) First, however, I want (in §1) to relate the topic of objections to animalism to debates about the notion of a person.

§1 Animalism and the Concept of a Person

In being asked to think about persons, what are we being asked to think about? 'Person' stands for a kind of entity, about which kind most people would agree on two things. (1) We – you, the readers, and I, the writer, of this paper – belong, at least currently, to that kind. It is a simple consequence of this that any defensible thesis about the conditions for being a person must contain only conditions that we currently satisfy. (2) In articulating the conditions for membership of the kind mention will, at some stage, have to be made of certain higher mental capacities, such as self consciousness and that kind of memory, called by some 'experiential memory' and by others 'personal memory', a form of memory in the exercise of which we can vividly recall the doings and happenings which we have previously enjoyed. These are, of course, two of the higher capacities mentioned by Locke in his famous and extremely influential definition of 'person'.[1] Since the present discussion is not too concerned with the details of the analysis of the concept of a person I shall talk of 'higher mental functions' without trying to pin down exactly what they should be. Until recently a third (slightly complex) condition would also have been generally agreed to. (3) The kind which 'person' stands for is a kind for which anything that is of that kind is so essentially, and it is also a kind which involves or is linked to distinctive conditions for existence and persistence of members of the kind. This

[1] See Locke 1975 Book 2, Ch. 21 sec. 9.

clumsy condition is intended to capture what would be meant by saying that 'person' is a sortal term. It is, of course, acceptance of claim (3) that leads people to talk of the problem of *personal identity*. It is acceptance of claim (3) together with claim (1) that confers on reflection about the notion of a person the supposed importance of revealing basic and fundamental truths about *ourselves*.

(3) has, however, recently been denied, or at least queried, by, amongst others, Olson and myself.[2] The reason for doubting (3) starts from the claim that animalism is correct. So we have: (4) we are essentially and fundamentally animals.[3] The currently influential reason for affirming (4) is that its denial seems to generate paradoxes.[4] Now, the suggestion that the denial of (4) leads to paradoxes has, of course, itself been denied, and there is currently an unresolved debate about it.[5] I do not propose to resolve that issue here, but I do wish to add the comment that even if the denial of (4) does not generate paradoxes of the currently alleged sort it might still be wrong to deny it, and reasons of a different kind might be available to recognise this. The importance of the debate about the paradoxicality of denying (4) should not, therefore, be exaggerated.

If, however, we do grant (4) then we can bring with it a relatively undisputed understanding of some aspects of the relation between conditions for animal existence and the presence of psychological capacities. Something that most people accept is that, if it is right to ascribe psychological functions to an animal, it could not be an essential property of the animal that it possesses such functions. One reason is that in the nature of the case there will have been periods in the animal's life before it acquired the functions when it was, rather, in the process of developing them. Another reason is that, for all sorts of possible causes, the animal might not have developed normally and so might not have even acquired them. Another reason for saying that such advanced psychological functions are not essential properties of the animal is that it is clearly possible for an animal which has acquired them to carry on existing but lose them, due to accidents or diseases which destroy such functions without killing the animal. So we can conclude: (5) if (4) is true then we are not essentially possessors of such advanced psychological capacities as self consciousness (and experiential memory). However, (2) seems to claim that it is a condition of being a person that someone possess such advanced psychological capacities. So, if we accept (4), (5) and (2) on that reading, it follows that (3) is false because of the non-essentiality to us of such higher mental properties.

---

[2] See Olson 1997, esp. ch. 5, and Snowdon 1990 and 1996.
[3] In this part of the paper I shall regard (4) as the formulation of animalism.
[4] For exposition of the paradox claim see Ayers 1992 ch. 25, Olson 1997 chs. 4 and 5, and Snowdon 1990.
[5] See Garrett 1998 ch. 2, and Baker 2000 esp. ch. 8.

In place of (3) the obvious proposal is something along these lines: (6) x is a person at t iff x is genuinely capable at t of such higher mental functions as self-consciousness (and experiential memory). This makes, or seems to make, 'person' logically akin to 'baker' and 'candlestick maker'. It does not stand for an essential property of things to which it applies, but rather marks capacities that they happen to have.

It might seem, therefore, that the animalist is committed to defending an account of the notion of a person along such lines.[6] Now, I am far from wanting to say that such an account is indefensible, but I wish, rather, to suggest that it is by no means obligatory for an animalist to endorse it. In developing this suggestion I shall not present a comprehensive catalogue of the options that remain open, but shall, rather, in a series of three remarks, describe (or half describe) a few of them. There is a second limitation to the present discussion which needs stressing. What I wish to do is to indicate how an animalist could theorise about the notion of a person in ways which avoid assigning to the term 'person' the same logical properties we would assign to such expressions as 'baker' and 'candle stick maker'. I am not trying here to show how an animalist can reinstate (3) in *all its aspects*.

(i) The argument presented above to show that an animalist should reject (3) seems to me to be correct. It rests, though, on a particular understanding of (2), which is that the higher mental capacities, whatever they are, that should figure in the articulation of conditions for being a person must figure there as capacities actually possessed by someone who counts as a person. If (2) is so understood, then according to the animalist, since we only contingently possess the capacities, we are not essentially persons.

An alternative way to understand (2), though, is to hold that the specification of the conditions for being a person must mention certain higher mental capacities but need not cite them as required to be actually present. One way of understanding some of the writings of Professor Wiggins on the notion of a person is as attempts to provide a defensible formulation of just such an understanding of (2). Thus, in *Sameness and Substance* Wiggins proposed what he called the *Animal Attribute Theory* of persons (hereafter abbreviated to AAT). In a slightly shortened version it says: '... x is a person if and only if x is an animal ... of a kind whose typical members perceive, feel, remember (etc.) ... , conceive of themselves as perceiving, feeling (etc.) ...'.[7] Since for Wiggins a defence was

---

[6] Believing, in the 1980's, that animalism required such an account of the term 'person', I devoted some time to trying to find and assess the evidence in favour of the standard view that 'person' stood for an essential property of the item to which it applied, and concluded that there was no such overwhelming evidence. My present point is that animalists can be somewhat more concessive about this claim about the logic of 'person'. For a presentation of the view of 'person' which animalist have so far found congenial see Mackie 1999.
[7] Wiggins 1980 p. 171.

needed of the idea that the psychological condition should be attached to the more general condition of being an animal, he sought (or, at least, so it seemed) to meet that need by providing arguments which tried to *derive* the condition of being an animal from the satisfaction of the psychological condition. It is, I think, quite reasonable to be sceptical of these arguments, but even if that type of criticism is right, it does not amount to an objection to the correctness of AAT, but merely to Wiggins's attempts to support it.[8] However, the crucial question here is whether this condition picks out an essential property of us. I want to allow that we are essentially animals of a certain kind (homo sapiens) but does the extended psychological characterisation apply to each of us essentially? To answer that question we need to attend to the significance in AAT of the talk of typical members of an animal kind. If by 'typical' is meant the way that most members of the kind are, then, although we do, as a matter of fact, typically end up fulfilling the psychological conditions cited in AAT, it does not seem that it is a necessary truth that humans as a kind do so. The reason for saying this is that what is in fact our normal psychological development might be blocked by, say, an evil scientist or an environmental hazard, so that we reproduce without getting anywhere near to fulfilling our psychological potential. In that case, we would not have belonged to an animal kind which fulfils the AAT condition.

The examples used in this argument, however, suggest a different way to understand 'typical'. Roughly, the properties of a typical member of an animal kind are those properties which animals of that kind would acquire if developmental conditions are optimal, that is, if nothing in the conditions which influence those developments is preventing the animal from achieving what would be called its general potential. Now, understanding 'typical' this way, it is, surely, correct to think that humans do fulfil the requirements in AAT, and further, the examples that counted against the essentiality to us of the property that the AAT condition on its first interpretation picks out do not count against its essentiality on this second interpretation. However, that does not mean that we *do* essentially possess the property picked out by the AAT condition on this second interpretation. In fact, pursuing this issue would raise too many complex and rather imponderable problems to make it suitable for the present paper. I want, therefore, to modify AAT yet again and consider the following proposal: (7) x is a person if and only if x is such at its origins that, if developmental conditions are optimal, then it would become something that perceives, feels, remembers (etc.) ... and conceives of itself as something which perceives, feels etc. ... . My question is whether elucidating 'person' this way might make it essentially true of what it applies to. To defend that two assumptions would need to be

---

[8] For an exposition of such criticisms of Wiggins see Snowdon 1996. The present discussion represents an attempt to get a little more out of Wiggins's proposals than I then thought possible.

defended. The first is that the initial physical condition of a thing is essential to it, and the second is that the causal dispositional powers possessed by it represent necessary properties of something of its physical sort. All I want to say here is that despite the existence of a strong feeling that neither claim is true, there is some chance that they can both be defended. If they are defensible then this theory of what it is to be a person would make it an essential property of us and one which the proper analysis of which must mention the higher psychological features. So (7) would be consistent with animalism, and yet represent an account of personhood which satisfies (2) *in some sense*, and makes it an essential property of us.

(ii) Another way of getting an elucidation of 'person' which both satisfies (2), again *in some sense*, and makes it an essential property of us, while acknowledging animalism, is to analyse it this way; (8) x is a person if and only if x is of that fundamental kind that we in fact are of, and, where, as introduced, the term 'person' is linked to a stereotype picture of ourselves in which the standard higher mental functions are made central.[9] The idea, that is, is to allow that an expression for a kind can be linked to certain features, not by being necessary conditions for its correct application, but by their figuring in a conception, which the standard process of teaching the meaning of the expression ensures is internalised by the learner, of the normal or stereotypical developed case. Further, in elucidating, as philosophers, the significance of the expression in question it is assumed that the components in this stereotype need citing. Fixing the reference of the term this way and then alluding to tis associated stereotype constitutes another treatment of the term 'person'.

(iii) Finally, we could confer on 'person' a different logic from that conferred on it by the baker/candlestick maker model, by defining it this way; (9) x is a person if and only if x possess the higher mental capacities *or has at some stage done so*. This would mean that the principle 'once a person, always a person' would be true, and again it would satisfy (2) in some sense.

I want to suggest, therefore, that animalism does indeed rule out elucidating 'person' as both requiring the presence of higher mental capacities *and* as being essential to us. However, apart from that, it can happily explore different accounts all of which satisfy (2) in some sense and which confer on it different logical properties from those associated with the account that animalists were initially inclined to suggest. When the final sifting of these proposals is over it remains to be seen which works out best.

With this conclusion I want to turn to the task of classifying the objections to animalism.

---

[9] This may correspond fairly closely to what Wiggins was proposing in Wiggins 1980.

§2 Objections to Animalism

2.1 There are lots of current objections to animalism, but I want to suggest a classification or grouping of them that might prove useful when considering the debate about animalism. By describing this as a classification or grouping of 'current objections' I mean to include in it only objections which are, or are supposed to be, consistent with (that vague thing) physicalism. Assuming that physicalism is true involves at the very least assuming that there are no parts to us, human beings, other then the physical parts of our bodies, and so any objections which presuppose the existence of such non-bodily parts are excluded from the present classification. Undoubtedly, the major objections that are currently influential are based on a belief in the possibility of what I shall call *dissociations* between ourselves, us, and the animals with which, according to (4), we are identical. Candidate dissociations come in different forms and can be categorised in different ways. The ones that I wish to begin with, because they are the ones most usually presented, all start with a person, that is to say, one of us, and an animal, a human being, in the same place at the same time. The fundamental division within these cases is between those where, supposedly, either the case develops in such a way that at the end there is the animal but not the person, or it develops in such a way that at the end there is the person but not the animal. I call cases of the first sort [A&~P] cases, and those of the second [P&~A] cases.[10] The crucial question is, of course, whether *any* such [A&~P] case or *any* such [P&~A] case represents a genuine possibility.[11]

Purported [A&~P] cases themselves, or what I am counting as such, can be divided in a rough way into three groups. The first group, which I call type-1 cases, and which is rather heterogeneous, contains cases about which there is some inclination to think that they involve the continuation of the animal, but the total ceasing to exist of the person. Why might it be thought that the person is not there, even though the animal is? The answer is that what is imagined is a fairly radical loss of the psychological capacities associated with the animal, and that loss tempts some people to describe what has happened as the extinction of the person. This is the verdict that is offered by some on, for example, cases of Alzheimer's disease, irreversible coma, and the kinds of occurrences imagined by philosophers, and sometimes labelled 'brain zaps', in which a process destroys the structures in the brain that are necessary for consciousness and cognition. The degree of loss that is necessary to tempt people to adopt the verdict that the person is

---

[10] Pronounced 'A and not P cases' and 'P and not A cases'.
[11] I have used the term 'person' in labeling the different groupings, but what must be remembered is that 'P' stands for there still being at the end that one of us with which the case started out, and '~P' stands for that not being so. This labeling does not reflect any interest in the question whether the thing remaining falls under the term 'person'.

no longer there can vary. Some are so tempted if certain of the higher cognitive activities or capacities are lost. For others, the temptation exits only if *all* mental capacities are lost.

Now, a verdict along these lines is correct only if we (or persons) are essentially possessors of psychological capacities of some sort. The proposition, vague though it is, that we, persons, are essentially possessors of psychological properties of some sort, I call (EP) (short for the essentiality of psychological properties). (EP) is not very precise, but to some people it is a plausible thought or intuition. So the fundamental question about supposed type-1 [A&~P] cases is whether anything like (EP) is true.

The second type of what I am counting as [A&~P] cases (type-2 cases) are ones where people are tempted to offer the verdict that despite there being, over a period, a single animal, there are, as we might say, 'based' in that animal, or associated with it, different persons at different times. This is the verdict some offer as applicable to cases of Multiple Personality Disorder (though, that is, of course, not necessarily the only possible example). The slight strain involved in classifying this as an (A&~P) case is that when such a verdict is endorsed little thought is given to the question as to what exactly has happened to the currently displaced person (who is, of course, usually envisaged as reappearing later). One option, though, is certainly to think that the displaced person is, at least for a time, *not* there housed in the animal. If that option is taken then the case is literally an [A&~P] case.

Why, though, is the multiplicity of successive persons verdict adopted? The fundamental commitment of this verdict is to the general thought that there must be certain *links* between the psychological states of a single person over time. It is believed that these necessary links are broken in the psychological discontinuities exhibited by MPD patients, at least as philosophers imagine such cases to be. The general proposition that there must be certain links between the successive psychological states of a single person over time, I call (EPL) (short for the essentiality of psychological links). Whether that general thought is true is the crucial question raised by type-2 cases.

The third rough category of [A&~P] cases is where although there remain psychological properties linked to the animal and there are also appropriate links over time, there seem to be a multiplicity of subjects or persons housed in the animal simultaneously, as a result of the destruction of various interconnections between parts of the cognitive structures present in the animal. The most obvious candidate for such a description is what results from operations of brain splitting. With the supposed emergence of a multiplicity of subjects the original subject is thought of as having ceased to exist. Since the animal is certainly still there we would, if this description were correct, have an [A & ~P] case. The basic assumption of the endorsement of this third category is that there must be a high degree of unity amongst the psychological states of a single subject at a time. Whether that assumption is correct is the crucial issue raised in the assessment of such cases.[12]

I turn now to the second general group of purported dissociations, the [P&~A] cases, where supposedly a process or occurrence preserves the person but does not, or need not, preserve the animal with the person. I think that it is sensible to subdivide candidate scenarios of this sort into five categories. The first I call *Pure Person Transfers* (PPT's). The idea of a PPT is that it is possible for a person (one of us) to be housed in, associated with, a certain animal at t, and then to be housed in a different animal (or thing) at t+n, and there be no need to specify any process or occurrence of a more basic sort (say, the transfer of a certain part of the animal's body, or the scanning of the original brain followed by implanting the 'information' extracted into another brain) which is needed for the person transfer to occur. We can, according to believers in this possibility, make sense of what is simply and purely a person transfer. The basic question raised by this sort of case is whether a PPT represents a *real* possibility. Should we allow that it is a genuine possibility for a person to transfer between locations without any more basic physical link between the locations?[13]

The remaining four categories of [P&~A] cases, in contrast, rest on the idea that certain possible physical processes, with their attendant psychological consequences, constitute the preservation of the person but not of the animal. The divisions concern significant differences between the physical processes. Thus, the second category of [P&~A] cases is special because the cases which supposedly constitute the survival of a person in a distinct place from the earlier housing animal are supposed to do so in virtue of a physical process which links them but which does not involve any material continuity between the object housing or supporting the person initially and the object supporting that person after the process. I call these *Non-Substantial Transfers* (NST's) This may seem obscure, but one example, introduced by Parfit, is where instructions are sent to the far side of the universe to create a new body with certain psychological properties based on a pattern provided by a person on earth. No substantial part of the earlier animal is transferred in the process, indeed it is usually envisaged as being totally destroyed,

---

[12] A preliminary engagement with [A&~P] cases from an animalist point of view is given in Snowdon 1995.
[13] A recent defense of such a possibility as genuine is given by Baker 2000 pp. 141-145. One might ask current proponents of this type of possibility whether a PPT is more of a possibility than what might be called a PPD, that is a Pure Person Demise. A PPD would be a case where we start with a person and a human animal at the same place at the same time and where absolutely nothing untoward happens to the animal but, supposedly, the original person simply and purely ceases to exist. This is, of course, the analogous [A&~P] case to PPT's. I did not include this in my [A&~P] cases because no-one seriously suggests it, but what is the difference?

but to some it seems that the person has been transplanted.

The third sort of case is where, supposedly, the original human animal is so modified physically that it counts as being replaced by something else but the original person remains, despite the physical changes, in virtue of the psychological continuities that are imagined as preserved. I call these Animal Replacement Cases (AR cases). Possible examples of AR cases are where the parts of the animal are gradually replaced by, say, inanimate parts, so that at the end there is something more like a robot, where, however, these new parts sustain both the mental functioning and the links between the stages that would have happened if the animal and person had continued normally. Other examples are imaginary cases where one animal is transformed into another one, but the person again remains because of psychological continuities. Some care, though, needs to be taken in considering such cases. If it is held that an animal that is initially of one sort, say a dog, can itself become an animal of a different sort (say a sheep), or, indeed, can itself become a non-animal, then the cases are not [P&~A] cases. They count as examples only if the transformation is understood as involving the elimination of the original object which was the animal together with the preservation of the original person. It is not easy to formulate a claim that the belief in the possibility of such cases rests on or reflects. The central idea is, roughly, that the preservation of a person – of one of us – requires nothing more than the preservation of a battery of psychological states. The question is whether this is a totally attenuated conception of our nature.[14]

Fourthly, there are cases in which a particularly crucial *part* of the animal is transferred, where, because of the psychological role of the part, its transferral is supposed to preserve or take with it the person but because it is only a *part* of the animal the animal is not preserved. I call these Animal Part Transfers (APT's for short). The most discussed case is that of brain transplants. Thus, it is supposedly possible in principle to remove a person's brain, and to keep it sustaining consciousness (and other mental states). It has seemed to many that it is true to say that the person would, in those circumstances, go with the brain, but the animal would not. So, in these possible circumstances, the person and the animal come apart. The most difficult question, I believe, to be faced in considering the truth of (4) is whether this is the right verdict on such cases. It is, though, important to remember other possible examples of the same sort, for example, head transplants.

Finally, there is a sort of case, not developed, as far as I know, in the literature, which resembles the APT's, but which does not itself involve a transfer. In these cases parts of

---

[14] This is not completely fair to some of those who believe in the possibility of such cases and who would stress the importance in them of the presence of a sort of physical continuity. So the underlying commitments of endorsing such cases as possible needs more careful description than given in the main text.

the human animal's body are allowed to atrophy but other parts have their functioning artificially preserved. The most interesting example would be to keep the brain functioning within an otherwise dead body. Some would judge, in the light of the supposed preservation of psychological processes, that this means that the person remains but that the general degree of atrophy means that there is no longer an animal. I call these Animal Part Atrophy cases (APA cases). Such examples raise issues like those raised by APT's but without the complications of transfers.

This completes the list of possible [P&~A] cases that I wish to categorise. There is one general comment to make on the [A&~P] and [P&~A] cases so far described. For most of them, to think that they represent genuine possibilities when specified in terms of animals and persons (as we are understanding that term in this section) is to assume that we, (or persons), are, as we might say, deeply psychological entities. We are such that, either to remain in existence certain psychological properties must be possessed by us, or, it is enough for us to remain in existence that certain psychological processes are continued in what are non-standard ways or circumstances. A fundamental question, therefore, is; are we psychological entities in the sense of this assumption?

There is, though, something about the logic of anti-animalist dissociation arguments that I wish to make explicit (perhaps unnecessarily). So far I have formulated animalism as; (4) we are essentially and fundamentally animals. But the more basic and usual formulation is in terms of an identity proposition, namely; (4*) each of us is identical with, is one and the same thing as, an animal. In considering the logic of dissociation arguments, therefore, it is better to consider them in relation to (4*). So consider now the proposition;

(O) each of us is identical with a rugby player.

Now, (O) is formally parallel to (4*), but one cannot object to the truth of (O) on the grounds that we might cease to be rugby players, that is, that there might be a time when we are there but there are no rugby players. But this possibility seems to be what I was calling a dissociation; it is like saying that there can be an animal without there being a person. So, why are dissociations of the [A&~P] kind, or of the [P&~A] kind, problems for (4*)? To provide an explanation of this we need to distinguish two sorts of sort. Let 'N' be a sort. For some sorts we can say;

an N can cease to be an N.

Thus we can say; a rugby player can cease to be a rugby player. But there seem to be other sorts for which we cannot say this. We cannot say;

a material object can cease to be a material object.

I call sorts of this latter kind - abiding sorts. Now, the reason that the dissociations I have cited are problems for (4*) is that both 'animal' and 'person' seem to be abiding sorts. We are surely, reluctant to say that an animal can cease to be an animal. Assuming that that is correct, then [P&~A] cases become inconsistent with (4*). Thus, (4*) says that this person (one of us) is identical with an animal; if being an animal is an abiding sort then this person, being an animal cannot cease to be an animal; but according to the imagined case, the person can come apart from the animal. If so, the person cannot *be* identical with the animal.

Further, on the face of it, being a person is an abiding sort. However, this is not really the crucial claim, for I have been using 'person' as shorthand simply for being one of us. So the abidingness of this notion comes down to the following claim (or something like it);

I cannot cease to be me, and,

You cannot cease to be you.

These claims certainly seem true. If so, 'person' as I have used it is an abiding sort. And that means that [A&~P] cases conflict with (4*). Therefore, involved in assessing the significance of both [A&~P] and [P&~A] dissociations must be a consideration of whether these two sorts are abiding sorts.

2.2 Now, the cases I have listed so far are not the only dissociations that might be used against (4*), and this fact reflects another apparent logical property of the A and P categories. Thus, what I am calling [A&~P] and [P&~A] cases all concern possible dissociations between a person, one of us, and an animal that might develop in a *life under way* where at some time and place there has been a person and an animal. But it would seem to be equally an objection to the claim that each of us is identical to an animal if either it was possible for there to have been the animal without there being one of us at all or if it was possible for the person to have existed without there being an animal at all. I call the former Animal Only cases (AO cases) and the latter Person Only cases (PO cases). If the physicalist constraint is accepted then it is difficult to see how there could be candidate PO cases, so I shall ignore that type of case. It is, however, not at all obvious that within that constraint there cannot be AO cases. Thus, it might be claimed that there are stages of foetal development where there is already a developing animal or organism, but where there is not yet a person, one of us. Or it might be claimed that it is quite possible for a foetus that did in fact develop normally so that consciousness emerged, to have not done so, if, say, it had been damaged by drugs. So, even if in the normal course of events there is both one of us and an animal, there might only have been the animal in this sort of case. If this is a description of a possible case then, it would have to be concluded, putting it in the first person, that I am not identical to, am not one and the same thing as, this animal. The reason is that just as I cannot cease to be me (which I expressed by calling being me an abiding property) so I cannot *not* have been me. I am, it seems, *essentially* and always myself.

It is crucial, though, in thinking about what I am calling AO cases to keep in mind what supposing that there was no person amounts to. It does *not* amount to supposing that there was nothing present to which the noun 'person' could be applied. It amounts to supposing, rather, and again putting it in the first person, that there was nothing present at these early stages which I can correctly think of as *myself*. So understood, the animalist might well ask whether really we do not think of the early stages of the animal's development as a foetus as stages in *our own* development, and also think of ways that might have gone wrong with it as ways our own development might have gone wrong. Might this not be a case of – there but for the grace of God go *I?*

2.3 This completes my classification of what I have called dissociation arguments against animalism. My purpose here is classificatory rather then evaluative, but at this point I wish to voice and comment on one thought that the classificatory list might prompt. Someone might say that the list of suggested dissociation counterexamples is so long and varied that some of them must be correct. Clearly, the defence of animalism, if it is possible, requires that no dissociations are possible. In response to the comment, though, I want to say two things. First, it is not reasonable to be impressed by the *number* of arguments in favour of a certain claim, since they could all be unsound. Second, part of the significance of the classification that I have been suggesting is that many counterexamples can be seen to rest on what is basically the same conviction, so it turns out that there are fewer fundamental difficulties with animalism than it initially seems.

However, and at this point the classificatory argument resumes, once we are using the general notion of dissociation arguments we can obviously define a further category of arguments, namely, arguments not based on premises claiming the possibility of any type of dissociation. We can then ask what kinds of arguments they might be. But the importance of such a category of argument can be appreciated also by raising the following question which it is natural to raise at this stage in our discussion; *must* someone who rejects (4*), that is who rejects animalism, endorse the possibility of at least one of the sorts of dissociation case distinguished above? Putting that in the first-person, might it be that I am *not* identical to the human animal here but that necessarily wherever and whenever I exist this animal exists also (and vice versa)? I think that the most reasonable answer to this question is 'yes'. In the first place, there are no arguments that I can think of to establish that the non-identity of A and B entails the possibility of conditions in which one exists but the other does not. Second, there are what seem to be counterexamples to the claim that there is such an entailment. For example, this table does not seem to be identical to the surface of this table, but there are no conditions under which there can be this table without the surface of the table and vice versa. Again, I am not identical to the set containing just me, but there are, or seem to be, no circumstances in which one exists without the other. Finally, 1 is not identical to 2, but there are no circumstances under which one might exist without the other. An anti-animalist, then, need not endorse the possibility of what I have called dissociations. This leads on to the next question; what, according to an anti-animalist position that rejects the possibility of dissociations, would reveal that the person is not identical to the animal? That would have to be revealed, if it could be revealed at all, by discernible property differences between the person and the animal other than dissociation possibilities. It remains, therefore, at least a possible strategy for an opponent of (4*) to try to demonstrate a non-identity without relying on arguments which claim that there are what I have been calling possible dissociations. Arguments of this sort, which would be essential for the justification of such a view, are just instances of the contrasting general category of argument to those based on dissociations which I have been so far classifying. I shall call them non-dissociation arguments.

Within this category of non-dissociation arguments we can further draw, or acknowledge, a distinction between those which if sound would justify an overall position according to which there would be the possibility of dissociations, and those arguments which, if sound, would refute the animalist's thesis but need not justify a belief in possible dissociations. Although this distinction is sound, it does not overturn the idea that both types of arguments are in an important sense of a single type.

The question that should be raised now is whether there is any chance that such a non-dissociation argument might be sound. I do not, however, see any general proof that there could not be a sound argument of this type, and want, rather, to proceed in a more piecemeal way by scrutinising, in the last section, some examples of such arguments which have been put forward by Professor Baker in her recent book *Persons and Bodies*. In the course of this scrutiny I hope that some more general points might emerge.

§3 Some Non-Dissociation Arguments

I have chosen to consider Professor Baker's discussion because she has attempted, in her book, to formulate in a serious way, some non-dissociation arguments. She does not rely on them exclusively, or even, perhaps, mainly, and she certainly formulates and endorses arguments based on dissociations. Further, my exposition and discussion here of these arguments has to be rather selective, because of space constraints, but I hope that this does not lead to any significant unfairness. I shall consider initially what I take to be three arguments presented in an early part of the book, in a section entitled 'Beyond Biology'.[15]

The argument that I shall consider first, although it does not come first in her exposition, is the simplest. The argument is based on the existence of significant differences between *us* and those things which everyone would so far agree to be animals. She says; 'We are not limited to goals derived from those of survival and reproductiion. This partial control is quite compatible with our being unaware of much that motivates us ... The point is that animals have no control over their goals; but that we ... have a certain control over some of our goals ...'[16]. Obviously, there is something incautious about Baker's expression here. Someone who is an animalist and who thinks that we have control over our goals will simply not allow that 'animals have no such control'. Equally, someone who is unsure ot the truth of animalism should not agree either.It is, therefore, best to say that the argument bases itself on this contrast (and other contrasts) between us and what are agreed to be animals. If this is the correct way to state the argument then it seems that we can represent it in the following way.

(A) We, (in virtue of self consciousness etc.), have properties $P_1...P_n$
(B) Things which are agreed so far to be animals lack $P_1...P_n$, therefore,
(C) We are not animals.

I want to make four comments arguing that this reason ought not to impress us. (i) The argument is formally speaking parallel to the following evidently fallacious argument.

(A*) Rolls Royces can cruise silently at 150 mph.
(B*) Things that are agreed to be cars so far cannot do that, therefore,
(C*) Rolls Royces are not cars.

It is evident that (A*) and (B*) might be true but that (C*) is false, so (C*) cannot follow from them. What does follow, of course, is;

(C*D) Either Rolls Royces are not cars or they are a different/new type of car.

Similarly, what follows form (A) and (B) is;

(CD) Either we are not animals or we are a different type of animal.

Nothing at all is presented in this argument for favouring the first disjunct in the conclusion. We might say, therefore, that the argument commits the Rolls Royce Fallacy!

[15] Baker 2000 pp. 12-20.
[16] Baker 2000 p. 14.

(ii) We should be struck, too, when considering this argument, by the manifest and colossal diversity within the class of what are agreed to be animals. There are enormous differences between amoeba and gorillas. Why should some more differences within the class of animals be significant?[17] (iii) Should we be confident that (B) is true? Three things should be noted. First, we are at a comparatively early stage of close observation of actual animals.[18] Second, it is a highly contentious and complex area of research. So we can hardly be confident about its outcome at this stage. Third, in considering what animals should be agreed to be capable of we ought to remember that the animals we can observe and sample are only a subset of those that have existed. Many sorts of animals are now extinct, and these include the animals which were the immediate predecessors of homo sapiens. It seems clear that they must have been much closer to humans than other extant animals. So the issue cannot be settled simply by observation of agreed present animals. (iv) Suppose it should turn out that our stereotype conceptions of some higher animal psychologies are mistaken and that other higher mammals have $P_1...P_n$. What should Professor Baker's attitude be? I take it that she would not conclude that we have found out that animals can have $P_1...P_n$ and so animalism is defensible, but would rather conclude that we have found out that these other higher mammals constitute persons (with $P_1...P_n$), just as she says about human animals. This means that the argument that I have been considering is not any sort of basis for the philosophical attitude it is needed to support. It can hardly be a justification for thinking that there could not be an animal with $P_1...P_n$ that we happen not to have found one as yet.

A comment that might be made on the discussion of the first argument, and one that I would not particularly insist on opposing, is that the criticised argument does not represent anything that Professor Baker was really relying on. The justification for considering it, as I see it, is that it does resemble some things that Professor Baker says and that we are, in the light of the criticism, warned off a certain style of unsound argument and forced to focus on what anti-animalist arguments which are not based on possible dissociation claims had better appeal to.

Before looking at the next argument I want to consider this general issue in the light of the failure of the first argument. The anti-animalist is trying to show that each of us is not identical to an animal (that is, that (4*) is false). The most straightforward way to show that an entity is not an animal (or organism) is to show that it lacks the basic features that animals must possess. Amongst such features are that it has a certain composition, that certain processes go on in it, and that it has a certain sort of life history. On this

---

[17] For a concise presentation of such differences see Mayr 2002 ch. 8. Think, for example, of the differences between organisms that reproduce sexually and those that do not.
[18] There is much to learn in this respect from what seem to me to be the wise words of De Waal 2001.

basis we might conclude after investigating the entity that it was not an animal but, say, a plant or a machine or a model. Evidently, no observation and reasoning of this sort will justify the conclusion that we are not animals, since any ordinary and biologically informed investigator would conclude that *we do* possess all these features.

It seems to me, therefore, that any argument which aims to establish a property difference, and hence a non-identity, between ourselves and animals (and which does not appeal to possible dissociations) must base itself on the idea that what we might call a Full and Proper Theory of Animals will imply that if something is an animal then it has a certain unobvious and theoretically grounded property which we can be shown to lack. Has Professor Baker provided plausible candidates for this sort of property?

She seems, in the following passage, to suggest one candidate. 'If we are nothing but animals, then either goals that people die for – for example, extending the rule of Allah, furthering the cause of democracy, or something else – should be shown to promote survival and reproduction or those people who pursue such goals should be deemed to be malfunctioning. ... But no one, I think, would suggest that our pursuit of happiness and virtue should be chalked up to biological malfunction.'[19] So the second argument can be represented thus;

(D) Animals which are not malfunctioning can only have goals which promote survival and reproduction.
(E) We have other goals without malfunctioning, therefore,
(F) We are not animals.

I have three comments. (i) The argument is valid, and so it is the premises that must be scrutinised. (ii) Of course, we would naturally agree to (E), but the nature of the argument means that we should be cautious about assenting to it. The strategy of this argument is that an unobvious property of animals has been derived from a full theory of such things, where, obviously, the full theory includes our current conception of the evolution of animals. In the nature of the case, therefore, it can hardly be *obvious* that *we* lack it. It is not the kind of property the presence or absence of which can be obvious. Why would it matter if we thought that we were malfunctioning in pursuing, for example, virtue? That thought would not licence the conclusion that we should not carry on being virtuous. (iii) The most important point, though, is that we have no reason at all to accept (D). Professor Baker herself gives no reasons, but merely cites its endorsement by others. What reason might there be? Obviously, whatever reason there is, it is supposed to start with the claim that animals are the products of evolution. I do not wish, though, to scrutinize possible reasons building on this premise, but shall try to show that there

[19] Baker 2000 p. 14.

cannot be any such sound reason by providing counter-examples to its conclusion. The principle that must, presumably, be correct if premise (D) is to be true is that it is inconsistent with the nature of animals (as the products of evolution) to possess properties that, if they are not malfunctioning, do not promote survival or reproduction. Here are three counterexamples to this generalisation. (a) It may be that there is an advantage in having arms which are three feet long, (given the role of arms) and the gene for that has been selected, and also an advantage in having a waist which is three feet below the neck, (given the role of that area) and that has been selected for, which means that we are genetically endowed with arms which come down to our waists, but that is a genetic endowment which confers on us a property which in itself does not promote survival or reproduction. Plainly, our biological inheritance of such a property is not ruled out by evolutionary theory. (b) It may be that there is an advantage to us in having the capacity to solve fairly advanced practical problems and we are genetically endowed with the physical means to do so. However, this inherited physical system may also endow us with a capacity to engage with intellectual problems, which engagement in itself does not promote reproduction or survival. There is no basis for describing this as a malfunction since nothing has gone wrong in the physical system when it is so employed. (c) Suppose a certain type of insect has evolved with eyes, and the eyes aid the insect's survival. Later there emerges a predator which kills insects with eyes. The eyes no longer promote survival. It clearly does not follow that the eyes are malfunctioning. They are still working perfectly as eyes. (d) Baker herself thinks that human animals genuinely possess the property of constituting persons who are capable of acting in a way not conducive to their reproduction or survival. She can, therefore, hardly think that the possession by animals of such a property is ruled out by the correct theory of animals. This discussion is far too brief, of course, but I conclude that (D) is baseless.

The third argument from Baker is contained in the following remarks. 'Those who take us to be essentially like nonhuman animals want to describe and explain our traits in terms of general biological traits share by other species. But the first-person perspective, whether selected for or not, is a biological surd in this respect. ... Our personal lives are made possible by our organic lives, but they are not exhausted or even fully explained by the facts that professional biologists traffic in'.[20] (pp 16 and 18). These remarks suggest that Baker is moved by the following argument.

(G) If something is an animal then its nature and life is fully explained by biology.
(H) Our nature and life is not fully explained by biology, therefore,
(I) We are not animals.

[20] Baker 2000 pp. 16 and 18.

Premise (G) is obviously the problem here, and I shall make four remarks. (i) Lots of other disciplines than biology contribute to the scientific study of animals as things are. There is ethology and animal psychology. So it is a strange dogma to hold that everything about an animal has a purely biological explanation. (ii) There are plainly lots of facts about animals which do not permit of explanation if the explaining categories are restricted to those of biology. For example, the fact that there are a lot of sheep in New Zealand does not have a purely biological explanation. It requires explanation in terms of the role in human life of that place and those animals. Obviously, with human animals there are endless facts which do not have a biological explanation. Biology cannot explain what language the human animal speaks, what it wears, how it spends its time, and what it knows. Once the existence of such facts about animals is conceded then (G) has to be abandoned. (iii) Baker can hardly accept (G) herself, since she thinks that there are many facts about human animals which lack a biological explanation, for example, that they constitute persons. (iv) There is a significant truth in (G) and that is that it is in the nature of animals to have myriads of central properties genetically determined and there will have to be biological explanations of the origins in each animal of such features, and further, these features will determine in a fundamental way the kinds of lives that such creatures can lead. To this extent biological explanations *are* crucial to animals. But these biological explanations will never totally explain the lives of animals, and, moreover, if the biological endowment of an animal precisely makes it highly sensitive to social influences, endows it with extraordinarily advanced learning capacities, and rich cognitive abilities, then the increased extent of non-biological explanations of its life will merely be a reflection of the underlying biology. This, an animalist might feel, is precisely how it is with *us*.

In the last two arguments it has been the attempt to derive some unobvious restrictive consequence about animals that has been their weakness. It cannot be concluded that no such argument could work, but it is hard to see what extra resources they could draw on. Baker, however, offers (in chapter 9) another non-dissociation argument against animalism, urging the general conclusion that animalism does 'not take persons seriously'. The argument has two stages. In the first stage it is claimed that an animalist must say one of two possible things about being a person. In the second stage it is claimed that both alternatives are inadequate because they 'do not take persons seriously'. The two possible things according to Baker that an animalist can say about persons are these; either (I) being a person is a contingent property that essentially nonpersonal beings have, or (II) 'being a person does not entail any mental properties'. It is then argued that option (I) does not take persons seriously because it entails that every person could be eliminated without eliminating any single individual. It is argued that option (II) does not take persons seriously because it entails that having mental states is irrelevant to what a person is and it also means that 'in a sense, there seems to be nothing that is distinctive of persons'[21]. On this argument I have two main comments. (i) It contains some claims that are mistaken. First, to take option (I) does not mean that persons are 'essentially nonpersons' but only that they are not essentially persons, and, second, taking option (II) does not have the consequence that there is nothing distinctive of persons but merely that the distinctive features are not mental. (Baker's remark is like saying that there is nothing distinctive about human animals because what is distinctive is not mental.) (ii) However, as I see it, animalists must take one of the options that Baker distinguishes with roughly their respective consequences. The problem then is that nothing is really presented by Baker to show that there is anything theoretically undesirable about either position. Why should we not allow that there might be no persons without any individuals being eliminated? Again, why should we not allow that being a person is not necessarily to have certain mental states? Baker's criticism merely comes down to the claim that it *must* be wrong to accept a position which does not hold both that persons are essentially persons and that necessarily being a person involves having certain mental states. As was seen earlier, animalism cannot accept both claims, but such a position has merely been labelled as deficient without any evidence being produced to show that it is deficient.

This brief survey of some non-dissociation arguments, suggested by Baker's discussion, has failed to find any sound arguments. I am not able, though, to show the impossibility of a sound argument belonging to this category and do not claim to have done so.

§4 Conclusion

The main purpose of this paper has been to provide a classification of objections to animalism, which if acceptable, might enable critical discussion of that position to be more systematic, but also to assess the strength of some examples which belong to one important category. I have argued that the latter examples are uniformly weak. In section 1 I tried, in a sketchy and brief way, to determine part of the relevance of this debate about animalism to the account of the concept of a person. My claim is that animalism rules out only one complex and, until recently, popular account of personhood, but that it is otherwise consistent with a variety of accounts of the logic of the term 'person'.[22]

---

[21] Baker 2000 p. 221.
[22] This paper was completed in the congenial environment of Dunedin, during a visit to the University of Otago. I am very grateful to University College London for granting me sabbatical leave, and to the Philosophy Department at Otago for organizing the visit. In particular I wish to thank Professors Grant

Bibliography

Ayers, M. (1992) *Locke* Vol 2, Routledge, London
Baker, L.R. (2000) *Persons and Bodies*, Cambridge, Cambridge University Press
Garrett, B. (1998) *Personal Identity and Self-Consciousness*, London, Routledge
Locke, J. (1975) *An Essay Concerning Human Understanding*, edited by P.H. Nidditch, Oxford, Clarendon Press
Mackie, D. (1999) 'Personal Identity and Dead People' in *Philosophical Studies* 95, 219-242
Mayr. E. (2002)*What Evolution Is*, London, Phoenix
Olson, E. (1997) *The Human Animal*, Oxford, Oxford University Press
Snowdon, P.F. (1990) 'Persons, Animals and Ourselves' in (ed) C.Gill *The Person and the Human Mind*, Oxford, Oxford University Press
Snowdon, P.F. (1995) 'Persons, Animals and Bodies' in (eds) J.L. Bermúdez, A. Marcel, N. Eilan, *The Body and the Self*, London, M.I.T. Press
Snowdon, P.F. (1996) 'Persons and Personal Identity' in (eds) S. Lovibond and S. Williams, *Essays for David Wiggins; Identity, Truth and Value*, Oxford, Blackwells
De Waal, F. (2001) *The Ape and the Sushi Master*, London, Allen Lane
Wiggins, D. (1980) *Sameness and Substance*, Oxford Blackwells

Gillett and Andrew Moore for making the visit so enjoyable. Thanks also to Stephan Blatti discussion with whom has stimulated my thinking about these matters and to Klaus Petrus for the invitation to contribute to this collection and patience waiting for the contribution.

Kevin J. Corcoran
Biology or Psychology?
Human Persons and Personal Identity

Recent discussions of personal identity[1] have been cast in terms of a debate between two broad approaches: The Biological Approach, defended by the likes of Eric Olson[2] and W.R. Carter,[3] and the Psychological Approach, defended by nearly everyone else, including, most recently, Peter Unger.[4] In this paper I develop an alternative to both accounts of personal identity, one which appropriates the insights of each without giving in to their excesses. Along with defenders of the biological approach, I believe that it is right to think of human persons as essentially physical, and that bodily continuity is *necessary* for their persistence. I also believe, along with defenders of the psychological approach, that it is right to think that human persons are essentially psychological beings (i.e, beings capable of, at a minimum, certain kinds of intentional states), and that a kind of psychological continuity is *necessary* for their persistence. Where the biological and psychological approaches go wrong, I shall argue, is in supposing that either biological or psychological continuity *alone* is sufficient for the persistence of persons, and that persons are either essentially physical or essentially psychological, but not both. I will argue that human persons are essentially physical *and* essentially psychological, and that both bodily and psychological continuity are not only necessary for their persistence, they are jointly sufficient.

**1. Problem Cases: Human Vegetables,
Cerebrum-Complements and Tibetan Buddhists**

As a way of introducing the biological and psychological approaches to personal identity I will follow Eric Olson's approach in the beginning of *The Human Animal* and elaborate

---

[1] By situating my discussion on physicalist turf, I do not intend to imply or suggest that dualism is a non-starter. My paper should be read, therefore, not as assuming the falsity of dualism without argument, but rather as an intramural squabble among more physicalist-minded philosophers. In fact, for recent defenses of various versions of dualism see the essays by John Foster, Williams Hasker, Brian Leftow, E.J. Lowe and Charles Taliaffero, in Soul, Body and Survival (Cornell University Press, 2001), ed. Kevin Corcoran.
[2] See his *The Human Animal: Personal Identity without Psychology* (Oxford University Press, 1997). See also his "Was I Ever a Fetus?," *Philosophy and Phenomenological Research* (1997) 95-110 and "Human People or Human Animals," *Philosophical Studies* (1995) 159-181.
[3] See his "Why Personal Identity is Animal Identity," *LOGOS* 11 (1990) 71-81.
[4] "Survival of the Sentient," *Philosophical Perspectives* 14 (2000) 325-348.

several thought-experiments. Consider first what Olson refers to as the Vegetable Case.[5] Imagine that what we commonly call your body comes to exist in a persistent vegetative state. Your brain, let us suppose, is deprived of oxygen for a time sufficient to result in the death of the neurons in your cerebral cortex. Because brain cells do not regenerate, and because higher mental functioning requires an intact cerebral cortex, your higher mental functioning is irretrievably and permanently lost. Suppose too that the subcortical parts of your brain survive the destruction of your cerebrum (upper brain) and continue to maintain respiration, digestion and other functions vital to biological life. Olson asks "[I]s ... the human animal that results when the cerebrum is destroyed strictly and literally you, or ... [is it] no more you than a statue erected after your death would be you?"[6,7]

Now consider another kind of case. Call that part of a human being that includes all of her except her upper brain or cerebrum *cerebrum-complement* and call the kind of case I have in mind the Cerebrum-Complement Case.[8] Suppose the cerebrum-complement of John is beginning to peter out but John's cerebrum, that part which subserves John's mental functioning, is perfectly healthy. Suppose Peter's cerebrum-complement is perfectly healthy but Peter's cerebrum, having suffered traumatic damage to the point that it no longer has the capacity to subserve Peter's mental functioning, is removed from his cerebrum-complement. Imagine an ingenious surgeon removes John's healthy cerebrum from his cerebrum-complement before his cerebrum-complement peters out and implants it into Peter's healthy cerebrum-complement such that John's cerebrum comes to be causally related to Peter's cerebrum-complement in precisely the way it had been causally related to John's cerebrum-complement. And imagine further that after the delicate grafting our ingenious surgeon returns to John's cerebrum-complement and is able, with some effort, to keep it alive and prevent it from petering out. The result, then, according to some philosophers, is that at the end of the story there is a *person* psychologically indistinguishable from John, insofar as he will have the same memories as John had before the surgery and think and feel just as John would have had he persisted into the future in the ordinary way, and a cerebrumless *human animal* that has inherited John's vital biological functions. The question is obvious: What happens to John in this story? Is John the metabolizing, respiring, cerebrumless animal that inherited all of

---

5 See *The Human Animal*, 7-9 (hereafter THA).
6 THA, 9.
7 I pass over the difficulties associated with Olson's naming of this case. For example, it seems at the very least what we have is a "human animal" at the end of the story and certainly not a "vegetable". Indeed, if some entity is human it surely is not a vegetable. Olson's animal/vegetable problem may just be inherited from garden variety discourse of cases of this kind.
8 This is an adaptation of Olson's Transplant Case presented in THA, 9-11.

John's vital biological functions? Or is John the person who ends up with John's cerebrum and John's psychology?

Before moving on to consider the Biological Approach to personal identity, let us lay before us one more kind of thought experiment. We will call this the Tragic Tibetan Buddhist Case. Imagine that I permanently lose all my present conscious memories, personality traits, aptitudes and all dispositions to act this way or that under various circumstances, but that my brain is otherwise in perfect working order, even retaining its very basic capacity to subserve mentality. Suppose my body is shipped in this condition to Tibet where, in time, a devout Buddhist emerges in my skin with a completely different psychological makeup than me. This is not a case of amnesia. Instead we are to suppose that this is a case involving the total oblivion of my past and present psychological life, my brain being rendered much like a new born infant's, and the beginning of a completely new psychological life. What happens to me in this story?

2. The Biological Approach to Personal Identity

According to Eric Olson's Biological Approach to personal identity, "[w]hat it takes for us [human persons] to persist through time is ... biological continuity: one survives just in case one's purely animal functions ... continue."[9] Thus, according to Olson, "... if things go badly I may end up a human vegetable – as long as my biological life continues." Moreover, on Olson's view, "psychology is completely irrelevant to personal identity."[10]

There is no mystery, therefore, surrounding how Olson would interpret the three cases with which we opened. Since, according to Olson, one survives just in case one's purely animal functions continue, it follows that in the Vegetable Case *you* are, strictly and literally, identical with the respiring, metabolizing, cerebrumless animal at the end of the story. And the interpretation of the Cerebrum-complement Case would be that John is, strictly and literally, identical with the empty-headed, respiring and metabolizing human animal, and assuredly *not* with the person who ends up with John's cerebrum and John's memories. What happens to me in the Tibetan Buddhist Case? The answer to which Olson must surely be committed is that what happens to me in this case is tragic:[11]

---

[9] THA, 16-17.
[10] "Was I Ever A Fetus?," 97.
[11] I say "tragic" because although I would be, on Olson's view, identical with the Tibetan Buddhist there might be certain self-involved desires I had before oblivion, e.g., my living long enough to see my son and daughter marry, about which it would be of little comfort for me (now) to know that the Tibetan Buddhist would one day fulfill this desire of mine by observing the wedding ceremonies of my children. I am the Tibetan Buddhist, of course, but the immeasurable discontinuity in my psychological life makes the fulfillment of my desires by the Tibetan Buddhist profoundly tragic.

I am, strictly and literally, identical with a person who is, in perhaps the most important of senses, psychologically discontinuous with me.

2.a Problems with the Biological Approach

I am of the opinion that Olson's Biological Approach offers the wrong interpretation to two of our three thought experiments. And the one case to which his Biological Approach gives the correct interpretation, i.e., the Tragic Tibetan Buddhist Case (which I discuss in due course), does so, I believe, for insufficient reason. Let me explain.

Consider first the Vegetable Case. At the end of the story you are, according to the Biological Approach, the human vegetable. The reason I believe that this cannot be the correct interpretation is this. Whatever else you may happen to be you are surely a *person*. Although it is a tall order to state conditions that are individually necessary and jointly sufficient for something's being a person, a view as plausible as it is modest would be that persons (human or otherwise) are, *minimally*, beings with a capacity for certain types of intentional states: believing, desiring, intending, etc. On such a view, if a being lacks *all* capacity for these types of intentional states, then that being, whatever else it may be, is not a person. Since the human vegetable at the end of the story has an intact but completely destroyed cerebrum, and therefore lacks all capacity for higher mental functioning, it is plausible to believe that that being is not a person. And if the human vegetable is not a person, then surely the human vegetable is not you: for you *are* a person!

The Biological View also gives, I believe, an incorrect interpretation to the Cerebrum-complement Case, and for the same reason. Since the respirating, metabolizing human animal at the end of the story lacks all capacity for intentional states, that being is not John. For John is a person. Is John the person who ends up with John's cerebrum and John's psychology? I want to postpone my answer to this question until I have had the opportunity to present the constitution account of persons and, in particular, an account of human bodies and their conditions for persistence. What I want to insist on here, however, is that John is not identical with any human animal.

2.b Objections and Replies

Objection: The response you have just offered assumes that persons are *essentially* persons, a claim the falsity of which is entailed by Olson's biological view of persons and his biological approach to personal identity. For according to Olson the sortal property 'person' is more like the phase-sortals 'boy' and 'girl' than like the substance-sortal 'human being'. Therefore, just as it is necessarily true that

(a) All U.S. presidents are (or have been) Commander in Chief of the U.S. armed forces,

and also true that it does not follow from (a) that George W. Bush has the property of being Commander in Chief *essentially,* insofar as George W. Bush is not *essentially* president of the U.S. (the president, in other words, could have failed to be president), so it might be necessarily true that all persons are psychological beings without it also being true that I, who am a person, have the property of being a person essentially.

If Olson is committed to the claim that being a person is of the same metaphysical nature as being president of the U.S. or being a girl, (i.e., that being a person is a "phase-sortal"), then you (a person) *could* exist without being a person; you could be, in other words, quite literally the human animal at the end of the stories under discussion.

Reply: The problem I have with Olson's approach to personal identity is *not* what kind of property he takes being a person to be, although my own view is that the property of being a person is a property had essentially if had at all. My problem has more to do with Olson's utter failure to make clear just what it is *to be* a person. Olson is supposed to be giving us an account of *personal* identity. The problem is that Olson focuses solely on the question, What does it mean to be a *human*?, and completely ignores the equally important and, given his aims, explanatorily prior question, What does it mean to be a *person*? Olson appears to believe that in answering the former question he is thereby answering the second. But this seems mistaken. As I will suggest shortly, I believe, like Olson, that *human* persons are *essentially* physical. But since I believe that what it means to be a *person* is minimally to be a being with a capacity for certain types of intentional states I do not believe that the human animal at the end of the Vegetable and Cerebrum-complement Cases is any person whomever. The question to which Olson's Biological Approach actually provides an answer is the question, What does it mean to be a *human* and what does it mean to be 'the same human'? But the answers provided by the Biological Approach to those questions at best only *partially* specify the conditions for the persistence of human *persons.* Insofar as Olson gives us nothing in terms of what it is to be a person, his Biological Approach to *personal* identity is, I believe, pretty thin soup.

Objection: Suppose what it is for an entity to be a person is just for that entity to be a human animal. That would certainly be compatible with, though perhaps not entailed by, the relation Olson takes human persons to stand in to human animals. For Olson takes a human person to be numerically identical with a human animal.[12]

---

[12] If one accepts the notion of relative identity, then one might agree that human persons are identical with human animals without also believing that in order for an entity to be a human person it is enough just for that entity to be a human animal. For further discussion of the relation between per-

Reply: But this presents the Biological Approach to personal identity with a problem. Considered strictly as biological organisms humans fail to differ from other kinds of biological animals in any metaphysically significant way.[13] Of course one might claim that the significant difference is a functional difference. Human animals differ *functionally* from non-human animals and it is this functional difference that is significant. But surely the most salient functional difference would be a human being's capacity for the types of *intentionality* already discussed, a feature that plays no role at all in the account of personal identity provided by the Biological Approach. So even if Olson believes that what it is to be a person is *more than* just to be a biological organism of the species *homo sapiens*, his Biological Approach to personal identity still faces a stiff problem. For insofar as the Biological Approach fails to include intentionality in its understanding of proper functioning for human beings it fails to capture the "more" that it means to be a person. And insofar as it fails in this regard it fails utterly as a candidate account of *personal* identity. In the end, I find the Biological Approach to personal identity wholly unsatisfying as an account of *personal* identity.

Since the most promising alternative to the Biological Approach to personal identity has seemed to many to be the Psychological Approach, let us turn now to a consideration of it.

3. The Psychological Approach

The Psychological Approach to personal identity comes in several varieties. What all such approaches have in common is that what it takes for a human person to persist through time is some sort of psychological continuity or, in the words of Owen Flannagan, some sort of continuity of narrative self-representation.[14] If a human person S at t_n is the same person as a person S' at t_{n+1}, then S' at t_{n+1} can *remember* some experience of S at t_n, or S' at t_{n+1} is continuous with S at t_n in virtue of having partially overlapping concatenations of psychological connections of one sort or another. Friends of the Psychological Approach include Derek Parfit,[15] Sydney Shoemaker,[16] and Peter Unger. Since Unger has

---

sons and bodies on a relative-identity construal see my "Persons, Bodies and the Constitution Relation," *Southern Journal of Philosophy* (37:1) 1999, 1-20, especially 6-8.

[13] Lynne Baker makes the same point in her "What am I?," *Philosophy and Phenomenological Research* (LIX) 1999, 151-159. See especially 158.

[14] See *Self Expressions: Mind, Morals and the Meaning of Life*, Oxford University Press (1996), 67ff.

[15] *Reasons and Persons* (Oxford University Press, 1984).

[16] See his "Self and Substance," *Philosophical Perspectives* (1997) 283-304, as well as "Personal Identity: A Materialist's Account," in *Personal Identity*, eds. S. Shoemaker and R. Swinburne (Basil Blackwell, 1984) and *Self-Knowledge and Self-Identity* (Cornell University Press, 1963).

presented the most recent version of this approach, I will focus on it.[17]

3.a Unger's Psychological Approach

In "Survival of the Sentient," Peter Unger claims that we human persons must be whatever it is we care about when we care about ourselves. Despite the odd and uninformative sound of this claim, Unger believes that it reveals something important about our deepest beliefs about ourselves. What it reveals, according to Unger, is this. If there is someone that, from a thoroughgoing and purely egoistic perspective, you care deeply whether he or she will experience great pain, then so far as you can tell you believe that person is *you*! Likewise if there is someone that, from a thoroughgoing and purely egoistic perspective, you do *not* care deeply whether he or she will experience great pain, then so far as you can tell you believe that person is *not* you.[18] Unger believes that any concept of ourselves that comports well with this insight about self-concern will be a philosophically adequate account of human persons and any account that fails to comport well with it cannot be an adequate account of ourselves. The Biological Approach, according to Unger, fails miserably to comport well this insight, whereas the Psychological Approach succeeds.

In order for our previous thought-experiments to plumb our deepest intuitions about ourselves, Unger would have us employ an apparatus that is based precisely on the insight of self-concern. He dubs that apparatus the Avoidance of Future Great Pain Test (AFGPT). The idea is this. Take the three thought experiments we examined earlier and imaginatively insert yourself into the beginning of each. Now ask yourself this question: With your choice solely motivated by self-concern will you choose to have yourself suffer great pain just before the events or processes involved in those cases if not suffering pain then means that soon after the event or procedure the emergent person will suffer even greater pain? If you answer, No, and would choose instead to have the person emergent after the procedure suffer even greater pain, then from Unger's perspective, this shows that so far as your most deeply held beliefs are concerned you do not believe yourself to be the person who will suffer that pain. If you answer, Yes, and would choose to have yourself suffer great pain just before the events in order to spare the person emergent from the procedure from suffering even greater pain, then this would indicate that as far as your deepest beliefs run, you believe yourself to be that emergent person.

---

[17] See his *Identity, Consciousness and Value* (Oxford University Press, 1990) and, most recently, his "Survival of the Sentient," *Philosophical Perspectives* 14.
[18] This point of Unger's is consistent I think with the claim that I can, from a purely egoistic perspective, care deeply about (say) my wife's suffering great pain. But I leave discussions of that putative assumption to those competent in ethical theory.

3.b The Psychological Approach and the Vegetable Case

Application of the AFGPT to our thought experiments should deliver a view of ourselves that comports well with our well founded and most deeply held beliefs about ourselves. So let's begin by applying it to the Vegetable Case. Since at the case's end there emerges no thinking, desiring, mentally engaged person to suffer any pain at all it must be tweaked. Just imagine that our earlier ingenious surgeon is also a gifted duplicator. Imagine she dutifully and with great care creates a molecular and healthy duplicate of your cerebrum just before its demise. Suppose she then removes your diseased cerebrum and replaces it with the molecular duplicate. At the end of this modestly tweaked Vegetable Case, there is a person with your inherited biology but no person with your *inherited* mentality. The person that emerges at the end of the story has a numerically distinct, *uninherited* but exactly similar mind that is functioning normally and fit to experience pain.

Now here's Unger:

> From your egoistic concerns, at the beginning you are to choose between (1) your suffering some significant pain, before a human vegetable's in the situation, so that, near the sequence's end, the person with the new (upper) brain suffers no pain at all and (2) your suffering no early pain and having it that, near the end, that person suffers terrible torture. Rationally you choose (2) over (1).[19]

What does this show? Well, according to Unger, it shows that "as far as you know or believe, you *won't* be the entity that's inherited your biology". To see the absurdity of the Biological Approach, Unger goes so far as to suppose that *you* exist as a human vegetable for a brief time just after the deprivation of oxygen and just before the implantation of the duplicate cerebrum. With the implantation of the new cerebrum, however, you would cease to exist. But that's absurd, thinks Unger. "Are we really to believe that, though it's possible for you to come to have *no* mind, what's impossible is for such a mindless *you* to survive your coming to *have a mind?* Such a suggestion as that, I'll suggest, is quite an absurd idea."[20]

3.c A Problem with Unger's Psychological Approach

Even if we suppose that Unger's psychological criterion tells us as much about reality, and what it takes for some future person to be you, as it does about our habits of thought, there are still problems with the view. It strikes me, for example, that Unger draws the wrong conclusion from the application of his AFGPT to the modestly tweaked

---

[19] "Survival of the Sentient," 336.
[20] "Survival of the Sentient," 336.

Vegetable Case. He thinks that what is shown from the fact that you would choose to have the emergent person suffer greater pain at the end of the procedure (and your foregoing suffering any pain before the procedure) is that you do not believe yourself to be the entity that's inherited your biology. Actually, all it shows is that you do not believe yourself to be the *person* that emerges *after* the procedure. Your choice is silent, so far as I can tell, on the question of what you believe about the human animal that persists through the procedure. Your choice is consistent, for example, with your believing that *you* are the same human animal as the human animal that exists after the procedure but *not* the same human person as the human person that exists after the procedure, a response surely open to a relative identity theorist. Likewise, if *you* exist as a human vegetable for a brief time just after the prolonged deprivation of oxygen and just before the implantation of the duplicate cerebrum, then, with the implantation of the new cerebrum, you would *not* (or at least not necessarily) cease to exist. For one persuaded by relative identity could hold that you would continue to exist, but that you would not be the same person as the person that emerges after the procedure.[21]

As for Unger's charge of absurdity concerning the possibility of your coming to have *no* mind, but the *impossibility* of a mindless *you* coming to *have a mind*, Olson himself could simply claim that since whatever is actual is possible it certainly *is* possible for a mindless *you* to come to have a mind. After all, Olson claims that each of us human persons was once a mindless entity as a fetus, and each of us has also come to have a mind. All that follows from all of this, Olson might point out, is just that you are only *contingently* minded. And there is no absurdity in saying that.

3.d Unger's Psychological Approach and the Cerebrum-complement Case

How about our Cerebrum-complement Case. How would the Psychological Approach handle it? Consider first the person who would end up with your cerebrum and Peter's cerebrum-complement. With your choice flowing solely from self-concern, will you choose to have yourself suffer considerable pain just before the procedure if your not suffering then means that, soon after the procedure, the person with your cerebrum (and thus your mind) will suffer even greater pain? Unger thinks you would. And what this "strongly" indicates is that you believe yourself to be the person with your cerebrum and hence your mind. Now suppose, again, that our deft surgeon duplicated your cerebrum after inserting your cerebrum into Peter's cerebrum-complement and then inserted the duplicate cerebrum into your original cerebrum-complement. What's even more

---

[21] Of course a relative identity theorist must also be committed to the denial of the claim that personhood is a property had essentially if had at all.

suggestive than the answer to the first question, thinks Unger, is your answer to this second parallel question: with your choice flowing solely from self-concern, would you choose for yourself to suffer considerable pain before the process begins if your not doing so then means that soon after the process the person with your original cerebrum-complement, but with a duplicate of your cerebrum, will suffer even greater pain? Unger thinks most assuredly not. Though not decisive, Unger thinks these questions are quite conclusive enough: "*you haven't even the slightest belief that here you're the being (with your healthy body) who's inherited your vegetative biological functioning.*"[22] Indeed, "... this negative response may be indicating a very bad fate for the Biological Approach in any of its versions. As well, it may also be indicating doom for any view on which the survival of our *bodies* is central to our own survival."[23]

But Unger moves much too fast here. Again, even if we suppose that Unger's psychological approach tells us as much about reality, and what it takes for some future person to be you, as it does about our habits of thought, it is still the case that Unger's response to the second question is perfectly consistent with the claim that the persistence of bodies is a *necessary* condition for the persistence of persons. Why? Well, consider our Tragic Tibetan Buddhist Case, for example. It is plausible to believe that at the end of the story I am the Tibetan Buddhist. This is so not *only* because there is the *mental* continuity for conscious experience, for rudimentary reasoning and for formulating beliefs, desires, intentions, etc, but also because there is *bodily* continuity. It is plausible to believe that since the core of my psychology (the capacity for certain types of intentionality) is continuously realized *in the numerically same, mental-sustaining human animal* that I am the Tibetan Buddhist.

According to Unger, absent "sufficient" mental continuity, animal or bodily continuity isn't sufficient for the continued existence of sentient beings like you and I.[24] Of course it isn't. But that's perfectly consistent with its being a *necessary* condition for your persistence that your body persist. Unger, however, seems to think that bodily continuity is *not even necessary*, at least not "most basically necessary".[25] He suggests that over the course of a year the neurons in your brain could be replaced with inorganic entities in such a way as to preserve psychological continuity. During the course of this re-

---

[22] "Survival of the Sentient," 331.
[23] "Survival of the Sentient," 331.
[24] "Survival of the Sentient," 342.
[25] If F is basically necessary for y's persistence (as opposed to only causally necessary), then there is an entailament relation from F to y's persistence. Unger's claim is that if biology were necessary for people's persistence, then should be an entailment relation from sentience to biology; but there is no entailment relation from sentience to biology. Therefore, biology is not necessary to our persistence, at least not basically necessary in the sense that sentience is.

moval and replacement process there would be a person whose partly organic and partly inorganic brain continues to subserve your mind. By the end of the year there would be a person whose wholly inorganic brain still subserves your mind. Now suppose this inorganic brain is grafted onto an inorganic "canine" body such that the nonbiological entity that emerges is capable of engaging with the environment and registering this engagement in all of the first person ways the original, biological *you* ever did. The conclusion to which we are supposed to be ineluctably drawn is that bodily continuity is not even necessary for *your* continued existence.

But surely that doesn't follow, at least not without accepting certain controversial claims about identity over time and replacement of parts. For it could be argued that your body *does* persist in Unger's story, albeit, in diminished and inorganic form. From this it would follow only that our bodies are contingently organic. Perhaps Unger's modal intuitions lead him to believe that our bodies are *essentially* organic. Fine. But in order for such intuitions to rise above mere philosophical prejudice, we are owed some argument or story. Indeed, what we are owed is some account of just what it is for some entity to be a body and some account of what its persistence conditions are. In the next section, I provide just such an account and tease out its implications for questions about personal identity.

Just as Olson's Biological Approach seems to come up short for failing to say what it is for some entity to be a *person*, Unger's Psychological Approach comes up short here insofar as it fails to say what it is for some entity to be a body or to persist as the same body.

In the end, neither the Biological Approach to personal identity nor the Psychological Approach is without difficulties. In what follows I will first present a constitution account of human persons and then draw out some of its implications for questions concerning personal identity.

4. The Constitution Relation

Since I have defended elsewhere the particular version of a constitution account of human persons that I will be discussing,[26] I will simply presuppose in what follows that account's plausibility. Before we begin, however, perhaps a word or two on the general relation of constitution is in order.

Among medium-sized physical objects that stand in constitution relations are statues, which are often constituted by pieces of marble, copper or bronze. But statues are

---

[26] See my "Persons and Bodies," *Faith and Philosophy* (15:3) 1998, 324-340 and "Persons, Bodies and the Constitutional Relation," *Southern Journal of Philosophy* (37:1), 1-20.

not identical to the pieces of marble, copper or bronze that constitute them. Likewise, dollar bills, diplomas and dust-jackets are often constituted by pieces of paper. But none of those things are identical to the pieces of paper that constitute them. Here's why defenders of constitution believe that the relation of constitution is *not* identity. Take the statue and the piece of copper, for example. It is possible for the piece of copper to survive being hammered flat, say, but not the statue. But a single thing cannot both survive and fail to survive through the same changes. Therefore, if the piece of copper can *survive* through changes that would *destroy* the statue, the piece of copper is not identical to the statue. Similar distinctions apply, *mutatis mutandis*, to dollar bills, diplomas and dust-jackets; not to mention tables, physical organisms of various kinds, and the things that constitute them.

On a constitution view, two material objects, x and y, stand in the constitution relation just in case (a) x and y are spatially coincident[27] and (b) x and y fall under different sortals. More formally, x constitutes y only if:

(i) x & y wholly occupy the same space, and (ii) there are different sortal-properties φ and ψ, and an environment E such that (a) (φx & x is in E) & (ψy & y is in E) and (b) (∀z) [(φz and z is in E) ⊃ (∃w) (ψw & w is in E) & (w ζ z)]

Since constitution is a relation between things falling under different sortals, constitution is neither reflexive nor symmetric. The piece of paper, for example, constitutes the dollar bill, not the other way around. Constitution is, however, a transitive relation. If the piece of paper is constituted by some molecules and the dollar bill is constituted by the piece of paper, then the dollar bill is constituted by those same molecules.

5. Persons, Bodies and Constitution

On a consitution account of *human persons*, persons are said to be constituted by bodies without being identical with the bodies that constitute them. Why think that? Well, consider what it is in virtue of which some object is a person and what it is in virtue

---

[27] There is historical precedent for the acceptance of coincident physical objects. On at least one reading of Aristotle he accepted them, as did Locke. Today friends of coincidence include Corcoran, "Persons, Bodies and the Constitution Relation," *Southern Journal of Philosophy* (1999) 1-20; Baker, "Why Constitution Is Not Identity," *The Journal of Philosophy* 94, 12 (1997) 599-621; Chappell, "Locke on the Ontology of Matter, Living Things and Persons," *Philosophical Studies* 60 (1990) 19-32; Doepke, "Spatially Coinciding Objects," *Ratio* 24 (1982) 45-60; Johnston, "Constitution Is Not Identity," *Mind* 101 (1992) 89-105; Lowe, "Instantation, Identity and Constitution," *Philosophical Studies* 44 (1983) 45-59; and most influentially, Wiggins, "On Being in the Same Place at the Same Time," *The Philosophical Review* 77 (1968) 90-95.

of which some object is a body. As mentioned earlier, it is a tall order to state conditions that are individually necessary and jointly sufficient for something's being a person, but many would agree that persons (human or otherwise) are, *minimally*, beings with a capacity for certain types of intentional states: believing, desiring, intending, etc. On such a construal, if a being lacks all capacity for such intentional states, then that being, whatever it is, is not a person. Moreover, it seems plausible to say that *human* persons in particular are *essentially* bodily beings insofar as they are now constituted by biological bodies.[28] And assuming that there is no problem in saying of a certain body that it is mine now, then there is no problem in saying at any future time that it is mine then. This is so because it is plausible to believe that if any body is my body, it is essentially my body. Human persons, therefore, cannot be constituted by bodies other than the bodies that originally constitute them. If a person S comes into existence at tn and at t_n is constituted by a body B, then, if some future person S' at t_{n+1} is the same person as person S, necessarily, S' at t_{n+1} is constituted by B. This is just to say that for any human person S S can be constituted by at most *one* body.

At this point perhaps it would help to get clear on just what I mean to pick out with the word "body". By *body* I mean, for starters, that entity we normally refer to with the words *physical organism*. According to a constitution account, physical organisms are themselves constituted objects being constituted by masses of cell-stuff. So according to a constitution account of bodies what the term "biological body" picks out is to be distinguished from the mass of cell-stuff that constitutes it. One but not the other is a mere *mass* or aggregate. And a mass just is a mereological sum. Therefore, the one but not the other is able to survive material part replacement.

So by "body" I mean to refer to the same kind of object that Locke speaks of when he says that a "living animal is a living organized body"[29] and a "man" "nothing but a participation of the same continued Life by constantly fleeting particles of matter, in suc-

---

[28] Thus I agree with those who claim that whatever is a physical object is *essentially* a physical object. Not all sober-minded philosophers agree, however. Michael Hooker apparently disagrees. See his "Descartes' Denial of Mind-Body Identity," in *Descartes: Critical and Interpretative Essays*, ed. Michael Hooker, (Baltimore: The Johns Hopkins University Press, 1978) 171-185. Trenton Merricks also disagrees. See his "A New Objection to A Priori Arguments for Dualism," *American Philosophical Quarterly* 31 (1994) 80-85. I suspect there are no conclusive non-question-begging arguments for the claim that physical objects *are* essentially physical. Nevertheless, the consequences of its denial strike me as simply unacceptable. For if the denial is true, then it is possible for a thing at this world that is spatially extended and weighs two tons (an elephant, say) to exist (that very thing!) at another world without any mass whatsoever and without, in fact, being a physical object at all. For a critique of Merricks, see my "Persons and Bodies," *Faith and Philosophy* 15 (1998) 324-340.
[29] John Locke, *An Essay Concerning Human Understanding*, XXVII, §5, ed. Nidditch (Oxford: Clarendon Press, 1991).

cession vitally united to the same organized Body."[30] Now by "Life" I take Locke to have meant an individual physically complex event of a remarkably stable sort, one that is well individuated, self-directing and self-maintaining. Those familiar with contemporary metaphysics will recognize this way of talking. For according to Peter van Inwagen, for example, physical organisms are "things that are composed of objects whose activities constitute lives,"[31] where once again by "life" van Inwagen means the special sort of self-directing physically complex event just mentioned.

This view suggests the following criterion of identity:

> If x and y are human bodies, then x is identical with y if and only if x and y are constituted by (sets of) physical simples participating in the same continued life.

Now one reason for denying that persons are identical with the bodies that constitute them is that the sortals "person" and "body" have different persistence conditions associated with them. For example, there is nothing in the criterion of identity for a human body that involves having intentional states. Therefore, there is no conceptual impossibility involved in thinking about my body continuing to exist while completely lacking a capacity for intentional states; if what I said above is true, however, then there is such an impossibility involved in the idea of *my* continuing to exist while lacking all capacity for intentional states; for I am a person.

This is so, of course, only if I am *essentially* a person. Am I? As I said earlier, I think so, and here's why. If persons are not essentially persons, then not only is it the case that a thing that is now a person could possibly exist at some future time without being a person, but it is also true that I – the very thing that at this world is a person – could exist at some other world without *at any time* being a person. Now I can imagine my life having gone a lot different than it has. I can imagine myself still being a practicing social worker, never having left Ferndale, Maryland and gone off to college, even never having developed crossed eyes thirty-two years ago. But I cannot imagine that I – the very thing that I am – could have existed without ever having been a person, without ever having any beliefs or desires at all. Defenders of the Biological Approach to personal identity like Olson may be willing to accept the claim that persons are not essentially persons. I'm not. Olson and I might, however, both agree that if human persons are numerically identical with human animals, then human persons are *not* essentially persons. But whereas Olson would accept the antecedent to this conditional and so too the consequent, the constitution account of human persons that I favor makes it clear that I deny the consequent, and so deny the antecedent as well.

---

[30] Locke, *An Essay Concerning Human Understanding*, XXVII, §6.
[31] Peter van Inwagen, *Material Beings* (Ithaca: Cornell University Press, 1990), p. 92.

6. The Identity and Persistence Conditions Of Bodies

What are the persistence conditions for a person's constituting body, on a constitution account of them? There are good reasons for believing that spatiotemporal continuity is normally merely a consequence of the persistence of a body and not its ground.[32] What is absent in the simple spatiotemporal continuity criterion of persistence for material objects of any kind is any mention of the role of *causation*. Yet surely, if the rug on the floor under my feet has persisted into the present then its existence in the immediate past must be causally relevant to its existence now. So too with human bodies. If the human body sitting across the table from me at 12:59 p.m. is not causally connected with the one across from me at 12:58 p.m., then it is plausible to think that the human body across the table from me at 12:59 p.m. is not a continuation of the body that was there at 12:58 p.m., but rather is a numerically distinct replacement.

Causal considerations, therefore, seem especially pertinent to the giving of persistence conditions for material objects of any sort. Of course the kinds of causal dependencies relating an object at earlier and later stages of its career will very likely differ according to the kind of object whose career we are tracing. Different kinds of persisting thing, in other words, have different persistence conditions. What it is in virtue of which a person's *body* persists is different from what it is in virtue of which a *statue* persists. But even so, it is causal considerations that are relevant to the persistence of each.

Peter van Inwagen offers the following principle for the persistence of organisms.

> If the activity of the xs at t_1 constitutes a life, and the activity of the ys at t_2 constitutes a life, then the organism that the xs compose at t_1 is the organism that the ys compose at t_2 if and only if the life constituted by the activity of the xs at t_1 is the life constituted by the activity of the ys at t_2.[33]

It seems certain that the activities of the simples caught up in a life are *causal* activities given the fact that a life, as we've said, is a self-preserving *event*. Restating van Inwagen's principle so as to make explicit the causal element involved, and with a view to arriving at a necessary and sufficient condition for the persistence of a human body, we might say:

> If an organism O that exists at t_3 is the same as an organism P that exists at t_1, and P persisted from t_1 to t_3, then the (set of) simples that compose P at t_1 must be causally related in the life-preserving way to the set of simples that compose O at t_3.

Let's call this condition for the persistence of a human body the life-preserving condition, or *LP* for short. *LP* makes it a requirement on the persistence of a human body that

---

[32] See for example David Armstrong's "Identity Through Time," p. 76.
[33] van Inwagen, *Material Beings*, p. 145.

immanent causal relations hold among the different stages of a body's career.[34]

A human body B that exists at t_3 is the same as a human body A that exists at t_1, *in virtue of persisting from t_1 to t_3*, just in case the temporal stages leading up to B at t_3 are immanent causally connected to the temporal stage of A at t_1.[35]

So much for bodies. What of the persons they constitute?

7. The Identity and Persistence Conditions of Persons

A person, said Locke, is "a thinking intelligent being, that has reason and reflection, and can consider itself as itself, the same thinking thing, in different times and places."[36] To Locke, and to others inspired by him, continuity of consciousness has seemed to be essentially what is at issue in deciding if a person S' at t_{n+1} is the same person as person S at t_n. As far as consciousness can be extended backwards to past thoughts and actions so far "reaches the identity of [the] *person* ...," said Locke.

My characterization of persons as beings with a capacity for certain types of intentional states is broadly Lockean insofar as what it means to be a person, on my view, gets cashed out in *mental* terms (beliefs, desires, intentions). Likewise, on my view, what it means to be the *same* person might seem to be an entirely mental affair. But several problems emerge from the fact that on my account human persons are *essentially* bodily beings, being constituted as they are by biological bodies of the species *homo sapiens*. It might also seem that my capacity for intentional states of all kinds owes precisely to my being constituted by a biological organism of a certain physical complexity. These considerations may make it look as though there is a clash involved in giving the persistence

---

[34] Such *stages* need not be thought of as temporal parts of the persisting organism; like the life lived by an organism, they need only be thought of as events. Thus, following Zimmerman, we can define "temporal stage of an organism" as follows:

s is the temporal stage at t of an organism O $=^{df}$ there is a set R of all the intrinsic properties and internal relations O has at t, and s is the event of O's exemplifying R at t.

See his "Immanent Causation," forthcoming in *Philosophical Perspectives* volume 11 433-471. Whereas Zimmerman offers the definition of "temporal-stage" for objects in general, I have taken the liberty to make the relevant substitutions so that the definition applies to organisms in particular.

[35] Immanent causation, then, is supposed to contrast with so called "transeunt causation," in that in the latter the state of one continuant, A, brings about state-changes in a numerically distinct continuant, B. In the former type of causation, however, a state x of thing A brings about a consequent state y in A itself. For more on the notion of immanent causation see Zimmerman's "Immanent Causation". For a definition of "temporal-stage," see previous footnote.

[36] Locke, *An Essay Concerning Human Understanding*, II.xxvii.2.

conditions for human persons; for it may look as though *both* mental and bodily criteria *alone* provide *sufficient* conditions for their persistence.

I think it is the case that the persistence conditions for *human* persons necessarily include reference to both the mental and the physical. I do not, however, believe that this involves a clash of any kind. The illusion of a clash is fostered by various thought experiments like those we have been discussing. Consideration of cases like the Cerebrum-Complement Case, for example, may lead us to believe that it is possible for me to continue to exist even if my body should either fail to exist altogether or continue to exist disassociated from any mind whatever. On the other hand, cases like the Vegetable Case may lead us to believe that bodily continuity is *enough* to secure sameness of person.

Mark Johnston believes that our intuition to judge even cases of annihilation and psycho-physical *duplication* as cases of 'body-*switching*' owes to the distorting presence of psychological continuity between the two bodies, a continuity that under normal circumstances is co-present with identity.[37] Johnston maintains, however that once it is recognized that human consciousness is subserved by the proper functioning of a human brain, it becomes most difficult to deny that one's psychology persists only in the case that one's functioning brain persists. Given the empirical data, which Johnston claims strongly suggests psychological functioning in human beings is crucially related to human brains, it appears that bodily criteria are at least *necessary* for the persistence of persons.

I think Johnston is basically correct in his assessment. A *necessary* condition for the persistence of a person is that her constituting *body* persist and what is both necessary and *sufficient* for personal survival is that *this* persisting body preserve its capacity to subserve a range of intentional states of the sort that have been under discussion. In this way I take my stand against those who claim that bodily continuity is not only not sufficient, but not even necessary (e.g., defenders of the Psychological Approach like Unger), and also against those like Olson, who see the persistence of the body as being enough for the persistence of a human person.

Let us return now to our thought experiments in order to see just how the view I propose handles them.

8. Personal Identity And Psychological Continuity

The quasi-Aristotelian metaphysics of bodies that I favor leads me to a different interpretation of Unger's organic/inorganic brain-replacement case than his own. So let us begin by looking more closely at that case.

---

[37] Mark Johnston, "Human Beings," *Journal of Philosophy* 84 (1987) pp. 59-83.

It would seem that Unger's case is not, with respect to loss of identity, unlike a case of Unger's neurons being gradually removed and replaced with nothing at all. Thus, there would seem to be a terminus in the series of removal and replacements beyond which Unger does not exist, since it would seem plausible to suppose that with the removal of a certain bunch of neurons what is Unger's constituting body would cease to exist.

Of course, Unger's body *can* persist through a definite number of neuron *replacements*. But just as Unger's body could plausibly be said to diminish in size with a series of digit and limb detachments, until a point is reached at which his body ceased to exist (quite likely at the boundary of his head), so does it seem eminently plausible to suppose in the imagined case that there would come a point beyond which Unger's body could not be said to persist, namely, the point at which the natural organism that is that body was no longer self-maintaining. If a person psychologically continuous with Unger should exist after the demise of Unger's body, we have no reason to believe that he or she is identical with Unger and every reason to believe that he or she is not.

On my view psychological continuity is not, therefore, sufficient for survival. But is it necessary? Recall our earlier example of the Tibetan Buddhist. The answer to the question, Am I the Tibetan Buddhist?, is, of course, Yes. This is not surprising once it is recognized that what it takes for the persistence of a person is the persistence of the person's constituting body *and* its preservation for subserving intentional states of the requisite sort. What follows from this is just that, on my view, personality and mental content are not essential properties of persons, i.e., persons can change, even radically, with respect to them without ceasing to exist. But there must be *some* minimal, mental continuity, if only the continued capacity for conscious experience – for basic reasoning and for formulating beliefs, desires and intentions. On my view, then, neither biological nor psychological continuity *alone* is sufficient for personal identity, but each is necessary and together they are jointly sufficient.

We have so far seen some changes of a sort through which a person can be said to persist on a constitution account of them. These involve alterations in psychology, even quite drastic alterations. But how does the view of the persistence conditions for persons that I favor handle cases like our Cerebrum-Complement and Vegetable Cases?

Certain tinkerings with my body are sufficient to bring it about that I cease to exist, even if those same tinkerings should not bring it about that my body ceases to exist. Suppose my cerebrum suffers severe trauma as a result of an automobile accident without my brainstem being affected in the least. If the trauma suffered by the cerebrum were such that it no longer was capable of subserving mental functioning, then I would cease to exist even although my body would not. My body would not cease to exist since the brainstem is the command center of the autonomic nervous system, regulating metabolic processes and directing an organism's vital biological functions. The fact that it remains functionally intact, and in the right sort of environment, is sufficient for the persistence of my body. So my answer to Olson's Vegetable Case is that I am assuredly not the respirating, metabolizing human animal at the end of the story.

Recall, now, our Cerebrum-Complement Case. Suppose it were possible to graft my healthy cerebrum onto the cerebrum-complement of a cerebrumless human animal. If the cerebrum is that organ of mine that subserves my mental functioning, and it were transplanted as imagined, would I go, as the Psychological Approach suggests, where my cerebrum goes? Not necessarily. If it is possible that my *body* should come to shrink and the boundaries of its life should come exactly to overlap the boundaries that once contained my cerebrum, then the answer is, Yes. But if it is not possible for the simples composing my body to be immanent causally connected (in the mentally-relevant way) with those that now occupy the region occupied only by my cerebrum, then the answer is, No – I do not go where my cerebrum goes. The important point is that for some future person to be me it is not enough that there be psychological continuity. What is needed as well as psychological continuity is bodily continuity. I suppose what would happen if my body cannot shrink in the way imagined is that it would be possible for a numerically distinct body to come to constitute a person psychologically indistinguishable from me. The resulting person, however, could not be me.

9. Baker's Prince and Cobbler Account

Although Lynne Baker defends a constitution account of human persons in her book *Persons and Bodies*,[38] she also offers there an account of the persistence conditions for human persons that I find woefully inadequate. To see what I find problematic about her view it will be helpful to lay her view out in some detail.

Baker begins by distinguishing two questions,

(i) "Under what conditions is a person x at t identical to a person y at t'?" and
(ii) "Under what conditions is x at t identical to y at t', where x is a person at t?"[39]

The difference between (i) and (ii) is that (i) is, where (ii) is not, asking for conditions of personal identity over time. In (i) both x and y are specified as persons, but in (ii) it is an open questions as to whether y is a person or not. Since both Baker and I believe that persons are essentially persons, we would give the same answer to both (i) and (ii). This is for the plausible reason that if x = y and x is a person, then y is a person also. Alter-

[38] (Cambridge University Press, 2000), esp. 118-146.
[39] Baker, p. 138.

natively, if you believe (like Olson) that it is possible for a single thing to be a person at one time but not a person at another, then you might well give a different answer to (ii) than to (i).

Baker also makes another distinction, that between asking (i) and (ii) and that between asking:

(i') "Under what conditions is a human person x at t identical to a human person y at t'?", and asking,
(ii') "Under what conditions is x at t identical to y at t', where x is a human person at t?"

Now these last two questions are explicitly questions about sameness of *human* persons. And Baker would give the same answer to (ii') as to (ii), since human persons are essentially persons. In other words, if x = y and x is a human person, then y is a person too. Of course, all of this is consistent with another claim to which Baker is also committed; namely, the claim that x could be the same person as y even if x is a *human* person and y is not. Put succinctly, Baker believes that although human persons are essentially persons they are *not* essentially human. And this, of course, is at odds with what I claimed earlier; namely, that if any human body is my body it is essentially my body.

In any case, since both x and y are specified as *human* persons in (i') (i') receives a different answer from Baker than the answer to questions (i), (ii) and (ii'). (i') is a question about human personal identity *across* time. And Baker offers the following principle for determining if a human person P at t is the same human person as a human person S at t'.

(T) "For all objects, x and y and times t and t', if x is a human person at t and y is a human person at t', then x = y if and only if for all human bodies z, w, necessarily: (z constitutes x at t if and only if z constitutes y at t) and (w constitutes x at t' if and only if w constitutes y at t')".[40]

Now, according to (T) "[s]ameness of human person considered at two times consists in necessary sameness of constituting bodies at each of the times."[41] And this allows for the possibility of body transfer given the fact that (T) does not require that z = w, where, again, z and w are human bodies.

While I grant that (T) is compatible with body transfer, and true even, I fail to see how it does any interesting work at all with respect to providing persistence conditions for human persons. Granted Baker does not think that (T) is *epistemologically* very in-

---

[40] Baker, 139.
[41] Baker, 139.

formative, but she does think it provides a *metaphysically* sufficient condition for the persistence of human persons across time. And in that regard it seems to me to fail. Here's why. First, note that (T) rules out that a single human person can be constituted by more than one body at a time. So far so good. But persistence conditions for human persons ought to tell us what it takes for a human person to persist *through* time. (T) does not do that. In fact, to see just how metaphysically unhelpful (T) is consider that it is also compatible with

> (T') For all objects, x and y and times t and t', if x is a human person at t and y is a human person at t', then x = y if and only if for all human bodies z, w, necessarily: (z constitutes x at t if and only if z constitutes y at t) and (w constitutes x at t' if and only if w constitutes y at t') and (z = w).

(T') rules out that a single human person can be constituted by *different* human bodies at *different* times. And that, of course, is compatible with the claim that a single human person cannot be constituted by more than one human body at a time. So (T') rules out the following scenario. Suppose Prince is constituted by human body b at t and Cobbler is constituted by human body b' at t. Following Baker, let's call the person with b' at t' "Joe". Since Baker's commitment is to (T) only she can imagine that Prince = Joe. It's not that (T) entails that Prince = Joe, of course; rather, (T) is simply compatible with the identity of Prince and Joe. (T) is, so far as I can see, also compatible with nearly every view of human personal identity over time that does not deny that human persons persist. (For example, it's compatible with certain versions of dualism, with Olson's animalism and with Trenton Merricks' anti-criterialism.) In any case, my commitment to (T'), on the other hand, entails that Prince ≠ Joe. And so, given (T'), it is inconceivable that Prince = Joe.

Admittedly, I don't see any way to argue for (T') that doesn't beg any relevant questions against Baker. But what's important to see is that, contrary to Baker, the theory of constitution *as such* does not lead us to believe that a single human person could be constituted by different human bodies at different times. Nor (again contrary to Baker) is it part of the theory of constitution as such that would lead one to believe that a human person can cease to be human without ceasing to exist.[42] These further beliefs are the result of constitution-independent, metaphysical commitments and not anything like entailments of a constitution account of human persons itself. Indeed, as I hope to have shown, one can embrace a constitution account of human persons without embracing either of these controversial beliefs.

---

[42] See Baker, p.11.

Conclusion

A constitution view of persons is not without its own costs and difficulties. I have tried to address some of those costs and difficulties in different places.[43] What I have tried to do here is to show how a constitution account of persons provides a view of personal identity that is a plausible alternative to the two dominant views in the current literature. I have also tried to show that a constitution account of human persons does not alone and all by itself commit one to two controversial claims; namely, that a single human person can be constituted by numerically distinct human bodies at different times, and that a human person can cease to be human without ceasing to exist.[44]

---

[43] See my "Persons, Bodies and the Constitutional Relation," *Southern Journal of Philosophy* (37:1) 1999, 1-20 and "Physical Persons and Postmortem Survival without Temporal Gaps," *Soul, Body and Survival* (Cornell University Press, 2000) ed. Kevin Corcoran, 201-217.

[44] I wish to thank the Tuesday afternoon philosophy colloquium at Calvin College, especially Greg Mellema, Del Ratzch and Steve Wykstra for helpful discussion, as well as audiences at Purdue University and Gordon College. I also wish to thank the following individuals for helpful comments and criticisms: Lynne Baker, Michael Bergman, Jan Cover, Michael Grant Schweiger, Gerrit Neels and Patrick Kain. I must also thank Eric Olson and Dean Zimmerman for saving me from making some gross errors. Thanks also to the Council for Christian Colleges and Universities and the Calvin Center for Christian Scholarship for financial support during the writing of this chapter.

Käthe Trettin
Persons and Other Trope Complexes
Reflections on Ontology and Normativity

1. Introduction

Most of the recent debate on personhood is guided by moral and judicial considerations. Questions like "When does personhood begin?" and "When is somebody no longer a person?" preoccupy the field of bioethical discussions in order to determine morally justified legal acts, for instance, whether one is justified in using fetal material for research or implantation, or whether people who presumably will never awake from a coma should be helped to die. These are serious questions which implicitly show that being a person or personhood is understood as a pre-eminent value – a value which seems to be considered as the very criterion of deciding over life and death. However, it is not very clear what a person or what personhood is, *i.e.*, on what's beginning and ending everybody in this debate is talking about. This is not to say that ontological reflections are absent. As far as I can see, the respective discussions deal with the following questions. First, what are the criteria of personal identity, especially, what are the diachronic persistence conditions of persons? Secondly, what are the defining features of personhood? Classical candidates are rationality, consciousness, self-consciousness, memory, free will of action, and responsibility for one's free actions. Thirdly, are persons *entia per se* or do they fall under a more general category of being?

There may be other important questions, but I shall not deal with them here. What seems to be a common presupposition of these and perhaps further major questions is the assumption that the paradigm cases of persons are very well human beings, but that human beings are not *eo ipso* persons. Personhood might therefore be regarded as a certain stage of a human being's biography, depending on how personhood is defined. Moreover, if the traditional equation of human being and person is given up or, at least, challenged, then the hitherto natural substrate of personhood, *i.e.* the human being, appears to be no longer a necessary condition for being a person. Doesn't one have to accept animals or artefacts of a specified kind as equally well appropriated bearers of personal features? Once the strict connection between human being and person is removed, the burden of explication hangs on defining personhood in a principled way without invoking human features.

In what follows I shall concentrate on the ontology of persons. Presumably the most widespread framework for categorising persons and personhood is some version of a substance-attribute-ontology. On this framework, persons are individual substances, *i.e.*

independent entities, which have certain properties. The debate then might concentrate on the category of attributes and divide philosophers over the question of what the crucial attributes or properties would be which taken together are necessary and sufficient for being a person. As this ontological framework not only allows for focusing on the category of attribute, the dispute might shift to the category of substance and thereby acquire a different tenor: Either persons are sharply distinguished from other individual substances like bodies, animal beings, and human beings (Lynne Rudder Baker), or persons are conceived of as just a phase of certain organisms (Joshua Hoffman and Gary S. Rosenkrantz). The first option might result in admitting persons as *entia per se* (Roderick Chisholm), whereas the second is open for further naturalistic accounts.

One of the difficulties with the substance-attribute-view is, however, that the debate is stuck in a controversy over persons *versus* physical bodies.[1] Is there *one* substance with personal properties, or are there *two* substances – bodies and persons? If the latter, how are they linked together? It's the old tune of monism *versus* dualism in the philosophy of mind which is played once again in debating the ontological status of persons. Another difficulty – not only due to this particular although widespread ontological framework – concerns the fusion, if not confusion, of ontological and moral questions. Nearly everyone in this debate seems to be obliged to grant persons a grade A ontological status. One recent example is Lynne Baker's passionate account of persons being "essentially persons". The basis for this conception is that persons differ radically from "human animals", as she terms it, in virtue of having a first-person perspective. One might object, however, that this way of upgrading the ontological status of persons implies a problematic downgrading of human beings. Are human beings *simpliciter* just animals? And even if so, are animals simply physical bodies? Would it not be better to ally with David Wiggins whose analysis of personal identity is based on a Human Being Principle on which the identity of persons coincides with the identity of human beings?

I shall say a little bit more on the views of Baker and Wiggins and probably some others, but it is not the aim of this paper to critically rehearse recent theorising on persons. Instead I should like to analyse how persons and personhood fit into an ontological framework which is solely based on the category of Trope, *i.e.* the category of Particular Property or Individual Quality. One reason for this attempt is the supposition that this framework – a world of individual qualities – allows for a very smooth integration of personal traits. A metaphysic based on tropes or individual qualities seems very hospitable to intentional or mental states which are usually ascribed to persons, including phenomenal states or *qualia*. On this supposition persons are just trope complexes which differ

---

[1] R. Chisholm (1996, 4), for instance, writes: "Material things are substances and persons are substances. But it is problematic whether persons are material things."

from other such complexes in virtue of some tropes or sub-complexes of tropes. The trope view thus provides the picture of a continuum which includes besides other trope configurations such highly sophisticated trope complexes as persons. There is a bit of a holistic idea behind it: no essential divides, no problematic gaps (between organisms of different degrees of complexity, between mind and body, etc.). The other reason for confronting trope theory with the concept of person simply consists in testing a theory. If ontology is mainly an empirical science – and I presume that it is, then the fact that we encounter persons in the world and have experiential access to their personal features provides an important test case for any ontological theory. That is not to say that the different phenomena require ontological categories *per se*. But surely those "highly sophisticated trope complexes", as I have called persons against the background of a continuum of individual qualities, should gain a contour of their own. A first step will be to provide a ground-level on which all trope complexes are based, from which, in a second step, such trope complexes as persons are considered.

2. Rich Entities and Ontological Dependence

To begin with, I shall confront my reconstruction of persons with the classical view which presupposes the category of substance, "in the 'rich sense of substance'", as Wiggins put it (2001, 194), that is to say, not in the sense of bare particulars or non-qualitied substrates. The equivalent of such a substance, *i.e.*, an individual in which qualities are supposed to inhere, is a rich trope complex, *i.e.*, a composition of different individual qualities (tropes) which are linked together by being existentially dependent on one another. Before going deeper into the explanatory advantages and disadvantages of these categorial distinctions, it is interesting to note that metaphysical dependency plays a role in both of these conceptions, although in a different way. Whereas on the substance view qualities are dependent on (first or individual) substances, on the trope view it is the complexes that are dependent on the individual qualities (tropes) which constitute them. To be more exact, the mutual dependency of tropes which explicates that there be a trope complex is *eo ipso* the foundation base for an integrated whole or rich trope complex. The trope complex itself is then one-sidedly dependent on the tropes which constitute it. Briefly: Whereas the qualitatively rich or complex entity is somehow presupposed on the substance view, it is metaphysically reconstructed on the trope view.[2]

So far the analysis is on a very general and topic-neutral level: Both Substance and Trope Complex don't convey which qualities the different entities that fall under these categories might have. In order to track certain entities, e.g. horses, trees, human beings,

---

[2] For a detailed account of ontological dependence in trope theory cf. K. Trettin (2001).

one might ask whether further dependencies have to be taken into account. This question arises, at least and foremost, when the identity of the respective entities is being discussed. For whenever one asks, whether *a* is the same as *b*, and simply knows that for *a* or *b* any entity falling under the category of Substance or Trope Complex can be filled in, the perplexity of asking 'the same what?' arises, as David Wiggins has nicely pointed out. A response to 'the same-what-question'[3] seems to require information about the kind or species to which the respective entities belong. Therefore, or so Wiggins argues, it is sortal terms ('horse', 'tree', 'human being') that play an ineliminable logical role in determining the identity conditions of individuals, a condition from which one might deduce a substance's general ontological dependency on a kind or species. This line of reasoning which is at the core as Aristotelian as it is in the spirit of John Locke has also been taken up in a pronounced way by Jonathan Lowe. In his *Kinds of Being* (1989, 4) he writes: "[...] the notion of an 'individual' and of a 'sort' or 'kind' are opposite sides of a single coin: each is only understandable in terms of the other. Individuals are necessarily individuals *of a kind*, and kinds are necessarily kinds *of individuals*." This sounds very much like a mutual dependency of categorially different entities, whereas for Wiggins an individual substance seems to be one-sidedly dependent on a kind (or 'its' kind).

At this point, however, substance ontologists and trope ontologists might part company (a company which has been very loose, anyway), for a trope philosopher surely will ask what qualities are apt to make up a species or kind. How could there be natural (and perhaps also artefactual) kinds in the world – if they had not been constructed out of salient qualities of trope complexes in the first place? How can a species exist separately from the special exemplars or instances? In connection with these problems the traditional question of essences might emerge: Are there any 'essential tropes' which by constituting a class stand in for the ontological correlate of sortal terms?

3. Kinds, Essences and Determinables

Although it seems to be intuitively plausible to posit or assume such things as kinds, essences or determinables in order to provide a sorting principle, it is far from clear whether (a) these things are ontologically necessary and, even if so, whether (b) they are to be construed as *entia per se* or, rather, as *entia per alio*.

On the substance-*cum*-kinds view, the response to (a) is surely in the positive. Kinds provide the necessary conditions of identity and identification. That is not to say that

---

[3] This question was originally introduced into the more recent identity debate by P. Geach (1962). For Geach, however, sortal dependence is sortal relativity. Two individuals might be the same relative to one sortal and different relative to another. Generally on sortal dependence see also Ch. Rapp (1995) and more recently M. Quante (2002).

every philosopher who invokes kinds is a realist about this ontological category. There always is the possibility of sneaking out of this metaphysical commitment by taking kinds to be purely linguistic items (sortal terms) and combining this position eventually with a pragmatic theory of language use. Concerning (b) substance-*cum*-kinds proponents, be they realists or anti-realists, usually suppose that kinds are entities (or terms) of their own which cannot be derived from some other category (or term).

On the trope view, things are different. A response to question (a) would be twofold: *First*, kinds or species are not the ontological providers of a principle of identity of trope complexes. A trope complex T_i and a trope complex T_j are identical, if they are constituted by the same tropes. *Secondly*, however, kinds or species seem to be useful in epistemological respects. The question whether T_i is the same trope complex as T_j might be decided more easily and conveniently, if some salient tropes of each complex are gathered in a further, second-order complex of tropes, *i.e.*, a kind. What the respective salient tropes are and whether they coincide with essential or necessary tropes (if there are any) is an empirical question. So, it remains to be seen whether one should be a realist concerning these higher-order trope complexes. The response to question (b) simply follows from the response to (a): If there are kinds, or higher-order trope complexes, then they are certainly derivative entities.

So far the reconstruction has just reached, in a very general and sketchy way, what I have called 'the ground-level'. Tropes constitute individual complexes in virtue of being dependent on one another and some of those tropes might constitute higher-order complexes. To recur to a prominent Aristotelian example, recast on the trope view, one would say, accordingly: The individual qualities of biped, featherless, and rational which have been discovered at a time as salient constituents of individual trope complexes, constitute a kind or species named 'human being'. Notice, however, that by citing Aristotle in a modified way, it has been left open whether all of these constituents are essences. And this for obvious reasons. For, surely, the (negative) quality of lacking feathers would not count as a necessary or essential feature of human beings, but as purely contingent. From this we may deduce that kinds or species are made up by a mixed selection of essential and contingent tropes.

Although, so far, a decided abstention from generally *naming* trope complexes (apart from *mentioning* examples) has been observed, the reconstruction is on the brink of a second step, namely, analysing two kinds of trope complexes: human beings and persons. This is so, because two decisive claims have been made: first, trope complexes are identical in virtue of the tropes that are their constituents; secondly, kinds or species are not *entia per se* but higher-order complexes which are constituted by some salient tropes derived of resembling first-order complexes, regardless of whether the salient tropes are contingent or essential.

In order to further explain these claims and elucidate the sense of frequently applied concepts such as "constitution" and "dependence", it seems useful to have a brief look at a theory, not at all a trope theory, which has been proposed by Lynne Rudder Baker and which she calls "the constitution view of persons".

4. Constitution and Identity I – the Substance-*cum*-Kinds-View

In her recent book *Persons and Bodies* (2000) as well as in her essay on "The Ontological Status of Persons" (2002), Lynne Baker makes the remarkable claim that constitution is not identity. By 'identity' she means 'strict identity' in the sense that if x is identical with y, then, necessarily, x is identical with y. On her Constitution View, however, there is only room for 'contingent identity'. Nevertheless, Lynne Baker seems to be strongly committed to the modal notion of necessity, since she invokes 'primary kinds' or 'primary-kind properties' which are necessary features or essences. A primary-kind property is a property "a thing has essentially", *i.e.*, without which it could not exist; it "determines what a thing most fundamentally is" (Baker 2002, 372). Constitution is then "a relation that things have in virtue of their primary kinds" (373). So a "thing" – which is probably meant to be an individual substance – seems to be one-sidedly dependent on a kind or kind-property.[4]

As the introduction of the term 'primary kind' already indicates, there are probably also 'secondary' kinds in the offing. And so it is. This is made explicit when she turns to works of art and persons. What is the primary kind of a marble statue? Answer: Although a piece of marble constitutes the respective statue, the primary kind of the marble statue is not Marble but Statue. The marble constitutes the statue only "derivatively". What is the primary kind of a person? The answer deserves citing:

> Person is your primary kind. Human animal is your body's primary kind. You are a person nonderivatively and a human animal derivatively; and your body is a human animal nonderivatively and a person derivatively. Although you are a person and your body is a person, there are not two persons where you are: This is so because constitution is a unity relation. (Baker 2002, 374)

There are two claims involved in this explanation. First, what a *primary* kind is for *one* thing might be a *derivative* kind for *another* thing, and *vice versa*. Secondly, constitution is being construed as a *relation* which *unites* primary and secondary (derivative) kind-properties. Although the ontological strategy behind this construal is quite obvious,

---

[4] From her examples – horses, passports, cabbages – one might deduce that "things" are individual material objects, be they natural or artefactual. Moreover, Baker does not distinguish categorially between Kind and Property. It is also left undecided whether kinds and properties are regarded as universals or particulars.

namely, that of saving persons from being reduced to merely material objects and, at the same time, of avoiding a conception of persons as totally immaterial beings or at least as totally disconnected from material things, these claims are open to objections or, at least, warranted demands for further explanations.

To begin with, I should like to say that I am quite in favour of Baker's non-reductive motivation. But I doubt that her suggestion really holds as a general ontological explication. A minor critical point would be that her splitting up kinds into primary and derivative sub-kinds is somewhat *ad hoc*. At least, there seems to be no way for empirical findings to demarcate the purportedly insurmountable border between "human animals" and "persons" in a new way. Although ontology as a science should be guided, *entre outre*, by our successful common-sense differentiations, it should not preclude scientific progress. Or, to put it in a more principled way, ontology should be methodologically guided not only by a *Principle of Phenomenological Adequacy* (PA), but also by a *Principle of Scientific Compatibility* (SC). Baker, or so it seems to me, is far too much on the side of PA. Therefore, I agree with Gary Rosenkrantz's objection to Baker's splitting up of kinds, because "many contemporary philosophers of biology reject the notion that biological species are natural kinds, along with the related notion that biological species properties are essences".[5] That is not to say that I endorse the Organism View of Rosenkrantz as a whole (which is labelled by Baker as an example of the so-called Animalist View), but I am inclined to demand a more empirical answer to the question of how species or kinds, provided there are any, are established in the respective domains. Baker's view seems to involve an oversimplified picture of "bodies" and "human animals". At least, it is an open question whether there are clear-cut species boundaries which are to be acknowledged in a general ontological theory.

The major critical point, however, is that Lynne Baker's cited statement seems to be circular. Persons, she says, are essentially persons – period. On her construal this means that an individual entity is a person if and only if it is one-sidedly dependent on a Person Kind, provided this kind is primary for the respective entity. If this is meant as a definition, then the term to be defined, the *definiendum* ("person"), recurs in the *definiens*, and nothing is gained by such a definition. The notion of 'person' would simply circulate from individuals to primary kinds and back. Perhaps Baker had just this in mind, namely to show that persons cannot be defined, *i.e.*, reduced to something more basic, because every definition would turn out to be circular (although she does not say so). If, on a charitable interpretation, we then rule out the circularity objection, there still remains the question how illuminating it is to say that persons are dependent on a Person Kind if and only if this kind is Primary. Apart from the fact that Baker is obviously committed to

---

[5] Cf. G. Rosenkrantz (2002, 391) in his Commentary on Baker's 2002 essay.

acknowledging an ontological category of Kind or Species, the crucial question is: Whence the primacy? What justifies a distinction between 'primary' and 'derivative' on the level of kinds? Isn't here eventually a second – and more hidden – circularity at work, namely that of tacitly harking back to the individuals which are to be elucidated by pointing to kind levels, from which we started – given that we start with kinds and kinds levels at all? Or, to put it another way, how is it to be explained that a kind has the – purportedly essential – attribute of being primary or of being merely derivative? Do kinds have different tags according to how they are related to individuals? Perhaps also here, circularity may be ruled out in virtue of some presupposed dialectic between kinds and individuals, but, nevertheless, one is thrown back on mere speculations.

Finally, constitution is supposed to be a *unifying relation*. Concerning persons, Lynne Baker argues that bodies and persons are united, because a body's derivative-kind properties and a person's primary-kind properties constitute a person. Both of these kind properties are supposed to be united in virtue of each being constituents of a person. The question here is, however, whether the notion of constitution implies the notion of unity. Although 'constitution' is surely to be regarded as a very basic concept in general ontology, because it challenges philosophers to find out the elementary categories of being, *i.e.*, the *constituents* of everything, it is an open question whether 'constitution' *per se* is apt to explain the *unity* of the constituents which are regarded as the ingredients of some integral whole, such as persons on the construal of Baker. If constitution has a unifying quality at all, then – or so one might argue – it depends on the very constituents themselves. At least some of them have to be such that they require other constituents or are 'unsaturated' in the Fregean sense in order to form a unity without requiring a further uniting relation.

To sum up, Baker's Constitution View is problematic in the following respects: (i) It cannot explain personal identity in terms of constitution, because the notion of identity which is usually implied by the notion of constitution is rejected; (ii) Constitution is construed, instead, as a unity relation and cannot serve its metaphysical purpose, at least on a substance-*cum*-kinds theory. Substance and Kind, if taken seriously as ontological categories – and Baker is committed to taking them seriously, – are totally independent categories of being. How, then, can entities belonging to those categories unite without any further uniting relation? (iii) The logical and ontological ground for distinguishing *primary* from *derivative* kinds is not very clear. What is it that makes "bodies" or "human animals" *derive* from "persons"? It seems as if someone has put the cart in front of the horse. Why not say that persons are necessarily embodied and then try to figure out features which might be labelled as 'personal properties'? (iv) Explaining 'persons' by saying that they are 'essentially' persons and thereby invoking primary kinds, *i.e.* necessary properties, would be circular and therefore fail as a definition. In case the explanation is meant as an elucidation, it might state, at best, that the category of Person is to be taken as primitive, *i.e.*, as not further analysable. But then one might ask whether showing just this, the primitiveness of Person, has to be demonstrated by putting into operation a very special theory of kinds.

However critical my short assessment has been, there is a point in Baker's theory which might serve as a link to a different 'constitution view', namely, the fact that properties figure greatly in her approach, since admitting properties is a promising starting point for trying out tropes. The question then is whether and how those 'kind properties' – be they 'primary' or 'derivative' – can be further analysed.

5. Constitution and Identity II – the Trope View

On the trope view, overt or hidden circularity problems do not arise simply because kinds or kind-properties are not presupposed. Moreover, the notion of constitution is preserved as a metaphysical concept which permits a definition of identity, according to Leibniz's *Principle of the Indiscernibility of Identicals* (necessarily, trope complexes T_i and T_j are identical if and only if T_i is constituted by the same tropes as T_j, and *vice versa*). In other words, trope constitution is equivalent to the identity of a trope complex. Last, but not least, a certain unifying aspect of constitution can be saved in virtue of the metaphysical fact that tropes are ontologically dependent entities. Let me briefly explain the implications and consequences of these claims, especially concerning change and persistence of a trope complex.

On trope philosophy it is not necessary to distinguish between the notion of full or 'strict' identity and identity 'in the loose or popular sense'.[6] All trope complexes – be they purely physical, be they physical and mental or be they purely mental (if there are any) – are each defined by their respective constituting tropes. On this construal changes within complexes can be easily explained, since change is nothing other than alteration of trope composition. But there might be problems concerning the persistence through change. A somewhat stereotyped example may illustrate the case.

Consider Mary. As a new-born baby, she could stare, yell and grope, suck and defecate, and possibly sleep for a while – at least these are the salient tropes of a complex called Mary at this stage. About three months later, another salient trope can be observed: a smiling in addition to the trope of purely staring. And everybody who observes Mary's smiling is very happy, because Mary seems to be responsive to her environment in a new way. As a two-year-old child, she has gained enormously in trope complexity: ob-

---

[6] Bishop Butler's prominent differentiation (1736) has been taken up by R. Chisholm (1976, 92-113) and is discussed by D. Wiggins (2001, 197-205) and M. Loux (1998, 226-230).

viously, there is a trope of bodily stability which seems to allocate a whole slew of other tropes: creeping, sitting, standing upright, going, running, climbing, falling – while all the tropes which constituted her as a new-born are still in operation. At about the same stage, one can observe that Mary is talking and not merely babbling. Perhaps this talk is still very much guided by pointing to something and articulating words like 'yellow', 'car', 'dog', or 'hot' and 'cold', a language which, according to Quine, is constituted by one word-sentences. At the age of eighteen, Mary is (at least according to the German law) a full-fledged citizen. She has rights and obligations. She can participate in elections, acquire a driver's license – and she is fully responsible for her free actions. Suddenly she is 'independent' in a new way. Let's skip Mary's further career (a career which we shall imagine as a nice and brilliant one) and consider the tragic moment when Mary, at the age of, let's say, seventy-eight, loses her memory and is no longer able to definitely state who she is or where she is. Surely, even at this stage, a lot of the 'old tropes' which have constituted the complex called Mary from the beginning of her existence are still in operation, e.g., there might be tropes of moving and talking, as well as the smiling trope, but quite a lot of the physical and, especially, the mental tropes are missing.

On this scenario, Mary is changing all the time, physically and mentally, in virtue of gaining or losing individual properties (tropes). In which sense then – if in any sense at all – can one speak about Mary's personal identity? On the trope view, Mary obviously does not have a once and for all determined personal identity. Instead she is something like a plurality or aggregate of 'identities', which are temporally determined by the actual tropes which constitute the complex that is identical with 'her'. Whenever a trope is gained, or a trope is lost (which is due to a certain sub-relation of ontological dependency – namely – causality), Mary changes her personal identity. All that she is depends on the tropes which constitute her, including eventually the tropes she memorises or anticipates.

The first objection will probably be that on this construal there is no personal identity whatsoever. 'Mary' could be any trope complex constituted by the properties of staring, yelling, groping, sucking, excreting and sleeping. At least, Mary-as-a new-born human would be very similar to any nameless new-born calf, dog, or walrus and lots of other animals which have been classified biologically as 'mammals'. Is there no difference? How could one distinguish Mary, the human infant, from Mary, the new-born walrus (if some zoologists have baptised the animal Mary)? Or, is Mary considered as a person only from that moment on when she talks or even from the later moment on when she is regarded as responsible for her free actions? Finally, what about Mary, the human being, when she develops Alzheimer's? Is Alzheimer-Mary no longer a person? But even if she's not, what else would she be?

A short answer to these questions is that persons can flourish without requiring a strict borderline. Mary-the-human and Mary-the-walrus are constituted by tropes which are similar and which in virtue of being so gather in 'resemblance classes', in this case, in a class or kind called 'mammals'. What distinguishes Mary-the-human and Mary-the-walrus, however, are lots of tropes which assemble in different classes, two of which I shall discuss below, namely tropes of intentionality and tropes of normativity. And there I shall come back also to the problems concerning Alzheimer-Mary.

Another objection might be that whenever something changes, there must be a permanent or unchanging thing or at least core of features which remains stable – otherwise talk of change misses the subject of discourse , *i.e.* 'change', altogether. This would be the 'endurantist' reminder against a 'perdurantist' approach which also seems to be at work in trope ontology. If, on the trope view, a complex is changing according to the tropes which actually constitute the whole complex, what we have – so the endurantists would say – is a mere sequence of different qualitative stages but no real change in *one* thing.

Although an appropriate response to this objection would require discussion which is beyond the scope of this paper, a short answer would be that trope theory, *i.e.*, a theory based on the ontological category of individual qualities, is neutral with respect to the different time ontologies mentioned. First, a trope theorist is not prevented from constructing a core of tropes, *i.e.*, a nucleus of (essential) tropes which remains stable as long as the trope complex exists, while changes are (accidental) alterations in the trope periphery which surrounds the nucleus.[7] Therefore, the endurantist option is not precluded. Secondly, also the perdurantist theory is open to trope theorists, for they can easily construct 'temporal parts', 'stages' or 'time slices' as temporal tropes. So, a definite answer depends on further arguments. My favourite option, until now, is that time is best reconstructed as *modes* depending one-sidedly on tropes, *i.e.*, I do not suppose that there are purely temporal tropes along with the rest, but, rather, that a trope might have a temporal mode of existence.[8] That means, to return to our example, that, for instance, Mary's different tropes of smiling persist each as long as these tropes actually constitute the complex called Mary. So Mary might smile, even if she has lost many tropes which have connected her to her social environment.

6. Intentionality

By 'intentionality' I understand mental activities like perceiving, thinking and feeling. They are classes of qualities which might overlap and which presuppose agents, such as

---

[7] Cf. P. Simons (1994).
[8] Cf. K. Trettin (2002).

animals, human beings and persons. Mental activities are, however, not representational. What a thought or belief 'is about' or has as 'its content' is a particular part of the world itself and not a particular representation of the world. Moreover, mental activities are qualities of some entities within the world and therefore as real as anything else. A *forteriori*, mental activities belong to the basic qualities, because they establish the access of agents to their own and many other qualities of the world.

This would be in a nutshell the *Credo* of a realist and particularist metaphysic of mind and body.[9] The interesting point here is the talk of 'agents'. Surely, the employment of 'agent' has to be elucidated, not only, because at least the following two queries will turn up. First, are trope theorists really entitled to employ this term? Isn't agent talk only conceivable, if clear-cut substances are presupposed? Secondly, even if this point can be settled in favour of trope theory, there still remains the question of why animals and persons appear in the list of examples – with just a comma between them. Are they really on a par? Aren't there enormous differences?[10] I shall discuss both of these objections together and try to clarify the notion of agent as applied within trope theory.

An agent is a trope complex which can act, *i.e.*, do something intentionally. Consider, first, a singular piece of marble (Aristotle's and Lynne Baker's example). Surely it is a nice solid trope complex, but it will not act in any way or do something. Neither can it intend to become a statue, nor can it plan to fall down in order to hit some hikers. Either there is the external causal power of an agent (an artist) involved, or some, equally external, entities (other non-intentional tropes or complexes thereof) cause the particular piece of marble to fall down and accidentally injure the hikers. An agent, in contrast, is a trope complex which is constituted not only by physical tropes but also by mental or intentional tropes. Mental or intentional tropes are such that they are individual qualities which might be summarised in a first approximation as a sentient appeal or direction towards the environment. This emotional groping for anything near can be noticed already in living beings far below the level of mammals. Whoever has come near a medusa, not always visible in the blue waters of a Mediterranean coast, will be convinced that her tentacles are surely directed towards something – although probably not at you personally, but at least generically at some trope complex which appeals to the individual medusa. What I want to illustrate by this example is that agency is not restricted to human beings. It covers a larger group of entities. The reason for this supposition is that species-borders are, as far as intentionality – conceived of in a very broad sense – is concerned, not major obstacles. Remember Mary-the-infant-human and Mary-the-infant-walrus. Surely, there will be enormous differences, but their resemblance is striking: both of these trope

---

9 For details see K. Trettin (2003, forthcoming).
10 I owe the last question to conversations with Ulrike Ramming, University of Stuttgart.

complexes are at least constituted by similar tropes of intentionality, for they act similarly towards their environment. And so, on the trope view – at least on my version – there is nothing wrong with gathering 'animal-tropes' and 'human being-tropes' in one and the same resemblance class of intentional tropes. So far, just one broad feature of agency, volitional and emotional intentionality, has been briefly touched on. How about cognitive intentionality?

By cognitive intentionality I understand a family of activities such as a perceiving, believing, thinking, or knowing, each of which is a trope, more precisely, a trope which has a temporal mode of existence.

If, for instance, Andrew is thinking of the Golden Gate Bridge, then what we have here, is a trope complex called Andrew (A), a trope complex called the Golden Gate Bridge (B), and a think-trope (T) which connects A to B in virtue of T's being ontologically dependent on both, A and B. But Andrew's thinking is not restricted to existent objects. He sometimes also thinks of a golden mountain or a mermaid. And there have been also moments when Andrew thought of a square circle, although he was quite aware of the fact that such a thing is an impossible object.[11]

The case of Andrew is not only presented in order to illustrate that cognitive intentionality such as a thinking involves more than straightforward directedness to something which exists, but also to emphasize that it involves imagination and fantasy. Moreover, I want to point to a feature of cognition which may be decisive for distinguishing some intentional trope complexes from others. The decisive feature may be that Andrew is able to differentiate between a real and a purely imaginative thought content, and nevertheless knows that his thoughts – whatever they are 'about' – are as real as himself. Or, to recast this statement in trope terminology: that Andrew's first-order think-tropes are supplemented by higher-order think-tropes which 'make Andrew aware' of the difference between the factual and the fictional. This sort of cognitive awareness may, surely, be regarded as a salient feature of rationality.

A further criterion for distinguishing between purely sentient, volitional and emotive trope complexes and those which are constituted additionally by cognitive tropes will be the faculty of learning and employing a language. Linguistic capability, in turn, seems to require as a precondition a social environment, *i.e.*, probably no rational cognitive agent can exist all on its own. So, a trope complex which has cognitive tropes among its constituents is a rational, language performing, and social agent.

The salient intentional tropes taken together might then be regarded as specifying a class or kind of trope complexes – the class or kind of human beings. I should like to

---

[11] For a more detailed discussion on thinking about non-existent and impossible objects cf. K. Trettin (2003 forthcoming).

add, however, that talk about the presumably specifying features of human beings, at least against the background of a long philosophical tradition, has either a pompous ring or may be suspected of merely summing up platitudes. I am quite aware of this awkward situation, but it was not my intent to come up with totally new and original features. Rather, I wanted to indicate in very broad outline how kinds may be reconstructed by employing trope theory. That is not to say that every philosopher who admits tropes in her ontology is committed to a reconstruction of kinds along these lines or to any reconstruction of kinds. There may be a separate argument – neutral towards different ontological categorising – which simply presupposes the human kind.

7. Normativity, Personal Identity, and the Human Being Principle

The separate argument for constructing a class which has as its members salient intentional features is normative rather than logical or ontological. The supposition of a human kind seems to give us a fundamental reason, perhaps the only reason, for understanding what persons are. For without this supposition personhood would be either a totally alien concept or its application would be arbitrary. In either case, the normative and ethical consequences would be disastrous. Therefore I shall ally myself with David Wiggins and his Human Being Principle. The following passage of his *Sameness and Substance Renewed* is not only illuminating in itself, but also shows that Wiggins invokes this principle for logical rather than normative reasons:

> So, *given* the human beinghood of A and B, this furnishes a perfectly good covering concept for the identity 'A is the same as B'. 'Person' and 'human being' differ in sense. They may even differ in their extension. But that is immaterial. What matters is that here, in so far as they assign any, the concepts *person* and *human being* assign the same underlying principle of individuation to A and to B, and that that principle, the *human being* principle, is the one that we have to consult in order to move towards the determination of the truth or falsehood of the judgment that A is B.[12]

While Wiggins is looking for the appropriate kind term or sortal concept in order to determine the identity of persons and therefore his Human Being Principle serves as a principle of individuation, my appreciation of that principle has purely normative motives. As I have tried to show (§5), on trope theory there is no need for *presupposing* kinds or species in order to explicate the identity of trope complexes. I am not sure whether even Wiggins presupposes kinds in the strict ontological sense. He may refer in this respect only to 'covering concepts', hoping that his 'rich' substances will shoulder all the ontological work to be done. When it comes to being a bit more explicit on what human beings are, Wiggins is equally as platitudinous as I have been.

[12] D. Wiggins (2001), Chapter 7, §1, 193f.

Human beings are substances possessed of a specific principle of activity to which, in the course of life, each one of us gives his own yet more specific, more and more distinctive, determination. Prominent among the specifically human activities is our exercise of cognitive faculties.[13]

I didn't quote this passage, however, just in order to show that the idea of human beings as cognitive agents coincides across categorial systems. The interesting point is that Wiggins conceives of his (human) substances as determinables which, in the course of their lives, gain in determination. This conception is interesting, because it may be interpreted in two different ways, each of which will throw light on the Human Being Principle and the concept of 'person'.

On the first interpretation, a human being starts its life as a mere stand-in or representative of a presupposed human kind. Although this sounds very plausible, if one has additional concepts in mind, such as potentiality and development, there seems to be a logical and ontological confusion at the outset. (1) Either the categories of 'individual substance' and 'generic substance' collapse and what we have here is just one category. But then the whole Thesis of Sortal Dependency, which David Wiggins has carefully laid out in his book, is in danger. Why should one pose 'the same-what-question' in order to judge whether A is the same as B, if A and B are nothing other than determinable kinds? Which further kind concept or sortal term would be needed or could be useful in order to decide the question of identity? (2) Or the categories don't collapse, but preserve a distinction – 'individual human substance', on the one hand, 'human kind', on the other. On this reading both categories would be understood as determinables of a different order, each of which allows for determinations. But then one is surely justified in demanding more details concerning the categorial distinction.

On a second interpretation (and with the pitfalls of the first one in mind), Wiggins' passage might be understood as a statement which implicitly indicates that trope theory would be a good solution, because then the problem of explicating 'enrichment' or 'growth of complexity' of 'individual substances' would vanish. Conceived of as trope complexes from the very start, an 'individual substance' would be as simple or as complex as it actually is, depending on which different tropes (with their dependent temporal modes) are the constituents of this complex. Moreover, trope ontology would have the advantage that sorts or kinds can be construed out of the salient features which intentional trope complexes convey. So the Human Kind Principle would not be based on common-sense intuition alone (which is surely in most cases a good intuition), nor would it be a mere conceptual or explanatory postulate. Whoever has followed the hermeneutic proposal (2) up to this point, will undoubtedly have noticed that at the very moment we switch to a consequent trope-theoretic interpretation, the logical considera-

[13] D. Wiggins (2001), Chapter 7, §13, 226.

tions – which are, of course, necessary to guide any philosophical investigation – will no longer be the only guide concerning personal identity.

I prefer the second reading, because on this interpretation, the concept of 'person' would turn out to be a *normative* concept – a concept, however, that has a safe ontological and epistemical grounding – a Human Being Principle Renewed.

8. Conclusion

I have argued that 'person' is a derivative concept. It derives from the salient intentional tropes which constitute a class of entities – human beings. Surely, Person is not an *ens per se*. Moreover, 'person' is a normative concept based on a Human Being Principle. Consider once again the situation of Mary when she develops Alzheimer's. Is she still to be regarded as a person, although many intentional tropes, especially those of cognitive, rational agency, which once constituted her, are missing? On the trope view of constitution the answer is: Yes, she is. That Alzheimer-Mary is to be respected and recognised as one of us follows, first and foremost, from the fact that she is a member of the class of human beings. Notice, however, that on trope theory a 'human kind' is not an ontological category of its own, but a derivative, second-order category. It derives from salient features of trope complexes which are constituted by a whole family of intentional tropes. What is really basic, is intentional tropes. So, if they exist, and they seem to be existent in many trope complexes which we would assemble in the non-human animal kind, trope philosophy allows for a smooth connection between different kinds of intentional beings: from a Mediterranean medusa to Mary-the-walrus, and further on from Mary-the-infant to Alzheimer-Mary. All of these, which have served as illustrative examples, are wonderful trope complexes, as is Andrew-the thinker-on-impossible-objects. Therefore, 'person' is a normative and not a metaphysical or ontological concept, a concept, however, which can only be applied in a non-arbitrary way, if it is based on a Human Being Principle.[14]

---

[14] I am very grateful to Louise Röska-Hardy, not only for checking my English, but for further philosophical discussions on this topic.

References

Baker, Lynne Rudder (2000), *Persons and Bodies: A Constitution View*, Cambridge: Cambridge University Press.

Baker, Lynne Rudder (2002), "On the Ontological Status of Persons", *Philosophy and Phenomenological Research* LXV, 370-388.

Butler, Joseph (1736), *First Dissertation* to the *Analogy of Religion Natural and Revealed to the Constitution of Nature*.

Chisholm, Roderick M. (1976), *Person and Object: A Metaphysical Study*, London: Allan & Unwin.

Chisholm, Roderick M. (1996), *A Realistic Theory of Categories: An Essay on Ontology*, Cambridge: Cambridge University Press.

Geach, Peter T. (1962), *Reference and Generality*, Ithaca: Cornell University Press.

Hoffman, Joshua and Gary S. Rosenkrantz (1997), *Substance: Its Nature and Existence*, London: Routledge.

Loux, Michael J. (1998), *Metaphysics: A Contemporary Introduction*, London: Routledge.

Lowe, E. Jonathan (1989), *Kinds of Being: A Study of Individuation, Identity and the Logic* of *Sortal Terms*, Oxford: Basil Blackwell.

Quante, Michael (2002), *Personales Leben und menschlicher Tod: Personale Identität als Prinzip der biomedizinischen Ethik*, Frankfurt am Main: Suhrkamp.

Rapp, Christof (1995), *Identität, Persistenz und Substantialität*, Freiburg: Alber.

Rosenkrantz, Gary S. (2002), "Reflections on the Ontological Status of Persons", *Philosophy and Phenomenological Research* LXV, 389-393.

Simons, Peter (1994), "Particulars in Particular Clothing: Three Trope Theories of Substance", *Philosophy and Phenomenological Research* LVI, 555-575. Reprinted in: Laurence, Stephen and Cynthia MacDonald (eds.), *Contemporary Readings in the Foundations of Metaphysics*, Oxford: Basil Blackwell, 1998, 364-384.

Trettin, Käthe (2001), "Ontologische Abhängigkeit in der Tropentheorie", *Metaphysica* 2, No. 1, 23-54. Reprinted in: Löffler, Winfried (ed.), *Substanz und Identität: Beiträge zur Ontologie*, Paderborn: mentis, 2002, 41-66.

Trettin, Käthe (2002), "Tropes and Time", in: Beckermann, Ansgar und Christian Nimtz (eds.), *Argument und Analyse*, Paderborn: mentis, 506-515.

Trettin, Käthe (2003 forthcoming), "Trope Theory on the Mental / Physical Divide", in: Kanzian, Christian, Josef Quitterer and Edmund Runggaldier (eds.), *Persons: An Interdisciplinary Approach / Personen: Ein interdisziplinärer Dialog*, Wien: Verlag öbv& hpt, 43-51.

Wiggins, David (2001), *Sameness and Substance Renewed*, Cambridge: Cambridge University Press.

Michael B. Burke
Is My Head a Person?

0. Introduction

Is the head of a whole-bodied human person itself a person? Are the head and other brain-containing parts of whole-bodied human thinkers themselves thinkers? There is pressure to answer such questions affirmatively. That pressure creates a problem, especially for those of us with conservative metaphysical inclinations. If we succumb to the pressure, we depart from ordinary ways of speaking and thinking. And we find ourselves propelled toward such radical theories as mereological essentialism. But the currently available means of resisting the pressure are themselves radical, problematic, or both. I offer a novel, conservative solution. Making the (unfavorable) assumption that human persons are wholly material, I explain why their heads and other brain-containing parts are neither persons nor thinkers. And I do so without sacrificing the broadly Aristotelian metaphysic implicit in ordinary ways of thinking.

1. Terminological Preliminary

Those who discuss the status of brain-containing person-parts ask, variously, whether such parts are "persons," "thinkers," "conscious beings," or "rational, conscious beings." Not infrequently they use the first or second of these terms to mean something like the fourth. I will use the term 'person' in its ordinary sense, not in any stipulative sense, and will offer no clarification of it, except to say that I assume that no nonthinking part of a thinking person is itself a person, even if *some* nonthinkers, such as human embryos, *are* persons. I will use the term 'thinker' in a special (Cartesian) sense, to mean 'conscious being who perceives, believes, desires, emotes, wills, and reasons, one whose perceptions, beliefs, desires, emotions, volitions, and reasonings are as complex as those of a normal, adult, human person'. I will not use the term 'rational, conscious being', but will take those who do to mean roughly what I mean by 'thinker'. Finally, I will use 'part' to mean 'proper part'.

2. The Argument that Creates the Problem

The problem is created by the existence of an imposing argument for the personhood, or at least the thinkerhood, of the brain-containing parts of (normal, adult) human persons. For the sake of concreteness, let's consider the (normal, adult) human organism

Percy, whom I'll assume to be a thinker and a person,[1] and two of his brain-containing parts: Heddi, which is Percy's head (or *one* of his heads, if some parts of heads are heads themselves), and Finn, which is the complement of Percy's left index-finger. (The "complement" of a part, relative to some one of the wholes of which it's a part, is the part of that whole which consists of all of the whole except that part.) So, *Percy* is a whole-bodied *person*; *Heddi* is Percy's *head*; and *Finn* is one of Percy's ten *finger-complements*.

The argument for the thinkerhood of brain-containing person-parts is straightforward. As we will see in section 3, it has provoked a variety of radical responses and has lent support to efforts to relativize or graduate identity. Applied to Finn, the argument is this:

The thinkerhood or nonthinkerhood of a being depends solely on its microphysical properties (i.e., the qualities and interrelations of its microphysical parts). Its purely relational properties are irrelevant. But Finn differs negligibly in its microphysical properties from the thinker Percy. And Finn is virtually identical in its microphysical properties to Finn*, the thinker its cells would compose if the finger of which Finn is the complement were suddenly annihilated. Therefore, Finn is a thinker.

To apply the argument to Heddi, we would change 'negligibly' in the third sentence to 'in no relevant way'. (The brain, or perhaps just the cerebrum, is the seat of thought.) And at the end of the fourth sentence, directly after 'annihilated', we would insert 'and if the head that remained were kept alive and functioning by medical technology'.

The argument is applicable to *all* brain-containing thinker-parts. And if it is supplemented with the premise that thinkerhood (in the special sense specified in section 1) entails personhood, it leads to the conclusion that such parts are persons as well as thinkers.

The argument seems potent, at least when confined to the *thinker*hood of the parts. But even thus confined, it presses us to accept something that seems absurd: that we all share our bodies with other thinkers. So we have a problem.[2]

---

[1] Some will want to say that the organism Percy *constitutes* a person, but is not identical with one. For the purposes of this paper, I need not and will not object to that view. But I have objected to it elsewhere. In Burke 1997b, I sought to remove its principal motivation by showing that to identify persons with their bodies, or with the human organisms with which they are coextensive, is not incompatible with accepting a psychological criterion of personal identity. (One might deny the thinkerhood of Percy on altogether different grounds. One might contend that it is only some *part* of Percy that thinks – his brain, for example. Any such contention should be rejected, for reasons that will emerge in section 7.)

[2] There is a related problem, Peter Unger's "problem of the many," that arises when we ask whether

3. The Existing Solutions

My purpose is to present a novel solution, not to quarrel with those already on the scene. But to provide perspective, I will survey the solutions with which mine must compete, and briefly indicate their drawbacks. All of the solutions to be discussed presuppose, as does mine, that human persons are wholly material.

Let me acknowledge at the outset what is acknowledged too seldom in such surveys: The writings surveyed are masterful treatments of the problems of material constitution. I am indebted to them for my understanding of many points. Whatever the merits of the ideas to which I critically advert, the writings by no means reduce to – and their value is by no means limited to – those ideas.

(a) Olson

Eric Olson (1995) would have us deny the very *existence* of Heddi and Finn. Unlike more thoroughgoing eliminativists, such as Unger (1979) and Heller (1990), Olson does believe in persons; but like van Inwagen (1981; 1990, 81-97), Olson denies that persons have such parts as (undetached) heads, brains, hands, and hand-complements. The only person-parts he recognizes are elementary particles. According to Olson, we need to deny the existence of Heddi, Finn, and the like precisely because we would otherwise be forced to accept the repugnant conclusion that such parts are "rational, conscious beings" (182). We would be forced to accept this, Olson says, because (a) such parts have what it takes "internally" to be rational, conscious beings, and (b) "... a thing cannot fail to be rational or conscious simply because of its relation to some *other* thing [such as a finger] – simply by having the wrong neighbours" (183).

Olson's solution might seem *ad hoc*, since the only reason he offers for denying the existence of macroscopic person-parts is the utility of that denial in forestalling their claims to thinkerhood. However, as van Inwagen has shown (1981), the denial also forestalls Tibbles-type problems, so there is some independent motivation for it. Still, the denial represents a radical departure from ordinary ways of thinking. I will show how we can comfortably deny the thinkerhood of brain-containing parts without denying the *existence* of those parts. (Elsewhere, in my 1994b and 1996, I offer a conservative solution to the Tibbles-type problems that motivated *van Inwagen's* denial.)

---

there is a precise set of particles such that Percy is definitely composed of just those particles. Unger's problem will not be addressed. But the solution I offer to the problem posed by certain *parts* of Percy is compatible with the principal solutions available to the problem of delineating the *whole* of Percy. In particular, it is compatible with the supervaluational and epistemic accounts of vagueness, and also with the competing view (which I favor) that persons are vague objects. For a superb discussion of Unger's problem, see Lewis 1993.

(b) Merricks

Trenton Merricks (1998a; 1998b; 2001, Ch. 4) focuses on the property of consciousness. Like Olson, he holds that consciousness is an intrinsic property, one that Finn could not lack simply in virtue of its relation to Percy's left index-finger. But despite the fact that Finn differs little from Percy (and hardly at all from Finn*) in its microphysical properties, Merricks, like Olson, would find it absurd to think that Finn and the other brain-containing parts of Percy constitute a "mighty host of conscious ... objects" (Merricks 2001, 95). For Merricks, what such cases show is that even though (human) persons are wholly material, the psychological does not supervene on the microphysical, not even globally.

What, then, *does* account for the difference between Percy and Finn with regard to consciousness? Merricks simply doesn't say. He says that normal, adult, human organisms are conscious and that their parts are not, but he denies that it's in *virtue* of their parthood that the parts fail to be conscious. (In his [2001], he decides that there *are* no undetached super-cellular parts, only detached ones, but denies that the former fail to exist in *virtue* of their undetachment.) Is the correlation between consciousness and nonparthood a brute fact? Is it the result of divine ordination? Or what? Merricks says only that it's "mysterious" (1998b, 845). It will be hard to take his view seriously until he has more to say about the mystery.

(c) Geach

A third solution is to concede that many person-parts are persons, but to avoid a *multiplication* of persons by relativizing identity to sort. One might acknowledge that Heddi and Finn are persons but insist, *a la* Peter Geach (1980, 215-18), that Heddi, Finn, and Percy are the *same* person (and the same thinker), although different lumps of person-stuff.

I doubt that this solution is coherent. If Percy and Heddi are the same one person, how much does that one person weigh? Might we say that he weighs 80 kilos *qua* person with a head, trunk, and limbs, but only 10 kilos *qua* person with merely a head? Presumably not. An entity can have a property "*qua*" F only if the entity *is* F. But the terms 'person with a head, trunk, and limbs' and 'person with merely a head' are undeniably contrary. (In this they differ from, say, 'person' and 'hunk of person-stuff'.) In any case, the Geachian solution relies upon a theory of identity that few identity theorists accept. I will show how we can deal with Percy-parts without surrendering the absoluteness of identity.

(d) Lewis

A fourth solution is to concede that Percy contains many *different* persons, but to make this concession less disagreeable than it initially seems. David Lewis (1993, 33-34) is willing to allow that the many hair-complements of a cat are themselves cats, and to agree that no two of them are completely identical, but he would add, invoking Armstrong's theory that numerical identity comes in degrees (Armstrong 1978, 37-38), that a cat and the many slightly smaller cats it contains are *almost* completely identical, because they almost completely overlap. Lewis remarks, "The cats are many, but almost one. By a blameless approximation, we may simply say that there is one cat on the mat." It appears that Lewis is willing to take the same line with regard to persons (24).

There are several grounds on which to object. First, many of us will be reluctant to allow that numerical identity comes in degrees. Second, some of us will find it implausible that Percy contains within himself a host of persons, even when it is added that those persons differ numerically from Percy and from one another only slightly. Third, there is the point stressed by Eric Olson (1995, 192-96): If we allow that brain-containing person-parts are persons, we must also allow that persons never know just who they are. Neither Percy, Heddi, nor Finn would have any way of knowing which person he is. Finally, and most seriously, Lewis acknowledges that his solution is inapplicable to cases, such as that of Percy and Heddi, where the overlap between whole and part is far from complete.

Lewis also offers a second, alternative account (28). He considers it acceptable to say that the hair-complement of a cat fails to be a cat simply in virtue of being "almost all of a cat with just one little bit left out" (Lewis 1993, 28). Perhaps he would also consider it acceptable to say that the hair-complement fails for that reason to be conscious. I call this an alternative *account*, rather than an alternative solution, because Lewis doesn't attempt to make the account acceptable to those who find it *un*acceptable, especially as applied to consciousness. If personhood and consciousness are indeed maximal (in a sense soon to be defined), what is needed is what I hope to provide: an understanding of why that should be so.

(e) Carter

Finally, there is the solution I associate with W. R. Carter. Actually, it's more aptly termed a position than a solution, since it contains no suggestion for mitigating its counterintuitiveness. It involves acquiescing in the threatened multiplication of persons, and then *heightening* the paradox by noting and accepting an apparent consequence of that multiplication: that persons cannot survive the loss of any of their parts, not even such small parts as fingers.

Although I attribute this position to Carter, I know of no one publication in which Carter endorses all of its elements. In Carter 1983, he declares his belief in a variety of undetached person-parts, including brains, leg-complements, and finger-complements. In a much later article (1997), he argues that brain-containing person-parts must, if they exist, be counted as persons, but nowhere in that article does he take a stand on whether brain-containing person-parts exist. In both articles, Carter claims that the existence of such parts would argue strongly for the conclusion that persons perish when any of their parts do. As regards Percy and his finger-complement, the argument (briefly and roughly) is this: Assuming that Finn exists, Finn is a person. But since Finn is *part* of Percy, not *identical* with Percy, Finn and Percy are *different* persons. Suppose now that Percy has lost the finger of which Finn was the complement. If both Percy and Finn have survived that event, they are two persons composed of just the same cells and occupying just the same place, which is absurd. But if only one has survived, surely it must be Finn, since Finn is the closer predecessor of the post-loss person. (Carter 1997, 374)

Of course, such arguments drive us toward mereological essentialism, the doctrine that every part of a thing is essential to its identity. And Carter does indeed warn (1983, 126-27, 142) that there may be no good alternative to accepting that doctrine, one very much contrary to his own intuitions (126).

4. Maximality

So much for my survey of the existing solutions. I will offer a conservative alternative to those solutions, one on which consciousness, thinkerhood, and personhood are maximal. So I will begin with a definition of maximality. On the usual definition, personhood is maximal just in case necessarily, no part of a person is itself a person. (Reminder: I use 'part' to mean 'proper part'.) This definition makes maximality claims needlessly and inadvisably strong. Although it's plausible to deny the personhood of those person-parts whose personhood is here at issue, it would be risky to claim that *no* person-parts are persons. It would be riskier still to claim that it's *impossible* for person-parts to be persons. Perhaps somewhere there are multicellular persons composed of unicellular persons. Or, if there aren't, perhaps there *could* have been. Although Quine (1981, 92-93) claims that the innumerable table-like entities nested within an ordinary table are not themselves tables, I doubt that he'd deny the possibility of making a Brobdingnagian table from a large number of Lilliputian tables.

Except for those few theorists who are mereological essentialists, maximality can more usefully be defined as follows: kind/property/term/concept C is *maximal* just in case necessarily, no identity-sufficient part of a C is itself a C. (Of course, 'a C' is short for 'an object that belongs to the extension of C'.) Something is an *identity-sufficient* part of a *C* just in case the particles composing the part would immediately compose *that very C*, if the complement of the part suddenly (as a rare, uncaused quantum event) ceased to exist. For example, Finn is an identity-sufficient part of the person Percy, for if the finger that is Finn's complement suddenly disappeared (ceased to exist), the particles composing Finn would then compose Percy. (What the relationship would be between Finn and the diminished Percy is controversial.[3]) Heddi, too, is an identity-sufficient part of Percy: Upon the sudden disappearance of Percy's head-complement, the particles composing Heddi would, if only briefly (or with the prompt employment of advanced life-support technology), compose Percy.[4] So personhood is maximal, in the sense defined, only if neither Finn nor Heddi is a person so long as it's part of Percy. Of course, this is the desired result.

Now consider a giant, multicellular person composed of tiny, unicellular persons. If the whole of the giant, except for one of the unicellulates composing him, suddenly disappeared, the particles composing that unicellulate would indeed compose a person, but not one identifiable with the giant. Thus the unicellular parts of the giant person fail to qualify as *identity-sufficient* parts. So their personhood is not inconsistent with the maximality, in my sense, of personhood. Again, this is the desired result.

5. Initial Arguments for the Maximality of Personhood and Thinkerhood

Heddi and Finn are neither persons nor thinkers. That's because (1) they are identity-sufficient parts of the person Percy, and (2) identity-sufficient parts of persons are nei-

---

[3] There are *several* accounts, however, that are compatible with the means I will offer of denying the personhood (and thinkerhood) of Finn. Three examples: On the single most widely accepted theory of material constitution (see, for example, Baker 2000), the disappearance of the finger would cause Finn suddenly to *constitute*, but not suddenly to *be*, the person Percy. I have offered an alternative theory of material constitution (Burke 1994a, 1994b), one that avoids coinciding objects. On my theory, the disappearance of the finger would cause Finn to cease to exist. That's because Finn is a nonperson, because nonpersons are *essentially* nonpersons (in my view, persons include embryonic animals capable of *maturing* into thinkers), and because Finn would *become* a human if it survived the disappearance of the finger. Finally I'll mention a temporal-parts account, on which the disappearance of the finger would cause Finn to "become" Percy, in this sense: the post-disappearance temporal part of Finn would be numerically identical with the post-disappearance temporal part of Percy. (See Lewis 1993, 24-25.)

[4] Compared to the sudden, uncaused disappearance of one's head-complement, decapitation by guillotine is more jarring and results, consequently, in greater immediate change in the intrinsic properties of one's head. But even guillotining does not immediately terminate consciousness. At least, this is what some evidence suggests. For some of that evidence, as well as a medical explanation of why consciousness, perception, and thought might continue not just for a fraction of a second but for seven seconds or more, see Abbott 1994, 203-5.

ther persons nor thinkers. For the commonsensical (1) I will give no argument. My purpose is not to refute the radical views (such as those of Olson and Carter) on which (1) would be denied, but to provide a conservative defense of (2) and, thereby, a conservative basis for denying the personhood and thinkerhood of Heddi and Finn.

So, what reason is there for believing (2)? Let's start with personhood. The first thing to say is that it certainly appears that our *concept* of personhood is maximal. Its maximality is evident in what we do and do not count as *instances* of the concept. When determining whether to ticket Percy for driving in the lane reserved for cars containing at least three people, the traffic officer will not count the likes of Heddi and Finn. Nor will the divorce court, when considering Percy's claim that his wife is an adulterer. Nor will the census taker. In general, we simply do not count person-parts as persons.

Some say that ordinary counts of persons can be construed as counts of *distinct* persons, and therefore need not be taken to reflect a view of the status of person-parts. (See Olson 1997, 264.) But even if they are right (which is far from clear), there remains the point that we don't count person-parts as persons even in the sense of *regarding* them as persons. The maximality of our concepts of personhood and thinkerhood is evident in what we ordinarily do and do not *view* as persons and thinkers.

Here's evidence, if any is needed, that we ordinarily view heads neither as persons nor as thinkers. During the spring of 2001 there was a period of two or three weeks during which colleagues and viewers of Neil Cavuto, a Fox TV business-news anchor, jokingly discussed Cavuto's head. The main issues were whether his head is unusually large for his frame and, if so, whether its magnitude contributes to or detracts from his sex appeal. Although there were frequent references to Cavuto's head, I heard no one refer to his head with a personal pronoun. Nor did I hear anyone express concern that Cavuto's head (as opposed to Cavuto himself) might be offended by the sometimes unflattering references to it. Indeed, viewers would have been baffled if someone *had* done so.

What about *larger* brain-containing parts, such as Finn? Well, it's doubtful that we ordinarily *think* of such parts. True, we might say, "Although Percy's finger is broken, the rest of him is fine." But when we do, it's doubtful that we are thinking of "the rest of him" as a single object. Perhaps we're just thinking and reporting that his other *parts* are fine, or that his only injury is to his finger. However, if we *are* thinking of the rest of him as a single object, we evidently are not thinking of it as a person, since we never add, "Happily, that slightly smaller person was uninjured." Moreover, we would be perplexed if someone else *did*. We would be equally perplexed if the reference were to "that slightly smaller thinker," even if Percy were famous for his intellect and were referred to frequently as a thinker.

My first point, then, is that we regard person-parts neither as persons nor as thinkers. I take this to evidence the maximality of our concepts of personhood and thinkerhood. Now for a second point: It would be surprising if those concepts were *not* maximal. It would be surprising because maximal concepts (or the terms that express them) are handier for referring and counting, and because (as noted in Burke 1997b, section II) we have no practical need for *non*maximal concepts of personhood and thinkerhood. We have no such need because there is no practical need to attribute thoughts or other mental states to person-parts. Any part of Percy that has beliefs has the same beliefs that Percy has, except that its first-person beliefs might (or might not) refer to a different subject and its introspective beliefs might (or might not) refer to numerically different but qualitatively identical mental entities. In any case, we would make just the same prediction of the part's behavior whether we based the prediction on *its* beliefs or on Percy's. Suppose we look toward Percy's 10-kilo head, Heddi, and say, "Any listeners who weigh less than 30 kilos should now wriggle their noses." Even if Heddi is a listener, a believer, a desirer, and an agent, we would expect the same nonresponse from Heddi that we expect from Percy, since Heddi believes itself to be the 80-kilo man Percy. In general, attributing personhood or thinkerhood to Heddi would in no way enhance our ability to predict Heddi's "behavior."

Furthermore, the attribution would give us no practical reason to change our behavior toward Heddi. We wouldn't bother to greet Heddi separately, if only because the courtesy would go unappreciated: if Heddi has beliefs, it believes itself to be Percy. (Moreover, there is no way for Heddi to discover its mistake.) Nor would we bother to minimize harm to Heddi when punishing Percy for strangling Fred. (If Percy and Heddi are both thinkers, then it's plausible to say, as Carter would, that amputating Percy's hands would destroy Percy without destroying either Percy's hands-complement or Heddi.) We wouldn't bother because we would think Heddi just as guilty as Percy, and not merely because of its equally malicious intentions. It would be reasonable to say that Heddi actually carried out its intentions, using hands under its control. (If Heddi is a thinker, Percy's hands are as responsive to Heddi's will as to Percy's.) In general, there would be no practical reason to behave differently toward Heddi, if we came to view Heddi as a person or a thinker, because in continuing to behave appropriately toward Percy we would, for all practical purposes, be behaving appropriately toward Heddi.

Let's recapitulate. Given what we ordinarily do and do not regard as persons and thinkers, it appears that our concepts of personhood and thinkerhood are maximal. Since we have no practical need for *non*maximal concepts of personhood and thinkerhood (and since maximal concepts are preferable for referring and counting), it would be surprising if our concepts were *not* maximal. We may reasonably conclude that our concepts of personhood and thinkerhood *are* maximal. Furthermore, we may reasonably infer that the *properties* of personhood and thinkerhood are maximal. (More on the latter point momentarily.)

The arguments of this section suffice, not to *prove* the maximality of personhood and thinkerhood, but to create a *presumption* in favor of their maximality. In sections 7 and 8, we'll see that the philosophical argument against their maximality fails to *overcome* that presumption; indeed, we'll see that there's a weighty philosophical argument that *reinforces* it.

6. Reply to an Objection

I will state the objection only as it applies to personhood, but both the objection and my response apply, *mutatis mutandis*, to thinkerhood. The objection might be formulated thus: Suppose for the sake of argument that our concept of personhood is indeed maximal. It doesn't follow that personhood itself is maximal. Perhaps persons (or human persons) form a natural kind. And perhaps our concept of persons is not a fully accurate representation of that kind. Perhaps our conception of the property of personhood is partly a *mis*conception. Furthermore, Kripke and Putnam have argued persuasively that the extension of terms denoting natural kinds is properly determined not by reference to the ordinary employment of those terms, and not by philosophical argument, but by extralinguistic, extraphilosophical facts ascertainable only through scientific inquiry. The facts cited in section 5 would be relevant if the issue were the content and extension of our *concept* of personhood; but they are out of order, as are the philosophical arguments awaiting us in sections 7 and 8, when the issue is the nature and extension of personhood itself.

Well, the existence of natural kinds is, of course, disputable. And even if there *are* natural kinds, it's not clear that persons, or even human persons (as opposed to humans generally), form a natural kind. But suppose they do. It is still unlikely, even from the perspective of Kripke and Putnam, that scientifically ascertainable facts are dispositive with regard to *all* questions concerning the extension of personhood. Consider animals, which, arguably, form another natural kind. There is an exciting new genealogical definition of animality, one that promises nonarbitrary decisions for such "borderline" cases as sponges and Mesozoa (Slack et. al. 1993, 490, 492). But while the new definition would enable us to decide on the animality of those borderline cases, it provides no more guidance than the older biological definitions on certain matters of interest to philosophers, such as when in the process of animal reproduction there first appears a new animal, or whether dead but undecomposed animals are still animals. The scientific definitions enable us to distinguish animals from plants and other kingdoms of living things, but not from *precursors* of animals or *remains* of animals. Nor do they rule on the animality of the brain-containing *parts* of animals. There is little prospect, if any, of a strictly scientific resolution of these questions – or of the question of interest to us. Even if persons form a natural kind, some candidates for personhood will have to be evaluated by philosophers. As always, philosophers will be guided by anything of relevance that science has to say. But they will be guided as well by the rich perspectives embodied within ordinary ways of thinking, and by philosophical arguments concerning the merits of those and competing perspectives.

7. The Differences between Percy and His Brain-Containing Parts

We don't view Heddi and Finn as thinkers. And there is no practical reason for us to start doing so. But is there good reason to believe that they nevertheless *are* thinkers? Let's focus on Finn, since (if there actually *is* such a thing as Finn, which I won't dispute), Finn's claim to thinkerhood may seem stronger than Heddi's. The principal argument for Finn's thinkerhood is the one previewed in section 2. It's the argument that drives Olson, Merricks, and Carter toward their radical positions. (See section 3.)

> The thinkerhood or nonthinkerhood of a being depends solely on its microphysical properties (i.e., the qualities and interrelations of its microphysical parts). Its purely relational properties are irrelevant. But Finn differs negligibly in its microphysical properties from the thinker Percy. And Finn is virtually identical in its microphysical properties to Finn*, the thinker its cells would compose if the finger of which Finn is the complement were suddenly annihilated. Therefore, Finn is a thinker.

The argument fails. It fails because there are differences between Percy and Finn (and similar, equally pronounced differences between *Finn** and Finn) that are far from negligible. Indeed, there are differences that can plausibly be held to ground a difference between the two with regard to thinkerhood. Those differences derive largely from their microphysical differences. The latter are consequential, although small taken in themselves.

'Percy' is our name for a certain human organism. It is undisputed (in the context of our discussion) that at least one thinker *overlaps* Percy (partially or completely). We have been assuming that Percy (or, if preferred, a purely physical person *constituted* by Percy) is *one* such thinker, if not the only one. That assumption will now be justified. As we are about to see, Percy's claims to thinkerhood are stronger than those of his parts, even if we set aside the arguments of section 5. So Percy is indeed a thinker.

Continuing to take Finn, the complement of Percy's left index-finger, as representative of brain-containing Percy-parts, I will now cite six differences between Percy and Finn, differences that can plausibly be thought to ground a difference between the two with respect to thinkerhood. (The sufficiency of the differences will be defended in section 8.) For ease of expression I'll use personal pronouns when referring to any thinker, although it's an open question whether all thinkers are persons.

(1) Percy, unlike Finn and every other Percy-part, is an organism. (It is generally acknowledged, I believe, that organicity is maximal, even if personhood and thinkerhood are not. See, for example, Olson 1997, 261.) This difference is relevant if only because of the leading role that Percy's organicity would play in explanations of each of the *other* differences.

(2) All who think with Percy's brain (be they one or many) have I-thoughts ascribing the very same nonreferential properties. Many of those I-thoughts are true of Percy but false of Finn. Examples: "I am called Percy"; "I am (or my body is) an organism"; "I am a full-bodied human person"; "I am wearing a ring"; "I weigh 80 kilos, not 79.8 kilos." Conversely, none is true of Finn but false of Percy (unless its subject is misinformed about the properties of the 80-kilo physical object that he regards as his body). Since the I-thoughts are differentially true of Percy, it's plausible that Percy alone is their subject. And it's plausible that Percy alone is their subject at least partly *in virtue* of their being differentially true of Percy.

(3) There is a thinker who is immediately conscious of all and only those tactile and kinesthetic sensations that are felt in some part of Percy, but no thinker who is immediately conscious of all and only those tactile and kinesthetic sensations felt in some part of Finn. Any thinker who is immediately conscious of sensations felt in Finn is immediately conscious, in a natural, normal, and ordinary way, of sensations felt in something, a finger, that lies *outside* Finn.

(4) There is a thinker who has direct voluntary control over all parts of Percy over which any thinker has direct voluntary control, and over nothing that *isn't* part of Percy. But any thinker who has direct voluntary control over parts of Finn has direct voluntary control, in a natural, normal, and ordinary way, over something, a finger, that is *not* part of Finn.

With regard to differences (3) and (4), note that the following is plausibly viewed as a conceptual truth: the "body" of a conscious being contains at least part of any physical object, x, such that (a) the conscious being feels sensations in x, in a natural, normal, and ordinary way, and (b) the conscious being has, in a natural, normal, and ordinary way, direct voluntary control over x. (The qualification 'at least part of' might be needed to deal with such objects, if such there are, as the one consisting of Percy's left index-finger and the dirt caking it.) Plausibly, Finn fails to be a thinker in virtue of failing to extend as far as the sensations and direct voluntary control that would be attributable to Finn if Finn were a thinker. Even more plausibly, Finn fails to be a thinker at least *partly* in virtue of that failure.

(5) There is a thinker whose self-regarding concern is limited to parts of Percy, but

no thinker whose self-regarding concern is limited to parts of Finn. Any thinker who has concern of the distinctively self-regarding kind for Percy's right index-finger has it also for his left. When such concern is natural, normal, and in no way extraordinary, it is plausible (to say the least) that its object is part of its subject. And it is plausible that Finn fails to be a thinker at least partly because Finn does not contain every object of the self-regarding concerns that would be attributable to Finn if Finn were a thinker.

(6) All who think with Percy's brain (be they one or many) show differential concern for Percy over Finn. For example, all would favor the annihilation of Percy's left hand, if they believed that the gain for Percy would even slightly outweigh the loss for Percy, even though annihilation of the hand would result in the outright destruction of Finn. It's plausible that Finn fails to be a thinker at least partly because of the indifference to its own survival that would be attributable to Finn if Finn were a thinker.

Why would annihilation of the hand destroy Finn? If Finn survived, so would the complements of the *other* four fingers of the hand, and also, presumably, the complements of the host of other *parts* of the hand, resulting in a host of coinciding hand-complements. Some theorists accept the coinciding of objects of different *sorts*, such as a diminished organism and the hand-complement (or sum of particles) that has come to "constitute" it. But I know of none who would countenance the coinciding of a host of hand-complements.[5]

I have cited six differences between Percy and Finn. Before discussing their sufficiency, let me note that analogues of the first, second, fifth, and sixth differences serve to distinguish Percy from a certain entity, hitherto unmentioned, to which Percy is all but identical microphysically. That entity – call it *Adam* – is the complement of a certain one of the atoms composing Percy's left index-finger. Although no one has suggested that atom-complements might be thinkers if finger-complements are not, it will be reassuring to have the means of dealing with even the largest of Percy's parts. So I want to note a particularly striking difference between Percy and Adam, one that probably does not hold between Percy and Finn. I'll label it difference (7).

Difference (7), stated in the paragraph following this one, hinges on Adam's mereological rigidity. Why is Adam mereologically rigid? Suppose that Atom, one of the atoms composing atom-complement Adam, is about to be annihilated. And consider Adam-Minus, the *pair-of-atoms*-complement that is composed of all and only the atoms composing Adam except Atom. (Surely there is no one who believes in Adam but not in Adam-Minus.) If Adam survives the annihilation of Atom, the diminished Adam will coin-

---

[5] The argument of this paragraph presupposes an endurantist view of objects. I will not consider the matter from the opposing, perdurantist point of view, on which objects as well as events have temporal parts. I believe, however, that perdurantists are likely to reach the same conclusion, although by a different argument.

cide with the undiminished Adam-Minus. But Adam-Minus will no longer be a *pair-of-atoms*-complement. Adam and Adam-Minus will be coinciding *atom*-complements, which provides ample reason for holding that Adam will *not* survive the annihilation of Atom. It provides ample reason for conceiving of Adam as something merelologically rigid, whether a sum of atoms, a quantity of stuff, or a hunk of stuff.

(7) Percy, a human organism, endures through decades. Adam, a mereologically rigid portion of an organism undergoing rapid mereological change, is either *ephemeral* (if conceived as a hunk) or ephemerally *intact* (if conceived as a sum or quantity). (One online source – www.vsar.org/vocab.html – states that humans shed an average of 650 skin cells per second.) Adam appears and disappears within the blink of an eye – or else exists intact for but a fraction of a second, existing subsequently as a conjunctive object consisting partly of atoms that compose part of an organism and partly of scattered atoms that interact neither with that organism nor with one another. It's certainly plausible that Adam's transitoriness, or transitory intactness, could help to ground a difference between Adam and Percy with regard to thinkerhood.

8. The Sufficiency of the Differences

In virtue of the striking differences cited in section 7 (and quite apart from the points of section 5), Percy has a stronger claim to thinkerhood than does Finn (or any other Percy-part). However, I have not demonstrated that the differences, individually or collectively, defeat Finn's claim to thinkerhood. And it may be said that the claims of Finn and other Percy-parts are strong *enough*, even though weaker than Percy's. Despite the differences, we may be told, Finn is sufficiently similar to the thinker Percy that it's hard to believe that Finn fails to be a thinker.

I have three replies. First, the differences cited are intended, initially, to rebut an *argument* for Finn's thinkerhood. That argument rests on the claim that there are *no significant differences* between Finn and Percy (and none between Finn and Finn*), that is, none that might ground a difference between the two with respect to thinkerhood. One supporter of the premise describes the differences as "paltry" and "piddling" (Merricks 1998, 845). Surely, the six differences we noted between Finn and Percy (and the similar, equally marked differences between Finn and Finn*) provide ample reason for doubting that premise.

Second, the differences between Percy and Finn need not be as great as one might assume, because the difference they are to ground is *less* than one might assume. If Finn fails to be a conscious, thinking being, it does not follow that Finn is *devoid* of consciousness and thought. We can say that consciousness is *present* in Finn, that thoughts occur *within* Finn, that Finn is a *container* of thoughts and consciousness (because Finn is a container of the cerebral *realizations* of thoughts and consciousness),[6] even as we deny that Finn is a *subject* of thoughts and consciousness. That there indeed is such a distinction, one that would be explicated by reference to differences of the sort identified in section 7, may seem clearer when considering such thought-containers as these: (a) Conjunct, the conjunctive object consisting of Percy's brain, liver, and left thumb; (b) Gerrymander, the (nonscattered) object consisting of Percy's brain, the portion of Percy that lies between his brain and his left ear, and the first 17.43 inches of Percy directly *under* that portion; and (c) the universe. (Are Conjunct, Gerrymander, and the universe deliberating about whether to go for a walk? Or is it rather that such deliberations are occurring *within* them?) Of course, not everyone allows that such scattered or gerrymandered objects are possible, never mind actual. But it's as reasonable to hold that counterpossibles differ in truth value as to hold that counterfactuals do. And I think that most disbelievers in such objects as Conjunct, Gerrymander, and the universe will want to affirm that *if* such objects existed, then even though conscious thoughts would be present within them, they would not be *subjects* of those thoughts.[7]

Third, the differences will seem altogether decisive, if we proceed on the plausible assumption that there is just *one* consciousness present within Percy and just one *subject* of that consciousness. The differences will then be relevant to this question: to which *one* of the entities overlapping Percy is that consciousness appropriately assigned? And when there's a competition for a single prize or honor, as in an election, a gymnas-

---

[6] Two points. First, when I say that Finn "contains" thoughts, I'm using 'contains' not in the weak sense in which rooms contain everything located within them, but in the stronger sense in which Finn contains thoughts only if there are thoughts constituted by the activities of *parts* of Finn. Second, it is indeed reasonable to claim that Finn contains thoughts, in this sense. On the dominant theory of thoughts, (token) thoughts are (token) brain events. On this theory, the claim that Finn contains thoughts is straightforwardly true. On one dissenting theory, on which actions are not events, some thoughts, such as deliberatings, are not events of *any* kind. But recall that we are using 'thoughts' in a technical sense, in which such nonactions as sensations and desires count as thoughts. Provided that mental *events* are brain events, it is still straightforwardly true that Finn contains thoughts. On another dissenting theory, one associated with the property-exemplification theory of events, thoughts are coextensive with their subjects. On this theory, Finn contains part, a *large* part, though not the whole, of every thought contained by Percy. And Heddi contains a much smaller part, although (one presumes) a centrally important part, of the Percy-wide event that is the thought. So even on this theory, which I hereafter ignore, Heddi and Finn do not lack psychological properties, even if (as I contend) they are nonthinkers. They still have the property of containing centrally important *parts* of conscious thoughts. (I will ignore altogether the unpopular theory that events are locationless universals.)

[7] Don't (narrow content) psychological states supervene on brain states? Perhaps they do, in this sense: necessarily, two subjects are in identical psychological states if their *brains* are in identical states. But the subjecthood of a brain-containing object isn't determined solely by the states of the contained brain.

tics event, or a horse race, there need be no *dramatic* difference – indeed, no more than a "paltry," "piddling" difference – between the winner and the losers.

On what basis might we say that there is only *one* consciousness, only *one* stream of thought, present within Percy? Note first that we are under no pressure to say otherwise from the empirical facts. The case is not like one of brain bisection, where the partially uncoordinated functioning of the left and right hemispheres results in uncoordinated behavior suggestive of *separate*, partially *independent* streams of thought. In our case, there would be no reason to postulate multiple thought-streams unless there were a prior reason to postulate multiple subjects. And there is no reason to postulate multiple subjects, as opposed to multiple containers, since there are not multiple physical *realizations* of thought streams.

It's plausible, to say the least, that for every thought-constituting brain event there is one thought token, not many, that it constitutes. And it's plausible, to say the least, that for every thought token there is one thinker, not many, whose thought token it is. No doubt we could call these plausible propositions into question, if we *had* to. But since we can distinguish between thinkers of thoughts and containers of thoughts, we *don't* have to. And if we do proceed on the assumption that there is just one thinker overlapping Percy, then the differences cited in section 7 provide abundant justification for assigning that status to Percy rather than to Finn, or to any other of Percy's parts. More generally, they enable us to understand why thinkerhood, and therefore personhood, are maximal.[8]

9. Conclusion

There is an argument that presses us to acknowledge the personhood, or at least the thinkerhood, of brain-containing person-parts. With the notable exception of Carter (see section 3e), who evidently is ready to allow not just the *multiplication* of persons, but their mereological petrification, philosophers have generally sought either to resist the pressure or else to mitigate the consequences of yielding to it. But as we saw in section 3, the measures by which they have sought to do so are radical, problematic, or ineffec-

---

[8] Analogues of some of the differences will be useful to those who believe that one or more objects *coincide* with Percy. As noted earlier, some theorists hold that human persons are *constituted* by, not identical with, human organisms. And some hold that a human organism is itself constituted by an object: a sum of particles (or a quantity or hunk of stuff). I oppose the first of those views in Burke 1997b and the second in Burke 1997a. But proponents of the second view can counter the sum's claim to thinkerhood by appealing to analogues of the first, second, sixth, and seventh differences. Proponents of the first view can appeal to analogues of the sixth and second. When viewed in light of the considerations adduced in section 8, those differences should suffice.

tive. Happily, there is a conservative alternative that is both effective and defensible. We can maintain the maximality of personhood, thinkerhood, and consciousness. Moreover, we can do so without relativizing or graduating numerical identity; without denying that the thinkerhood of purely physical thinkers supervenes on their purely physical properties (intrinsic and relational); without denying the existence of heads and other brain-containing person-parts; and without denying the existence of the fingers, hands, and feet whose existence is denied, for the sake of "consistency," by those who deny the existence of finger-, hand-, and foot-*complements*.[9]

As we saw in section 5, we do not ordinarily view person-parts either as persons or as thinkers; moreover, we have no practical *reason* to regard them as such. In section 7, I examined the main philosophical reason for thinking that some person-parts nevertheless *are* thinkers, and found it uncompelling. I noted six differences between Percy and Finn, differences that can plausibly be held to ground a difference between the two with regard to thinkerhood. Those differences are largely in the *intrinsic* properties of Percy and Finn. Contrary to what many assume (I had long assumed it myself), the maximality of thinkerhood does not stand or fall with the proposition that purely relational differences can ground a difference with regard to thinkerhood.[10]

In section 8, I defended the sufficiency of the differences cited in section 7. I did not prove that because of those differences, Finn is a nonthinker. But the differences refute the main argument in *favor* of Finn's thinkerhood. Furthermore, when viewed in light of the considerations adduced in section 8, and taken together with the points of section 5, they argue strongly *against* Finn's thinkerhood. Consciousness and conscious thoughts are indeed *present* in Finn. So Finn is by no means *devoid* of consciousness and thought. But that is not to say that Finn is a *subject* of them. We can say instead that Finn and

---

[9] I don't myself see an inconsistency in asserting the existence of natural sorts of body parts, such as fingers, hands, brains, and heads, while denying the existence, or rather the objecthood, of arbitrary portions of bodies. I doubt that there is any such *object* as Finn or Adam, although I don't doubt the objecthood of Heddi.

[10] Theodore Sider (forthcoming) is perhaps the only theorist now willing to attribute the nonconsciousness of person-parts solely to their possession of a disqualifying relational property. He writes of one such part, "Although Martha-minus isn't literally conscious, she has what it takes intrinsically to be conscious. ... All that disqualifies her is a seeming 'technicality': the failure of the maximality condition ... ." He then introduces the concept of "consciousness*," which he defines as "consciousness stripped of any maximality requirement," and allows that Martha and many or all of her brain-containing parts are conscious*, although only Martha is conscious. On my view, by contrast, only Martha is either conscious *or* conscious*. Sider's defense of maximality, although nicely crafted, is unsatisfying both because its denial of the consciousness of person-parts does rest on a seeming technicality and because it concedes that brain-containing person-parts are conscious*.

Heddi, as well as Conjunct, Gerrymander, and the universe, are mere *containers* of conscious thought.[11]

Since there is no suggestion that such entities might be persons *without* being thinkers, we can deny their personhood as well as their thinkerhood. And we can do so without denying their *existence*. We can blithely acknowledge heads, brains, cerebra, and central nervous systems, as well as fingers, toes, noses, and the many other person-parts with brain-containing complements. In short, we have established the tenability of the *conservative* view of person-parts, the view implicit in ordinary ways of thinking.[12]

References

Abbott, Geoffrey. (1994)*The Book of Execution* (London: Headline Book Publishing).
Armstrong, D. M. (1978) *Universals and Scientific Realism*, Vol. 2 (Cambridge: Cambridge University Press).
Baker, Lynne Rudder. (2000) *Persons and Bodies: A Constitution View* (Cambridge: Cambridge University Press).
Burke, Michael B. (1994a) "Dion and Theon: An Essentialist Solution to an Ancient Puzzle," *The Journal of Philosophy* 91: 129-39.
Burke, Michael B. (1994b) "Preserving the Principle of One Object to a Place: A Novel Account of the Relations Among Objects, Sorts, Sortals, and Persistence Conditions," *Philosophy and Phenomenological Research* 54: 591-624.
Burke, Michael B. (1996) "Tibbles the Cat: A Modern *Sophisma*," *Philosophical Studies* 84: 63-74.
Burke, Michael B. (1997a) "Coinciding Objects: Reply to Lowe and Denkel," *Analysis* 57: 11-18.
Burke, Michael B. (1997b) "Persons and Bodies: How to Avoid the New Dualism," *American Philosophical Quarterly* 34: 457-67.
Carter, W. R. (1983) "In Defense of Undetached Parts," *Pacific Philosophical Quarterly* 64: 126-43.
Carter, W. R. (1997) "Dion's Left Foot (and the Price of Burkean Economy)," *Philosophy and Phenomenological Research* 57: 371-79.
Geach, Peter. (1980) *Reference and Generality* (Ithaca and London: Cornell University Place).

---

[11] And we can deny that it would be far worse to cause anguish to Percy than to a bodiless (but morally and psychologically comparable) angel.
[12] For valuable comments and suggestions, I am grateful to John Tilley.

Heller, Mark. (1990) *The Ontology of Physical Objects: Four Dimensional Hunks of Matter* (Cambridge: Cambridge University Press).

Lewis, David. (1993) "Many, but Almost One," in *Ontology, Causality and Mind: Essays in Honor of D. M. Armstrong*, ed. J. Bacon *et. al.* (Cambridge: Cambridge University Press), 22-38.

Merricks, Trenton. (1998a) "Against the Doctrine of Microphysical Supervenience," *Mind* 107: 59-71.

Merricks, Trenton. (1998b) "On Whether Being Conscious is Intrinsic," *Mind* 107: 845-46.

Merricks, Trenton. (2001) *Objects and Persons* (Oxford: Clarendon Press).

Olson, Eric T. (1995) "Why I Have No Hands," *Theoria* 61, Part 2: 182-97.

Olson, Eric T. (1997) "Dion's Foot," *The Journal of Philosophy* 94: 260-65.

Quine, Willard Van Orman. (1981) "Worlds Away," reprinted (from *The Journal of Philosophy* 73, 1976) in *Theories and Things* (Cambridge: Harvard University Press).

Sider, Theodore. (Forthcoming) "Maximality and Microphysical Supervenience," *Philosophy and Phenomenological Research*.

Slack, M. W., Holland, P. W. H., & Graham, C. F. (1993) "The Zootype and the Phylotypic Stage," *Nature* 361: 490, 492.

Unger, Peter. (1979) "Why There Are No People," *Midwest Studies in Philosophy* 4: 177-222.

Unger, Peter. (1980) "The Problem of the Many," *Midwest Studies in Philosophy* 5: 411-67.

Van Inwagen, Peter. (1981) "The Doctrine of Arbitrary Undetached Parts," *Pacific Philosophical Quarterly* 62: 123-37. Van Inwagen, Peter. (1990) *Material Beings* (Ithaca and London: Cornell University Press).

Klaus Petrus
Human Persons
Some Conceptual Remarks

In this paper, I shall not primarily deal with the question what human beings or persons are. As regards the former, others, biologists for instance, are much more competent. As far as the latter concers, there are by now a great number of philosophical theories about the ontological, psychological, or moral status of persons. What I am interested in is the *concept* we have of a human being and of a person, or, more precisely: what matters to me is *our* concept of a *human person*.

To be sure, it is not easy to specify what is meant by *our* concept, or indeed by a *concept*. I shall have to say nothing about this here (see Petrus 2002, p. 29ff.). I rather take it as a fact that human persons are individuals, and as such they are part of our daily experiences. We meet them in bars, we dance with them, we wonder how they feel or guess their desires. These and countless similar experiences are mirrored in the concept of a human person and because they are *our* experiences this concept is *our* concept and thus *our* subject. Of course, if we engage in conceptual analysis, it may turn out that our concept of a human person is confused or obscure, that it is incompatible with some other, related concept, or that it is connected with another concept in an unexpected way. But even then it still remains our very own concept – at least as long as we do not misuse familiar or similar sounding concepts to change the subject imperceptibly. I know that this is not always the case. But more on this later.

Mere Human Beings and Mere Persons

To begin with, it is a striking fact that our concepts of human beings and of persons differ considerably. On the one hand, the concept of a person is *broader* than that of a human being. When a person dies, they remain a person. When a human being dies, they turn into a corpse. This difference is notable. While corpses decompose, dead persons do not – at worst, they fall into oblivion, at best, they live on in people's memories. Furthermore, the concept of a person is allowing more and more for the possibility that someone is a person who is not a human being, but, for example, a higher primate possessing mental properties, or one specific property (something like a "first-person-perspective"; cf. Baker 2003). On the other hand, the concept of a person is *narrower* than that of a human being. Someone may lose their capacity of perceiving, feeling or thinking, and so be lacking those properties that would define them as a person. Yet he isn't one. Such a being is indeed a human being, but this human being is not a person.

The fact that the two concepts diverge enables us to regard someone as a *mere* human being. Thus it is the job of the biologist to study Gioacchino (or you and me) as a complex cell structure, and the job of a neuroscientist to examine him from the perspective of his brain functions. Of course, it is arguable how specific such *perspectives* can be and still reveal something about Gioacchino as a human being. What, for instance, is contributed in this regard by someone who analyses neurophysiological processes at the molecular level, or someone who delves even deeper down to the subatomic level? However, these questions should not really distract us, for they mainly concern problems of hierarchy between the so-called special sciences. More important is this: whenever we're dealing with human beings, we can consider them from the perspective of their being-a-mere-human-being – a biological organism, or even just a brain. This perspective, though not customary in everyday life, is habitually adopted in the natural sciences, and there is no problem with that.

What I have said about the concept of a human being equally holds for the concept of a person. Here, again, nothing prevents us from regarding somebody as a *mere* person. The humanities do so when they consider individuals as creators of cultural artifacts, or the phenomenologists and psychologists when they focus on mental phenomena. However, not every analysis of mental phenomena leads to statements about persons. It is surely true that the concept of a person includes the idea of having mental properties (in a broad sense): a person is, inter alia, able to perceive, feel, think, judge, consider, speculate, decide, to know something of themselves and perhaps also to know something of themselves as themselves. And it is certainly an essential characteristic of these properties that they are properties of persons. As far as this goes, it may be okay to say of Gioacchino that, viewed as a mere person, he is a mind. For a mind is something that displays mental properties.

Yet this (more or less Cartesian) sense of "mind" is not always on the agenda. Those for instance who are interested in the totality (or a conglomeration or cluster or the like) of mental properties are not concerned with the mind a person *is*, but rather with the mind a person *has*. The difference between "is a mind" and "has a mind" is conceptually crucial (see also Kemmerling 2001, p. 53). While, taken as a mere person, I am identical to the mind in the first sense (i.e., identical to the x that possesses those-and-those mental properties), I am *not* identical to the mind in the second sense (i.e., to the x that is the totality or a conglomeration of mental properties). The mind I am perceives, feels, thinks, etc. while the mind I have does not. The mind I have is the totality of what I perceive, feel, think, etc., and such a totality is nothing that is itself able to perceive, feel, or think. To put the nub in other words: while some analysis of mental phenomena lead to statements about the mind which I am as a mere *person*, others concern the *personality* that I am as a human being. The difference between "person" and "personality" will play its part later. For the moment, what we should take on board is this: whoever is a person can be regarded from the perspective of being-a-mere-person. This is done in the human and social sciences and now and then in daily life, and everything is right with that, too.

Human Persons

On the one hand, our concepts of human beings and of persons differ clearly. For instance, the biological organism that Gioacchino, as a mere human being, is is not the same as the mind that he, as a mere person, is.[1] On the other hand, these concepts are, in a certain way, closely interlinked. (I say "in a certain way" because, as you shall see, I'm not really dealing here with two concepts, but only with a single one.) Let's suppose once again that someone loses her ability to perceive, feel, or think. In such a case one typically speaks of an injured, irreparably impaired, degenerate human being – perhaps even of a "vegetable" – and thereby indicates that she lacks much of what constitutes the *person* that this human being essentially is. By "essentially" I mean "by nature". For human beings are naturally related to the property of being a person. Certainly, there are cases where human beings who are not persons are conceived as mere human beings – as biological organisms, for instance. But even then, they are still naturally predisposed for "personness". Hence, a human being who is not yet a person is already a rudimentary person, just as somebody who is a mere human being and no longer a person is a fragmentary person (see also Kemmerling 2000a, p. 235).[2] This kind of link between being a human being and being a person is not a matter of hazard – it's strictly and permanently the case, even after death: a dead human being is a corpse, not a carcass.

Note that by all this I am not saying that we have to add the concept of a person to that of a human being in order to justly say of Gioacchino that he is a *complete* human being. For a complete human being is not: a mere human being + a mere person. Neither do I want to suggest that it's somehow bizarre to imagine a human being that is not a person. At least, there is nothing contradictory about this. The fact that we can imagine a mindless human being just goes to show that it is *not* part of the concept of a mere hu-

---

[1] The conceptual difference also becomes manifest in this: when I, as a mere person, refer to my brain, I am not referring to myself. In contrast, it is a case of self-reference if I refer to my mind, since I, as a mere person, am my mind.

[2] Thus, when I speak of mere (or complete) human beings (and, equally, about mere or complete persons), what I mean is a certain 'natural' *perspective* from which human beings are viewed, and not their physical or biological condition. So, even a perfectly fit and healthy human being can be viewed as a mere human being, and someone who has a prosthetic arm can be considered without difficulty from the perspective of a complete human being.

man being to be or to have a mind, or that human beings can be regarded under exclusion of those properties that they exhibit as mere persons.

I'm aiming at something else. What matters to me is the concept that we have of a human being taken as a complete human being. As a complete human being he is naturally related to the property of being a person (or, if you like, he is predisposed for "personness"). If he were not, he wouldn't be what he is – he would be something that is at odds with his nature. There is, then, no sense in viewing a complete human being as somebody who is not a person. For the concept of a complete human being is evidently not a concept of somebody who is regarded under a blinding out of that property that makes him what he is. If someone is conceived under exclusion of the property of being a person, the concept that applies is that of a mere human being. If, on the other hand, he is viewed as a complete human being, then he is seen as someone who is by his nature or essence related to the property of being a person, or, more adequately, to the property of being a *complete* person. For a person is in fact more than a mind: persons do not just perceive, feel, or think, they also speak, promenade, smooch or just wave to each other.

In other words, complete persons have *personal* properties and personal properties are the properties of *complete* persons. By a "personal property", I mean either a mental property, or a property which presupposes that x has mental properties. Thus when one says of x that she is waving to someone, one is attributing mental properties to x, because waving entails reasons (desires, beliefs, intentions) which cause x to move her arm as one generally does when one waves. (If x had no such properties, then what she is doing would more properly have to be characterized as something that is "happening to her"). Keep in mind that personal properties constitute the total set of properties that (complete) persons have. The mental, purely mental properties only form part of it. This is important in that it implies that Gioacchino could not have certain personal properties (namely, the not purely mental ones) if he were only a mind – he obviously possesses these properties by virtue of being a human being. Seen thus, the person Gioacchino is is closely connected to the property of being a human being. However, we should not jump to any conclusions at this point. For we might change our tune and expand the concept of a person to, for instance, non-human animals. In short, then, it may be that Gioacchino could not have certain of his essential properties if he were just a mind. But that, in turn, doesn't mean that Gioacchino must necessarily be a human being to have these properties.

Needless to say that one can speak of just about anything as if it were a person. However, if we take it that in some cases, such talk is not literal (but adopted, for example, for heuristic purposes), while it is indeed literal in other cases, it's after all noteworthy that the boundary between literal and figurative speech is located in an area where we are still concerned with man-like beings. I admit that this just a hint that our strong tendency to attribute mental properties to human beings is anchored in a concept of a person that is closely linked to the concept of a human being.[3] But there is an underlying reason why this tendency is not just simple and convenient, but indeed reflects what is, at least for us, the *most natural* point of view. This reason is connected with language in the widest sense, more precisely, with the fact that language is (at least for the time being) the most efficient tool at our disposal for articulating our concepts and for making it explicit to you and me what concepts are presently at issue. Mind you, it's wholly irrelevant here whether we justly speak of certain creatures as persons. The crucial point is this: when *we* speak of ourselves as persons, we always do so as *complete* persons. For *speaking* is a personal property, and indeed one of those properties which presuppose that their bearer has mental properties (since *speaking* in the relevant sense involves reasons). But not merely this. If the one who speaks were related solely or entirely to the property of being a (mere) person, it would be the mind that speaks. Yet minds do not speak. Speaking also involves all sorts of properties that render us capable of speaking, and which just belong to the human being that the person in question is.[4]

Again, I am not suggesting that it is contradictory to imagine a person that is not a human being. The fact that one is able to fantasize this way shows that it is *not* an integral part of the concept of a person to be, for example, a biological organism (for a person could have a bionic body), or that persons can be viewed under a blinding out of those properties that they may have as human beings. This notwithstanding, it would be, at least for us, rather perverse to view ourselves as persons who are *not* human beings. If we lacked the property of being human beings, we wouldn't be what we are – we would be something contra our nature. To see in ourselves someone who is not a human being would be to view ourselves under exclusion of just the property that makes us what we are: complete persons. In other words, to do so would only be appropriate under a

---

[3] Or perhaps, after all, just to our concept of mere "humanness", that is, to the human brain, which is to say to the neocortex, or is it perhaps rather the size of our brain in comparison with that of other animals that is decisive, or its size in proportion to body height, or is it perhaps rather ... ...? As is well-known, one does not get very far on this route. The question by what right one may attribute mental properties to what creatures is no doubt one of the most delicate and difficult problems of all. From a philosophical point of view, it leads to issues of justifying various types of explanations of behaviour. Good ideas on the topic are provided by Bennett 1991a; 1991b.

[4] I do not wish to imply here that only someone who has a complex vocal language (such as ours) can be a person. (In any case, I am, believe me, not in the slightest bit interested in any claptrap about our extraordinary or godlike position in the animal kingdom.) Quite the reverse, I think there are really good reasons to treat at least some kinds of (non-human) animals as persons, and that these reasons have nothing at all to do with language and the like.

change of subject, that is, under a shift from the concept of a complete person to that of a mere person.

The concept we have of ourselves is then essentially the concept of a complete human being or a complete person. In less clumsy terms: it's the concept of a *human person*. That sounds flimsy, but it bears important consequences (as I hope to show in the following sections). At any rate, my point is not just that human beings are paradigmatic examples of persons or that persons are typically embodied in human beings. If this were what I want to say, I would be concerned exclusively with the concepts of a mere human being and a mere person, or with some language-games in which these concepts merge to a greater or lesser extent. My interest lies in the concept of a human person, which differs clearly & distinctly from both the concept of a mere human being and the concept of a mere person. For the mind that a (mere) person is is not to be identified with the human person she is, as the brain a (mere) human being is is not to be equated with the human person this human being is (more on this in the next section). Note, above all, that the concept of a human person is *not* constituted by the concept of mere human being and the concept of a mere person – it is not an amalgam or mix of two (or more) concepts. It is, on the contrary, a *single, unified* concept, a concept according to which human beings are naturally and inextricably connected to their being persons, & vice versa. Hence, it would be wrong to split it into two components: a biological one concerning (mere) human beings, and a psychological one concerning (mere) persons (cf. also Strawson 1959, ch. 3, Kemmerling 2000a, p. 236). Since the concept of a human person is a unified one, there is nothing into which it could be divided. Where we are concerned with ourselves, we are concerned with "whole unified things": the person you are is the complete human being you are, just as the human being you are is the complete person you are.

Wrong Questions

If I'm right, then there is no point in asking what makes us what we are (namely, human persons). If someone – a philosopher, for instance – answered in all seriousness: "Brain is what I'm made of!", or even: "I am my brain!" (or temporal parts of a brain, or whatever), and if he moreover thought that he was saying something illuminating about ourselves, he would be pretending that the concept of a human person can be divided into the two components just mentioned. Only on this condition could he sensibly claim that a human being, seen as a brain, constitutes or even is the person this human being is. But he would not then be talking about human persons, but about mere human beings or mere persons. If taken to be speaking about *us*, he would not be making any sense at all. For the person somebody is, is the complete human being they are. The brain, however, is not a complete human being. Already for this reason, it can't be only the brain which makes us what we are. If there is anything at all that makes us what we are, it's the complete human being.

Things are similar with regard to the question of what it is that makes us the particular person we are (and not another one). I do not want to deny that it can be of some interest to speculate whether and to what degree one and the same human being can be different persons. But true here as well is this: anyone who muses on this topic is *not* pondering human persons! He deals with the concept of a mere human being or a mere person, and indulges in (rather tricky but also fairly dicey) thought experiments in which these concepts collide. (He may, for instance, be imagining a surgical procedure that puts two minds into his body.) Were he concerned with human persons, he couldn't even start to think that way. For he would then be forced to recognize that neither the concept of a mere human being nor that of a mere person allows one to say of a *human person* that she is one human being but two (or even more) persons, or the same human being, but a completely different person. The reason for this is simply that according to our concept of ourselves, human beings are closely linked to "personness", just as persons to "humanness". With regard to human persons, as long as we're dealing with one and the same human being, we're concerned with one and the same person, & vice versa.[5]

In making these points, I am not rejecting as senseless the question of what can "change" us. Also, I do not want to deny that the brain will play a leading role here. Changes in the brain demonstrably change perception, sensation, feeling and thinking. Thus there may well be a close connection between brain damage and impairment of mental processes. And it may, therefore, be perfectly sensible and accurate to say that Gioacchino has changed, in a certain way. But in which way exactly? What is it that has changed? The answer seems obvious: Gioacchino's brain has changed, and therewith – if we presuppose a law-like correlation between the neural and the mental – has changed a possibly considerable part of his mentality, which is determined by the totality of his mental properties. In a word: what has changed is Gioacchino's *personality*.[6]

---

[5] As far as I can discern, most of those who pore, for instance, over personal identity are not even interested in mere human beings or mere persons – at least not primarily. While, eventually, talking about us and the likes of us, they do not care about our concept of ourselves. This, it seems to me, is not without danger, given the tendency of such discussions to confuse concepts (i.e., the concepts of *human person*, of *mere person*, and of *personality*).

[6] Of course, this is a rather abstract concept of (one's) personality. There are hundreds of factors which can determine a personality and which have little to do with one's brain. So, even if it is true that the brain plays a significant role in the determination of personality, that certainly doesn't mean that one's brain (and nothing over and above it) *makes* or even *is* one's personality.

Notice however, that someone's personality is not their mind. Nor is their personality the personality of a mind. Someone's personality is the personality of a human person! Thus, if you claim that Gioacchino has changed and thereby mean that the human person that is Gioacchino has undergone changes in personality, then you're making perfect sense. For the concept of personality explicitly leaves room for the possibility that a human person – one and the same human person – displays different personalities, at different times. (You might even go a step further and say: there is something wrong with somebody who never undergoes any change in personality throughout their life.) In contrast, it is senseless to say that Gioacchino has changed if what is meant thereby is that the human person itself has changed. This would be to say that the complete human being or the complete person has changed, whereas what has changed – i.e., the totality or part of his mentality –, is not something that Gioacchino, seen as a complete human being or as a complete person, is.[7] The same goes for the claim that Gioacchino, this time regarded as a mere person, has changed. For the mind which Gioacchino is is not the complete person he is. If the purporter of this claim nonetheless insists that he is speaking of human persons, he is already conceptually wrong. Since he is then presupposing that the concept of a human person is a conglomerate of the concepts of a mere human being and a mere person. But exactly that's not, for it is a unified concept.

The risk of asking wrong questions is imminent not only in the domain of human persons, but also, *pars pro toto*, in the area of the human mind. Here, again, the point is not that we can't at all talk sensibly about ourselves as mere persons (some do so professionally). The problem starts only when one speaks about the human mind and, while doing so, forgets that the human mind is essentially the mind of a human person, that is: the mind of a complete human being or a complete person. In other words: the difficulty crops up if one pretends to be speaking about the human mind when one is de facto talking about the mind a mere person is, or about a mere human being, seen as a brain.

Thus, in some circles goes the word that the question of what the human mind is can be answered by finding out how the brain manages to think, for instance (and there indeed appear to be some who believe that). However, holding such a view once again involves the mistake of more or less tacitly assuming that our concept of human persons can be chopped up into the concepts of a mere human being and a mere person. If, on the other hand, one realizes that this concept is unified, it should be quite obvious why it

---

[7] Damasio 1994, ch. 1 illustrates the point in double respect. On the one hand, his discussion of various forms of personality change, referring to the famous case of Phineas Gage, illuminates quite well the relation between personality and the complete person. On the other hand, however, Damasio goes too far when he claims that Gage, because of his personality disorder, was no longer Gage, meaning thereby (as can be gathered from the context) that Gage was no longer a human person.

makes no sense at all to say that *brains* think. For *thinking* is a personal property, and as such essentially a property of human persons and thus of complete human beings. Accordingly, there are no personal properties in the sub-personal realm. A mere human being, however, belongs here. Therefore, anyone who seriously claims that a mere human being or even a brain is thinking is wrong. Perhaps, however, such claims are put forward with more caution than I've suggested here. For instance, one could try to answer the question as to the nature of the human mind by investigating how the brain achieves those feats which enable us to think. In this way, nothing is attributed to the brain which strictly belongs to the personal domain.

Unfortunately, the idea is mistaken and it's worth saying why. This time the problem results from a category difference between that which is to be explained and that which explains, i.e., between the human mind on the one hand and neurophysiological processes on the other. The difference is categorical for the following reason: to be a human mind is a property of human persons. For neurophysiological processes, this is not so: to be a process of this kind is a property of a brain or of a mere human being, seen as a brain. As a consequence, even the most rigorous description of such processes could not elucidate what the human mind is. (At most, it would tell us something about how the human mind works, for its part.) It may be into account here that it's not just the brain alone that provides those services that underlie mental activity, that the restriction to the brain (indeed, the restriction to cognitive activity) involves a great deal of simplification, and that a serious approach of this kind would have to take many other factors into consideration (for instance, the somatic and vegetative nerve systems, the ENS, or indeed the fact that the human mind is a product of phylo- and ontogenetic development). One may, in short, construe human persons not merely as brains, but adopt a somewhat more comprehensive perspective, when the human mind is at issue. Yet the problem remains. For, as I have argued, it emerges from a category difference – and category differences are not neutralized by trying to gradually assimilate one category to the other. Thus, even on a more comprehensive view, human beings are still considered from the perspective of their being mere human beings. And this means anew that just that property which is an essential feature of the human mind is not – nay, cannot – be taken into consideration. For the human mind is essentially a part of the complete human being and not (only) of a mere human being – no matter what, in detail, is subsumed under the mere human being. Things would of course be different if the question what the human mind is were approached by investigating how the *complete* human being achieves those feats that enable it to think. In that case the category difference between the explanans and the explanandum would disappear. But then there would be nothing left to explain. For anyone who delves into these matters has a concept of a complete human being, and anyone who has such a concept already has a concept of the human mind.

Strange Talk

I think the preceding observations clearly indicate that it's now and then worthwhile to keep an eye on how we speak, and the way we handle concepts. At this point, two general remarks (that will hopefully help to avoid possible misunderstandings).

First. In the above section, my mind was not primarily on category mistakes in the common sense of the word. Perhaps there are good reasons to hold that I am nothing over and above my brain – perhaps there are none. I'm not interested in the question of whether it makes sense to attribute properties of mere persons to mere human beings. What matters to me is a different question, namely whether it makes sense to attribute to a mere human being (or a mere person) properties which only someone who is a *human person* can have. I hope to have shown that this second question must be answered with a resounding "No!" – largely regardless of how one answers the first question, and therefore beyond the widely known *Isms* which are commonly adduced in answering it.[8] Because our concept of a human person does *not* demand an account which mediates between (supposedly) different domains (e.g., a psychological and a biological one), or tries to reduce one domain to the other, or even eliminates one of them. Rather, it calls for a global point of view from where human persons are seen as a whole, with all their properties and without any further differentiation (more on this in a minute).

Accordingly, I wasn't concerned with different language-games or different levels of description. These may come into play when one theorizes about mere human beings or mere persons; and they may raise problems when, for instance, one speaks about the mind in language that is normally used for talk about the brain, or when one tries to assimilate mind-language to brain-language, or even to translate the former into the latter. But in the area of human persons, we're not concerned with two (or more) ways of talking about them, and we could not be, given that the concept of a human person does not contain two (or more) concepts pertaining to different language-games. Where, in talk about human persons, different levels of description collide with each other, this re-

---

[8] By which I do not mean to say that I am indifferent to the first question. There are some *Isms* which strike me, once again for conceptual reasons, as fundamentally misguided. One can, for instance, argue that the so-called intentional states are simply not amenable to analysis in terms of the type/token-distinction. (If I understand him correctly, this is what Kemmerling 1997, p. 245f. has in mind.) If this is right, certain reductionist accounts (the type/ or token-identity theory, for instance) are revealed to be defective from the outset. I myself would want to say that even if such a theory were true, it would still be false if intended to tell us something about *human persons*. Of course this is not absolutely and generally true (therefore the "largely"): should it turn out that eliminativism is correct, the second question doesn't pose itself, since there are then no human persons. Although I do not think that eliminativism can be as easily refuted as is often believed, I am still of the opinion that it is mistaken (a convincing critique is provided by Baker 1987).

sults either from separating what conceptually belongs together, or mixing what in conceptual terms ought to be kept separate.

Second. I don't want to claim in any way that those sciences which deal with ourselves constantly and systematically change the subject, under the cover of familiar or similar sounding concepts. In other words, it's of no interest to me to demonstrate by hook or by crook that most scientists who apparently or explicitly talk about human persons actually speak about something else (about mere human beings or mere persons, for example). Quite the reverse, I assume that most of them content themselves with what they can achieve within their research programmes, and ask questions such as "How does the brain provide for our ability to think (to perceive, to feel, etc.)?" *without* taking their answers to be explanations of what the human mind is. And yet it is a fact that we hear things like that time and again: The human mind is central processor of a robot made of cellular tissue! It's a huge biological information processing unit! It's a great neural machine! It's the sum of the intricate behavior of a multitude of nerve cells!, and a lot – a lot – more along these lines.

Why the abundance of such talk on the part of experts? One answer typically given by philosophers is that scientists generally tend towards conceptual sloppiness. I, for my part, am not so sure. Besides the fact that also numerous philosophers (of mind) speak like this, the cognitive scientists concerned do at times themselves insist on conceptual distinctions. I think the reason lies somewhere else: talking like that simply sounds good! It's all the rage, trendy, cool, provocative, it is as irritating as it is fascinating when, for instance, someone propagates (in a postscript, yet still loudly) that free will is located in the anterior *sulcus cinguli*, and that's the answer! I, therefore, do not believe that too little attention is paid to conceptual issues here, but suspect that concepts are mixed for the sake of razzle-dazzle. This, however, seems unhealthy to me. For the discussion ultimately turns around us. It is all about finding out who we are, what we do and what we're capable of doing. And it is no doubt the case that also and especially those sciences that focus on human brain can contribute to a better understanding of us human persons. But it is difficult, at least for me, to see how *that* should work if crucial concepts are tossed about for pompous effect.

Naturalizing Ourselves

Can we do it better? That is, is there a way of saying something illuminating about ourselves which is in line with the above conceptual ruminations? I think that the answer is "Yes", and I want to show on the remaining pages where this might lead. To wit, I shall limit myself to the topic of "Human persons and their place in nature", or to the question: can human persons be naturalized?

The answer seems obvious: naturalizing ourselves is possible if it can be shown that *personal properties* are of a type of properties which is acceptable from a naturalistic point of view. For this to be the case, in turn, the following conditions a) to d) have to be fulfilled (cf. Kemmerling 2000b, p. 236): a) Personal properties globally supervene on non-personal (i.e., physical, etc.) properties. By this I mean that in (physically) indiscernible worlds, the same entities have the same personal properties. – b) Personal properties are properties of material entities, or at least of things which are, qua bearers of properties that fulfill a) to d), material. In other words, human persons are neither non-material individuals nor bearers of properties which are, from a naturalistic point of view, unacceptable. – c) All phenomena related to human persons can be reduced to personal or to non-personal properties. That is to say, there is nothing pertaining to the personal domain which is both an individual of a 'personal kind' and irreducible. – d) Personal properties are expressible by predicates that have *explanatory* power. That is to say, a science of human persons is possible.

At first sight, it looks as if the old story were just told anew here, perhaps in somewhat modified terms, and that we've once again reverted to mere human beings or mere persons, instead of tackling human persons. I'd like to show that this is not so by trying to explain which sense of "naturalism" is in play here, or what it means for a property to be naturalistically acceptable.

Firstly, this version of naturalism has hardly anything to do with physicalism. Of course, human persons – complete human beings, complete persons – are part of our single singular natural world, indeed with all that they are, that they do, and that they're capable of doing. Yet this is not the same as saying that they are part of the physical world. For what is commonly taken to be the "physical world" is the domain of physics, that is, that aspect of the world that can be accounted for solely with the means provided by (perhaps not present-day, but some future or ideal) physics (cf. Tetens 2000, p. 274, 279f.). Following this variety of physicalism, human persons have to be considered exclusively from a physicalistic point of view, and must be analysed within the conceptual scheme of an ideal physics. Such a way of looking at things is, however, inevitably abstract. It takes us for mere human beings, and thus leaves unaccounted for a great many of the properties which make us what we are. So, when I say that human persons are part of the single singular natural world, I mean this in a really big way: Human persons are part of our *Erfahrungswelt*, i.e., they are part of that world which presents itself to our experience in manifold ways (sensorially, aesthetically, morally, etc.), and which is accordingly investigable in manifold ways. I want to leave aside for the moment the question of which science or sciences would play a relevant role under this approach to human persons (I will touch on this point in the last section). But note that also under the viewpoint of the idea that the sciences involved might be ultimately reducible to physics, my version of naturalism has nothing to do with physicalism. For a physicalist Unified Science would be unable (and indeed would not want) to offer anything above a more or less abstract view of human persons.

Secondly, since this version of naturalism is a naturalism without physicalism, it is quite relaxed vis-à-vis the criterion which, as numerous fans of (even a minimal) physicalism hold, decides in all cases, and definitively, what is and what is not: namely, causality. "To be real is to have causal powers!", one often-cited slogan goes. According to it, objects, facts, events or properties exist only insofar as they are causally related to other objects, etc. In parallel to often quixotic ideas about what physics can or should achieve, there is frequently a concept of causality in play here which, to put it mildly, hardly corresponds to anything in natural scientists' practice.[9] Now, I'm not concerned with whether scientists really observe the adequacy standards for explanation which such an understanding of causality would require. I'm aiming at a different point, which strikes one when one delves into research reports of natural scientists, or browses through their textbooks (a nice example of this is provided by Cognitive Ethology; see Allen & Bekoff 1997): descriptions of physiological as well as mental processes enter into one and the same explanation, and it is not unusual that such explanations are based on mere correlations, or supported by contrafactual conditionals solely, and yet, they are naturally placed next to causal explanations in a stricter sense. Where certain philosophers imagine an explanatory gap, then, scientists simply proceed with their business and prove themselves flexible (or, as I would prefer to say, pragmatic): depending on their needs, they prefer one sort of explanation to the other, or, in certain situations, where one kind of explanation is unavailable, they simply content themselves with the other.

In other words, numerous scientists take for granted what many philosophers fail to accept: that it is wrong to apply standards of adequacy which are, trivially, only appropriate for a certain type of explanation (namely, for causal explanations in the strict sense) to every kind of explanation, by reference to a specific concept of causality (cf. Baker 1995, ch. 4). It is important to see that this point is not merely in accordance with the scientists' practice, but also has a philosophical facet. For it's altogether mysterious why, quite irrespective of considerations of (successful) explanatory practice, a physicalistic concept of causality should be given metaphysical priority over all other accounts (see, in a different context, Baker 1993 and Burge 1993). And even if one realizes that this concept is in its turn grounded in a certain ideology (one may call it a "physicalistic metaphysical Weltanschauung"), the question still remains: by what right should it be superior

---

[9] As should be obvious, I am here addressing the philosopher. It may be that my remarks are too rough and sweeping (which is surely true of my statements about physicalism). Nevertheless, it is a fact that these kinds of view are purported time and again implicitly or explicitly, and that they harbor serious philosophical problems (cf. Lowe 1996, ch. 3).

to others? This, then, is what matters to me: the version of naturalism I have outlined is not just a naturalism without physicalism, it's also a naturalism without causality – at least in the sense that in it causation surely doesn't have priority over explanation.

Philosophical Anthropology

These remarks are, as all my thoughts here, quite general and programmatic, but they will do for my purposes (for more details, see Petrus 2000, p. 140ff.). There is one point, however, that I think I should make explicit. For my taste, naturalism is not a position. It is at best a project, and a project is something which can succeed or fail. Thus, when I listed conditions a) to d) above, what I had in mind was that if one can show that they are fulfilled, then the project of naturalizing human persons has been successful. For it has then been shown that human persons are naturalistically acceptable entities: they are, although not physical entities, material things possessing properties which, although not physical properties, have explanatory power. Or, put more moderately: I consider it possible that a) to d) are fulfilled, and so I am optimistic that the project of naturalizing human persons will succeed.

Who should contribute to this project? Everyone possible, of course. For this is all about us, human persons. In academic terms, what is needed is a science beyond the common and established categories (i.e., faculties, disciplines, etc.), a science of the unity of man, or in a word: a *philosophical anthropology*. Thus, a philosophical anthropologist would be anyone interested in what human persons are, in what they do and what they're capable of doing – regardless of whether she is a biologist, a psychologist, a linguist, and so on.[10] Note that it is of secondary importance whether philosophical anthropology is conceived as a science of its own right or just as a central agency that coordinates the efforts of various disciplines. What is much more important is that from the philosophical anthropologist's standpoint, human persons are considered as a part of our *Erfahrungswelt* – under inclusion of everything, they are, do, and can do. Thus, even if investigation into the *Erfahrungswelt* remains shared among the specialized sciences (and this is a realistic assumption), from the perspective of a philosophical anthropologist, human persons are always seen as a unified whole and not just as mere human beings or mere persons. To make sure that this is heeded is, by the way, not the philosopher's task: he is neither head nor supervisor of philosophical anthropology. I mention this for a well-known reason: where naturalism is in play, philosophy is in danger.

---

[10] Cognitive science is exemplary here. Why, then, do we need a *philosophical anthropology*, and cannot simply content ourselves with cognitive science? Because, at least to date, cognitive science lacks a specific philosophical component (more on this at the end of my paper).

Well, philosophy is a conceptual activity. Its task is to identify and grapple with conceptual problems. That's what philosophy has to do and that's why philosophers are called upon more frequently than others to tackle conceptual issues. Not that they were specially ordained to do so – it's simply their job. However, this is also just what appears to shut them out of the naturalists' circle, since, as thinkers, philosophers draw on sources of insight which even the moderate naturalist seeks to avoid. In the latter's eyes, philosophical theories (i.e., rational reconstructions, in the main) can at best contribute to foundational issues – of course on condition that they are in line with the empirical facts. At any rate, from this point of view, philosophers have no say *within* the naturalist project. They stay outside, sometimes they are admitted entrance, but most of the time they keep among themselves (and muse about metaphilosophical stuff). This is just my opinion too: philosophy is, all along the line, a conceptual activity. And I also think that philosophy, while not standing under the dictate of empirical edification, should be in harmony with empirical research. However, I do not think that *this* decides the question whether philosophers can take part in naturalism. The crucial question is another one, namely whether they can contribute to conceptual issues which concern the heart of the matter – that is, in our case, the issue of what human persons, as a part of our all-encompassing *Erfahrungswelt*, are, what they do, and what they can do.

With this, I come to my final point: at least within the kind of naturalism I sketched out above, philosophy has a firm place. By this I do not mean that it is the sole task of philosophers to do what I have done, or rather begun to do, in this paper: to identify and analyze in more or less nitpicking fashion conceptual differences between, for instance, "mere person", "personality", and "human person". Of course, this is an important task. Because these differences are *real* differences, conceptual analysis of this kind may be of some use to the empirical sciences.[11] Yet this belongs under the heading of "basics". When I say that philosophy has a firm place *within* naturalism, what I mean is that phil-

---

[11] There are differences which are only logical differences, and others which are also of metaphysical import (cf. also Kemmerling 2000a, p. 229; 2001). Here is an example of the first: i) Gioacchino, and ii) the property of being Gioacchino. There is a logical difference here because one can ascribe ii) to someone, whereas not i). The difference, however, is metaphysically void, since whenever ii) is exemplified, i) is exemplified too. In traditional terms, we would speak here of a *distinctio rationalis*. – An example of a metaphysically relevant difference is the following: iii) being a human person, and iv) being such-and-such a personality. What we have here is a *distinctio realis*: iii) is a basic metaphysical property; if Gioacchino loses this property, he stops being, or starts being a specimen of a different kind. In contrast, iv) is a psychological property, the presence or absence of which in Gioacchino is not in itself critical for his belonging to one or another kind. – I hope to have shown that the conceptual differences I've elaborated are real differences: they are metaphysical ones, and as such they concern the ontological status of human persons. A proposal which, as far as I can tell, is compatible with my analysis, is Lynne Baker's constitution view (cf. Baker 2000).

osophers can contribute to answering a question that poses itself within the project of naturalizing human persons. The question is, roughly, this: why is the conceptual framework by which we categorize certain elements of our *Erfahrungswelt* as human persons, or in terms of which we try to explain, by reference to personal properties, what these elements are, what they do and what they can do – why is this conceptual framework as natural to us as it is?

This question turns on conceptual issues; it therefore falls into the philosopher's sphere of authority. And it is about issues of naturalness, which forces the philosopher to mingle with naturalists; for the question forms part of the project of naturalizing human persons. If philosophers failed to attend to it, the project would be incomplete and the science of man would not be a science of the unity of man – it would be an anthropology without philosophy.[12]

References

Allen, C. & M. Bekoff 1997, *Species of Mind*, Cambridge, Mass.
Baker, L. R. 1987, *Saving Belief*, Princeton
– 1993, Metaphysics and Mental Causation, in *Mental Causation*, ed. J. Heil & A. Mele, Oxford, 75-95
– 1995, *Explaining Attitudes*, Cambrigde
– 2000, *Persons and Bodies*, Cambridge
– 2003, The Difference that Self-Consciousness Makes, in *On Human Persons*, ed. K. Petrus, Frankfurt a. M., London, 23-39
Bennett, J. 1991a, How to Read Minds in Behaviour: A Suggestion from a Philosopher, in *Natural Theories of Mind*, ed. A. Whiten, Oxford, 97-108
– 1991b, Analysis Without Noise, in *Mind and Common Sense*, ed. R. J. Bodgan, Cambridge, 15-36
Burge, T. 1993, Mind-Body Causation and Explanatory Practice, in *Mental Causation*, ed. J. Heil & A, Mele, Oxford, 97-120
Damasio, A. R. 1994, *Descartes' Error*, New York
Kemmerling, A. 1997, Zur sog. Naturalisierung von Intentionalität, in *Sprache und Denken*, ed. A. Burri, Berlin, New York, 237-258
– 2000a, Ich, mein Gehirn und mein Geist: Echte Unterschiede oder falsche Begriffe?, *Das Gehirn und sein Geist*, ed. N. Elsner & G. Lüer, Göttingen, 223-241

[12] I have benefited from discussions with Paul David Borter, Sarah-Jane Conrad, Andreas Flury, Andreas Graeser, Katja Janz, Edi Marbach, Jonas Pfister and Charlotte Walser. Thanks to all of them, as well as to David Lüthi and Trant Luard for trimming my English, and to N. for making me feel good.

– 2000b, Selbstkenntnis als Test für den naturalistischen Repräsentationalismus, in *Naturalismus*, ed. G. Keil & H. Schnädelbach, Frankfurt a. M., 226-249
– 2001, Was ist menschlicher Geist? Neue Wissenschaft und alte Begriffe, in *Geist und Welt*, ed. Humboldt-Studienzentrum, Ulm, 37-65
Lowe, E. J. 1996, *Subjects of Experience*, Cambridge
Olson, E. T. 1997, *The Human Animal*, New York
Petrus, K. 2000, Die Autonomie der Emotionen, in *Studia Philosophica* 59, 129-154
– 2002, Philosophische Probleme, in *Internationale Zeitschrift für Philosophie*, 23-40
Strawson, P. F. 1959, *Individuals*, London
Tetens, H. 2000, Der gemässigte Naturalismus in den Wissenschaften, in *Naturalismus*, ed. G. Keil & H. Schnädelbach, Frankfurt a. M., 273-288

Daniel Cohnitz
Personal Identity and the Methodology of Imaginary Cases[1]

> Philosophical puzzle cases are an instance of the simplest and most powerful of our methods of inquiry, the method of differences, applied to the most interesting of human problems. The method can be abused, as can food, drink, and sex. As in those cases, even when abused it has its rewards.
>
> John Perry (Perry 2002, xi)

Introduction

An already well-known philosophical joke runs like this:

> A boy is about to go on his first date, and is nervous what to talk about. He asks his father for advice. The father replies: "My son, there are three subjects that always work. The famous three "F". These are Food, Family, and ... Filosophy."
> The boy picks up his date and they go to a soda fountain. Ice cream sodas in front of them, they stare at each other for a long time, as the boy's nervousness builds. He remembers his father's advice, and chooses the first topic. He asks the girl: "Do you like potato pancakes?" She says "No," and the silence returns.
> After a few more uncomfortable minutes, the boy thinks again of his father's suggestion and turns to the second item on the list. He asks, "Do you have a brother?" Once more, the girl says "No" and there is silence again.
> The boy then plays his last card. He thinks of his father's advice and asks the girl: "If you had a brother, would he like potato pancakes?"[2]

As the joke suggests, counterfactual reasoning and deliberating imaginary cases is one of the major activities in philosophy. Some have even argued that the reference to counterfactual cases and the method of thereby invoking philosophical intuitions is constitutive of this discipline and the key to defend the autonomy and authority of philosophy.[3]

Whether or not philosophy has a certain autonomy and (maybe therefore) a special authority is for most modern philosophers certainly a question of minor importance.[4]

---

[1] I would like to thank Gardar Arnason, Stefan Bagusche, Dieter Birnbacher, Manuel Bremer, Axel Bühler, Ross Cameron, David Chalmers, Tamar Szabó Gendler, Josh Parsons, Klaus Petrus, Agustin Rayo, Marcus Rossberg, Gerhard Schurz, Barry Smith, and Markus Werning for helpful suggestions on earlier versions of this paper. I also profited a lot from conversations with John Perry on the topics of this paper.
[2] Apologies to the numerous audiences which had to listen to this joke during the years I was struggling with this topic. I promise, never to tell the joke again from today onwards.
[3] See Bealer 1998.
[4] See Bühler/Kann 2002.

For *that* reason it might not be overly interesting whether or not the role of this practice within philosophical methodology is central or justified or better to be diminished in the future. But what seems to be true is that in large areas of philosophy the deliberation of imaginary cases and the invocation of intuitions as well as appeals to conceivability do play a role, in fact a role of such weight that it already provoked quite nasty reactions from inside and outside philosophy[5]. Hence the interesting questions are: what exactly is the role they play? Will the reliance on imaginary cases undermine our results if this method is not properly heeded (and what would that consist in)? Do imaginary cases undermine our results in that they by and large mislead us?

One of the areas of philosophy which is probably best-known for its reference to imaginary cases is the metaphysics of personal identity. Locke argued for the distinctness of men and persons with the example of the body swap of prince and cobbler[6], Leibniz argued for the importance of memory for satisfying immortality with the example of the irrational individual wishing to become the prince of China and thereby losing all its recollection of the past[7], Wiggins[8] and Perry[9] asked us to conceive the tragic story of Brown, Jones and Smith, who, due to a lubberly nurse, are involved in the branching of Jones into Brown-Jones and Smith-Jones, and Parfit[10] made us imagine how puzzling a world with continuous fission and fusion can be when there are no answers to the question of identity, but answers to the question of survival. There are numerous more examples like this, some involving strange creatures and characters like a very old Methuselah[11], some the invention of new fascinating technology like teletransportation[12].

No wonder that much of the methodological discussion concerning the function of imaginary scenarios and the reliance on intuitions in philosophical arguments started here and still accompanies many contributions to this area[13]. In this article I will give a

---

[5] See Hintikka 1998 for the thesis that the method of invoking intuitions is amongst the things which will eventually "kill" analytic philosophy.
[6] Locke 1975, 44.
[7] Leibniz 1996, 155-156.
[8] Wiggins 1967.
[9] Perry 2002.
[10] Parfit 1971.
[11] Lewis 1976.
[12] Parfit 1984.
[13] Especially if there is a thought experiment which seems problematic for one's own position, philosophers are likely to overthrow the whole method as unreliable in principle. Cases of this sort seem to be Daniel Dennett (Dennett 1991) and especially Mark Johnston (Johnston 1987). Positive exceptions of this practice are Wiggins 1980, Wilkes 1988 and Snowdon 1991 who argue rather carefully for disregarding certain thought experiments as inconclusive. See Snowdon 1991 for a critique of Johnston's way of dealing with thought experiments.

systematic survey of the state of this methodological discussion, focusing on the personal identity debate.[14]

In part I of this paper I start by looking at criticism that puts the methodology of imaginary cases generally in doubt for all areas of philosophy. In part II I consider arguments that criticize the role of imaginary cases in the personal identity debate especially, leaving the use of thought experiments in general (more or less) intact. In the final part III I conclude this survey by way of giving a brief sketch of a positive account of how we should deal with intuitions and imaginary cases, given what we've learned from the debate. As it will turn out, the result might be one which both the friends of thought experimentation and the friends of naturalism could learn to live with.

I. General Criticism of Thought Experiments in Philosophy

Before we can turn to the general criticism of thought experiments, we should clarify the issue.

(i.) The proper heading of the *methodological* discussion that is concerned with the role of intuitions, appeals to conceivability, imaginary cases etc. is "thought experiments in philosophy".[15] This will also be the subject of this paper. Another intimately connected topic but not quite the same is "modal *epistemology*".[16] Given a certain interpretation of the function of thought experiments in philosophy (hence some stand on the first topic), the question of how we can possibly have knowledge of non-realized possibilities and necessities is highly relevant (which is the second topic), whereas, given certain other interpretations of their role, it simply isn't.

Even if an alternative interpretation is accepted, modal epistemology might be of interest for other reasons: philosophers adopted the possible worlds framework in various areas of philosophy and, anyway, modal talk is an important part of scientific and natural language. Given this, we are facing an ontological/epistemological problem which will persist even if we foreswear imaginary cases. The Benacerraf-type problem we are facing in any case was aptly summarized by John O'Leary Hawthorne:

> Assume that our modal talk and thought is not really committed to the existence of possibilia, possible worlds, ways things might have been. A puzzle naturally arises. How are we now to explain away the apparent reference to such modal entities in our everyday talk about the space of

---

[14] Thus some interesting contributions to the topic "thought experiments in philosophy" will not be covered. These are contributions which I found irrelevant to the debate about personal identity. Dancy 1985 is such a case. For a detailed study of Dancy's criticism see Häggqvist 1996.
[15] This is the topic discussed by Wilkes 1988, Sorensen 1992, and Häggqvist 1996.
[16] This is the topic discussed by Peacocke 1999, Hale 2002, Yablo 1993, and Chalmers 2002, etc.

possibility [...]? Assume instead that our modal talk and thought is genuinely committed to the existence of possibilia. Now an epistemological problem looms large. How do we know that the entities we purport to refer to exist and how do we know what they are like? As we make the epistemological problem tractable we face an apparently intractable semantic problem. As we make the semantic problem tractable, we face an apparently intractable epistemological problem. (O'Leary-Hawthorne 1996, 183)

I personally think that both topics should be solved together, but there is no prima facie reason to assume this. For reasons of space I will focus on the discussion of the topic of thought experiments in philosophy, but highlight the points by which I think both topics are related.

(ii.) Some authors have felt a need to give a definition of what a thought experiment is or what 'thought experiment' in their usage will refer to, whereas others found that such an attempt is not really enlightening. I, too, think that giving such a definition isn't "enlightening", but that it can help a lot to structure the debate. I will focus here on thought experiments insofar as they are intended as counterexamples to a philosophical theory[17]. Saying this, it is clear that there are other intended roles for thought experiments in the sciences. For methodological reasons it is of some importance to direct attention towards them, if only to ignore them from then on:

Sometimes thought experiments are used as didactical or even propagandistic means, in order to illustrate an abstract theoretical consequence, or to maximize the acceptance of someone's own theory or to ridicule the acceptance of somebody else's. Under which conditions thought experiments are able to play that role is interesting from a pedagogical and political point of view. Such an investigation might even help understand certain peculiarities of the history of science, like Kuhn's observation that thought experiments are more frequent, and play their proper role in times of scientific crisis.[18]

From a *methodological* point of view, these cases are less interesting. If we want to include all kinds of thought experiments in our methodological investigation, we would find that they have little in common. Whereas thought experiments which are intended as counterexamples against a theory try to induce a *justified* belief revision[19], other uses aim – at best – at a mere belief revision, justified or not. As "all's fair in love and war", all's fair in didactics and scientific crises. If an imaginary case is helpful to teach physics students some abstract law and its implications, for some psychological (maybe mnemonic) reason, that's O.K. There is prima facie no methodological reason why these

---

[17] I will use 'theory' in a very broad sense which includes real definitions, conceptual analyses, and even entailment claims.
[18] See Kuhn 1964.
[19] See Gähde 2000.

thought experiments should not be question-begging, or not strictly metaphysically impossible, or not deeply flawed in any other respect in which thought experiments aiming at *justified* belief revision might be flawed.

Hence, if we want to understand why so many have criticized the use of thought experiments and have pleaded for their displacement, we will probably not gain much insight by including all the ways in which a thought experiment can be intended, within our working definition of 'thought experiment'.

It follows that, although philosophers[20] were right to draw our attention to these other uses of thought experiments, they were nevertheless wrong to include them in their working definitions, since most of their problems with thought experiments don't properly arise with these other usages of 'thought experiment'. Consider the following analogy: The question of why ripe tomatoes are red certainly makes sense and is interesting to investigate, whereas the question of why some objects are red, will not lead to the same interesting insights (although tomatoes, too, are objects). The latter is analogous to the question of why thought experiments are e.g. informative, when 'thought experiment' is thus defined that they generally aren't and don't have to be.[21]

To summarize: the phenomenon I am mainly interested in can be characterized by Ulrich Gähde's three "substantial properties" of thought experiments:

(G1) It's the aim of every thought experiment to induce justified belief revision in the addressee.

(G2) To achieve this aim, a certain state of affairs is described which is claimed to be conceivable.

(G3) The aim is intended to be achieved without realizing the described state of affairs or assuming that the state of affairs really obtains.[22]

---

[20] For example Brendel 1999.
[21] The question of why thought experiments are informative is one of the questions Elke Brendel discusses in Brendel 1999.
[22] Ulrich Gähde intends this to be a (partial) real definition of 'thought experiment', i.e. (G1)-(G3) are said to be *substantial* properties of *all* thought experiments. Real definitions can be true or false, and this one seems false. According to our linguistic practice there are thought experiments lacking (G1) (and therefore a considerable amount of (G3)). Most physics textbooks are full of thought experiments which do not aim at a justified belief revision, but are intended to illustrate. Still, Gähde could claim that they at least aim at belief revision in a certain sense. But what about the "thought experiments" we nowadays carry out on computers, like computer simulated quests for numerical solutions of differential equations, as was done e.g. for the problem of supersonic jets? (Norman et al. 1982) What about computer simulations in modern evolutionary game theory? What about classical game theory? The mere fact that we do the calculations and deductions on a computer and not anymore literally in thought is, by the way, wholly irrelevant here, for my point is that these exercises don't aim at belief re-

(iii.) Many philosophers start their discussion of thought experiments in philosophy from (a) the "surface grammar" of the expression 'thought experiment' and (b) the fact that there is a similar phenomenon in the natural sciences that goes by the same name. (b) might well be true in so far as the three "substantial properties" given above will often be properties of phenomena we can find in the methodology of physics. However, whereas for large parts of philosophy it can be said that they *proceed essentially* by the method of imaginary cases, the same cannot be said for the sciences. Thought experiments are much more crucial in philosophy than in physics. It is prima facie unlikely that they have the same systematic place within the respective methodologies (which might nevertheless turn out to be the case later in the investigation of the two phenomena[23]). Thought experiments in science will hence be dealt with rather stepmotherly in this paper. The guidance of the "surface grammar" of the expression 'thought experiments', i.e. that thought *experiments* have something important in common with *experiments*, will be followed though.

(iv.) Some authors have argued that there is a special epistemological dilemma with thought experiments for the reason that thought experiments make *counterfactual* assumptions. Now – so the "dilemma" goes – since the assumptions are counterfactual, and since they figure as premises in an argument, the argument itself is, though "trivially valid", not sound, for it has false premises.[24] To avoid this bulk of confusions, we will consider thought experiments to be – at least – embedded in modal arguments, which, by the explication of modal logic, satisfy our intuitive notions of validity and soundness of an argument. This will allow us to speak of counter*actual* premises as well as different sorts of possibility and necessity. Therefore, modal arguments will be sound, although one or more of the premises might be counter*actual*, as long as the argument is valid and the premises are true.

After these clarifications, we can now turn to the different forms of general criticism the method of imaginary cases has had to face.

---

vision in any non-trivial sense, although they intuitively are thought experiments in the sense relevant for a real definition.
[23] See Gähde 2000 for the thesis that thought experiments in philosophy and the natural sciences share their substantial properties, and Kühne 2001 for the thesis that their position within the respective methodologies is nevertheless downright different.
[24] See Mayer 1999 for a statement of this "dilemma", and Laymon 1991.

I.1. Thought experiments are to be abandoned in philosophy because there is no positive theory available to support them

Thought experiments are fun. They are entertaining and interesting, because the narratives accompanying them are often finished and from a literary point of view appealing. Although this may heighten the interest for modern philosophy[25], there is a large number of novices to philosophy for whom the method of thought experimentation is puzzling:

> As a newcomer to philosophy, one is soon treated, both in class and textbooks, to a steady diet of strange, exotic, or downright bizarre examples. The average undergraduate student's reaction to these examples is, I think it fair to say, one of bewilderment. Why should Olga's relatives take such pleasure in making soap of her? That's *unrealistic*! How could somebody acquire my memories, wishes, thoughts by stepping into a machine? Surely that's *not possible*! How could it be that a group of people gather to decide on the principles of society without even knowing their own age, sex, physical or psychological characteristics? What is the *point* of these exercises? (Häggqvist 1996, 11)

As Sören Häggqvists notes, some of those skeptic undergrads leave philosophy, whereas others gradually come to see the point. Nevertheless, there are philosophers who conserve their juvenile skepticism: Why should considering imaginary cases teach me anything about the problem at hand? I was interested in *x*, and not in *x* as it might turn out to be in philosophers' dreamland.

This is the criticism most commonly brought against the method of imaginary cases: there doesn't seem to be a clear justification for using this method (as Descartes might have had in his theory of innate ideas), therefore we should discontinue it, until someone comes up with such a justification. Given that the situation even seems to be deteriorating for the skeptic[26], a "scandalous" state of the profession is diagnosed.

To maintain a skeptical attitude towards scientific and especially philosophical methods is certainly good practice. Nevertheless, some forms of methodological skepticism seem too gung-ho. To simmer down, let's remind ourselves of David Hume's induction-skepticism and thus have a look at what (at least according to C. D. Broad[27]) is another major scandal of philosophy.

---

[25] See for example David Lodges beautiful novel *Thinks...* for the way it portrays the attractive impact thought experiments from the philosophy of mind have (at least on a certain female writer-in-residence at Gloucester University). Lodge 2001.

[26] Hintikka 1998, 257: "If I open at random a paper published in these days in an English-language philosophy journal, more likely than not I will find appeals to intuitions in support of the writer's views. Sometimes the entire task of a philosophical paper or book is said to be the regimentation of our intuitions about the subject matter in question."

[27] Broad 1952, 152.

What Hume found out was that all the obvious ways to justify our most central methodology, viz. that we learn from observed cases, are doomed to fail. Neither is there any obvious a priori principle by which induction might be justified, since it seems epistemically possible that the world could simply change its behavior. Nor does there seem to be any obvious a posteriori reason by which induction might be justified, for it would simply be question-begging to argue from experience to support arguing from experience. Now, what did Hume make out of this? Was his suggestion that since inductive inferences are not (yet) backed up by a justification that "this is enough to make them highly suspect"?[28] Did he think that the lack of a justifying theory was a reason better to "abandon" the method of induction?[29] Neither of these seemed to Hume to be reasonable:

> Though we should conclude [...], that, in all reasonings from experience, there is a step taken by the mind which is not supported by any argument or process of the understanding; there is no danger that these reasonings, on which almost all knowledge depends, will ever be affected by such a discovery. (Hume 2000, 41)

One certainly has to take the analogy as well as Hume's liberalism with a grain of salt, but the obvious moral to draw should be this: the mere lack of a sound justification for a method cannot *by itself* be a reason to abandon it; neither can it by itself be a reason to demand from everyone who wants to use it to first provide us with a justification. Philosophy of science and epistemology are important disciplines, but we usually feel neither inclined nor justified to knock on the doors of our colleagues in the science departments and order *them* to stop using method x, since – as it turns out – we have not been able to come up with a waterproof justification for it. To argue that the situation with philosophy is entirely different, is to argue either that (a) philosophers have never really found out anything by that method, or (b) if they ever found out anything by that method this must have been sheer luck, since the method is unreliable. For the sake of the arguments I will assume that (a) is false. A proponent of (a) would have to show that the progress made in philosophy was only achieved by using other methods than imaginary cases. Given that the method is so widely used, and that it is in so many areas almost exclusively used, the prospect for this seems dim. For (b), however, reasons must be provided. If one wants to claim (b), one has to argue why one thinks that the method is *unreliable*. This can be done by pointing to serious flaws (the results of this method are incoherent with other results we gained from a better justified method, or the results we

---

[28] As Jaako Hintikka suggests for the very same reason for the status of intuitions for philosophical arguments. Hintikka 1998.
[29] As Verena Mayer seems to suggest for the very same reason for the use of thought experiments in philosophy. Mayer 1999.

get by this method are (or can be) inconsistent), or by finding internal inconsistencies within the method which make serious flaws highly likely. Both sorts of arguments were put forward in the debate on thought experiments in philosophy. I will try to present them, again, by breaking them down to more specific objections.

I.2. We simply don't know what we would say

The objection is often raised that in answering to imaginary cases "we simply don't know what we would say". There are at least two ways to make sense of this objection: (Q1) that there is no fact of the matter to what we would say; and (Q2) that though there is a fact of the matter, it is inscrutable by the method of imaginary cases.

(Q1) There is no fact of the matter to what we would say

(Q1) seems to be an objection raised, for example, by Willard Van Orman Quine and maybe Ludwig Wittgenstein:

> The method of imaginary cases has its uses in philosophy, but at points [...] I wonder whether the limits of the method is properly heeded. To seek what is "logically required" for sameness of person und unprecedented circumstances is to suggest that words have some logical force beyond what our past needs have invested them with. (Quine 1972, 490)

> "It is as if our concepts involved a scaffolding of facts."
> That would presumably mean: If you imagine certain facts otherwise, decsribe them otherwise, than the way they are, then you can no longer imagine the application of certain concepts, because the rules for their application have no analogue in the new circumstances. [...] (Wittgenstein, 1967, §350)

> What would it be like if I had two bodies, i.e. my body were composed of two separate organisms? [...] Philosophers who believe you can, in a manner of speaking extend experience by thinking, ought to remember that you can transmit speech over the telephone, but not the measles. (Wittgenstein, 1975, §66)

What these brief remarks seem to suggest is that for situations which are contingently or necessarily unprecedented, our rules for describing them properly are indeterminate. As Häggqvist has pointed out, this objection is prima facie not very plausible. At least for mundane actual situations, our past needs were in general sufficient to invest words with the "logical force" to predict determinately what we would say – although these situations might well be novel – and the same holds for mundane *possible* situations. To give an example from Häggqvist: New cats I *will* call 'cat', and an animal which looks just like my friend's cat, but with differently colored fur, I *would* call 'cat'. Why should this change with less mundane or even alien situations?

In Quine's case the idea seems to be that a radical disruption of central parts of our web of belief would lead, given holism, to a disruption of meaning. Some imaginary cases involve such a radical disruption in our web of belief, e.g., when we consider cases incoherent with great parts of our background knowledge. Given certain strong forms of holism a problem might indeed follow. Anyway, I doubt that such forms of holism are plausible in themselves.

If a disruption in a part of our web of beliefs leads to *local* meaning change, it seems plausible that it is still determinate which changes would occur, and that we could reliably predict what we would say, given that enough counterfactual background is supplied[30] (for we might be able to say, e.g., that altering a fact about quantum mechanics in hypothetical scenarios involving teletransportation is not inferentially connected with our concept of personal identity[31]).

If, on the other hand, a change in the web of belief leads to a *global* meaning change spreading *uncontrollably* via absolutely *all* inferential relations, what we would say is indeed likely to be indeterminate. If the latter is the picture the holist wants to draw, she is faced with a slippery slope: if the meaning of a term or the content of a concept is determined by the *whole* inferential role in the system of beliefs, then if two systems differ anywhere with respect to the propositions they endorse, they differ completely with respect to the propositions they endorse. As Fodor[32] and others have pointed out, this would have the unwelcome consequence that *in the actual world* no two people would ever share a belief, that no two people would ever mean the same thing by what they say, that no two time slices *of the same person* would ever mean the same thing by what they say, etc. Therefore, the holism which would make indeterminacy of what we would say plausible or likely is itself implausible and unlikely.

Another, more proximate response is expressed in the following often quoted passage by Derek Parfit: "This [Quine's and Wittgenstein's] criticism might be justified if, when considering such imagined cases, we had no reactions. But these cases arouse in most of us strong beliefs."[33] More often than not, our words at least *seem* to have been invested with enough logical force to determine what we would say. We find that in general (and anyway in almost all cases which have found their way into the literature) our responses converge. This would have to be explained away first, (peer group pressure and mass hallucination are, for all we know, both unlikely candidates for the *expla-*

---

[30] For this argument see Häggqvist 1996, 37.
[31] For a brief discussion of the roles of coherence and holism for thought experiments involving teletransportation, see Bartelborth 1996, 206.
[32] Fodor 1994, 145.
[33] Parfit 1984, 200.

nans).[34] Therefore, it is at least not obvious, why there should be no fact of the matter to what we would say. But let's turn to (Q2):

(Q2) Though there is a fact of the matter to what we would say, it is inscrutable by the method of imaginary cases

One of the advocates of (Q2) is Jerry A. Fodor. His objection is of one of the forms we discussed at the end of (1.). He tries to show that the very conception of the method of imaginary cases proves the method to be dubious. Fodor distinguishes two kinds of cases in which philosophers seek answers to the question of what we would say, one rather unproblematic, the other dubious.

The unproblematic kind is the attempt to describe a language, i.e. to formulate and make explicit the internalized rules speakers acquire when they learn the language. One way of doing this is to observe the speakers' verbal behavior in different situations, pretty much the way Quine's field linguist tries to describe the language she is studying. Another way of doing this is to ask speakers of that language what they would say about certain imagined situations. The data so achieved might be somewhat less reliable than the data achieved by the first method, but this strategy seems generally unproblematic. Mistaken judgments can be revealed when the speakers are confronted with an actual situation and it turns out that the verbal behavior differs from the one speakers said to obtain when confronted with the description of the situation. We can hence test the reliability of the method and it is plausible to assume that the knowledge of the language provides speakers with some basis for claims about what they would say in novel situations. Indeed, this is what we tried to make plausible with the help of the cat example above.

The second way to ask what we would say, the one which Fodor finds problematic, rests on the distinction between logical and empirical characteristics of a word. These notions are defined as follows[35, 36]:

D1 A feature F is logically characteristic of a word w iff "If w is properly used then F is instantiated" is logically true.

D2 A feature F' is empirically characteristic of a word w iff:
1. There is some feature F which is logically characteristic of w; and

---

[34] Although this seems to be what Inwagen 1998 and Fuhrmann 2002 are suggesting.
[35] The exact wording of Fodor's definitions can be found in Fodor 1964.
[36] Häggqvist 1996 rejects Fodor's criticism already on the basis of this distinction. True, if you are a semantical holist, as Häggqvist is, Fodor's argument won't make sense since then there will be no question of what distinguishes empirically characteristic features from logically characteristic ones. There are problems with this reply, as we will see.

2. "If F' is instantiated then F is instantiated" expresses a true empirical generalization or a law of nature (but not a logical truth).

With D1 Fodor formulates the doctrine that some of the features which regularly characterize the occasions upon which a word is properly used are criterial, i.e. their presence is a necessary condition of the proper use of the word (like the presence of somebody who has the feature of being a male sibling is a necessary condition of the proper application of 'brother'). D2, on the other hand, describes the fact that some characteristic features of words are merely symptomatic, they are correlated with the occurrence of logically characteristic features, but not logically so. Now the question is how to distinguish between the logically and the merely empirically characteristic but perfectly reliable features of a given word. Obviously we won't be able to make that distinction by the methods of Quine's field linguist. This is because there are by definition of "empirically characteristic feature" no situations a speaker could come in by any natural way, such that in these situations only the empirically characteristic features are absent, we don't seem to be able to just look and see which features that accompany the occurrences of a word are features which just accidentally accompany these occurrences. Nevertheless, the method employed by philosophers to make that distinction is to ask what we would say if certain actual conditions which reliably accompany the occurrence of a word were absent. If what we claim we would say does not differ from what we say in situations *with* the actual conditions, these conditions are shown to be mere empirically characteristic features of the word in question.

Fodor gives a purported a priori argument against the reliability of that method. The argument proceeds as follows:

(i.) The method cannot in principle be vindicated by independent empirical evidence.
(ii.) (Therefore) we don't have any reason to trust this method.
(iii.) There are a priori reasons to distrust the method.
(iv.) Therefore the method should be abandoned.

Fodor finds (i.) to be obvious because the intuitive claims of speakers cannot be tested against the real world. This is so, Fodor argues, because in the real world situations cannot obtain in which a word is properly used and the reliably correlated characteristics are absent.

Nevertheless, it's easy to think of other tests: First, one could simply wait for a naturalized theory of meaning and check what happens in our brains when we are asked what-we-would-say-questions. If what our naturalized theory of meaning tells us about what the meaning thing is that happens in the brain indeed happens, we have *independently* tested the method of what-we-would-say-questions. Second, it doesn't seem at all necessary for the actual world not to behave according to the laws of nature to test the reliability of the speaker's intuitions by observation. It would be enough if the speaker *thinks* that she is in a situation that misbehaves and then compare whether what she says coincides with what she claimed she would say. Situations like these can be arranged without altering the laws of nature it is sufficient to deceive the speaker about which situation she is in. Third, one could cross-induce from situations observable to situations unobservable. If a speaker's intuitions prove to be generally reliable for situations we can observe we can inductively support the claim that she will be a reliable informant even for situations we cannot observe. Fodor takes the tests to be of poor potential evidence for a vindication of the method of imaginary cases, but doesn't say why he thinks so. Anyway, (i.) – in the way it is stated – is false. If the method of imaginary cases cannot be vindicated empirically then this is, as we have seen, an a posteriori matter. This essentially diminishes the conclusiveness of Fodor's argument.

Nevertheless, if it turns out that we have not yet undertaken such tests and do not yet possess a sufficiently fine-grained naturalized theory of meaning, we still seem to be left with empty hands – which means that (ii.) might still be true. However, as we've said in (1.) this does not yet make an argument against the method. It might be true that we are unable to find a justification for the method, but this is obviously not an a priori matter. Since, as Fodor argued, the intuitions of speakers are so far the only evidence we have to scrutinize the logically characteristic features of words, it would be "irresponsible" to abandon the method unless we have a further reason to distrust it. So the interesting part of this argument is why Fodor thinks the method is *a priori unreliable*.

Fodor wants to argue that it is a priori irresponsible to answer what-we-would-say questions on the basis of our linguistic intuitions, because there is no reason to assume that our linguistic intuitions might help us in predicting what we would say if current beliefs were proven seriously false:

> [T]o ask what we would say should certain of our current beliefs prove false involves asking what new beliefs we would then adopt. But to answer this question we would now have to be able to predict what theories would be devised were our current theories to prove untenable [...] Since there is no general way to determine [on the basis of our linguistic intuitions] how many of our beliefs may need to be altered as the result of such discovery [...] there can be no general way to determine how much of our talking such a discovery may require us to revise. (Fodor 1964, 207f)

In a way this reminds us of the Quine/Wittgenstein-objection we dealt with above already. Nevertheless, we will use this objection for another clarification of what is at issue in imaginary cases. What-we-would-say-questions can be asked in more ways than the ones Fodor distinguishes. Consider the question of what we would say if we all had quasi-memories of the pasts of our parents, phenomenologically indistinguishable from the memories of our own past experiences. One way to ask this question is to ask whether we had the same concept of a self, *if we were the inhabitants of this twin-earth*. Or consider what we would say *if we were the inhabitants of the Parfit-world*, in which fission and fusion are everyday phenomena. Would we have developed a concept like PERSON at all? Would we have the same concept of life? These questions are hard to answer intuitively, since they should rather be answered by a linguistic theory which explains how concepts evolve given the niche the language community is inhabiting. Fodor is right that it is somewhat irresponsible to answer them on the basis of linguistic intuitions alone. Our linguistic intuitions might make us experts for the meaning of *our* words, but not necessarily experts for the meaning of words language communities speak in other possible worlds. When we ask questions like these, we consider possible worlds as worlds whose makeup influences the descriptive sense of our terms.[37] Although this is an interesting and illuminating problem, it is not what we are asking for in philosophy in trying to distinguish logically characteristic features from empirically characteristic features.[38] What we want to elucidate is the meaning[39] of *our* terms and the content of our concepts as they are in the *actual* world. This is why we ask if and to what our concept would apply in counterfactual worlds. We ask whether we would apply 'self' to the "conscious thinking thing, which is sensible to pleasure and pain, as far as that consciousness extends" in a world of regular quasi-memories or whether it is 'the survival of persons' that we witness in a Parfit-world. It is plausible to assume that we can answer that, since the concepts we try to apply are *ours*.[40]

Though Fodor comes near to admitting that[41] he concludes his argument with the skeptical challenge that since we don't possess a theory of meaning-change, which can be confirmed independently from intuition, we could not be sure that we always succeed in considering a possible world as counterfactual in certain respects without thereby affecting the descriptive sense of our terms. It might be, he thinks, that whenever we turn to a possible world in which some of the propositions we believe are false, the meanings of our concepts change in an uncontrollable way.

[37] Whether there are descriptive senses for all our terms, or maybe only for some terms except the natural-kind terms, or whether there are no descriptive senses of our terms at all (or what that would mean for the method of imaginary cases) will be subject of part II.
[38] Wilkes 1988 and Gale 1991 fall prey to the same confusion, as Kanuck 2000 has convincingly argued.
[39] Better: their descriptive senses.
[40] Note that this doesn't involve fixing the reference of our concepts in the actual world. This presumably can't be done just by reliance on our linguistic intuitions alone.
[41] Fodor 1964, 211: "It may still be claimed that the speaker's intuitions suffice to determine when a revision in our ways of talking is tantamount to a change in the meaning of some word. I do not deny this is so, but I deny that it is a claim we entitled without argument."

It is not clear why this should be so. If reliance on our intuitions is the only way to distinguish empirically characteristic features from logically characteristic features, it seems that this distinction is due to our intuitions in the first place. Would we have made a conceptual distinction between empirically and logically characteristic features of words, if these intuitions were a rather unstable phenomenon? It doesn't seem to us that meaning changes occur frequently during these modal exercises, and we can obviously keep the question of what language we would speak on a possible twin-earth apart from the question how we would describe what there is on twin-earth in our language. We are not generally confused about this and therefore it is plausible to assume that we are generally reliable informants about what we would say. Moreover, we are interested in making that distinction and have no other method doing it anyway. How can this make a good case for abandoning the method? Fodor does not provide any a priori argument why we should distrust our intuitions. What he provides is an a posteriori argument, and an implausible one.

I.3. The Analytic/Synthetic Distinction and the Method of Metaphysics

There is a deep sea of problems closely related to what we just have discussed in response to Fodor's objection. We will only dip our toe into it here and take a quick dive in part II again, although most areas of this sea (especially the deepest parts where the seamonsters dwell) will be left unexplored in this paper.

What Fodor presupposes to get his objection off the ground is a distinction between the logically and the empirically characteristic features of words, which is nothing but the distinction between the analytic and the synthetic. Häggqvist tries to rebut Fodor's objection by denying that such a distinction can be made from the outset:

> It may plausibly be argued that the unsolvable problem confronting Fodor is spurious. For one may hold that a word's meaning is rather determined (insofar as it is) by its role in all (true or believed) sentences in which it occurs, and that no principled distinction between "criterial" and merely symptomatic, or empirical, or contingent, truths containing the word is feasible (or desirable). (Häggqvist 1996, 36)

It may be that Fodor's problem cannot arise in the same way if there is no analytic synthetic distinction. But what is it we try to find out with the help of thought experiments then? According to Fodor's suggestion it is the aim of deliberating imaginary cases to get clear about what belongs to the empirically characteristic features of words and what to their logically characteristic features. If there is no such distinction, why should we deliberate imaginary cases at all? We can sketch two answers here, one of which will be reconsidered in part II.

The Essential/Accidental Distinction

One way to answer the question raised above is to admit that we are not after the analytic/synthetic distinction, but after another distinction, the distinction between accidentally characteristic features and essentially characteristic features, not of words or concepts, but of persons, knowledge, consciousness and the like.

If this is what thought experiments are about, we enter the realm of *modal epistemology*. Although mere conceptual possibilities might not exist (if the analytic/synthetic distinction does not exist), many metaphysically impossible things are (or were) epistemically possible. Heat could not have been molecular motion, the morning star could have turned out to be distinct from the evening star, water could not have been H_2O, etc.

How can we manage not to confuse these kinds of possibility while thought experimenting? Why should our intuitions be reliable here? What did inform them? The problems we get by choosing this "solution" are thornier than the ones raised by Fodor. It is much less plausible to expect that our intuitions might inform us about what is metaphysically possible and what is not, than to trust that we have some intuitive insight into what is conceptually possible via our grasp of our language. Since we cannot enter the problems of modal epistemology in this paper, we have to postpone a full discussion. Nevertheless, in part II and III we will again say two or three brief things about it.[42]

Revisionary Metaphysics – Yet Another Ballgame

Metaphysics can be done with different tempers. One can do the bookkeeping of what we believe, or one can attempt to change them. According to Peter Strawson we can distinguish *descriptive* from *revisionary* metaphysics.[43] Descriptive metaphysics is what Strawson does in *Individuals* and what seems to be done if we try to explore the essential/accidental distinction with the help of thought experiments as characterized in the last paragraph. Revisionary metaphysics is what Parfit does. It is not the aim of this philosophical enterprise to *map* the contours of our common sense concepts, but to *shape* them. Again, there is not enough space here to discuss in full detail whether this way of doing philosophy is independent of the analytic/synthetic-distinction. The idea would be this: By finding out *what we would want to say* with the help of thought experiments, we regiment and shape what we mean by a concept and possibly end up with new beliefs about, e.g., persons, life and survival. Doing the thought experiments triggers new beliefs

---

[42] There is now a growing literature on the topic. One might start with Yablo 1993, Jackson 1998, Chalmers 2002, and then read Buekens/Dooremalen 2003 and Block/Stalnaker 1999 as an antidote.

[43] For even more ways in which one can do metaphysics see the introductory part of Cohnitz/Smith 2003.

with which other beliefs cohere better than the beliefs we had before. Häggqvist seems to have something similar in mind:

> [T]here is room to argue that thought experiments of the type Fodor considers may serve a normative function. So reaching a verdict about what we would say may be a matter of argued decision rather than, as it were, brute discovery. (Häggqvist 1996, 36)

That this might be difficult to disentangle from the analytic/synthetic distinction seems likely because of its methodological closeness to Rudolf Carnap's conception of *explication*[44]. What else is it, one could argue, that we (normatively) shape by this method, if not the semantical contours of concepts? But this form of implicit semantic conventionalism is almost identical with the target of *Two Dogmas*.

Another worry might be that it is unclear why it is thought experiments involving, e.g., teletransporters that will help us with reshaping our belief systems in any desirable way. Why should we suppose that? Because we expect teletransporters to be around soon and want to be prepared for this? Is it because teletransportation is something that we want to allow our possible world-counterparts to survive? Why shouldn't our *actual* needs and problems, like strong forms of dementia, multiple personality disorder, comissurotomy patients and their separated streams of consciousness, etc. be of much higher interest when we decide what to shape our concept of a person for?[45,46]

This, again, is another topic we will set aside for some other paper. What we will keep as results for the remainder of this paper are these: Fodor's challenge seems to be met if we endorse an analytic/synthetic distinction. If we give up the distinction, but still keep to the method, we have to have another objective. This can either be the aim to explore the essential/accidental-distinction or the aim to reconfigure our belief system (or, of course, something we haven't thought of yet). The former involves a study of modal epistemology, the latter at least an account of why we think that thought experiments

---

[44] Carnap 1950, see also Hempel 1974.
[45] For these problems posed by the actual world, see Wilkes 1988.
[46] Parfit himself is very quiet on this matter. Famously he defends the method of imaginary cases in the following way (in continuation of the quote given above): "[T]hese cases arouse in most of us strong beliefs. And these are beliefs, not about our words, but about ourselves. [...] Though our beliefs are revealed most clearly when we consider imaginary cases, these beliefs also cover actual cases, and our own lives." (Parfit 1984, 200) So far so good. Nevertheless, Parfit himself seems to hold that the method of imaginary cases itself reveals only what the metaphysical status quo is, rather than helps us to do metaphysical revisions. Thus he continues (ibid.): "In Part Three of this book I will argue that some of these beliefs are false, then suggest how and why this matters." Indeed, in the end he finds himself in agreement with Wittgenstein who wouldn't have trusted thought experiments in the first place (Parfit 1984, 273). This suggests that Parfit would not himself endorse the revisionary strategy offered by Häqqqvist and sketched above.

with strange cases might inform us about what we want. Neither of these options is one that cannot be argued for. We will just not pursue the matter here.

II. The very concept of a person makes it impossible to learn from thought experiments

In part II of this paper I will survey criticism which is less general and directed at the use of imaginary cases in the debate about personal identity. The objections we will discuss do not claim that thought experiments in general are unreliable instruments for the sciences, but that it is this peculiar subject or certain features of it that makes the method inapplicable.

II.1. 'Person' is not a natural-kind term and therefore thought experiments are unreliable

Famously, Kathy Wilkes argues that thought experiments are often successful in physics, but that they are usually unsuccessful in philosophy.[47] The only exception is when it comes to natural-kind terms, like 'water' or 'tiger' in which case imaginary cases can teach us something. But since most terms we explicate in philosophy and certainly the concept PERSON are not of this kind, we cannot apply the method successfully here:

> This helps to explain why thought experiments in physics have generally been effective and substantial [...]; why thought experiments in philosophy that pick on natural-kind terms, such as 'gold' or 'water', seem conclusive [...]; and why other thought experiments in philosophy in general, and those concerning personal identity in particular, are not so [...]. For it is improbable that 'person' is in any legitimate sense a term that can usefully be constructed as a 'natural kind' [...] (Wilkes 1988, 15)

To see why Wilkes deems thought experiments unreliable for terms which do not denote natural kinds, we need to take a brief look at her theory of thought experiments.

As we said already, most thought experiments ask us to conceive of some state of affairs. Then it is shown, that our judgment that such a state of affairs seems possible, is incompatible with the conceptual analysis, theory, or entailment claim at issue. If we agree that zombies, i.e. physical duplicates of us who lack phenomenal consciousness, are possible, then this is incompatible with physicalism, if we agree that persons can survive split-brain surgery and go with their memory, than this is incompatible with animalism, etc. *That* these judgments are incompatible with physicalism and animalism respectively seems to be a matter of logic. Certain forms of physicalism claim that mental states (like

---

[47] For a more detailed critique of Wilkes see Häggqvist 1996, Snowdon 1991, and Cohnitz forthcoming.

being in pain) are identical with physical states (like having one's C-fibres firing). This identity is assumed to hold necessarily, therefore it should be impossible that there is a possible world in which exact physical duplicates of us are in the relevant physical states (having their C-fibres firing) without being in the relevant mental states (feeling pain). Animalism claims that persons are essentially human beings, and that the conditions for identity over time for persons are the conditions for identity over time for human beings. Therefore it is impossible that one person can survive in another human being. The states of affairs which seem to be possible are *logically* incompatible with the modal claims the thought experiments are directed at. But how can we make sure that a state of affairs we found conceivable, and therefore *seems* possible, really *is* possible?

Wilkes idea here seems to be this: if we want to check whether a state of affairs under a certain description is possible, the best we can do is to check whether the description given is consistent with relevant background beliefs we hold. What is relevant seems to depend on our theoretical knowledge, i.e. our scientific theories. These theories are always relevant and tell us for a state of affairs of a certain type what else has to be the case in such a state of affairs for it to obtain. If we consider whether it is possible that iron bars can float on water, our theories about iron bars and water as well as our theory about what has to be the case for an object of some kind to float on a liquid of some kind, inform us about whether this is possible or not. Or if, to take another example, we consider whether water could be XYZ, we consider what our theories tell us about water and its molecular structure. Our theoretical knowledge will tell us in those cases, that for x to float on y, x must have a lesser density than y. Since iron has a density between 7.3 and 7.8, and water the density 1, iron bars can't float on water.[48] Respectively, water has the molecular structure H_2O. Therefore it is impossible for water to be XYZ.

For natural-kind terms like 'water' and 'iron' theories are usually available, which tell us what properties the kinds denoted by these terms have. Therefore, what is possible and what isn't is in these cases (a) metaphysically determinate, and (b) (in principle) accessible to us via our best theories.

Now, if we are asked to consider the possibility of states of affairs which are described in other than natural-kind terms, it is not clear whether what is possible is or is not metaphysically determinate, anyway, since we have no scientific theories available about these kinds, we cannot say what else would have to be the case for such a state of affairs to obtain. Therefore we cannot evaluate whether such a state of affairs really *is* possible (although it might *seem* possible).

Thus, if 'person' is (like, according to Wilkes, most terms which play prominent roles in philosophy) not a natural-kind term, thought experimenting about persons is futile.

---

[48] This argument is from Seddon 1972, the way it is presented follows Häggqvist 1996.

This is not the place to join the discussion about whether or not 'person' is a natural-kind term. In the next paragraph we will consider Wiggins' famous claim that 'person' is pretty close to a natural-kind term and that *therefore* thought experimenting about persons is futile. To understand how Wiggins could reach this (now somewhat) surprising conclusion, we have first to see what Wilkes got wrong in the argument reconstructed above.[49]

We were interested in thought experiments in so far as they are intended to lead to justified belief revision. Let's say that the belief intended to be revised by our thought experiment is T, a theory we hold about a certain domain, which has modal implications (it says something about what is the case in a certain domain in some or all possible worlds). This is what Häggqvist called the "target thesis". Now we are asked to conceive of a state of affairs (we call it R) which is incompatible with T. This is the thought experiment. According to Wilkes, we check whether this state of affairs is compatible with background information we have. This background information will tell us what other parts of our background knowledge are relevant to evaluate whether or not R is possible. Since the thought experiment is directed at revising T, T will be of relevance for the evaluation of R, and T (since we aim at belief revision) is part of our background knowledge. But if we consult T to evaluate the possibility of R, R will always turn out to be impossible, because R is constructed to be incompatible with T. Therefore T should better not be considered part of our background knowledge, if we want to evaluate R. (i) If T is a substantial theory which is consistent with other explicit theories we hold to be true, it is a trivial task to find some R which is incompatible with T, but compatible with the set of our explicit background beliefs, if T is taken away from this set. In this case, the fact that there is such an R is absolutely uninteresting. (ii) If T is not substantial, but implied by other background beliefs, it is impossible to find such an R. If T *was supposed* to follow from other background beliefs, to find some R is thus interesting. Unfortunately, the T's we are considering according to Wilkes are about natural kinds. They are metaphysical necessities in Kripke's sense which are not supposed to follow a priori from other background beliefs.[50] (iii) If T is inconsistent with other explicit background beliefs[51], it might well be possible to find some R which is compatible with the rest of our explicit background beliefs and incompatible with T, but, of course, we are unable to tell the differ-

---

[49] I think what Wilkes got wrong is the dialectic in which thought experiments take place. If Wilkes is right, then successful thought experiments in the sciences and philosophy are not only acceptable, but are in fact splashy instruments of research: they provide short-cut a priori insights into substantive a posteriori scientific knowledge. This would be rather difficult to explain, thus thought experiments better should work differently. Luckily, they do.
[50] At least not according to the orthodox picture. The unorthodox picture will be discussed in II.2.i.
[51] This is what Bunzl 1996 seems to have in mind as the proper role for thought experimentation.

ence between this case and (i) on this basis alone. Thus finding some R which can be shown to be consistent with all of our explicit background beliefs, but which is incompatible with T, does not itself show that the union of the set of our background beliefs and the set whose sole member is T is inconsistent. This *can* be done by deriving a contradiction from the union set of our explicit background beliefs, but this is nothing we would need a special method of thought experimentation for.[52]

What Häggqvist, Sorensen, Fodor and others have suggested is that thought experiments are not intended to play our explicit background beliefs off against themselves (as they are according to Wilkes), but rather to play them off against our *implicit* beliefs. In this case T is supposed to make explicit what we implicitly believe to be true. Thus finding some R we believe to be possible but which is in fact incompatible with T, proves T to be inadequate. But if T is supposed to follow from implicit background beliefs, we miss the point of thought experimentation if we ask for an explicit justification of R's possibility in Wilkes' sense. T is exactly what could serve as the basis of such an explicit justification, but the adequacy of T is what is at issue.[53]

If we take thought experiments to be primarily applicable to natural-kind terms, this seems misleading. That water is H_2O, or that heat is molecular motion is not a consequence of our a priori beliefs. If we accept natural-kind talk, these (purported) truths about water and heat are a posteriori. To reflect from the armchair what water and heat could be seems prima facie unreliable.[54] Let T be the claim that water is identical with H_2O. If I am ignorant of T [55], I can conceive water to be XYZ. Thus it seems possible to me (in this hypothetical epistemic situation) that water has some other molecular structure than H_2O. If water is H_2O, then it is necessarily so. But we just found water to be possibly XYZ. Therefore, we can conclude our thought experiment about natural kinds: water is not H_2O. It is at least not obvious why our implicit beliefs should be good informants about the metaphysical make-up of our world, as soon as we have accepted natural-kind talk in the sense of Saul Kripke and Hilary Putnam.

Hence, if we consider what seems prima facie plausible, our a priori intuitions (shaped by our grasp of our language) might be reliable for what is *not* denoted by a natural-kind term, rather than what *is* denoted by one. It seems even more plausible in this case

---

[52] Thus, such thought experiments rather illustrate the problem. As a means to *prove* the inconsistency they are redundant.
[53] If we possess an alternative explicit justification for R's possibility, then we are speaking of an alternative to T. But using this alternative justification is nothing but to beg the question against the proponent of T.
[54] We will come back to this later.
[55] We argued above that assuming T to be true for the purpose of the thought experiment would not lead anywhere either.

to assume that what we can conceive on the basis of our a priori beliefs is of relevance for the determination of meaning, contra Wilkes.

II.2. 'Person' is a natural-kind term (or pretty much like one) and therefore thought experiments are unreliable

We should be careful about what we have shown so far. We argued that if 'person' is not a natural-kind term, this does not ruin our chances to scrutinize by the method of imaginary cases what persons are, at least given the arguments we have considered; whereas if it is a natural-kind term, it seems dubious whether we can scrutinize by this method what persons are. In this paragraph we will concentrate on the latter and revisit the former option in the next paragraph.

In *Sameness and Substance*, David Wiggins makes us contemplate whether the thought experiment in which "a stream of consciousness divides at some point and flows into a delta of two consciousnesses that are separate thereafter" really uncovers a conceptual possibility. If this were conceptually possible, Wiggins' neo-Lockean analysis of personal identity over time in terms of a continuous stream of consciousness would be doomed to fail, since the person stages existing after the occurrence of the delta would both have to be identified with the person stage previous to the delta, and therefore, by transitivity of identity, identical with each other. But since they are clearly distinct, the analysans relation is not transitive and symmetrical, although the identity relation over time is.

Wiggins argument is that if 'person' were a natural-kind term[56], the situation described would not be a conceptual possibility, for

> any would-be determination of a natural-kind stands or falls with the existence of lawlike principles that will collect together the actual extension of the kind around an arbitrary good specimen of it; and [...] these lawlike principles will also determine the characteristic development and typical history of members of this extension. [...] If that is supposed, then the first thing we can expect is that the sense of the sortal predicate 'person' will exempt us from counting as genuinely conceivable any narrative in which persons undergo changes that violate the lawlike regularities constituting the actual nomological foundation for the delimitation of the kind we denominate as that of persons. (Wiggins 1980, 169-170)

---

[56] Wiggins eventually argues that 'person' is not in fact a natural-kind term, but that PERSON is a concept whose "defining marks are to be given in terms of a natural kind determinable, say ANIMAL, plus what may be called a functional component." Thus every person *belongs* to some natural kind. For these natural kinds the possibility of a delta in the stream of consciousness could still be essentially excluded as a result of the empirical investigations on the level of biology, neurophysiology, psychology and the like. See Wiggins 1980, 171-172. See Beck 1992 for a convincing critique of this move.

One feels immediately inclined to object that this argument rests on a confusion of conceptual and metaphysical necessity. Thus one might claim that the concept of a person we possess does indeed allow that persons undergo changes that violate lawlike regularities, whereas it might be that for the referents of our concepts this is nevertheless *metaphysically* excluded. But this metaphysical impossibility does not imply a conceptual impossibility. The set of metaphysical possibilities might be a proper subset of the set of conceptual possibilities. Anyway, as long as we are interested in *persons* and the conditions of *their* identity over time, rather than merely in our *concept* of a person and in our *concept* of their identity over time, Wiggins objection is prima facie plausible. What is possible for *persons* to survive, if 'person' denotes a natural kind, seems to be nothing we could determine a priori on the basis of our linguistic intuitions alone. This is a problem that we met in section II.3 already. We will briefly survey some of the possible stands one might take on this issue and consider what consequences follow for the method of imaginary cases: (i) neo-descriptivism, (ii) Putnam-Kripke orthodoxy, (iii) moderate descriptivism.

(i.) Neo-Descriptivism

David Chalmers and Frank Jackson have argued that serious metaphysics is concerned with what has been called the "location problem", viz. the problem how a true story about the world told in one vocabulary can be made true by one told in some allegedly more fundamental vocabulary. Hence the metaphysical problem of, e.g., physicalism is the problem of how the psychological account of our world can be made true by a physical account of our world. That one account "makes true" some other account is supposed to depend on entailment of one account by the other. One account is then "reductively explainable" by the other account via a priori deductions. The prime method to do metaphysics is to do conceptual analysis, "the very business of addressing when and whether a story told in one vocabulary is made true by one told in some allegedly more fundamental vocabulary"[57].

Conceptual analysis reveals what our ordinary conception of, say, *J*s and *K*s is and thus helps to answer the question whether *K*s are nothing over and above *J*s, whether an account of our world in terms of *J*s entails an account of our world in terms of *K*s, and so on. Unless we start from our ordinary conception of *J*s and *K*s in addressing the location problem, metaphysics becomes a pointless enterprise. If, for example, we simply stipulate what we mean – never mind what others mean – by *J*s and *K*s, and "solve" metaphysical puzzles on that basis, we turn "interesting philosophical debates into easy exer-

---

[57] Jackson 1998, 28.

cises in deductions from stipulative definitions together with accepted facts"[58]. The way conceptual analysis is done is by triggering our intuitions about possible cases:

> Intuitions about how various cases, including various merely possible cases, are correctly described in terms of free action, determinism, and belief are precisely what reveal our ordinary conceptions of free action, determinism and belief, or, as it is often put nowadays, our folk theory of them. (Jackson 1998, 31)

This position obviously leaves the method of imaginary cases in full standing, even for addressing the *metaphysical* questions of what the things are which are denoted by natural-kinds terms. But how do they bridge the gap between the conceptual and the metaphysical revealed by Kripke and Putnam?

First of all neo-descriptivists affirm the Kripke-Putnam doctrine about referential properties of natural-kind terms. 'Water' rigidly designates H_2O, due to way the reference of 'water' is fixed in the actual world. But they also affirm a substantial part of classical descriptivism, viz. that natural-kind terms indeed have (something like) descriptive senses[59], that these senses are what competent users of a language grasp, and that therefore descriptive senses yield substantial a priori truth.[60] We know a priori that 'water' refers to whatever plays the role of the watery stuff in our world, independent of what *actually* plays this role. If we consider other possible worlds *as actual*, e.g., a world in which XYZ would play the watery stuff role (is a pure liquid that quenches thirst, falls from the sky as rain, can be used to extinguish fire, is transparent, etc. but has the molecular structure XYZ) 'water' would refer to XYZ. We also know a priori that whatever 'water' refers to in a world considered as actual is what 'water' refers to in all possible worlds *considered as counterfactual*. Thus, if 'water' refers to XYZ, then water is necessarily identical with XYZ. In a nutshell: if we consider what a term or sentence refers to in a world considered as counterfactual, holding fixed the reference of that term in the actual world, we ask for the term's or sentence's *secondary intension*. If we ask for the reference of a term or sentence in worlds considered as actual, we ask for the *primary intension* of that term or sentence.

For an illustration, take the example of 'water' and suppose for simplicity that in addition to the actual world @, there are exactly two possible worlds: w_1, a twin earth

---

[58] Jackson, 1998, 31.
[59] These are supposed to be similar to Fregean senses. See Chalmers 2002b on this.
[60] As David Chalmers pointed out to me, this way of putting it is slightly misleading. I should better have put it in terms of epistemic possibilities or epistemic intensions, rather than descriptive senses. See Chalmers 2002b for more on this. The slightly misleading part is, that "descriptive senses" are usually understood to be the same for different speakers of a language. This does not have to be the case with epistemic intensions in Chalmers' sense.

where Putnam's potable fluid XYZ is found in the lakes and oceans, etc.; w_2, a world where the fluid in the lakes and oceans is a mixture of 95% H_2O and 5% XYZ. If we turn to the intension of sentences, of 'Water is H_2O.' in particular, what are the possible-worlds truth-conditions of the proposition expressed by this sentence?

According to neo-descriptivism the secondary intension and the primary intension are obtained by, respectively interpreting the sentence in accordance with the secondary and primary intensions of its terms. Thus 'Water is H_2O' is supposed to have the same secondary intension as 'H_2O is H_2O' and the same primary intension as 'The watery stuff is H_2O'. If we keep the reference of every other term fixed and consider the primary intension of this sentence depending on the primary intension of 'water', we can display the intensions of 'Water is H_2O' in the following matrix:

'Water is H_2O'

Counterfactual → Actual ↓	@	w_1	w_2
@	True	True	True
w_1	False	False	False
w_2	True	True	True

The primary intension of 'Water is H_2O' is represented in this matrix by the diagonal from top left to bottom right, evaluating the sentence in the very world in which the reference of 'water' is fixed.[61] The secondary intension of 'Water is H_2O', on the other hand, is represented just from left to right. We say that this sentence has a *necessary* secondary intension (it is true in all possible worlds considered as counterfactual if the reference is fixed in @), but a *contingent* primary intension (there are possible worlds in the primary intension in which it is false).

These two different perspectives on possible worlds are represented in what has been called "two-dimensional semantics" or "two-dimensionalism".[62] At the heart of two-

---

[61] The worlds in which the reference of the terms is fixed, are the worlds considered as actual, whereas the worlds in which we *evaluate* the sentence are "considered as counterfactual". Note that there are cases such that the world in which the reference of the terms is fixed coincides with the world in which the sentence is evaluated.

[62] See Cohnitz 2003 on two-dimensionalism.

dimensionalism lies the thesis that this a priori access we have via the descriptive senses of natural-kind terms, is helpful for solving the location problem. If the core thesis of two-dimensionalism is true, i.e.

(2D) For any sentence S, S is a priori iff S has a necessary primary intension,

and, e.g., the sentences which expresses the metaphysical doctrine of physicalism can be shown to have a necessary primary intension (because of the primary intensions of its component terms), the fact that we nevertheless find a world possible in which physicalism is false, falsifies physicalism[63] *metaphysically* speaking! Thus if neo-descriptivism is true, and natural-kind terms have descriptive senses, and if 'person' turned out to be a natural-kind term, thought experimentation would definitely not turn out futile.

(ii.) The Putnam-Kripke Orthodoxy

The second stand one could take would be a form of Putnam-Kripke orthodoxy and consist in claiming that there are no descriptive senses of natural-kind terms. Thus 'water' refers to H_2O not in virtue of H_2O being the watery stuff in our world, but in virtue of being the stuff we dubbed 'water', period. Now, if 'person' is a natural-kind term, what we have grasped when we acquired the concept PERSON is merely a prototype in Putnam's sense rather than a clear descriptive sense we could reasonably scrutinize by the method of possible cases.

Consider Putnam's joke about a patient who is on the verge of being discharged from an insane asylum. The doctors have been questioning him for some time, and he has been giving perfectly sane responses. They decide to let him leave, and at the end of the interview one of the doctors inquires casually, 'What do you want to be when you get out?' 'A teakettle'.

Putnam suggests that the joke "would not be intelligible if it were literally inconceivable that a person could not be a teakettle"[64]. If this is so, thought experiments may seem to tell us next to nothing, if persons are referred to by concepts which are represented as prototypes. The question of whether persons are referred to by such concepts is independent though of whether all or some or actually none of the natural-kind terms have descriptive senses, and thus independent of whether 'person' is a natural-kind term. For it might be that PERSON is a prototype structured concept, although 'person' does not denote a natural, but rather a social kind (just as Putnam argues that CHAIR, and PENCIL are prototype structured); or it might be that although 'person' denotes a natural kind, PERSON is by chance a not prototype-structured concept. Therefore we will

---

[63] For a complete presentation of the idea see Chalmers 2002a.
[64] Putnam 1975, 244.

consider whether *persons are referred to by concepts which are represented as prototypes* as an extra problem in section 3.

(iii.) Moderate Descriptivism

Defenders of moderate descriptivism would claim, just like neo-descriptivists and the orthodox, that the Kripke-Putnam doctrine concerning the referential properties of natural-kind terms is basically correct. But they would deny that metaphysical entailment-relations between, say the physical and the mental, should only be assumed to hold, if semantical entailment relations between the mental vocabulary and the physical vocabulary can be shown to hold as well. Thus it might be that there are metaphysical relations in our world, which are not (yet) mirrored in conceptual relations. Thomas Nagel seems to hold such view about materialism:

> [...] I believe that there is a necessary connection in both directions between the physical and the mental, but that it cannot be discovered a priori [...] I continue to believe that no purely functionalist characterization of a system entails – simply in virtue of our mental concepts – that the system is conscious. (Nagel 1998, 1)

Thus far this position agrees with the Putnam-Kripke orthodoxy. What moderate descriptivists would deny, though, is that considering imaginary cases is futile if they cannot (or sometimes cannot) inform us about the holding of metaphysical relations. The method of imaginary cases will (to a certain extent) reveal what our conception of persons or of consciousness is. They will reveal what matters to us when we ask questions like 'What is consciousness?', 'What are persons?', 'When are persons identical over time?', etc. Thereby they will help us to see what the kind of answer is we are wishing for and help us to understand why, e.g., an answer to the question what consciousness is in terms of a functionalist characterization of our neural system seems (yet) to some so absolutely unsatisfying. This is a valuable and important role imaginary cases play, because this is an important task of conceptual analysis. Even if this a priori inquiry (alone) will not help us answering the metaphysical question directly, it will help us answering the question indirectly, by helping us to understand better what it is we are looking for. And this *is* important (contra Putnam[65], Kornblith[66] and others), because it is of importance for *us*.

Imagine that we find out, incidentally, that art-essentialism as defended by Harold Osborne and Monroe C. Beardsley is correct after all in assuming that there is one property all artworks have in common. Say, it was a certain radiation, emanated by all artworks, even by theater plays and dances. Exceptions are (as we find out after investiga-

---

[65] Putnam 1975.
[66] Kornblith 2002.

tion) forms of conceptual art (where we cannot find the radiation anywhere, although most of us thought it was art), the music of Richard Wagner (where we cannot find the radiation, but which a significant number of us found always a little suspicious) and paper umbrellas (where we clearly find radiation, although most of us haven't regarded them as art yet). Moreover we find no causal connection which would explain any of the things we have always thought to be important features of art. It doesn't explain why we worship art or put it in museums or thought that aesthetic properties are of any importance, for we find that the radiation has no causal impact on us and our experience. Things like that are imaginable (this can be conceded to Putnam), but it seems equally clear that this could in no way refute or make futile the results of conceptually analyzing ART!

The remaining question is whether at least this much can be achieved by the method of imaginary cases, or whether it proves eventually futile because of the purported fact that the concept PERSON is represented as a prototype. To this problem we will now turn.

II.3. Because 'person' denotes a concept which is represented as a prototype, imaginary cases cannot inform us about what matters to us in actual cases

Parallel to the distinction between prototype structured concepts and concepts which are organized around a set of necessary and sufficient conditions, we can, following Tamar Gendler[67], distinguish two different strategies which might be employed when confronted with what she calls "exceptional cases". Exceptional cases are imaginary cases we can make sense of, but in which our evaluation does not conform to what we thought would be the necessary and sufficient application conditions of our concepts. These two strategies are the *exception-as-scalpel strategy* and the *exception-as-cantilever strategy*.

The exception-as-scalpel strategy is what we described as the standard method of thought experimentation in philosophy. We have a tentative conceptual analysis T of some concept C, which singles out some of the properties which accompany proper applications of C as necessary and sufficient conditions of C-hood.[68] Say, T is of the following form:

(*T*) $\forall x (Cx \leftrightarrow (P_1x \wedge P_2x \wedge P_3x \wedge P_4x))$

What T claims, is that entities which fall under C always have the characteristics or prop-

---

[67] Gendler 1998, Gendler 2000.
[68] For brevity I will describe this example in a rather "material mode". It would be better to keep the application conditions of a concept and the necessary conditions for having the property, which is the content of the concept, clearly distinct. I hope this does not lead to any confusion.

erties P_1-P_4. Suppose that we can make sense of an imaginary case, in which an entity e has P_1-P_3, lacks P_4, but nevertheless falls under C. We are then entitled to revise T in so far as P_4 can no longer be claimed to be a necessary condition for C-hood.[69] In Gendler's words:

> The exception-as-scalpel strategy uses exceptional cases as a way of progressively narrowing the range of characteristics required for the application of a concept by allowing us to isolate the essential features for concept-application from those which are merely ordinarily correlative. (Gendler 1998, 607)

But this is only one way to accommodate our judgment about the imaginary case. It presupposes that C is organized around a set of necessary and sufficient conditions. If we drop this assumption, there is a second strategy to react:

> [T]he exception-as-cantilever strategy views the category membership of exceptional cases as essentially reliant on the ordinary instances against which they can be seen as exceptions. (Gendler 1998, 607)

Now, if we apply this strategy to the case considered, what we would say about e is that it falls under C only because it is relevantly similar to more typical instances of C-hood, the instances described by T.[70] Thus, if C is prototype-structured, each of the P_1-P_4 could be absent in any single actual or imaginary case (although presumably not all of them), without making C inapplicable in this case, *and* without being less central for the proper application of C, as long as P_1-P_4 constitute the prototype which is central for the determination of the similarity relations for entities which fall under C.

What seems to follow from this is, that if we are convinced that the concept we study is actually prototype-structured, the consequences we should draw from finding an exceptional case differ radically from cases in which we are convinced that the concept under scrutiny is organized around some necessary and sufficient conditions. We are not anymore entitled to revise our tentative conceptual analysis, for the exceptional case might be really just that, *exceptional*.

But what is it that could convince us to regard PERSON as a prototype structured concept, rather than a concept which is organized around some necessary and sufficient

---

[69] On the other hand, we might be able to make sense of imaginary cases in which entities do have properties P_1-P_4, but do not fall under C. (An example are Gettier-cases in which C is our concept of knowledge and the characteristics are justified, true belief). In such cases we will revise T by finding new, relevant properties, we might *add* to the original list (like some causal constraint in the case of knowledge).

[70] Probably T would really be of a different form then. Let S denote some binary similarity relation, our new T^* could be

(T^*) $\forall x (Cx \leftrightarrow y((P_1y \land P_2y \land P_3y \land P_4y) \to Sxy))$.

conditions? Gendler's argument for this relies on Bernard Williams' well-known thought experiment from *The Self and the Future*:

Williams makes us consider the following case. Two persons, person A and person B, are told by Dr. Evil at t_0 that they will undergo some operation at t_1 which will result in a switch of psychological continuity. After the operation at t_2, the A-body will have the memories, interests and character traits, the B body had until t_1, and vice versa. They are also told, that one of them will be tortured after t_2, whereas the other will be given a large sum of money.

Now, if asked at t_0 to decide whether the A-body person or the B-body person should be tortured, what should A say? Intuitively we would advise A to say that the A-body person should be tortured at t_2, thereby evaluating the case in accordance with some psychological continuity criterion.

But consider the following case: one person A is told by Dr. Evil at t_0, that there will be an operation at t_1 such that A will lose consciousness during the operation, but will wake up at t_2 with a totally new set of memories and character traits and interests. Moreover, after t_2 she will be tortured. What should A's proper reaction to this case be? As Williams and Gendler suggest, the proper reaction would be pure horror. Not only is the prospect of having one's psychology busted not very pleasant, the outlook of being tortured in addition is certainly terrifying independently of what psychological state one might be in at that moment.

As it seems, we have rather clear intuitions about what A should think of both cases. It also seems that what A should think of the one case is rather different from what she should think of the other. In the first case she should not be concerned about what happens to the A-body at t_2, whereas in the second case she is absolutely right to be horrified about what she learns will happen to the A-body. Now Gendler and others have taken this to prove that one and the same imaginary situation, merely described in two different ways, can lead to two wholly different intuitive evaluations. How does this relate to the question whether or not PERSON is prototype-structured?

Consider the exception-as-scalpel strategy applied to both cases. The first thought experiment would suggest that bodily continuity is not what really matters for personal identity, since, instead of being concerned for her body, A should choose torture for the A-body at t_2. Given our pre-theoretic set of necessary and sufficient conditions for the diachronic identity of persons, bodily continuity should be dropped from the list of necessary conditions.

Considering the second case, according to the exception-as-scalpel strategy we should rather drop psychological continuity as a necessary condition for the diachronic identity of persons, since it seems that although psychological continuity gets busted, A has good reasons to be concerned about what happens to her body at t_2.

Thus applying the exception-as-scalpel strategy in the case of the concept PERSON makes us cut away too much. We end up denying both, psychological as well as bodily continuity its role as a necessary condition for personal identity over time. According to Gendler we reach a more appropriate verdict if we employ the exception-as-cantilever strategy. In this case we would not conclude anything about the lack of necessary and sufficient application conditions. What the stories tell us is that our judgments about personal identity over time are oriented on similarity with ordinary cases, either by focusing on psychology or by focusing on physical continuity. Our judgments depend on how we categorize the cases into similarity classes, which, in turn, depends on the way the cases are presented to us. Thus imaginary cases do not inform us reliably about our judgments of ordinary cases. We might be able to make sense of these cases, but the structure of our concept PERSON does not allow us to single out a clear set of necessary and sufficient conditions of what matters in survival.

There are basically two ways to respond to Gendler's analysis. One way is to reject Gendler's reasons to consider PERSON as a concept which is prototype-structured, the other way is to explain them away.

The easiest response to Gendler's analysis is to criticize Williams' thought experiment as partially question-begging.[71] It is obvious that A's reaction in the second case depends on the presentation of the future events as being events of *her* future. If the situation were interpreted in terms of psychological continuity, one should conclude that at t_2 A is long dead. This is still a pretty good reason for A to be horrified. And what if A hopes that (although Dr. Evil doesn't say so) there is still a chance that A is not dead (Dr. Evil's usage of personal pronouns even seems to imply that), but that some of her stream of consciousness is preserved in the A-body at t_2? It is clear that this would not mean relief, but would mean torture. Thus even interpreting the case according to the psychological continuity criterion gives a reason to be horrified. Williams' description of the case begs the question against the psychological continuity criterion. But if the thought experiment by Williams is question begging, there does not seem to be another reason to assume that PERSON is prototype structured. Moreover it seems that Gendler's only method to ever find out that a concept is prototype-structured is by imaginary cases (since she allows for concepts which are not so structured).

One might not be overly impressed by the argument just given, since one might suspect that it is still more likely that PERSON is indeed prototype-structured and that it is only a matter of time to come up with a modified thought experiment which is not question begging. What should we do then?

---

[71] See Kanuck 2000 for a more detailed version of this argument.

It seems that clashes of intuition might indeed occur. If there is no available strategy to explain them away, but if it seems that their muddledness brings our analysis to a halt, that's the way it is. Our scientific methods can only reveal as much as there is to reveal, they cannot do more, and if the world really does not have more to offer as our concept of a person than a prototype, than that's that. This is nothing we can blame a method for, nor is this anything we should feel inclined to shield a method from.

What sometimes *can* be done is to explain conflicting intuitions away by other strategies than by proving a thought experiment to be question begging. The classification in similarity classes Gendler has in mind, indeed opens an interesting topic not yet fully understood in the methodology of imaginary cases. This might even lead to a substantial positive theory of thought experimentation. We will turn to this in the final section.

III. Conclusion: The Psychology of Context and The Explaining Away of Intuitions

After reviewing different methodological attempts to reject a certain thought experiment in the personal identity debate, and finding all of them wanting, Snowdon chooses the last resort:

> [T]here is no counterintuition that can be generated, and there are no grounds of a general sort for being suspicious of such intuitions, no independent evidence that they do lead us astray. But this is just a case where we find ourselves with what, in the light of all the evidence, has to be recognized as a deviant, although recalcitrant, intuition. This is a case where what is genuinely possible for *us* is to be decided on the basis of what the best theory of us is – and we must swallow the consequences of that. (Snowdon 1991, 126)

Snowdon is aware of the fact that this is a rather weak response (especially if there is another theory available whose proponents might have a different opinion about what the best theory of us is). But he knows what should be done to make this kind of reply stronger than a mere keeping to a theory "come what may". What really would improve this reply would be an explanation of why we have an intuition which is, according to our theory, incorrect. These explanations are indeed sometimes available and help to resolve a clash of intuitions. Maybe one of the best examples is Perry's argument in *The Importance of Being Identical*.[72]

As all reductionists, the mentalist has to answer Butler's challenge, viz., why we find ourselves so immensely interested in our future survival, if this future survival is nothing but a future person stage standing in a certain abstract relation to us, a relation we don't seem to have the same intimate concern for. The problem is to explain how the impor-

[72] Reprinted in Perry 2002.

tance of identity can be derivative when it feels so intrinsic. What Perry offers is the sketch of an evolutionary explanation why we have this very sort of self-concern. If this explains how it comes that self-concern enters our person-theory as strongly as it does, the reductionist's conceptual analysis does no longer clash with this intuition.

Other strategies to explain conflicting intuitions away make use of the very mechanism Gendler refers to when considering how differently described cases are grouped into different similarity classes. As Goldman has argued, if we understood the psychology better that makes us group such cases together, the method of imaginary cases would rather be vindicated than affected. What we should inquire is how contextual factors influence our intuitive responses. That there are *systematic* connections between the specific framing of cases and our intuitive responses seems plausible from the psychological literature.[73] Thus Goldman writes about the analysis of 'knowledge':

> In general, it looks as if uniformities about knowledge could be predicted from the psychology of context effects together with the relevant-alternatives account of the meaning of 'know'. This illustrates how empirical psychology might lend credibility (or incredibility) to specific philosophical analyses. (Goldman 1992, 147)

It doesn't seem to us, after surveying various arguments, that the method of imaginary cases should be abandoned on a priori grounds. We admitted that a positive theory that supports thought experimentation is not available yet and might very well involve an empirical investigation of the stability, reliability, and context-dependence of our modal judgments.[74] But it is far from being a priori clear (i.) that language does not give rise to a stable modal structure, (ii.) that we are unable to make reliable judgments about this modal structure on the basis of our linguistic intuitions, and (iii.) that if there is a modal structure that transcendents the linguistic level there could be no systematic connection with the level which is accessible with the help of linguistic intuitions. We also argued that even if modal epistemology should prove (iii) to be true, there is still a valuable function for thought experiments. They might fail to inform us about the metaphysical relations that hold in our world but still provide us with valuable information about what really is of importance to us when raising a philosophical issue.

---

[73] The basis of this psychological theory of imaginary cases is the research undertaken by Daniel Kahneman and Amos Tversky (Kahneman/Tversky 1979). Goldman sketches in Goldman 1992 what such a theory could look like for the case of 'knowledge'. According to Kamm 1998, Kahneman himself seems to be less optimistic about the prospect of a psychological foundation for the method of imaginary cases than Goldman. See also Kamm 1998 and Horowitz 1998 for the connection between the results of Kahneman and Tversky and philosophical methodology in ethics.

[74] Empirical as well as theoretical research in that area is carried out by the research group on modal illusions of the Institut Jean-Nicod (Paris) and the Institut des Sciences Cognitives (Lyon), notably Sacha Bourgeois-Gironde, Ira Noveck, Anne Reboul, and Jean-Baptiste van der Henst.

It might turn out that one day we find better methods for answering our philosophical questions. Or it might turn out that our psychological investigations will even lead to a substantial improvement of the methods already employed.[75] Until then there is no reason to stop traveling these other possible worlds to learn what we would say. Buckle up!

References

Bartelborth, Thomas, 1996, Begründungsstrategien: Ein Weg durch die analytische Erkenntnistheorie, Berlin, Akademie Verlag.
Bealer, George, 1998, Intuition and the Autonomy of Philosophy, Michael R. DePaul and William Ramsey (eds.), Rethinking Intuition, The Psychology of Intuition and Its Role in Philosophical Inquiry, 201-239.
Beck, Simon, 1992, Should We Tolerate People Who Split? The Southern Journal of Philosophy XXX, 1-17.
Block, Ned, Stalnaker, Robert C., 1999, Conceptual analysis, dualism, and the explanatory gap. Philosophical Review 108,1-46.
Brendel, Elke, 1999, Gedankenexperimente als Motor der Wissenschaftsdynamik, J. Mittelstraß (ed.), Die Zukunft des Wissens (XVIII. Deutscher Kongress für Philosophie Konstanz 1999), Konstanz, Universitätsverlag Konstanz.
Broad, Charlie D., 1952, Ethics and the History of Philosophy, London, Routledge & Paul.
Bühler, Axel; Kann, Christoph, 2002, Wie besser sind wir? Thomas Spitzley, Ralf Stoecker (eds.), Philosophie a lá carte, Paderborn, Mentis, 147-148.
Buekens, Filip; Dooremalen, Hans, 2003, Three Grades of Conceivability, forthcoming in Dialectica.
Bunzl, Martin, 1996, The Logic of Thought Experiments, Synthese 106, 227-240.
Carnap, Rudolf, 1950, Logical Foundations of Probability, Chicago, The University of Chicago Press.
Chalmers, David, 2002, Does Conceivability Entail Possibility? Tamar Szabó Gendler and John Hawthorne (eds.), Conceivability and Possibility, Oxford, Clarendon Press.
Chalmers, David, 2002a, The Foundations of Two-Dimensional Semantics, Manuscript.

---

[75] Consider some concepts to be represented as prototypes, but homogeneously so. Reconsider (T^*) from FN 70. Two individuals could be said to have grasped the same concept C iff the right hand side of T^* truly captures the application conditions internalized by both of them. S could be substantiated along the lines sketched here, grounded in a psychological theory of how our reactions to imaginary cases depend on contextual factors. If there is homogeneity among the speakers of a language community with respect to T^*, imaginary cases would still be a valid tool for analysis, even though concepts might be prototype structured. This, of course, is an empirical question.

Chalmers, David, 2002b, On Sense and Intension, Philosophical Perspectives 16, 135-182.

Cohnitz, Daniel, 2003, Two-Dimensionalism and the Metaphysical Possibility of Zombies, B. Löwe, W. Malzkorn, T. Räsch (eds.), Foundations of The Formal Sciences II. Applications of Mathematical Logic in Philosophy and Linguistics [Trends in Logic]. Dordrecht, Kluwer Academic Publishers.

Cohnitz, Daniel, forthcoming, The Science of Fiction.

Cohnitz, Daniel; Smith, Barry, 2003, Assessing Ontologies: The Question of Human Origins and Its Ethical Significance. Proceedings of the 25th International Wittgenstein Symposium, in Press.

Dancy, Jonathan, 1985, The Role of Imaginary Cases in Ethics, Pacific Philosophical Quarterly 66, 141-153.

Dennett, Daniel C., 1991, Consciousness Explained, London, Penguin.

Fodor, Jerry A., 1964, On knowing what we would say, The Philosophical Review LXXIII, 198-212.

Fodor, Jerry A.; Le Pore, Ernest, 1994, Why Meaning (Probably) Isn't Conceptual Role, Stephen P. Stich and Ted A. Warfield, Mental Representation. A Reader, Oxford, Blackwell, 142-156.

Fuhrmann, André, 2002, Das Mögliche und das Vorstellbare, Logos, in print.

Gähde, Ulrich, 2000, Gedankenexperimente in Erkenntnistheorie und Physik: strukturelle Parallelen, Julian Nida-Rümelin (ed.), Rationalität, Realismus, Revision : Vorträge des 3. internationalen Kongresses der Gesellschaft für Analytische Philosophie vom 15. bis zum 18. September 1997 in München, Berlin, de Gruyter, 457-464.

Gale, Richard, 1991, On Some Pernicious Thought Experiments, Tamara Horrowitz and Gerald Massey (eds.), Thought Experiments in Science and Philosophy, Savage, Rowman & Littlefield, 297-305.

Gendler, Tamar Szabó, 1998, Exceptional Persons: On the Limits of Imaginary Cases, Journal of Consciousness Studies 5, 592-610.

Gendler, Tamar Szabó, 2000, Thought Experiments: On the Powers and Limits of Imaginary Cases, New York, Garland Routledge.

Goldman, Alvin, 1992, Liaisons: philosophy meets the cognitive and social sciences, Cambridge (Mass.), MIT Press.

Hale, Bob, 2002, Knowledge of Possibility and Knowledge of Necessity, Proceedings of the Aristotelian Society CIII, 1-20.

Häggqvist, Sören, 1996, Thought Experiments in Philosophy, Stockholm, Almqvist & Wiksell International.

Hempel, Carl G., 1974, Grundzüge der Begriffsbildung in den empirischen Wissenschaften, Düsseldorf, Bertelsmann Universitätsverlag.

Hintikka, Jaako, 1998, Who is about to kill analytic philosophy? Ana Biletzki and Anat

Matar (eds.), The Story of Analytic Philosophy, London/New York, Routledge, 253-269.

Horowitz, Tamara, 1998, Philosophical Intuitions and Psychological Theory, Ethics 108, 367-385.

Hume, David, 2000, Enquiries concerning human understanding and concerning the principles of morals, third edition, Oxford, Clarendon Press.

Inwagen, Peter Van, 1998, Modal Epistemology, Philosophical Studies 92, 67-84.

Jackson, Frank, 1998, From Metaphysics to Ethics: A Defence of Conceptual Analysis, Oxford, Clarendon Press.

Johnston, Mark, 1987, Human Beings, The Journal of Philosophy LXXXIV, 59-83.

Kahneman, Daniel; Tversky, Amos, 1979, Prospect Theory: An Analysis of Decision under Risk, Econometrica 47, 263-291.

Kamm, F. M., 1998, Moral Intuitions, Cognitive Psychology, and the Harming-versus-Not-Aiding Distinction, Ethics 108, 463-488.

Kanuck, Kathryn T., 2000, Personal Identity: The Significance of the Fission Thought Experiment, Manuscript.

Kornblith, Hilary, 2002, Knowledge and its Place in Nature, Oxford, Clarendon Press.

Kuhn, Thomas S., 1964, A Function for Thought Experiments, L'aventure de la science, Mélanges Alexandre Koyré, Vol. 2, Paris, 307-334.

Kühne, Ulrich, 2001, Die Methode des Gedankenexperiments: Untersuchung zur Rationalität naturwissenschaftlicher Theoriereformen, Manuskript.

Laymon, R., 1991, Thought Experiments by Stevin, Mach and Gouy: Thought Experiments as Ideal Limits and as Semantic Domains, Tamara Horrowitz and Gerald Massey (eds.), Thought Experiments in Science and Philosophy, Savage, Rowman & Littlefield, 167-191.

Leibniz, G. W., 1996, Philosophische Schriften, Vol. 1, edited and translated by Hans Heinz Holz, Frankfurt a.M., Suhrkamp.

Lewis, David, 1976, Survival and Identity, Amélie Rorty (ed.), The Identities of Persons, Berkeley/Los Angeles, University of California Press, 17-40.

Locke, John, 1975, Of Identity and Diversity, John Perry (ed.), Personal Identity, Berkeley, University of California Press, 33-52.

Lodge, David, 2001, Thinks ..., London, Secker & Warburg.

Mayer, Verena, 1999, Was zeigen Gedankenexperimente? Philosophisches Jahrbuch 106, 357-378.

Nagel, Thomas, 1998, Conceiving The Impossible and the Mind-Body Problem, Manuscript.

Norman, Michael; Winkler, Karl-Heinz; Smarr, Larry; Smith, M. D., 1982, Structure and Dynamics of Supersonic Jets, Astronomy and Astrophysics 113, 285-302.

O'Leary-Hawthorne, John, 1996, The Epistemology of Possible Worlds: A Guided Tour, Philosophical Studies 84, 183-202.
Parfit, Derek, 1971, Personal Identity, The Philosophical Review 80, 3-27.
Parfit, Derek, 1984, Reasons and Persons, Oxford, Clarendon Press.
Peacocke, Christopher, 1999, Being Known, Oxford, Clarendon Press.
Perry, John, 2002, Identity, Personal Identity, and the Self, Indianapolis / Cambridge, Hackett.
Putnam, Hilary, 1975, Mind, Language and Reality, Cambridge, Cambridge University Press.
Quine, Willard Van Orman, 1972, Review, Journal of Philosophy 69, 491-497.
Seddon, George, 1972, Logical Possibility, Mind 81, 481-494.
Snowdon, P. F., 1991, Personal Identity and Brain Transplants, David Cockburn (ed.), Human Beings, Cambridge, Cambridge University Press, 109-126.
Sorensen, Roy, A., 1992, Thought Experiments, Oxford, Oxford University Press.
Wiggins, David, 1967, Identity and Spatio-Temporal Continuity, Oxford, Blackwells.
Wiggins, David, 1980, Sameness and Substance, Cambridge (Mass.), Harvard University Press.
Wilkes, Kathleen V., 1988, Real People: Personal Identity without Thought Experiments, Oxford, Clarendon Press.
Williams, Bernard, 1973, Problems of the Self, Cambridge, Cambridge University Press.
Wittgenstein, Ludwig, 1967, Zettel, edited by G. E. M. Anscombe and G. H. von Wright, translated by G. E. M. Anscombe, Oxford, Basil Blackwell.
Wittgenstein, Ludwig, 1975, Philosophical Remarks, edited by Rush Rees, translated by Raymond Hargreaves and Roger White, Oxford, Basil Blackwell.
Yablo, Stephen, 1993, Is Conceivability a Guide to Possibility, Philosophy and Phenomenological Research LIII, 1-42.

Daniel von Wachter
Free Agents as Cause

The dilemma of free will is that if actions are caused deterministically, then they are not free, and if they are not caused deterministically then they are not free either because then they happen by chance and are not up to the agent. I shall propose a conception of free will that solves this dilemma. It may seem to many metaphysically more extravagant than other conceptions but I shall suggest that this should not deter us. However, I shall not undertake here to argue that there really are beings with free will; this would be a different project. Here I shall only discuss what free actions would be like.

Imagine a tidal wave at time t_2 that was caused by an earthquake in the sea at time t_1. There was a causal process, described by laws of nature, leading from the earthquake to the tidal wave. The tidal wave was a part of an ongoing causal process and was a result of this process. Let me define a few terms related to causal processes. An event that includes everything that belongs to a process at a certain time (instant or period) when the process is going on I call a *stage* of the process. An event that is a stage or a part of a stage of a process I call a *part of the process*. A stage or a part of a stage of a causal process is a *cause* of every later stage of the process. A stage of a causal process is the *complete cause* of every later stage of the process. A cause of this type, i.e. a cause that is a part of a causal process of which its effect is a later part, I call an *event cause*, in order to distinguish it from what some authors have called an 'agent cause'.

If an action is a part of an ongoing causal process and a result of this process, then, in an interesting sense of 'free', the action is not free, even if the agent feels free. Other authors define what is essentially the same concept of freedom by saying that free agents 'are not causally necessitated to do the actions which they do by brain-events or any other events' (Swinburne 1997, 231), or by saying that a free action is not caused by a preceding 'sufficient causal condition' (Chisholm 1976, 202). This kind of freedom is usually called libertarian freedom. We can, of course, form also other concepts of freedom, compatibilist freedom, which do not require that a free action is not the result of ongoing causal processes. For each concept of freedom we can form we can inquire whether there are beings that have such freedom. Further, one can argue that one concept of freedom is more similar to our usual concept of freedom and more relevant for questions of responsibility and guilt than others. To many it seems that if someone was caused to do what he did and if he could not have prevented the causes of his action to cause him to act in the way he did, then he is not responsible for his action. However, here I shall not discuss for which concepts of freedom there are beings with that kind of freedom, and I shall not discuss which concept of freedom is how adequate. I only want to discuss what libertarian free actions would be like.

Assume somebody freely raised his arm. There was a causal process leading to the rising of the arm, involving events in the muscles, nerves, etc. I call this the *action process*. As the action was free, it does not go back infinitely, it had a beginning. I call the first stage of the action process the *initial event*. It was not wholly caused by a preceding event. The initial event may have been a complex event, some parts of which were caused by preceding events. But, if the action was free, then at least an event that is a part of the initial event was not caused by preceding events. I call this event that was not caused by preceding events the *initiating event* or *choice event*.

How and why did the initiating event occur? According to the assumption that the action was free, it was not fully caused by preceding events. It is often suggested that an action is free if, and only if, there is 'indeterminacy' at a certain point. Clarke holds that the *decision* has to come about indeterministically: 'When a decision is freely made [...] there remained until the making of that decision a genuine chance that the agent would not make that decision.' (Clarke 2000, 21) Others hold that in a free action the decision is caused deterministically but the process of *deliberation* leading to the decision is indeterministic (Dennett 1978; Fischer and Ravizza 1992; Mele 1995). It is true that an action's involving an indeterministic process makes it true that, before the action occurred, it was possible that another action would occur instead of the one that did occur. But this is not what we are getting at when we say that a free agent 'could have done otherwise'. The trouble is that if it is a matter of indeterminacy which action occurs then it is not up to the agent what he does. An action that occurs by chance is not a free action because the agent lacks *control* over which action occurs. If an action is the result of an indeterministic process, then the agent has as little control over it as an agent has over an action that occurs as the result of a deterministic process. We are stuck at the second horn of the dilemma of free will. Can we avoid it?

If the action was free, then the initiating event was not caused deterministically, it was not uncaused, and it was not caused indeterministically. Is there another way how an event can come about? I suggest that there is another way. As the action was free, the action process had a beginning whose occurrence was due to the agent. If you trace back the causes of the action result, the rising of the arm, you reach a stage of the action process a part of which, the initiating event, did not have a preceding cause. It had neither a deterministic nor an indeterministic preceding cause. Its occurrence was due to the agent. The agent made an event pop up that initiated the action process. This initiating event, together with other events, caused the later stages of the action process and the action result.

We can call the initiating event also 'choice' or 'choice event'. A choice event is an event that has no preceding cause and whose occurrence is due to an agent. We can say that the event is the agent's choice, or that it occurs as the agent's choice. A free agent is somebody who can initiate causal processes by doing something for a reason and with an intention. However, the agent need not know what the choice event is and he need not know all the stages of the action process. Human agents (I assume for the sake of the argument that they are free) never know all the stages of the action process when they move parts of their bodies. If somebody raises his arm, then the rising of his arm is caused by certain brain events, but the intention governing the action is not about all the events that cause the action result. The agent does not do anything in or with his brain in order to raise his arm; he does not even know what brain events cause the rising. When he tries to raise his arm a choice event occurs that causes the rising of his arm, without the agent knowing all the events that cause the rising of the arm. What is needed for successful free action is that the agent knows what he has to try to do in order to achieve what, and that when he tries a choice event occurs that causes the intended result.

With choice events the dilemma of free action is solved. Free actions are neither caused deterministically nor are they uncaused or indeterministically caused. Choice events are the third way that avoids both horns of the dilemma.

What are the choice events in human free action? What answer one will give to this question partly depends on what view one takes on the mind body problem. A materialist will argue that choice events are certain physical events, presumably brain events. A dualist may hold that they are non-physical events of a certain kind. In either case, one promising candidate for choice events are *tryings*. Let me illustrate.

Imagine you want to drink a cup of tea. You take the handle of the cup in order to lift it. But due to an illness of yours your arm is paralysed and does not do what you want. You try in vain to lift your arm. Then you try again. This time you are successful: your arm obeys your command and rises. The mental event that occurred when you first tried to raise your arm, which is described by 'I tried to raise my arm', is an example of a trying. An exactly similar event occurred presumably when you raised your arm successfully. As I use the term, there are successful as well as unsuccessful tryings. Tryings are mental events of the kind that occur when someone undertakes an action.[1]

Perhaps all choice events in human actions are tryings. A dualist may take tryings to be non-physical events, a materialist will take them to be identical with certain physical events (or he will say that for each trying a physical event fulfils its causal role). However, we do not need to answer the question which events are choice events here. My thesis is

---

[1] Swinburne (1997, 95) uses besides 'tryings' also the term 'purposings'. Chisholm (1976, 201) uses 'undertakings'.

just that the action process in a free action involves an event that has no preceding cause and whose occurrence is due to the agent.

Is a choice event *caused* by the agent?

Often when a choice event occurs, another choice event could have occurred instead, or no choice event at all. Although choice events are not caused by earlier events, they do not occur by accident. Rather, they occur because agents choose. Should we then say that they are not caused at all or should we say that they are caused, but not by other events but by agents. Whether we say that a choice event is caused by the agent is mainly a question of terminology. To say that they are caused by agents may be adequate and useful as long as we are clear about the differences between how a choice event comes about and how an event caused by a preceding event comes about. Let me state these differences again.

Where an event caused another event the one event was part of a process that led to the other event. A person and his choice event, however, are not connected through a causal process. A choice event occurs because the agent makes a certain choice, and this bears little resemblance to the way how an event causes another event. Further, whereas an event that causes an event is always earlier than the caused event, the person is in no clear sense earlier than the choice event. There is nothing about the person which takes place at a certain time before the choice event which we could identify as the cause of the choice event. A choice event has no *preceding* cause. All this counts against saying that choice events are caused by agents.

On the other hand, it is quite in line with common talk as well as with the philosophical tradition to say of the result of a free action that it is caused by the agent. Furthermore, where a choice event occurred usually another choice event could have occurred instead (or none at all). And that the one rather than the other occurred was due to the agent. Now, something to which it is due that the world carries on in one way rather than in another is fittingly called cause of that which happens due to its activity. That counts in favour of saying that a choice event is caused by the agent. Further, we commonly say about the result of an action that it is caused by the agent. If you raise your arm, you are rightly called the cause of your arm's rising. You brought about your arm's rising, and this is synonymous to saying that you caused your arm's rising. Likewise, there is no reason why we should not say of a choice event that it was brought about, or 'caused', by the agent.

I conclude that it is adequate to say of a choice event that it is caused by the agent. Further, it is adequate to say of events that are effects of a choice event, that they are caused by the agent. We can say that a person was a cause of events that were caused by a choice event that occurred through his choice. Usually the context will make clear whether with a statement of the form 'x caused y' it is meant that y was, or was the effect of, a choice event that occurred in virtue of x's choice, or whether x was a part of a causal process that led to y. Where one wants to make clear that y occurred because of x's choice, one can say that x was the *agent cause* of y, or that y was caused through x's action. Where one wants to make clear that y occurred as the result of a causal process of which x was an earlier part, one can say that x was an *event cause* of y. However, I am not claiming that agent causation and event causation are somehow the very same relation,[2] in the one case relating an agent with an event and in the other case relating an event with an event.

Agent causation

Is my proposal in line with Chisholm's theory of 'agent causation'?[3] Surprisingly not. I shall now show that Chisholm's theory does not help to solve the dilemma of free action, and that Chisholm confuses semantical with metaphysical issues.

Chisholm holds that there is besides event causation another kind of causation, namely agent causation. The centre piece of his theory is the concept of undertaking, by which he means what I have called 'trying'. About an event that results from a successful undertaking Chisholm says that the agent 'contributed causally to' it (Chisholm 1976, 205); the agent is the cause of it. So if you raise your arm, then *you* are the cause of your arm's rising, which means the same as that you are contributing causally to your arm's rising. One might think then that Chisholm's 'undertakings' are what I have called 'choice events'. In order to solve the dilemma of free action we need to assume that there is a way how an event may come about other than through event causation or indeterministic processes. One should think that those who hold that there is agent causation do so in order to solve the dilemma of free action by introducing agent causation as the special way how an event comes about in a free action. Why else would one assume that there is besides agent causation another kind of causation?

However, Chisholm's theory fails to solve the dilemma of free action. A free action, for Chisholm (1976, 202), is an action that involves an undertaking for which there is no preceding 'sufficient causal condition'. But, according to Chisholm, *also non-free actions*

---

[2] Randolph Clarke proposes an account of agent causation of the kind I reject here. He writes: 'The relation that obtains between cause and effect in an instance of agent causation is the very same relation that obtains between cause and effect in an instance of event causation.' (Clarke 1996, 21)
[3] (Chisholm 1976; 1976, ch. 2). Very similar is Swinburne's theory: (Swinburne 1997, 89-96; 1994, 56-62; 1997, 87-90). The objections I raise below apply equally to Swinburne's theory. Other authors who have proposed agent causation are (Reid 1788), (Taylor 1966, chs. 8 & 9), (O'Connor 2000).

involve undertakings and hence agent causation (whereas I have argued that only free actions involve what I call choice events and what I call agent causation). The difference is only that in a non-free action the undertaking has a preceding sufficient event cause. I have two objections.

First, Chisholm rightly says that in a free action the undertaking has no preceding sufficient cause, but he does not specify how it comes about instead. He fails to consider the case where it occurs by chance, as the result of an indeterministic process. Surely if an undertaking occurs by chance, then the agent has no control over it, the action is not up to the agent, therefore the action is not free in the sense in question. But according to Chisholm's definition of a free action it is a free action. In my definition of a choice event I therefore not only say that a choice event has no event cause but additionally that its occurrence is due to the agent, the agent makes in pop up. So Chisholm's definition of a free action fails to exclude the case where an undertaking occurs by chance and not under the control of the agent.[4]

Second, to Chisholm's claim that there is agent causation in non-free actions I object that we have no reason to assume that in non-free actions there is another kind of causation besides event causation involved. Assume your raising your arm is fully caused by preceding events, for example through a machine that is connected to your brain. Chisholm would still say that your arm's rising is caused by you – but surely the full truth is that your trying to raise your arm as well as your arm's rising was caused by nothing but preceding events. Contra Chisholm, there is no extra kind of causation involved in non-free actions.[5]

Why does Chisholm hold that there is an extra kind of causation involved in non-free actions? The reason is that Chisholm by claiming that there is agent causation means something different from what one should think he means. He does not mean that when Smith raises his arm the way how the arm's rising comes about is dissimilar to the way how an explosion comes about that is caused by a spark. (Whereas I hold that the way

---

[4] Johann Christian Marek pointed out to me that Chisholm has addressed this objection in his (1979). There he answers the question what an undertaking in a free action has that an uncaused physiological event does not have as follows: 'What it has is this: it is the agent's undertaking. To put the matter somewhat loosely, it is a state of affairs that involves the agent himself. We can describe the physiological events in my brain without using expressions that refer to any person. But the property of undertaking – like that of thinking or believing – is a property that can be had only by persons.' (363f) I do not find this convincing because saying that it is the agent's undertaking does not rule out that it is a chance event whose occurrence is not up to the agent. It only says that the undertaking occurs in Jones's mind rather than in Miller's.
[5] In earlier writings Chisholm defended a theory of agent causation that is more similar to mine. There he postulated an event 'which is caused not by any other event, but by the agent' (Chisholm 1964, 54) (cf. Chisholm 1966). This seems to be getting at what I have called a choice event.

how a choice event comes about is dissimilar to the way how an explosion comes about.) His claim that there is irreducible agent causation is in fact not a claim about action but about certain *statements* describing actions. It is a child of the linguistic turn. This becomes clear in the following passage.

> The philosophical question is not – or at least it shouldn't be – the question whether or not there is 'agent causation'. The philosophical question should be, rather, the question whether 'agent causation' is reducible to 'event causation'. Thus, for example, if we have good reason for believing that Jones did kill his uncle, then the philosophical question about Jones as cause would be: Can we express the statement 'Jones killed his uncle' without loss of meaning into a set of statements in which only events are said to be causes and in which Jones himself is not said to be the source of any activity? And can we do this without being left with any residue of agent causation – that is, without being left with some such statement as 'Jones raised his arm' wherein Jones once again plays the role of cause or partial cause of a certain event? (Chisholm 1978, 622f, quoted in O'Connor 2000, 64)

So by his claim that there is agent causation Chisholm does not mean that there is something like what I have called choice events, he only means that statements like 'Jones killed his uncle' cannot be transformed into statements of a different kind. I suggest that investigating statements is the wrong method for finding out whether there is agent causation. Chisholm's mistake is that he tries to answer a metaphysical question just by answering semantical questions. That the statement 'Jones killed his uncle' cannot be transformed into a statement of a different type does not mean that Jones's action involved a kind of causation different from event causation.

Peter van Inwagen's mystery objection against agent causation

Peter van Inwagen, in his article 'Free Will Remains a Mystery' (2000), has claimed that free will 'undeniably exists' but that there is no way out of the free will dilemma and that free will is hence a mystery. He argues that agent causation offers no remedy; it 'is entirely irrelevant to the problem of free will' (van Inwagen 2000, 11). He comes to this conclusion because of the following thought experiment.

Imagine Alice being in a situation where she has a choice between doing A and doing B at time t_2. Before the decision, e.g. one minute before, at t_1, it was undetermined whether she would do A or B. Suppose she does A. Now suppose that God 'caused the universe to revert to precisely its state one minute before Alice' did A, i.e. to its state at t_1. (p. 14) Then 'let things go forward again'. Again it is undetermined what she will do. She might do A, she might do B. Suppose she does B. 'Now let us suppose that God *a thousand times* caused the universe to revert to exactly the state it was in at t_1. [...] What would have happened?' (p. 14). Probably Alice will sometimes do A and sometimes B.

Van Inwagen suggests that the frequency of her doing A would converge: 'As the number of "replays" increases, we observers shall – almost certainly – observe the ratio of the outcome' A to the outcome B 'settling down to, converging on, some value'.

Van Inwagen suggests further that we should infer from this that it is *'simply a matter of chance'* (p. 15) what Alice does. 'Is it not true that as we watch the number of replays increase, we shall become convinced that what will happen in the *next* replay is a matter of chance?' If it is a matter of chance what she does then she is not able to choose between A and B. It is not up to her what she does. 'If one confronts a choice between A and B and it is a matter of chance whether one will choose A or B, how can it be that one is able to choose A?' (p. 17)

Van Inwagen believes that 'there is something wrong with the argument' (p. 18), but he has no views about what is wrong with it. What he wants to show is mainly that the concept of agent causation offers no remedy here, that if it were of any use it would offer remedy, and that therefore it is of no use. *'The concept of agent causation cannot be used to undermine the intuitive plausibility of this argument.'* (p.16) He points out that even if we were to assume that Alice is an agent cause, given many repetitions of the situation of decision, the ratio between her doing A and her doing B would converge. Therefore, so van Inwagen argues, we should still assume that it is a matter of chance what she does, and hence she does not act freely.

I object that it is not true that in any case, if the ratio between Alice's decisions to do A and decisions to do B were to converge, we should accept that Alice's acting is a mere matter of chance. Whether the outcome of van Inwagen's experiment counts against the assumption that Alice has free will depends on whether we should expect a different outcome in the case of Alice having free will. What sort of outcome should we expect on the assumption that Alice is acting freely? If the situation is really as van Inwagen describes it, so that Alice has within one minute two and only two options, we should expect just the sort of outcome that van Inwagen describes: we should expect the ratio between her doing A and her doing B to converge in the long run. The difference between the case where it is a matter of chance whether A or B occurs and the case where Alice is choosing freely between A and B is *not* that in one case and not in the other there is convergence. The difference is that in the case where there is chance the action is the result of an indeterministic process, whereas in the case of Alice choosing freely there is a choice event initiating the action process, an event that is not the result of a causal process (deterministic or indeterministic). The reason why we should expect the convergence on the assumption that Alice is free too is the following. Whatever Alice does she does either following a natural inclination or following a belief why it would be good to do the one thing rather than the other thing. If she has an inclination to do A and no counteracting inclinations and no beliefs that B would be better, then she will invariably freely do A. If she has a desire to do A and an equally strong desire to do B and no further beliefs about which is better, then it is unpredictable in each case what she will do, and it is predictable that if the situation is repeated often then the ratio will converge to 1/1. If she has, besides the natural inclinations, certain beliefs about A being better than B, then the proportion of A-actions will be greater. In any case, if she has in each case the same beliefs, the same inclinations, and the same character, then the ratio will converge.[6] We should expect the convergence on the assumption that Alice is acting freely as well as on the assumption that she is not free.

If we have reason to believe that Alice is acting freely, then we have thereby reason to believe that her acting is not a mere matter of chance. As we should expect the convergence in any case, whether Alice is acting freely or whether her acting is a matter of chance, conducting the sort of experiment which van Inwagen describes does not help to find out whether Alice is acting freely. An experiment only makes improbable a certain hypothesis if the outcome is different from what we should expect on the hypothesis. The hypothesis in this case is that Alice is acting freely. The outcome of van Inwagen's experiment is that the ratio of A to B converges, and that is what the hypothesis leads us to expect. The fact that the hypothesis that Alice's acting is a matter of chance leads us to expect the same outcome does not speak against the hypothesis that Alice is acting freely. Therefore van Inwagen should not conclude from his thought experiment that Alice's acting is a mere matter of chance and therefore not free.

As the argument is flawed it does nothing to discredit the concept of agent causation. The concept of agent causation helps us to describe the difference between the case where Alice is acting freely and the case where she is not free. The cases differ in their causal structure. If Alice is acting freely, then the action result is the result of an action process that starts with an initial event, a part of which (the choice event) is not the result of a process and occurs because of Alice's choice. If, however, Alice's acting is a mere matter of chance, and hence if she is not acting freely, then the action result is just the result of a process – in this case an indeterministic one – which at no stage involves a choice event.

Van Inwagen's thought experiment does nothing to show whether we have free will and what free will is and how it works. Different considerations would be required in order to find out whether we, or some other beings, have free will. This is not the place to pursue this.[7] For our project here we only need to know what it would be like if someone had free will. I conclude that van Inwagen's argument also does nothing to discredit the concept of agent causation.

---

6 For similar arguments for this claim see (Swinburne 1997, 259-261).

Is agent causation mysterious?

To many agent causation as I have described it will seem metaphysically extravagant or mysterious. Consider two kinds of objections. First, one may object that the occurrence of choice events is incompatible with what we know about the causal structure of the world. Second, one may object that the relation between an agent and his choice event is mysterious or unintelligible.[8]

The first type of objection is based on the idea that any event is either 'necessitated' by a set of earlier events or it is the result of an indeterministic process. In event causation that involves no chance, according to this idea, which we may call *causal necessitarianism*, there is at a time t_1 a certain set of events, A, that makes it inevitable that at time t_2 later than t_1 event B occurs. Once A has occurred it is impossible that B does not occur.[9] There is no reason to believe that there is causation of this type. How should events at one time necessitate in this way what occurs at a later time? There is always the possibility that something occurs after t_1 and before t_2 that prevents the occurrence of B. Consider what the causal processes we know are like, e.g. a rolling billiard ball. Imagine even Newtonian physics to be true and hence the process to be deterministic. Even in that case the process is of course not so that nothing can stop it. If there is nothing that stops it, then it will carry on, but it is possible that something intervenes, e.g. another billiard ball or a cat jumping on the table. If there are entities that have the power to let certain events pop up (so that they have no preceding cause), then these events may well be interventions in causal processes. The question is whether there are such entities, but there is nothing in the nature of the causal processes we know (even the most 'deterministic' processes) that speaks against the existence of such entities.

The other way of how an event may come about which causal necessitarianism allows is that an event is the result of an indeterministic process. But this brings us only to the second horn of the dilemma of free will. An event that is caused indeterministically is still caused by earlier events and the agent has no control over it.

The second type of objection is that the relation between an agent and his choice event is mysterious or unintelligible. To this I reply that it is not more mysterious than the other ways how an event can come about. That an agent should make an event occur

---

[7] For arguments for free will see (Swinburne 1997, ch. 13).
[8] (Clarke 2000, 21), in this context, speaks of 'extravagant metaphysical commitments'. (Honderich 1993, ch. 3) makes both kinds of objections. Objections of the second kind (the unintelligibility objection) are raised by (Kane 1985, 72) and (Watson 1987, 167).
[9] Mellor, for example, thinks that there are causes which are in this sense 'sufficient' for their effects. He writes: 'By causes that determine their effects I shall mean ones that are in the circumstances both sufficient and necessary for them.' (Mellor 1995, 133) Similarly (Hausman 1998, 33) and (Bigelow and Pargetter 1990, 290).

in the way described is at least as mysterious as that an event at one time should make it that a certain event at a certain later time occurs. We have to try to make sense of how things seem to be, and if it appears that in some cases what occurs at one time has an impact on what occurs at certain later times, then we should believe that there are causal processes and that there is event causation; and if it appears that we (or other animals) have free will, then we should believe that there are choice events.[10]

References

Bigelow, John, and Robert Pargetter. 1990. *Science and Necessity*. Cambridge UP.
Chisholm, Roderick. 1964. Human Freedom and the Self. In *Free Will*, edited by R. Kane. Oxford: Blackwell.
–. 1966. Freedom and Action. In *Freedom and Determinism*, edited by K. Lehrer. New York: Random House.
–. 1976. The Agent as Cause. In *Action Theory*, edited by M. Brand and D. Walton. Dordrecht: Reidel, 199-211.
–. 1976. *Person and Object*. La Salle (Illinois): Open Court.
–. 1978. Replies. *Philosophia* 8:620-636.
–. 1979. Objects and Persons: Revision and Replies. In *Essays on the Philosophy of Roderick M. Chisholm*, edited by E. Sosa. Amsterdam: Rodopi, 317-388.
Clarke, Randolph. 1996. Agent Causation and Event Causation in the Production of Free Action. *Philosophical Topics* 24:19-48.
–. 2000. Modest Libertarianism. In *Philosophical Perspectives, 14: Action and Freedom*, edited by J. E. Tomberlin. Malden: Blackwell Publishers, 21-46.
Dennett, Daniel. 1978. On Giving Libertarians What They Say They Want. In *Brainstorms*. Brighton: Harvester Press, 1981.
Fischer, John M., and Mark Ravizza. 1992. When The Will is Free. In *Philosophical Perspectives, 6: Ethics*, edited by J. E. Tomberlin. Atascadero: Ridgeview.
Hausman, Daniel M. 1998. *Causal asymmetries*. Cambridge: Cambridge University Press.
Honderich, Ted. 1993. *How Free Are You?* Oxford UP.
Kane, Robert. 1985. *Free Will and Values*. Albany: SUNY Press.
Mele, Alfred R. 1995. *Autonomous Agents: From Self-Control to Autonomy*. New York: Oxford UP.
Mellor, D. H. 1995. *The Facts of Causation*. London and New York: Routledge.
O'Connor, Timothy. 2000. *Persons and Causes*. Oxford UP.

---

[10] I wish to express my gratitude to the Free State of Bavaria which enabled this work through the "Bayerischer Habilitationsförderpreis".

Reid, Thomas. 1788. Essays on the Active Power of the Human Mind. In *Inquiry and Essays*, ed. by R. E. Beanblossom and K. Lehrer. Indianapolis: Hackett, 1983, 297-368.
Swinburne, Richard. 1994. *The Christian God*. Oxford: Clarendon.
–. 1997. *The Evolution of the Soul (Revised Edition)*. Oxford: Clarendon.
–. 1997. The Irreducibility of Causation. *Dialectica* 51:79-92.
Taylor, Richard. 1966. *Action and Purpose*. Englewood Cliffs, NJ.
van Inwagen, Peter. 2000. Free Will Remains a Mystery. In *Philosophical Perspectives, 14: Action and Freedom*, edited by J. E. Tomberlin. Malden: Blackwell Publishers, 1-19.
Watson, Gary. 1987. Free Action and Free Will. *Mind* 96:145-172.

Thomas Spitzley
Identität und Orientierung

Die politische Philosophie der letzten Jahrzehnte ist geprägt von einer Debatte, die weit über die akademische Philosophie hinaus auch in der breiteren Öffentlichkeit Beachtung gefunden hat, nämlich von der Debatte zwischen Kommunitaristen und Liberalen. Im Kern handelt es sich dabei um eine Auseinandersetzung über die Rolle und die Aufgaben des Staates.

In modernen Gesellschaften findet sich eine Vielzahl unterschiedlicher und unvereinbarer religiöser und moralischer Überzeugungen. Es gibt keine allgemein geteilte Weltauffassung, keine Konzeption des guten Lebens, die von allen Gesellschaftsmitgliedern gleichermaßen anerkannt würde. Mit Verweis auf dieses Faktum des Wertepluralismus fordern die Liberalen einen gegenüber rivalisierenden Lebensentwürfen neutralen Staat, der nicht nur das Selbstbestimmungsrecht seiner Bürger zu respektieren hat, sondern darüber hinaus auch mit Hilfe bestimmter prozeduraler Regeln dem Einzelnen seine maximale Entfaltung ermöglichen soll. Im wesentlichen weisen die Liberalen dem Staat also nur die Aufgabe zu, die *Freiheiten* des Einzelnen rechtlich zu garantieren.

Die Kommunitaristen behaupten dagegen, eine wesentliche Bedingung für jede funktionierende Gesellschaft sei die Existenz allgemein geteilter Werte. Daher fordern sie, der Staat müsse eine sogenannte "Politik eines gemeinsamen Gutes"[1] verfolgen. Der Staat müsse solche gemeinsamen Werte nicht nur bewußt machen, sondern auch deren Umsetzung fördern. Nicht nur müsse er seine Bürger dazu ermutigen, Konzeptionen des Guten zu wählen, die mit diesen Werten übereinstimmen, sondern er sei darüber hinaus auch verpflichtet, die dafür erforderlichen Rahmenbedingungen zu schaffen.

Letztlich basieren die zwischen Liberalen und Kommunitaristen umstrittenen Auffassungen in bezug auf die Rolle und die Aufgaben des Staates auf unterschiedlichen Vorstellungen von der Verankerung des Individuums in der Gesellschaft. Die Kommunitaristen vertreten die Meinung, der Liberalismus ignoriere die Abhängigkeit des Menschen von gesellschaftlichen Beziehungen und propagiere ein zu individualistisches bzw. atomistisches Menschenbild. Ihrer Ansicht nach ist die Gesellschaft mehr als nur eine Gemeinschaft freier und gleicher Bürger; die Individuen seien in eine existierende soziale Praxis eingebettet, von der sie sich nicht freimachen könnten.

Während die Liberalen der Meinung sind, die Frage nach dem guten Leben erfordere von jedem Einzelnen, sich zu entscheiden, was für eine Person er sein oder werden möchte, glauben die Kommunitaristen, die maßgebliche Frage sei nicht "Was sollte ich

---

[1] Cf. M. Sandel, Morality and the Liberal Ideal, *New Republic*, 7.5.1984, 190, S.15-17.

sein, was für eine Art von Leben sollte ich leben?", sondern vielmehr "Wer bin ich?". Man *wähle* sich nicht sein Ziel, wie die Liberalen meinen, sondern man *entdecke* es.[2] Zu den Fragen, welche Stellung das Individuum in der Gesellschaft einnimmt, was seine Identität ausmacht und wie bzw. woran sich Menschen in ihrem Leben orientieren sollen, vertritt der den Kommunitaristen zurechenbare kanadische Philosoph Charles Taylor eine besonders dezidierte und ausführlich begründete Position. Unter dem Titel *Sources of the Self* hat er eine umfangreiche systematische und historische Studie zur "Geschichte der neuzeitlichen Identität" vorgelegt und anschließend aus deren Ergebnissen in seinen beiden Büchern *The Ethics of Authenticity* und insbesondere *Multiculturalism and 'The Politics of Recognition'* politische Konsequenzen gezogen. Dabei geht es Taylor, wie Habermas konstatiert, um "eine *Ethik des gegenwärtigen Zeitalters*".[3]

Taylor glaubt, es könne uns nur dann gelingen, ein gutes Leben zu führen, wenn wir uns unserer Identität bewußt seien und dadurch die nötige Orientierung erhielten. Die (richtigen) Ziele, welche Individuen in ihren Leben verfolgen müßten, ergäben sich ihrerseits aus einer genaueren Bestimmung der vorhandenen gemeinschaftlichen Werte. Taylor zeigt sich jedoch beunruhigt über den Individualismus und über den Vorrang, den die instrumentelle Vernunft mittlerweile eingenommen habe. Der Individualismus und der Vorrang der instrumentellen Vernunft hätten zu einem Verlust an Freiheit und zu einem Sinnverlust nicht nur des gesellschaftlichen, sondern damit auch des individuellen Lebens geführt.

Im folgenden möchte ich die von Taylor vertretene Position entwickeln und zugleich kritisch kommentieren. Dabei konzentriere ich mich darauf, was in Anlehnung an Taylor unter "Identität" zu verstehen ist, und welcher Zusammenhang zwischen Identität und Orientierung besteht. Ich gehe in vier Schritten vor: Zunächst entwickle und verteidige ich eine These zum hier relevanten *Begriff* der Identität; darauf folgt eine *inhaltliche Bestimmung* personaler Identität. Danach erörtere ich das Ideal der Authentizität, der "Treue zu sich selbst". Zum Abschluß versuche ich, das von Taylor geäußerte "Unbehagen an der Moderne" zu entdramatisieren und seiner These, der Verlust der Identität der einzelnen Individuen führe zu einer Auflösung der staatlichen Gemeinschaft, die Spitze zu nehmen.

1. Zum Begriff der personalen Identität

Wer versichert, Dr. Jeckyll und Mr. Hyde seien ein und dieselbe Person, oder seine neue Nachbarin sei niemand anderes als seine alte Jugendliebe, behauptet etwas über die

---

[2] Cf. W. Kymlicka, *Contemporary Political Philosophy*, Oxford University Press, Oxford 1990, S.213.
[3] J. Habermas, *Erläuterungen zur Diskursethik*, Suhrkamp, Frankfurt/M. ²1992, S.181.

Identität einer Person. Was in *diesem* Sinne unter personaler Identität zu verstehen ist, insbesondere wann es sich bei zu unterschiedlichen Zeitpunkten identifizierten Personen um *dieselbe* Person handelt, ist von Hume und Locke untersucht worden. Diese Art von personaler Identität wird *relationale* oder *numerische* Identität genannt.

Wenn wir dagegen wissen wollen, was für ein Mensch jemand ist, wenn man sich darum bemüht, einen verurteilten Mörder vor der drohenden Exekution zu retten, weil er im Verlauf seiner langjährigen Haft doch *ein anderer* geworden sei, oder wenn behauptet wird, es sei unmöglich, in einer multikulturellen Gesellschaft seine Identität zu bewahren, dann ist eine andere Art von personaler Identität gemeint, nämlich die *qualitative* Identität einer Person.[4]

In der Philosophie des Geistes geht es im Anschluß an Locke vornehmlich darum, unter welchen Bedingungen eine zu einem Zeitpunkt identifizierte Person mit einer zu einem anderen Zeitpunkt identifizierten Person numerisch identisch ist, also um die *diachrone* Identität von Personen. In der Kulturphilosophie, in der Moral- und in der Sozialphilosophie ist dagegen die *qualitative* Identität einer Person von größerem Interesse.[5]

Im *numerischen* Sinn verstanden, kann man seine Identität weder erwerben noch verlieren (höchstens mit dem Tode), man kann sie nicht verändern, und man kann auch nicht in eine Identitäts*krise* kommen. All diese Möglichkeiten bestehen jedoch, wenn man den qualitativen Sinn von "Identität" zugrunde legt. So spricht man z.B. davon, daß ein Jugendlicher seine Identität noch nicht gefunden hat. Hat er sie dann einmal gewonnen, muß er diese Identität aber nicht sein ganzes Leben lang behalten; er kann sie wieder verlieren, und ebenso kann es sein, daß er zu einem späteren Zeitpunkt eine andere Identität besitzt.

Es scheint auch möglich zu sein, eine andere Identität bloß *anzunehmen*, wie es manche gefährdete Zeugen nach ihrer Aussage vor Gericht tun. Wer eine andere Identität annimmt, wählt sich einen neuen Namen, sucht sich einen anderen Beruf, verändert sein Äußeres und erfindet vielleicht einen neuen Lebenslauf. Dies sind alles Merkmale, die man gängigerweise im Alltag verwendet, um die numerische Identität einer Person festzustellen. Wer eine neue Identität nur *annimmt*, ändert deshalb aber noch lange nicht seine Einstellungen, seine Vorlieben und Interessen, seinen Geschmack und seinen Charakter. Was er verändert, sind *extra*-mentale Merkmale, während die *mentalen* Merkmale dadurch nicht direkt berührt werden.

Meiner Auffassung nach sind es aber gerade die mentalen Merkmale, die bei der Bestimmung der qualitativen Identität einer Person eine entscheidende Rolle spielen:

---

[4] Zur Terminologie vgl. Tugendhat, *Selbstbewußtsein und Selbstbestimmung*, Suhrkamp, Frankfurt/M. 1979, S.234 und 284.
[5] Dasselbe gilt auch für die Psychologie.

Das, was man einer Person zuschreibt, wenn man von ihrer qualitativen Identität spricht, ist nichts anderes als ein bestimmtes Bündel von Einstellungen, insbesondere von Meinungen, Wünschen und Wertungen. Nun hängt die Identität einer Person natürlich nicht von *allen* ihren Einstellungen ab, sondern nur von einer noch näher zu spezifizierenden Teilmenge dieser Einstellungen. Der Frage, welche Einstellungen eine Rolle spielen, werde ich im nächsten Abschnitt nachgehen. Soviel sei an dieser Stelle jedoch schon gesagt: Ich halte es für unmöglich, eine sowohl eindeutige als auch generelle inhaltliche Charakterisierung des relevanten Einstellungsbündels anzugeben; ich bin aber auch der Meinung, daß es sich dabei keineswegs um eine beklagenswerte Unzulänglichkeit handelt.

In Taylors Werk ist weder die Unterscheidung zwischen numerischer und qualitativer Identität zu finden noch die von mir gerade vorgeschlagene Bestimmung dessen, was unter qualitativer Identität zu verstehen ist. Daher werde ich im folgenden zunächst kurz zeigen, daß mein Verständnis von personaler Identität im qualitativen Sinne auch als Interpretation von Taylors Ansicht zu vertreten ist, und in einem zweiten Schritt von einer Taylor-Interpretation unabhängige Gründe für die Gültigkeit meiner These anführen.

Das zentrale Merkmal der Identität, auf das Taylor in seinen Schriften an zahlreichen Stellen verweist, besteht darin, daß die Identität der jeweiligen Person Orientierung bietet,[6] und zwar eine Orientierung, die ihr von Fall zu Fall zu entscheiden gestattet, was gut oder wertvoll ist, was sie tun oder lassen sollte, was sie billigt oder ablehnt (QS, S.55). Ich würde sagen: Alles das gestatten mir meine Einstellungen, d.h. meine Meinungen, Wünsche und Wertungen.

In Taylors Essay *Multikulturalismus und die Politik der Anerkennung* gibt es jedoch eine Stelle, die zumindest auf den ersten Blick mit meiner These in bezug auf Identität unvereinbar zu sein scheint. Dort heißt es: "Was verstehen wir eigentlich unter *Identität*? Wir verstehen darunter, wer wir sind, 'woher wir kommen'. So bildet sie den Rahmen, in dem unsere Vorlieben, Wünsche, Meinungen und Strebungen Sinn bekommen."[7] Ich würde sagen: Woher ich *komme*, ist u.a. in meinen Erinnerungen und Überzeugungen festgehalten und nur in*so*weit Teil meiner qualitativen Identität. Wenn ich mich z.B. an ein bestimmtes Ereignis nicht mehr erinnere, so ist dieses Ereignis nur insofern für meine Identität relevant, als es möglicherweise anderen zu verstehen hilft,

---

6 Cf. Ch. Taylor, *Sources of the Self*, Cambridge University Press, Cambridge 1989, S.27, 28, 34, 63 (dt. Ch. Taylor, *Quellen des Selbst* (QS), Suhrkamp, Frankfurt/M. 1994), ders., *The Ethics of Authenticity*, Harvard University Press, Cambridge, Mass., 1991, S.34 (dt. Ch. Taylor, *Das Unbehagen an der Moderne* (UM), Suhrkamp, Frankfurt/M. 1995) und ders., *Multiculturalism and "The Politics of Recognition"*, ed. by A. Gutmann, Princeton University Press, Princeton, New Jersey, 1992, S.33f (dt. Ch. Taylor, *Multikulturalismus und die Politik der Anerkennung* (MPA), hrg. von A. Gutmann, Fischer, Frankfurt/M. 1993).
7 MPA, S.23; meine Übersetzung.

warum ich so geworden bin. Und wer ich *bin*, ergibt sich aus der noch näher zu bestimmenden Teilklasse meiner Einstellungen. Hier könnte Taylor allerdings einwenden, ich könne mich doch in Hinblick darauf, wer ich sei, täuschen, z.B. in bezug auf die Wertschätzung, die ich bei anderen Menschen genieße. Wird nicht 'wer wir sind' zumindest *mit*bestimmt durch das Bild, das Dritte von uns haben? Ja, das ist in einer Hinsicht richtig, wenn nämlich in Frage steht, wer wir in den Augen der anderen sind. Taylor geht es aber stets um das *Selbst*verständnis (cf. QS, S.67). Meine Identität, so behauptet Taylor zu Recht, beeinflußt mein Handeln, und zwar insofern, als mein Handeln durch das Bild bestimmt wird, das *ich* von mir, von meiner Identität habe. Auch wenn ich das Ansehen, das ich in den Augen anderer besitze, nicht richtig einschätze, so ist dann doch diese *falsche* Überzeugung Bestandteil meines Selbstbildes und hat dadurch einen Einfluß auf mein Handeln.[8]

Daß die Identität einer Person als maßgebliches Erklärungsmoment für das Handeln dieser Person aufgefaßt wird, ist im übrigen auch als indirekte Unterstützung für meine These anzusehen, wonach die qualitative Identität einer Person in nichts anderem als in einer bestimmten Menge von Einstellungen, d.h. von Wünschen, Wertungen und Überzeugungen besteht. In der philosophischen Handlungstheorie hat es sich nämlich etabliert, genau diese mentalen Merkmale einer Person, ihre 'beliefs' und 'pro-attitudes', für die Erklärung ihrer Handlungen heranzuziehen.[9]

Nun heißt es an der gerade zitierten Stelle aber weiter: "So bildet sie [sc. die Identität] den Rahmen, in dem unsere Vorlieben, Wünsche, Meinungen und Strebungen Sinn bekommen." Das klingt wirklich so, als sei meine Identität etwas ganz anderes als meine Einstellungen, denn meine Vorlieben, Wünsche, Meinungen und Strebungen sollen doch nur vor dem Hintergrund meiner Identität einen Sinn haben. Die Kompatibilität von Taylors Behauptung mit meiner These, qualitative Identität sei nichts anderes als eine Menge von Einstellungen, könnte man allerdings zunächst durch den Hinweis darauf plausibel machen, daß ja nicht *alle* meine Einstellungen Bestandteile meiner Identität sind. Dann ist Taylor so zu verstehen, daß die nicht zu meiner Identität gehörenden Wünsche, Vorlieben usw. ihren Sinn erst vor dem Hintergrund oder im Kontext der zu meiner Identität gehörenden Einstellungen bekommen. Das halte ich für richtig. Ich würde allerdings noch weiter gehen und vertreten, daß Taylor hier (vielleicht ohne es zu wissen) gar nichts behauptet, was speziell für die Identität der Person gilt, sondern etwas, das ganz

---

8 Mein Handeln wird zwar durch mein Selbstbild bestimmt (sei es richtig oder falsch), aber nicht ausschließlich: Wenn ich beispielsweise eine falsche Meinung in bezug auf meine tatsächlichen Wünsche habe, wird mein Handeln einerseits durch diese (falsche) Meinung über meine Wünsche, andererseits aber auch durch meine *tatsächlichen* Wünsche beeinflußt.
9 Cf. z.B. D. Davidson, Actions, Reasons, and Causes, in: ders. *Essays on Actions and Events*, Clarendon Press, Oxford repr. with corr. 1982, S.3-19.

generell auf *alle* meine Einstellungen zutrifft. Davidson drückt das so aus: "propositional attitudes [...] come only as a matched set",[10] "we make sense of particular beliefs only as they cohere with other beliefs, with preferences, with intentions, hopes, fears, expectations, and the rest."[11] Auch das halte ich für richtig.

2. Die inhaltliche Bestimmung personaler Identität

Die qualitative Identität einer Person besteht, so hatte ich behauptet, aus einer Teilmenge der Einstellungen der betreffenden Person. Doch wie läßt sich diese Teilmenge genauer charakterisieren? Einer Antwort kommt man näher, wenn man untersucht, wie eine Person zu beschreiben ist, die ihre Identität *verloren* hat oder sich gerade in einer Identitäts*krise* befindet. Man sagt von jemandem, er habe seine Identität verloren oder er befinde sich in einer Identitätskrise, wenn sein Leben z.B. ganz unerwartet einen anderen, schrecklichen Verlauf genommen hat, oder wenn er feststellt, daß er eine für ihn völlig untypische Handlung ausgeführt hat. Er weiß dann nicht, wie er sich selbst einschätzen, wie er sich weiterhin verhalten und welche Entscheidungen er treffen soll. Natürlich muß man hier genauer spezifizieren: Man denke z.B an jemanden, der sich im Restaurant nicht entscheiden kann, welches Menue er bestellen soll. Solche Trivialitäten sind klarerweise nicht gemeint; es muß sich um etwas Wichtiges handeln. Und es spielt auch eine Rolle, in welcher Hinsicht die Handlung oder Entscheidung wichtig ist: Wenn ich vor der Wahl stehe, ein Haus zu kaufen, oder wenn ich nicht recht weiß, welchen Titel ich für meinen Aufsatz wählen soll, befinde ich mich zum Glück noch längst nicht in einer Identitätskrise!

Darin befände ich mich eher, wenn ich nicht wüßte, was für mich bedeutungsvoll ist, wenn ich kein Ziel hätte, auf das hin ich mein Leben ausrichten wollte oder könnte, oder wenn mir die Maßstäbe für das verlorengegangen wären, was aus moralischen Gründen ge- oder verboten ist.[12]

In seinem Buch *Quellen des Selbst* schreibt Taylor: "[U]nsere im Sinne der jeweils grundlegenden Orientierung definierte Identität [sc. ist] im Grunde komplex und vielschichtig [...]. Wir alle bewegen uns innerhalb eines Rahmens, der aus nach unserer Anschauung allgemeingültigen Bindungen besteht [als Beispiele gibt Taylor hier an, Katholik oder Anarchist zu sein] [...] sowie aus nach unserem Verständnis partikularen Identifikationen (nämlich daß man [z.B.] Armenier ist oder Quebecer). Oft stellen wir es so hin, als wäre unsere Identität durch nur eines dieser Elemente definiert, weil es in unse-

---

[10] D. Davidson, Rational Animals, S.318, in: *Dialectica* 32, 1982, S.317-323.
[11] D. Davidson, Mental Events, S.221, in: ders. *Essays on Actions and Events*, Clarendon Press, Oxford 1980, repr. with corr. 1982, S.207-225.
[12] Es muß für mich allerdings *wichtig* sein, diese Orientierung zu haben.

rem Leben ausschlaggebend oder gerade in Frage gestellt worden ist." (QS, S.58) Versteht man Identität in dem von mir charakterisierten qualitativen Sinn, hat Taylor meiner Ansicht nach in mehrfacher Hinsicht recht: Das, was uns in unserem Leben Orientierung gibt, ist wirklich komplex und vielschichtig. Manches betrifft unser Leben als ganzes, anderes nur Teilbereiche, und wir neigen in der Tat leicht dazu, uns vor allem an *einem* Aspekt zu orientieren.

Taylor behauptet, es gebe eine wesentliche Verbindung zwischen Identität und moralischer Orientierung (cf. QS, S.56): Erst, wenn man weiß, welche Orientierung man in bezug auf das Gute hat, wo man relativ zu diesem Guten steht und in welche Richtung sich das eigene Leben entwickelt, hat man seine Identität bestimmt. "Wissen, wer man ist", schreibt er an anderer Stelle, "heißt, daß man sich *im moralischen Raum* auskennt, in einem Raum, in dem sich Fragen stellen mit Bezug auf das, was gut ist oder schlecht, was sich zu tun lohnt und was nicht, was für den Betreffenden Sinn und Wichtigkeit hat und was ihm trivial und nebensächlich vorkommt."[13] Wie unsere moralische Orientierung laut Taylor gelingt, läßt sich in Anlehnung an seine Metapher vom 'moralischen Raum' gut beschreiben: Man stelle sich eine Art Netz vor, dessen Knoten die verschiedenen moralischen Güter sind. Diese Knoten (und damit die Güter) sind mit elastischen 'Seilen' verknüpft, so daß die Distanz der Knoten variabel ist. Der Knoten oder die Knoten, an denen das Netz aufgehängt ist, entsprechen sogenannten Hypergütern, die für die anderen Güter eine Ordnungsfunktion erfüllen und deren relative Position zueinander und damit auch deren relative Wichtigkeit festlegen. Wenn man sich vergegenwärtigt, daß für Taylor als Hypergüter z.B. Gerechtigkeit, der Wert des Familienlebens oder das Verhältnis zu Gott in Frage kommen (QS, S.122f), dann wird plausibel, daß die Bedeutung *anderer* Güter, also ihre Position innerhalb des moralischen Netzes einer Person, stets vom jeweiligen Hypergut dieser Person abhängig ist. Außerdem wird verständlich, daß sich die Identität einer Person (verstanden als ihre *moralische* Orientierung) am ehesten mit Hilfe ihrer Orientierung an einem solchen Hypergut bestimmen lassen soll.

Taylor behauptet nun, man habe es zumindest in unserer Kultur immer mit ein und demselben Netz zu tun und brauche sich nur darüber zu 'streiten', wie es am besten zu drapieren sei. Ein Vergleich der moralischen Netze verschiedener Personen würde demnach also immer dieselben Güter zutage fördern. Von dem jeweiligen Hypergut ist jedoch abhängig, ob und, wenn ja, inwiefern die einzelnen Güter verdeckt bzw. überlagert sind und so möglicherweise der Aufmerksamkeit der betreffenden Person entgehen. Erst das richtig entfaltete moralische Netz, das den Blick auf die ganze Reichhaltigkeit von Gütern freigibt, gestattet aber, wie Taylor glaubt, die beste moralische Orientierung und

---

[13] QS, S.56; meine Hervorhebung.

ermöglicht dadurch auch das beste und erfüllteste Leben.

"Wissen, wer man ist", so hatte ich Taylor zitiert, "heißt, daß man sich *im moralischen Raum* auskennt [...]".[14] Doch das greift zu kurz: Wenn es wirklich um das geht, "was sich zu tun lohnt und was nicht, was für den Betreffenden Sinn und Wichtigkeit hat und was ihm trivial und nebensächlich vorkommt" (QS, S.56), dann gehört dazu manchmal mehr und manchmal anderes, als sich im *moralischen* Raum auszukennen. Die Identität von Heinrich Schliemann z.B. scheint uns nachdrücklich durch seine Suche nach Troja geprägt zu sein; er hat sein Leben danach ausgerichtet, doch war das eine Orientierung am *Guten*? Hier ist es plausibler, nicht der moralischen Orientierung, sondern einem außermoralischen *Ideal* die identitätsbestimmende Kraft zuzusprechen.[15] Oder denken wir an Extremfälle, z.B. an das von Alexandre Dumas geschilderte Leben des Grafen von Monte Christo, der alles daran setzte, sich für erlittenes Unrecht zu rächen. Auch in solchen Fällen scheint es mir sinnvoll, die Planung und Gestaltung des Lebens der betreffenden Person im Rekurs auf ihre Identität zu erklären. Doch es wäre in aller Regel abwegig, hier von der Orientierung an einem Ideal oder gar von einer *moralischen* Orientierung zu sprechen. In solchen Fällen ist sicher nur der Ausdruck "Ziel" angemessen.

Als Bestandteile des Bündels mentaler Zustände, das die qualitative Identität einer Person ausmacht, kann man also zunächst einmal ihre Moralprinzipien, ihre Ideale und/ oder Ziele identifizieren. Hinzu kommen sicher diejenigen Wünsche, welche die langfristige Planung und Ausgestaltung des eigenen Lebens betreffen, und solche Meinungen, die z.B. bei Wahlprognosen als "längerfristige Grundüberzeugungen" bezeichnet werden.[16]

Diese Charakterisierung der qualitativen Identität einer Person ist allerdings noch nicht hinreichend: Wer wissen möchte, was für ein Mensch jemand ist, wer die Handlungen und das Verhalten einer Person erklären oder verstehen möchte, darf nicht nur ihre Meinungen, Wertungen und Wünsche zu Rate ziehen, sondern muß auch ihre Vorlieben, Aversionen, Phobien etc. berücksichtigen. Es gehört nämlich beispielsweise auch zur qualitativen Identität einer Person, wenn sie regelmäßig unter heftigen Angstzuständen leidet.

Um einer Person zu Recht eine qualitative Identität zuschreiben zu können, muß das mittlerweile näher spezifizierte mentale Bündel in einem gewissen Maße beständig sein.

---

[14] QS, S.56; meine Hervorhebung.
[15] Cf. H. G. Frankfurt, Über die Notwendigkeit von Idealen, in: W. Edelstein, G. Nunner-Winkler & G. Noam (Hrg.), *Moral und Person*, Suhrkamp, Frankfurt/M. 1993, S.107-118.
[16] Solche Ideale und Wünsche zu besitzen, kann man sogar als Zeichen von und Bedingung für Personsein ansehen. Vgl. H. Frankfurt, Die Notwendigkeit von Idealen, S.114f, in: W. Edelstein, G. Nunner-Winkler & G. Noam (Hrg.), *Moral und Person*, Suhrkamp, Frankfurt/M. 1993, S.107-118.

Man stelle sich nur jemanden vor, der, wann immer er mit Autoritätspersonen zusammen ist, in jeder Hinsicht *deren* Meinung vertritt, und zwar nicht etwa nach dem Motto "wes Brot ich eß', des Lied ich sing", sondern weil er sich in dem jeweiligen Moment des Einflusses nicht erwehren kann. Er ist dann *wirklich* von dem überzeugt, was er behauptet. Er wechselt seine Meinungen und Wertungen also laufend. Objektiv gesehen, ist ein solcher Mensch extrem wankelmütig; *insoweit* können wir natürlich wissen, was für ein Mensch er ist. In einem anderen, interessanteren Sinne wissen wir dies allerdings nicht, denn wir wissen nicht, wofür er steht: Ihm fehlt nämlich insofern eine Identität, als er über keine Orientierung verfügt, an der er sein Handeln und Entscheiden ausrichtet.[17]

Auch wenn man, wie ich gerade zu zeigen versucht habe, die für die eigene Identität erforderliche Orientierung zumindest nicht vornehmlich oder gar ausschließlich als moralische Orientierung bezeichnen sollte: Kann man Fragen nach dem guten Leben trennen von Fragen nach dem moralisch Guten?[18] Nicht jede Änderung meiner Identität hat Konsequenzen für meine Orientierung auf das moralisch Gute, doch wohl jede Änderung meiner Orientierung auf das moralisch Gute hat Auswirkungen auf meine Identität.[19]

Wie entwickelt sich unsere Identität? So, wie Kleist von der allmählichen Verfertigung der *Gedanken* beim Reden spricht, behauptet Taylor, die *personale Identität* entwickele sich im Dialog mit anderen und mit Hilfe von Artikulation. Aufgabe der Artikulation sei es, uns insbesondere unsere moralischen Intuitionen bewußt zu machen, ja mehr noch: Artikulationen seien Versuche, etwas zu formulieren, das anfangs unentwickelt, konfus oder schlecht formuliert ist. Etwas zu artikulieren oder ihm eine bestimmte Artikulation zu verleihen, bedeute, unser Verständnis von dem zu formen, was wir wünschen oder was wir in einer bestimmten Weise für wichtig halten.[20]

---

[17] Wie die gerade angestellte Überlegung zeigt, müssen die zur qualitativen Identität gehörigen Grundüberzeugungen oder Ziele über eine gewisse Zeit stabil sein. Für manche Bestandteile der qualitativen Identität genügt aber eine andere Art von Beständigkeit: Angstzustände beispielsweise gehören nämlich nicht erst dann zur Identität einer Person, wenn diese jahrelang *ununterbrochen* unter ihnen leidet; es genügt, wenn sie über einen längeren Zeitraum *immer wieder* unter ihnen leidet.
[18] Taylor glaubt, das sei unmöglich. Cf. Ch. Taylor, Comments and Replies, S.244, in: *Inquiry 34*, 1991, S.237-254.
[19] Cf. E. Tugendhat, Korreferat zu Charles Taylor: "What is Human Agency?", S.445f, in: ders., *Philosophische Aufsätze*, Suhrkamp, Frankfurt/M. 1992, S.441-452.
[20] "[A]rticulations are attempts to formulate what is initially inchoate, or confused, or badly formulated. [...] To give a certain articulation is to shape our sense of what we desire or what we hold important in a certain way." (Ch. Taylor, What Is Human Agency?, S.36, in: ders., *Human Agency and Language. Philosophical Papers*, Vol.1, Cambridge University Press, Cambridge 1985, S.15-44. – Sprache hat für Taylor eine dreifache Aufgabe: "making articulations, and hence bringing about explicit awareness; putting things in public space, thereby constituting public space; and making the discriminations which are foundational to human concerns, and hence opening us to these concerns." (Ch. Taylor,

Wenn man sich einmal klar gemacht hat, daß die personale Identität in etwas Mentalem, nämlich in den wesentlichen Überzeugungen und Wertungen der betreffenden Person besteht, dann ist die Frage nach der Genese und dem Wandel dieser Identität eine Frage danach, wie bestimmte *Einstellungen* entstehen und sich ändern. Darüber gibt es insbesondere innerhalb der Sozialpsychologie eine Fülle von Theorien, denen meines Wissens eines gemeinsam ist: Keine von ihnen leugnet und viele von ihnen betonen die von Taylor nachdrücklich hervorgehobene Bedeutung anderer Menschen oder der Sprache.

Weder verfügt man also immer schon über eine Identität noch gewinnt man sie durch schlichte Rückbesinnung auf sich selbst. Sie ist vielmehr etwas, das wir in Auseinandersetzung mit uns selbst *und anderen* entdecken, entwickeln und erwerben, wobei wir auf die (gleichberechtigte) Anerkennung der anderen angewiesen sind (vgl. MPA, S.34f). Und sowohl der Erwerb als auch die Veränderung der eigenen Identität erfolgt in der Regel im Verlauf eines längeren und mehr oder weniger langsamen Prozesses. Manche Ereignisse, sogenannte Schlüsselerlebnisse, bewirken allerdings, daß sich die eigene Wertorientierung innerhalb ganz kurzer Zeit, wenn nicht gar von einer Minute auf die andere radikal ändert. Das vielleicht berühmteste Beispiel für ein solches Schlüsselerlebnis ist die Episode, die sich vor knapp 2000 Jahren vor den Toren von Damaskus abgespielt haben soll, nämlich des Saulus' wunderbare Verwandlung zu Paulus.[21]

Bis jetzt läßt sich zusammenfassend folgendes festhalten: Die qualitative Identität einer Person entsteht im dialogischen Umgang und in der Auseinandersetzung mit anderen. Ein entscheidendes Element ist dabei die identitätsbildende (sprachliche) Artikulation. *Welche* Einstellungen für die Identität relevant sind, läßt sich nur insofern charakterisieren, als es sich bei ihnen um Einstellungen handeln muß, die für die Lebensausrichtung oder die Lebensplanung der betreffenden Person von Wichtigkeit sind. Ob dazu im konkreten Fall moralische Wertungen, Ideale oder nur nicht weiter charakterisierbare Ziele gehören, ist jedoch völlig offen und nicht generell angebbar.

Taylor behauptet, es sei eine "Grundbedingung des Selbstverstehens [...], daß wir das eigene Leben im Sinne einer *narrativen Darstellung* begreifen müssen" (QS, S.94), und ist so – wie Dilthey – der Meinung, daß "Selbstbiographien [...] der direkteste Aus-

---

Theories of Meaning, S.263, in: ders., *Human Agency and Language. Philosophical Papers*, Vol.1, Cambridge University Press, Cambridge 1985, S.248-292)
[21] Die Konversion des Saulus von einem Verfolger der Christen zu einem ihrer überzeugtesten Anhänger ist übrigens kein Gegenbeispiel zu Taylors entscheidender These über die Entstehung von Identität. In der Apostelgeschichte wird nämlich berichtet, daß Saulus "zu Boden [stürzte] und hörte, wie eine Stimme zu ihm sagte: Saul, Saul, warum verfolgst Du mich?" (Apg 9, 4) Der Überlieferung zufolge hat Saulus auch geantwortet, so daß das für Taylor unverzichtbare dialogische Moment der Identitätsbildung sogar in diesem Beispiel erkennbar ist.

druck der Besinnung über das [sc. eigene] Leben"[22] sind. Damit greift er einen Topos auf, der in der Philosophie der Geschichte seit Mitte der sechziger Jahre große Bedeutung erlangt hat.[23] Eine narrative Darstellung ist von einer rein chronologischen insofern verschieden, als es sich bei ihr (kurz gesagt) um eine retrospektive Beschreibung handelt, die zu der Zeit, als das zu beschreibende Ereignis stattfand, in dieser Form nicht hätte gegeben werden können.[24] So hätte man z.B. im Sommer 1914 über das Attentat auf den Erzherzog Ferdinand nicht mit den Worten berichten können: "Mit seinem Schuß auf den Erzherzog löste Gavrilo Princip den Ersten Weltkrieg aus."[25] In der Philosophie der Geschichte zieht die Forderung einer narrativen Darstellung die These von der prinzipiellen Unabgeschlossenheit der Geschichtsschreibung nach sich; dasselbe gilt *mutatis mutandis* für die narrative Darstellung eines Lebens. Stets sind zeitlich früher liegende Ereignisse im Lichte späterer Ereignisse und Erkenntnisse zu beschreiben, und der Autor einer narrativen Selbstdarstellung hat sowohl die Möglichkeit, einzelne Ereignisse seines Lebens hervorzuheben, als auch andere im Interesse der zu erzählenden Geschichte unerwähnt zu lassen.

Stellen wir uns vor, Herr A überfährt mit dem Auto seinen ärgsten Feind. War es ein Unfall? Konnte Herr A sich endlich rächen? Ist er seinen moralischen Standards untreu geworden? Von der Interpretation, die A *selbst* für sein Verhalten wählt, hängt maßgeblich ab, wie er sein bisheriges Leben beurteilt: ob z.B. als erfolgreich oder als letztlich verfehlt. Diese Beurteilung scheint mir genau das zu sein, was Taylor meint, wenn er von der Position eines Menschen in bezug auf das Gute spricht, also davon, wie A sich selbst in Hinblick auf das von ihm als Gut Anerkannte verortet.

Von *Handlungen* wissen wir, daß sie stets nur unter bestimmten Beschreibungen als *absichtlich* angesehen werden können. So mag es in dem gerade angeführten Beispiel

[22] W. Dilthey, *Der Aufbau der Geschichtlichen Welt in den Geisteswissenschaften*, Gesammelte Werke Bd. VII, Teubner, Stuttgart, und Vandenhoeck & Ruprecht, Göttingen, 41965, S.198. Vgl. auch: "Die Selbstbiographie ist nur die zu schriftstellerischem Ausdruck gebrachte Selbstbesinnung des Menschen über seinen Lebensverlauf." (a.a.O., S.200)
[23] Vgl. A. C. Danto, *Analytical Philosophy of History*, Cambridge University Press, Cambridge 1965, W. B. Gallie, *Philosophy and Historical Understanding*, Chatto and Windus, London 1964, und M. White, *Foundations of Historical Knowledge*, Harper & Row, New York 1965.
[24] Bei den Beschreibungen, die man im Rahmen einer narrativen Darstellung seines Lebens wählt, muß es sich um sogenannte dichte Beschreibungen im Sinne Ryles handeln. (Vgl. G. Ryle, *Collected Papers*, Vol.2, Thoemmes, Bristol 1990, S.474ff und S.482; vgl. dazu aber auch C. Geertz, *The Interpretation of Cultures*, Basic Books, New York 1973, Kap. 1.)
[25] Besonders plastisch wird der Unterschied, wenn man eine Life-Reportage eines Sportereignisses mit der zusammenfassenden Berichterstattung über dasselbe Ereignis vergleicht: "... der Ball kommt von links auf Ballack, der läßt ihn fallen; sein Gegenspieler nimmt ihm den Ball ab und gibt ihn weiter an..." und "... als der Ball von links auf Ballack kam, hatte dieser seine schwächste Phase; sein Bewacher dagegen hatte leichtes Spiel ...".

sein, daß Herr A nur rückwärts fahren wollte, aber nicht beabsichtigte, irgendjemanden zu überfahren. Unter einer Beschreibung ("rückwärts fahren") war sein Handeln absichtlich, unter einer anderen ("jemanden überfahren") jedoch nicht. Ganz analog kann man sagen: Wer sein früheres Verhalten im Rahmen seiner narrativen Lebensbeschreibung interpretierend darstellt, gibt an, unter welcher Beschreibung er sein Handeln als *sinnvoll* versteht.

Kann man das Konzept "unter einer Beschreibung" gar auf ein ganzes Leben übertragen? Kann man vielleicht sagen, ein Leben sei auf *eine* Weise erzählt, sinnvoll oder geglückt, auf eine *andere* Weise erzählt, aber womöglich gar gescheitert?[26] Ebenso wie eine Handlung nicht unter jeder Beschreibung absichtlich ist, ist ein Leben nicht gemäß jeder narrativen Darstellung sinnvoll. Doch für Handlungen gilt auch: Jede Handlung *ist* unter mindestens einer Beschreibung absichtlich. Sollte auch jedes Leben im Lichte mindestens einer narrativen Darstellung sinnvoll sein? Eine so starke *ontologische* These würde Taylor meines Erachtens nicht vertreten.[27] Taylor macht drei Grundannahmen: (1) jeder Mensch braucht eine und sucht seine Identität; (2) man findet seine Identität, indem man seinen Standort relativ in bezug auf das Gute bestimmt; und (3) ein Abweichen vom 'rechten Weg' käme für den Einzelnen einer Katastrophe gleich (cf. QS, S.123). Diese Annahmen machen es plausibel, Taylor die folgende *anthropologische* These zuzuschreiben: Jeder Mensch strebt danach, sein Leben, wenn er es narrativ darstellt, als *sinnvoll* darzustellen.[28]

Wenn man berücksichtigt, daß Menschen den Wunsch nach einem sinnvollen und erfüllten Leben haben, birgt die Notwendigkeit, immer wieder aufs neue eine narrative Darstellung der eigenen Lebensgeschichte zu geben, um sich dadurch seiner Identität bewußt zu werden, eine Gefahr in sich: Es ist nämlich leicht möglich, einer ex post Rationalisierung zu erliegen und so Schönfärberei zu betreiben. Mit Blick auf ein und dieselbe Kette von Ereignissen eines Lebens lassen sich stets unterschiedliche und gleichwohl

---

[26] Cf.: "It is really a problem about the interpretation of the familiar role-reversal argument in ethics: 'How would you like it if somebody did that to you?' The answer that has to be dealt with is 'How would I like it if somebody did *what* to me?' There is often more than one way of describing a proposed course of action, and much depends on which description is regarded as relevant for the purpose of moral argument." (Th. Nagel, Moral Conflict and Political Legitimacy, S.225, in: *Philosophy & Public Affairs 16*, 1987, S.215-240; cf. auch ebd., S.226.

[27] Vgl. dagegen Dilthey: "*Jedes Leben hat einen eigenen Sinn.* Er liegt in einem Bedeutungszusammenhang, in welchem jede erinnerbare Gegenwart einen Eigenwert besitzt, doch zugleich im Zusammenhang der Erinnerung eine Beziehung zu einem Sinn des Ganzen hat. Dieser Sinn des individuellen Daseins ist ganz singulär [...]." (Dilthey, a.a.O., S.199; meine Hervorhebung)

[28] Vgl. "Die spezielle Identität einer Person besteht [...] in dem Aufbau bzw. der Konstruktion der sinnhaften Ordnung einer jeweiligen Lebensgeschichte." (N. Meuter, *Narrative Identität*, M & P, Stuttgart 1995, S.32; vgl. auch S.28.)

kohärente Geschichten erzählen. So haben z.B. am Ende der vierziger und auch während der letzten Jahre viele Deutsche ihre Lebensgeschichte ganz anders erzählt als noch einige Jahre zuvor. Es gibt aber nicht nur zwanglose und ungehinderte Weiterentwicklungen in Richtung auf ein einmal gewähltes Ziel. Das Leben der meisten Menschen beinhaltet auch Elemente des Scheiterns und der mehr oder weniger radikalen Umorientierung. Derartige Brüche sind selbst durch noch so schöne Neubeschreibungen nicht zu kitten. Nicht immer kann, wie Taylor zu glauben scheint, die Zukunft die Vergangenheit 'erlösen' und aus einem Leben ein bedeutungsvolles Ganzes machen (QS, S.100f). Was fehlt, ist ein Kriterium für die Angemessenheit oder Objektivität einer narrativen Darstellung.[29]

Insofern, als in den Handlungen einer Person deren bedeutsame Überzeugungen, Wünsche und Wertungen zum Ausdruck kommen, kann man die narrative Darstellung eines Lebens als indirekten Bericht über Art, Konstanz und gegebenenfalls auch Veränderung der wichtigen Überzeugungen, Wünsche und Wertungen der betreffenden Person auffassen. Von diesen *Einstellungen* gilt aber zu jedem Zeitpunkt: man hat sie, oder man hat sie nicht; daher gibt es hier insofern kein Problem der Objektivität. Man darf jedoch nicht übersehen, daß es hier ein *Erkenntnis*problem gibt: Wie läßt sich herausfinden, welche relevanten Einstellungen und damit welche (im qualitativen Sinne) personale Identität wir zu einem bestimmten Zeitpunkt haben oder hatten? Wäre dies nur auf dem Weg einer narrativen Darstellung unseres Lebens möglich, gäbe es keine Kontrolle dafür, ob wir über ein zutreffendes Selbstbild oder Selbstverständnis verfügen.

3. Das Ideal der Authentizität

In seinem Buch *The Ethics of Authenticity*, das auf deutsch unter dem Titel *Das Unbehagen an der Moderne* erschienen ist, beklagt Taylor mit Blick auf den Liberalismus die "Ausbreitung einer Einstellung, die die Selbstverwirklichung oder Selbsterfüllung als wichtigsten Wert im Leben hinstellt" (UM, S.65). Die Rede von Selbstverwirklichung hat – und darauf weist Taylor selber hin – starke Ähnlichkeit mit der These, daß es "eine bestimmte Weise, Mensch zu sein, [gibt], die *meine* Weise ist [...] [und ich] dazu aufgefordert [bin], mein Leben in ebendieser Weise zu führen, ohne das Leben irgendeiner anderen Person nachzuahmen" (UM, S.38). Diese Idee[30] hält Taylor für ein einflußreiches moralisches Ideal, nämlich für das Ideal der Authentizität. Jeder Mensch sollte danach stre-

---

[29] Vgl. D. Carr, *Time, Narrative, and History*, Indiana University Press, Bloomington/Indianapolis 1986, S.91: "The question [...] is not: 'How does this or that event or action fit into the story?' but rather: 'What *is* the story?'"
[30] Sie soll auf Herder zurückgehen; cf. Herder, *Ideen*, 8. Buch, 1, in: ders., *Sämtliche Werke*, hg. von B. Suphan, Bd.13, S.291: "Jeder Mensch hat ein eigenes Maß, gleichsam eine eigne Stimmung aller seiner sinnlichen Gefühle zu einander."

ben, dieses Ideal zu erfüllen, da nur so ein gutes Leben erreichbar sei. Mit Bezug auf die weit verbreitete *Praxis* der Selbstverwirklichung spricht Taylor dagegen von Egoismus und von einer "Kultur des Narzißmus". Die *Bedeutung des Begriffs* der Authentizität ist unstrittig: Gemeint ist damit "Treue zu sich selbst". Strittig ist jedoch das *intentionale Objekt* der Treue: was genau es denn ist, worauf die Treue sich richten soll. Authentizität als Ideal fordert, der eigenen Identität die Treue zu halten. Und das von Taylor bedauerte "Abgleiten in den Subjektivismus" (UM, S.65) läßt sich – wie sich gleich zeigen wird – gut unter Rekurs auf den oben entwickelten Begriff der qualitativen Identität beschreiben.

Wenn ich meiner Identität treu bleiben soll, dann heißt das, daß ich meinen für die eigene Lebensorientierung bedeutsamen Meinungen, Wünschen und Wertungen treu bleiben soll. "Treu bleiben" kann hier nur bedeuten, daß ich mich nach ihnen richte. Und dieses Sich-nach-ihnen-Richten betrifft zwei Bereiche: zum einen mein Handeln, zum anderen aber auch mein Urteilen. Wenn ich *urteile*, sollte ich das – wo erforderlich – im Lichte meiner mir wichtigen Meinungen, Wünsche und Werte tun, und diese Einstellungen sollten es auch sein, an denen ich mein *Handeln* ausrichte.

Die Charakterisierung des Ideals der Authentizität als ein Sich-nach-eigenen-Einstellungen-Richten ist in einer Hinsicht von dem *Gehalt* dieser Einstellungen unabhängig.[31] Obwohl es sich um *meine* Meinungen, Wünsche und Wertungen handelt, brauchen sie natürlich nicht nur *mich selbst* zu betreffen, sondern können sich auch auf andere Menschen, auf die Natur oder auf Gott richten.

Das von Taylor konstatierte drohende Abgleiten in den Egoismus und 'sozialen Atomismus' (UM, S.68), bei dem ich von der gesamten Umwelt absehe und nur mich berücksichtige, ist jetzt leicht zu beschreiben: Egoismus ist es, wenn ich bei meinem Versuch, authentisch zu sein, nur einen Teil der Meinungen, Wünsche und Wertungen berücksichtige, die meine Identität ausmachen, nämlich diejenigen, deren Gehalt vornehmlich mich selbst betrifft. Diese Beschreibung deckt genau das ab, was Taylor meint, wenn er in *Das Unbehagen an der Moderne* schreibt, in gewisser Weise böten sich die moralischen Ideale dazu an, ein wenig verzerrt oder, wenn es gelegen komme, vergessen zu werden (UM, S.113), und wenn er dann behauptet, die Kultur des Narzißmus bleibe systematisch hinter dem Ideal zurück, dem gemäß sie lebe (UM, S.66).

Nun macht es aber einen Unterschied, ob jemand über Meinungen und Wertungen, die andere Menschen, die Natur oder Gott betreffen, verfügt, sie aber in seinem Handeln unberücksichtigt läßt, oder ob ihm solche Meinungen und Wertungen schlicht *fehlen*.

---

[31] Cf. Taylors Unterscheidung zwischen Form und Stoff oder Inhalt (UM, S.93f). – Natürlich besteht die Unabhängigkeit nicht in jeder Hinsicht, denn die gemäß dem Ideal der Authentizität zu berücksichtigenden Einstellungen sind doch inhaltlich als die für die Lebensorientierung bedeutsamen Einstellungen gekennzeichnet!

Taylor ist (wie ich finde: fälschlicherweise) nicht bereit, einer Person Authentizität zuzuschreiben, die sich zwar ihren für sie selbst bedeutsamen Meinungen und Wünschen entsprechend verhält, aber keine im selben Sinne bedeutsamen Einstellungen besitzt, die *auf andere* gerichtet sind. Aus diesem Grund, so scheint mir, fügt er der Bestimmung von Authentizität als Treue zu sich selbst noch einen dynamischen Aspekt hinzu und behauptet, Authentizität beinhalte auch die "Wiedergewinnung des eigenen 'Gefühls des Daseins'" (UM, S.104). Dabei ist mit der Metapher 'Gefühl des Daseins' nichts anderes gemeint als Meinungen und Wertungen, die das eigene Eingebettetsein in eine soziale Umwelt, in die Natur und in eine größere Ordnung der Dinge zum Gegenstand haben (cf. UM, S.93-104).

Hier wird deutlich, daß Taylor den dynamischen Aspekt nur aus inhaltlichen Gründen integriert. Etwas salopp formuliert, lautet *sein* Ideal der Authentizität nämlich nicht nur "Bleib Dir selbst treu", sondern unter der Hand ergänzt er "... aber sorge dafür, daß Du die *richtigen* Einstellungen hast"! So ist Authentizität für Taylor also nicht Treue zu der Identität, die man *hat*, sondern zu der Identität, die man haben *soll*.

Daß die Erläuterung des Ideals der Authentizität als Treue zu sich selbst in irgendeiner Form um einen dynamischen Aspekt ergänzt wird, erscheint auch mir wichtig, allerdings nicht aus dem Grund, der Taylor dazu motiviert. Nur mit Hilfe einer dynamischen Komponente kann man nämlich in der Beschreibung der Möglichkeit gerecht werden, sich selbst ändern zu wollen (oder auch nur zu einer Änderung bereit zu sein) und dennoch zugleich authentisch (d.h. sich selbst treu) zu sein. Sonst stände Authentizität sogar im Widerspruch zum Streben nach moralischer Vervollkommnung.

4. Das Unbehagen an der Moderne

Das Ideal der Authentizität führt zu dem letzten Aspekt von Identität, auf den ich eingehen möchte: Auch wer das Ideal in seiner recht verstandenen Ausprägung anerkennt, sich danach zu richten bemüht und sogar über eine zutreffende Selbstinterpretation verfügt, kann scheitern. Dann gerät er in eine ganz andere Art von Identitätskrise.

In diese Art von Identitätskrise kann nur geraten, wer über eine Identität *verfügt*. Es ist möglich, daß jemand weiß, welche wichtigen Wertungen und Überzeugungen er besitzt, daß er an ihnen sein Leben ausrichten möchte, daß ihm dies aber dennoch nicht gelingt. Daß jemand nicht seinen Überzeugungen und Werten entsprechend leben kann, mag an überzogenen Idealvorstellungen liegen, es kann aber auch darauf zurückzuführen sein, daß sich die soziale Umwelt oder die natürlichen Gegebenheiten gravierend geändert haben. Ein solches Schicksal wurde z.B. den nordamerikanischen Indianern zuteil und droht vielen kulturellen Minderheiten. Derartige Fälle sind keine Exempel für *intra*individuelle Identitätskrisen, sondern hier ist ein *Verhältnis* gestört, und zwar das zwischen dem Individuum und seiner Umwelt. Grundlegende Beziehungen zwischen Personen und ihrer Umwelt zu regeln, ist eine Aufgabe des Staates. So stellt sich die Frage, ob und, wenn ja, wie der Staat reagieren soll, wenn Identitätskrisen auftreten, die im Verhältnis zwischen Individuum und Umwelt begründet sind. Hier liegt der eingangs erwähnte entscheidende Dissens zwischen Liberalen und Kommunitaristen. Kommunitaristen wie Taylor plädieren für etwas, das Habermas 'administrativen Artenschutz' genannt hat.[32] Sie behaupten, es gehöre zur Aufgabe des Staates, Rahmenbedingungen zu erhalten oder gar zu schaffen, die ein 'Ausleben' der eigenen Identität ermöglichen.[33] Wenn die einzelnen Individuen ihre Identität verlören, verliere auch die staatliche Gemeinschaft ihre Identität, und daraus resultiere die Auflösung der staatlichen Gemeinschaft.

Die in dieser Argumentation anklingende Dramatik verdankt sich aber meines Erachtens nicht zuletzt der Ambiguität des Identitätsbegriffs, die ich zu Beginn des Vortrags erläutert habe. Wenn man unter "Identität" (die hier gar nicht relevante) *relationale* oder *numerische* Identität versteht, kann ein Gegenstand diese Identität nicht verlieren, ohne damit zugleich seine Existenz zu verlieren, und das ist natürlich dramatisch. Versteht man unter "Identität" jedoch – wie man sollte – *qualitative* Identität, so ergibt sich eine ganz andere Situation: Verliert eine Person ihre qualitative Identität, bleibt sie doch zumindest am Leben. Aber kann dieses Leben noch ein *gutes* Leben sein, wo wir doch festgestellt haben, daß der Verlust der Identität zur Orientierungslosigkeit führt? Hier entfaltet eine zweite Mehrdeutigkeit ihre Kraft: Seine Identität zu verlieren, kann heißen, anschließend keine Identität mehr zu besitzen; daraus folgt in der Tat die beklagte Orientierungslosigkeit. Man kann aber auch *eine* Identität verlieren und eine *andere* dafür gewinnen; dies geschieht stets, wenn die eigene Identität sich *ändert*. Nicht immer also, wenn man seine Identität verloren hat, besitzt man anschließend *gar* keine!

Mit Hilfe dieser Einsicht läßt sich die Dramatik der kommunitaristischen Krisendiagnose zumindest teilweise entschärfen. Wer es befürwortet, eine gegebene Identität zu bewahren, müßte z.B. dafür plädieren, jedem Menschen seinen Kinderglauben zu erhalten, und dürfte keine Resozialisierungsprogramme gutheißen. Daß sich die Identität einer Person im Laufe ihres Lebens ändert, halte ich nicht nur für normal, sondern sogar für wünschenswert.

Taylor und die Kommunitaristen würden vermutlich erwidern, es gehe doch eigentlich gar nicht um die Identität des Einzelnen, sondern um die kulturelle Identität von

---

[32] J. Habermas, Anerkennungskämpfe im demokratischen Rechtsstaat, S.173, in: Ch. Taylor, *Multikulturalismus und die Politik der Anerkennung*, hrg. A. Gutmann, Fischer, Frankfurt/M. 1993, S.147-196.
[33] Vorausgesetzt ist hierbei allerdings, daß das Individuum die 'richtige' Identität hat, d.h. sich an den in der Gesellschaft tradierten und von den Mitgliedern der Gesellschaft allgemein geteilten Werten orientiert.

Gruppen oder *Gemeinschaften*. Was aber könnte *die* Identität einer staatlichen Gemeinschaft sein? Mir scheint, daß es sich dabei – ganz analog zu dem entwickelten Konzept der *personalen* Identität – um die von den Mitgliedern der Gesellschaft geteilten wichtigen *Einstellungen*, also um Wertvorstellungen, Wünsche und Überzeugungen handelt – nicht umsonst spricht man doch von der *Mentalität* einer Gesellschaft.

Und jetzt ist, wiederum ganz analog zur *personalen* Identität, zu fragen, weshalb sich die Identität einer Gesellschaft denn nicht ändern dürfen sollte. Darauf gibt es meines Erachtens nur eine überzeugende Antwort: Die Identität einer Gesellschaft dürfte sich dann nicht ändern, wenn es sich bei der betreffenden Gesellschaft um die beste aller möglichen handelte. (Genau genommen, sind hier natürlich die in der Gesellschaft geteilten Einstellungen und Werte gemeint.) Wenn man den Slogan vom 'Identitätsverlust der Moderne' vor *diesem* Hintergrund verstünde, ginge es also nicht darum, daß die moderne Gesellschaft keine Identität mehr hätte; die Mitglieder der Gesellschaft würden zwar Werte und Überzeugungen *teilen*, aber es wären, genau wie wir es bei der Erörterung der Authentizität gesehen haben, einfach nicht die richtigen.

Diese Diagnose ist jedoch ergänzungsbedürftig. Könnte man sich nicht auch eine Gesellschaft vorstellen, deren Mitglieder nicht nur nicht die *richtigen* Einstellungen teilen, sondern in der es *gar keine* hinreichend große Menge gemeinsamer relevanter Einstellungen gibt? Dann würde die Rede vom Unbehagen an der Moderne, vom Sinnverlust und insbesondere von der 'Zerstörung der Gesellschaft' besser verständlich, denn unter solchen Umständen könnte man nicht mehr von *der* Identität oder von *der* Mentalität der Gesellschaft sprechen, sondern vielleicht nur noch von *verschiedenen* Mentalitäten der einzelnen, in einer staatlichen Gemeinschaft zusammengefaßten Gruppen oder Kulturen: man hätte es mit einer multikulturellen Gesellschaft zu tun. Aber selbst wenn eine derartige Gesellschaft nicht über eine eigene Identität verfügt – warum sollte uns deshalb unbehaglich werden? Aus Sicht der Kommunitaristen fällt die Antwort nicht schwer: Die Identität eines jeden *Mitglieds* der Gesellschaft wird von der Identität der Gesellschaft *als ganzer* nicht nur beeinflußt, sondern wird von ihr (mit)*konstituiert*. Wenn die Identität des Einzelnen sich nur unter Rückgriff auf die in der Gesellschaft geteilten Werte ausbilden und auch nur innerhalb dieses Kontextes Bestand haben könnte, dann stellte eine multikulturelle Gesellschaft in der Tat eine direkte Bedrohung unserer Identität dar.

Diese Beurteilung ist meines Erachtens jedoch nicht haltbar. Es kann und soll nicht geleugnet werden, daß sowohl die Bildung als auch die Änderung der Identität jedes Einzelnen in vielfältiger Weise vom gesellschaftlichen, familiären oder beruflichen Einflüssen (um nur einige zu nennen) abhängig ist. Doch wer dies einräumt, braucht deshalb nicht zugleich auch die kommunitaristische These über die Abhängigkeit der individuellen Identität von der gesellschaftlichen Identität zu akzeptieren. Daraus, daß es nicht der Fall ist, daß wir von jeder kulturellen Gemeinschaft *un*abhängig sind, folgt nicht, daß es *genau eine* solche Gemeinschaft gibt, von der wir abhängig sind. Die Identität einer Person ist weder schlicht gegeben wie die Haarfarbe, noch kann man sie so auswählen, wie ein Menue im Restaurant.[34] So lernen wir beispielsweise durch die Gesellschaft, was überhaupt ein Wert ist und was als Wert in Frage kommt, doch sobald wir 'reif' genug, selbständig und eigenverantwortlich sind, stellen wir anerkannte Werte in Frage und können und müssen wir entscheiden, welche Werte wir selbst gutheißen.

Die eigentliche Befürchtung, die mit dem Multikulturalismus verknüpft ist, scheint mir eher darauf abzuzielen, daß in einer bestimmten Gesellschaft möglicherweise nicht mehr die 'richtigen' Werte tradiert werden. Bei Licht besehen, haben wir es also mit einem *normativen* Problem zu tun. Die richtigen Werte *als* richtige Werte zu charakterisieren, scheint mir nur mit Hilfe einer universalistischen Moral möglich zu sein. Doch das ist ein (zu) weites Feld ...

5. Schluß

Zu Beginn dieses Aufsatzes habe ich zwei Identitätsbegriffe unterschieden, nämlich relational und qualitativ verstandene personale Identität. Ich habe erläutert, worin personale Identität im qualitativen Sinne besteht, inwiefern sie uns eine Lebensorientierung bietet und was es heißt, im wohlverstandenen Sinne authentisch zu sein. Außerdem habe ich gezeigt, daß und wie man bei einer sorgfältigen Anwendung der beiden Identitätsbegriffe Taylors immer wieder geäußertem Unbehagen an der Moderne begegnen kann.

Auf mindestens zwei Fragen bin ich bislang die Antwort schuldig geblieben: 1.) Welcher Zusammenhang besteht zwischen relationaler oder numerischer Identität und qualitativer Identität? 2) Wie läßt sich das, was zur qualitativen Identität gehört, *genau* bestimmen?

Zu 1): Die Frage, wann zu verschiedenen Zeitpunkten identifizierte Personen *numerisch* identisch sind, wird in Anlehnung an Locke oft im Rekurs auf die psychischen Zustände der betreffenden Personen beantwortet. Die Standardantwort lautet: Eine zu t_1 identifizierte Person ist genau dann numerisch identisch mit einer zu t_n identifizierten Person, wenn zwischen der zu t_1 identifizierten Person und der zu t_n identifizierten Person eine psychische Kontinuität besteht.[35] Nun läßt sich der Zusammenhang zwischen

---

[34] Cf. A. Gutmann, Das Problem des Multikulturalismus in der politischen Ethik, S.283, in: *Deutsche Zeitschrift für Philosophie* 43, 1995, S.273-305.

[35] Darunter ist (vereinfacht) folgendes zu verstehen: Zu allen aufeinanderfolgenden Zeitpunkten zwischen t_1 und t_n gilt, daß die Mengen der zu diesen beiden Zeitpunkten (also beispielsweise zu t_3 und t_4) bestimmten psychischen Zustände eine nicht-leere Schnittmenge besitzen. Falls diese Bedingung erfüllt ist, so folgt daraus allerdings *nicht*, daß auch die zu t_1 und t_n bestimmten Mengen psychischer

der numerischen und der qualitativen Identität einer Person ganz leicht angeben: Zur Bestimmung der *numerischen* Identität einer Person muß man *alle* psychischen Zustände berücksichtigen, in denen sie sich zu einem (oder zu mehreren) Zeitpunkt(en) befindet. Um die *qualitative* Identität einer Person anzugeben, bedarf es dagegen nur einer (in der Regel echten) *Teil*menge der psychischen Zustände, in denen sich diese Person zu einem gegebenen Zeitpunkt befindet.

Taylor wehrt sich *expressis verbis* dagegen, die Identität einer Person mit Bezug auf einzelne Zeit*punkte* zu bestimmen; seiner Ansicht nach ist vielmehr stets eine Zeit*spanne* von Bedeutung, nämlich die des ganzen Lebens der betreffenden Person (vgl. QS, S.99f). Aber auch er muß die Frage beantworten können, wann wir es nur mit einer und wann wir es mit zwei *verschiedenen* Personen zu tun haben. Selbst wenn die These von der psychischen Kontinuität nicht überzeugte oder gar falsch wäre: Wir brauchen nun einmal ein Kriterium, mit dessen Hilfe wir z.B. entscheiden können, ob eine Kennedy-Biographie wirklich nur, wie der Titel verspricht, von John Fitzpatrick handelt, oder ob der Autor zwischendurch unwissentlich über dessen Bruder Robert berichtet. Die Frage nach einem *solchen* Kriterium kann man nicht schlicht dadurch beantworten, daß man auf die Bedeutung des *ganzen* Lebens für die Identität der betreffenden Person verweist. Strittig ist doch gerade, von *welcher* Person da die Rede ist und um *wessen* Leben es geht.

Man sollte numerische und qualitative personale Identität nicht als *rivalisierende* Konzepte auffassen, wie Taylor es zu tun scheint. Viel fruchtbarer ist es, die beiden Begriffe als *komplementäre* Aspekte dessen aufzufassen, was wir unter personaler Identität verstehen. Es ist unmöglich, daß *verschiedene* Personen *dieselbe numerische* Identität besitzen; es ist aber nicht ausgeschlossen, daß mehrere Personen über dieselbe qualitative Identität verfügen.

Zu 2): Die genuin moralischen Einstellungen einer Person sind – wenn vorhanden – auf jeden Fall Bestandteil des Bündels von Einstellungen, welches die qualitative Identität der betreffenden Person ausmacht. Doch von denen einmal abgesehen, kann man meiner Meinung nach keine klarere Aussage über den Rest des Bündels machen, als daß all jenes dazu gehört, was für die Lebensorientierung der jeweiligen Person und für die von ihr selbst für wichtig gehaltenen Entscheidungen von Bedeutung ist. Weder läßt sich da a priori ein Bereich auszeichnen noch ausklammern, wenn auch die Geschichten womöglich sehr umfangreich sein müssen, mit denen wir uns die Relevanz prima facie irrelevant erscheinender Meinungen oder Wünsche verständlich machen können. Um nur

---

Zustände eine nicht-leere Schnittmenge besitzen, denn die Relation "steht in psychischer Kontinuität zu" ist nicht transitiv. (Vgl. hierzu auch D. Parfit, *Reasons and Persons*, Oxford University Press, Oxford 1984.)

ein (einfaches) Beispiel zu nennen: Einstellungen, die die Zeitrechnung oder unseren Kalender betreffen, scheinen auf den ersten Blick nicht zu den für die Lebensorientierung wichtigen Einstellungen zu gehören, doch dann braucht man nur an jemanden zu denken, der sich aus religiösen Gründen an der jüdischen oder muslimischen Zeitrechnung orientiert ...

Diese (allgemein betrachtet) inhaltliche Unbestimmtheit, ja Unbestimm*bar*keit dessen, was die Identität einer Person ausmacht, ist allerdings, so möchte ich betonen, auf gar keinen Fall ein Manko! Sie spiegelt nur die Vielfalt der bei den Menschen vorfindbaren Identitäten wieder, für die es – Gott sei Dank! – kein Prokrustesbett gibt.[36]

---

[36] J. Kulenkampff, Th. M. Schmidt und E. Dierks danke ich für orientierende Gespräche und hilfreiche Kritik!

Timm Lampert

Klassische Logik

Einführung mit interaktiven Übungen

Studien zur Logik, Sprachphilosophie und Metaphysik
Hrsg. von Volker Halbach • Alexander Hieke
Hannes Leitgeb • Holger Sturm

λόγος

Das Buch vermittelt die Grundlagen der Aussagen- und erweiterten Prädikatenlogik in 12 Lektionen. Neben Techniken zum Überprüfen der Schlüssigkeit von Argumenten bilden die Kunst des Formalisierens wissenschaftlicher Argumente und metalogische Fragen den Inhalt des Buches. Das Buch eignet sich in Verbindung mit begleitenden interaktiven Übungseinheiten und Klausuren, die über Internet frei zugänglich sind, sowohl zum Selbststudium als auch für Einführungskurse in die Logik.

ontos verlag 2003
ISBN 3-937202-29-3
385 Seiten, Paperback € 28,00

Diese Arbeit erläutert und interpretiert Platons Dialog *Phaidon*. Vor dem Hintergrund der Ausführungen zu *Eidos, Psyche und Unsterblichkeit* und deren Relationen zueinander stellt diese Untersuchung einen präzisen Kommentar dar, der eine synchrone Lektüre des *Phaidon* stützt. Die Interpretationen der Dialogaussagen zu den *Eide*, zur Seelenkonzeption und zur Unsterblichkeitslehre werden ergänzt durch den Vergleich mit den grundlegenden philosophischen Todes- und Jenseitsauffassungen der Vorsokratik. Neben der eng am Text entwickelten Überprüfung aller Unsterblichkeitsbeweise, der Einwände des Simmias und des Kebes und der Widerlegungen dieser Einwände durch Sokrates, beschäftigt sich diese Arbeit ferner mit einer detaillierten Explikation des Hypothesisverfahrens.

ontos verlag 2003
ISBN 3-937202-33-1 ·
204 Seiten, Pb € 21,00

Torsten Menkhaus

Eidos, Psyche und Unsterblichkeit

Ein Kommentar zu Platons *Phaidon*

---

ontos verlag
Postfach 61 05 16
60347 Frankfurt / Main
Tel. 069-40 894 151
Fax 069-40 894 169
info@ontos-verlag.de
www.ontos-verlag.de

ontos verlag

Frankfurt • London

PHILOSOPHISCHE ANALYSE
PHILOSOPHICAL ANALYSIS

Hrsg. von / Edited by
Herbert Hochberg • Rafael Hüntelmann • Christian Kanzian
Richard Schantz • Erwin Tegtmeier

Volume 9

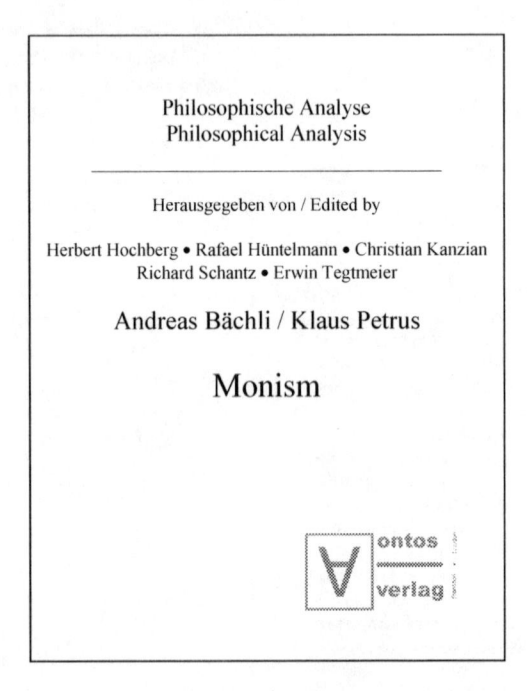

Philosophische Analyse
Philosophical Analysis

Herausgegeben von / Edited by

Herbert Hochberg • Rafael Hüntelmann • Christian Kanzian
Richard Schantz • Erwin Tegtmeier

Andreas Bächli / Klaus Petrus

Monism

ontos verlag

Monism is not a particular theory or even a school. However, monistic intuitions or doctrines are grounded in many different ways of philosophizing. For instance, one may argue that there is ultimately only one thing, or one kind of thing, or that there is only one set of true beliefs, one truth, one type of action, one sort of meaning, one way of analysing, explaining and understanding; or, alternatively, one may pursue the project of the unity of knowledge or even that of the unity of science. Taken in this broad sense, monism is often opposed to varieties of pluralism or numerous versions of dualism, since so much philosophical debate has focused on the question whether there are two different kinds of thing, mind and matter, or only one. The aim of the present volume is to discuss some of these aspects historically and systematically. With original contributions by Scott Austin, Andreas Bächli, Alex Burri, Thomas Grundmann, Herbert Hochberg, Mark A. Kulstad, E.J. Lowe, Eduard Marbach, Alex Mourelatos, Klaus Petrus, Matjaz Potrc, Wolfgang Röd, Richard Schantz, Ralf Stoecker, Karsten R. Stueber, Leonardo Tarán, and Jean-Claude Wolf.

ontos verlag 2003
ISBN 3-937202-19-6
340 pages / Hardcover € 70,00